Praise for

Travel with the Aunts

"This is a story filled with great humor, adventure, insights into places we all should visit, and revelation. As the trip advances, the hidden stories of the three sisters emerge, and their experiences with love and loss, struggle, and victory offer us all wisdom and an invitation to develop compassion—and a good spirit toward life."

—David Hazard, Author

"This is a delightful story, based on real life and evocative of current issues. It is not only a travelog, but a study of personalities who love adventure. The tale is heartwarming, very funny, and includes fascinating bits of Americana. I found myself caring about each of the aunts and their grandniece."

—Mary Louise Days, Historian and Author

"Look out! Here come three senior sisters on an epic journey, showing their young niece that you are never too old. Great fun!"

—Karen Stupak, Well-Traveled Senior

"This is a fabulous, insightful, intergenerational road trip with Allison and her aunts. There is an abundance of laughter for the characters and the reader, proving that growing and being old does not have to be boring."

—Tamara Jordan, Librarian and Educator

"When a college student reluctantly agrees to chauffeur her three octogenarian great aunts on a four-week road trip, she has no idea what a delightful romp they will have. While some of the colorful family stories will prove to be true, more importantly, she will discover the depth of their family relationships."

—Barbara Coger, Librarian

Travel with the Aunts

By Barbara Linsley

ISBN 978-1-64663-486-6

Published by

◣ köehlerbooks™

3705 Shore Drive
Virginia Beach, VA 23455
800–435–4811
www.koehlerbooks.com

Travel with the Aunts

Barbara Linsley

VIRGINIA BEACH
CAPE CHARLES

DEDICATION

To my mom and her grandmother, Josie Shaddack Sweers. Josie and her sisters, Daisy and Rosie, were strong, independent women who traveled, explored, and when in their seventies and eighties, dyed their hair red, blonde, and brunette and went bar hopping.

Chapter 1

Job Offer

One more day of finals, and undergraduate college was over. No job. No money. Allison kicked a stone off the path which led by the ivy-covered dorms. Dark clouds masked the sun, bringing gusts of chilly wind.

"*CumuloNimbus New Yorkus.*" That's what her brother called the near-constant cloud cover. That brought a hint of a smile as Allison pulled the sweatshirt free that she had tied around her waist. Mid-May and snow flurries were predicted up in Oswego and the Tug Hill. Well, that about summed up her mood—cool and dreary with a threat of snow.

She pulled on her sweatshirt. *It's not hoarding if it's Books* the sweatshirt proclaimed.

Allison could always get a job at Walmart, or waitressing. *Gross!* She viciously kicked the head off a dandelion, snarling at the decapitated flower. *I'm going into school counseling. I need to work with kids.* She tried to shut down the follow-up thought. *Even if I don't like it.*

There it was, the nagging suspicion that she really didn't want to work with kids.

She sighed. The summer camp where she had been employed for the past two summers had burned down. *Cripe!* It was the Adirondacks. The snow hadn't even all melted. Everything was still soggy. How could a building in the woods, surrounded by dripping trees and covered with wet, moldy leaves burn down? She shook her head and sighed again. Last week, the letter had arrived, saying, *"We're sorry to inform you. . . "* blah blah. She had been a counselor there for the past two summers. She would have reported in mid-June, a week before public school ended. The counselors would clean and rake, haul the docks out into the freezing cold lake, battle black flies, and then the first batch of kids would come. After two weeks, and just when the black flies would relent, the next batch of kids would come, along with mosquitoes. By the end of summer, it was the deer flies. And the newest addition— ticks, carrying the threat of Lyme Disease.

The main building had burned down, though, and now the entire summer was cancelled. So, no job. Allison had sent out applications to two other camps, but at this late date it was pretty much a lost cause unless someone quit, had a burst appendix, or got pneumonia from giving swimming lessons in a freezing Adirondack lake.

Ride of the Valkyries played from her jacket pocket. She pulled out her cell phone, checking the incoming caller. Her mom. Again. She waited for the tune to finish, smiling at the memory. Her father had given her the phone when she left for college. He'd chosen the ringtone. *Ride of the Valkyries* had been her favorite piece of music when she was young.

Allison flipped the phone on. "Yeah, Mom?"

"Allison. Have you found a job yet?" her mother asked brightly.

Allison fought an urge to be really snide. "No, Mom, I have not found a job since you asked me last night. I didn't have time to look during my Psychological Development of Adolescence exam this morning." Okay, so she was a little snide.

"I think I have something for you. It involves travel."

Allison's radar beeped a warning. Her mother was being way too chipper.

"Really?" Allison prodded.

"Yes!"

Allison waited, looking both ways before crossing the final road to her dorm. Maybe a car would hit her, and all this suspense would end. She sighed as she reached the far side safely, phone still to her ear.

"Mom?"

"Well, you like history, right? And you like travel, right? And you need money, right?"

"So, is this some kind of tour guide?" Allison knew that if she entered the dorm lobby, she'd lose the cell connection. It was tempting.

"Well, sort of, yes."

"Mom! Just out with it. Tell me." Actually, a job as a tour guide sounded interesting.

It came out in a rush. "You know your great aunts? They want to travel. All three of them have decided to take a road trip, and you've heard what they're like when they get together. They go to bars. They try to pick up men. They aren't safe driving at their ages. Allison, we need to convince your aunts to let you chauffeur them for the next month."

Allison clicked her phone shut. This was going to take some serious thought. Yes, she'd love to travel. Yes, she needed money. But her father had a low opinion of his three aunts and their wild behavior.

Key-swiping her way into her senior dorm, Allison climbed the stairs to her third-floor cell. Through the open door, she saw her roommate, Meghan, poring over her history notes for their last final the next morning.

"Okay, history genius," Meghan greeted. "Why was J.E.B. Stewart late in arriving at Gettysburg, why was Benjamin Franklin told NOT to allow British Parliament to give the colonies representation, and why on earth do I need to know this stuff to be a school counselor?!"

"Because one of your roles will be to help kids with their homework, so you'd darn well better know at least the basics of science, history, and math," Allison snapped.

"Oh my! What's wrong?" Meg wasn't the best history student, but she was a real girl when it came to reading people.

Allison slouched on her bunk. "I got a call from my mom." Meghan waited with that *oh-so-hard-to-resist-talk-to-me* expression. "She wants me to chauffeur my aunts on a road trip."

"Oh, Allie! That's wonderful! You must be SO excited." Meghan was also one of the best gushers Allison knew. "Oh, but you're not excited? What's wrong?"

Allison shook her head. No one was allowed to call her Allie except Meghan. From her, it didn't sound like a narrow, dirty side street. She sighed, kicked off her sandals, and wiggled her toes. The nails were chipped and broken. One was black from dropping her heavy Adolescent Development book on it. That was the other problem. Meghan would be a perfect counselor; she listened and really cared. Allison was unsure of her own abilities.

"You don't know my aunts."

Meghan went into full sympathetic-listener mode. "Then you'd better tell me, Allie. What are they like?" She shifted her weight forward, leaning in and focusing.

"Rosie, Josie, and Daisy, the Shattuck sisters, my great aunts, are not . . . well . . . normal. Rosie is the youngest at eighty-two, I think, and sang backup for various bands. She met some really amazing people, way back in the fifties, sixties, and into the seventies. She never married and now lives in an apartment in Rochester, New York.

"Daisy is about eighty-six and married an inventor. They've stayed married, on paper at least. My dad called him a vagabond. He bought one of those silver tin-can trailers and wandered the country.

Daisy hated traveling in the thing. They spent years going to rallies and big meetups of Tin-Canners. They now share a bungalow in an old neighborhood in Toledo, Ohio.

"Then there's the oldest, Josie, who's eighty-seven or eighty-eight. She's been married four times. The first husband died soon after they were married. He fell off a boat in Boardman Lake in Traverse City, Michigan. That was the official report. People who knew them said he jumped. A few said Josie pushed him off, except that she was hanging out in Little Bo's, a Bohemian bar, at the time. Her second marriage resulted in a son. Josie took off as soon as the kid hit college, and she went on to marry two more times. The third, she apparently liked, but he died in his early seventies, leaving Josie once more on the hunt. She married the fourth time in her late seventies to an Italian waiter in California. He was young enough to be her son, but she outlived him and moved back to Traverse City."

Meghan giggled. "You've got to be kidding. Those are your genetics? What happened to you, Missy Nun? But if those were all aunts, who was your grandparent? Was there another sister?"

"Yeah, that was Anna. She was the normal one. She married at twenty, had four children, and died. Well, not immediately. I was three when she died of breast cancer. She was the third youngest of the four girls." Allison made a sour face. "I only remember her when she had cancer. She had a bad smell, you know, that sick smell. And every time Mom and Dad visited her, they came home crying. I hated those visits, so Mom stopped taking me."

Meg shook her head. "Sad. I really liked my gran. Anna sounds like the one you took after, but let's hope not the cancer part. You know, really, it sounds exciting, Allie. And if they're going to pay you, well, you said you needed money for grad school."

Meghan could see Allison wasn't convinced. She leaned in, eager listening mode again.

Allison took a deep breath. "Yeah, I could sure use the money. But taking after Grandma Anna is part of the problem. Dad never liked those three. He wanted nothing to do with them. He said Grandma always referred to her sisters as 'wild, wayward, uncouth, and loose.' What if I don't like them? I haven't had any contact with Josie and Daisy since Grandma's funeral. I was three. What if I find I can't stand being around them?"

"Didn't you ever get together for holidays? When was the last time you saw the third one?" Meg slid forward, one knee touching Allison's leg, sympathy oozing from her.

Allison shook her head, once more feeling inadequate around her much more sensitive roommate.

"Once or twice a year, we drive to Rochester with our camping stuff, stay in a state park nearby, and go to some concert or church choir Rosie's singing in. She's really good. She was in a performance choir. They'd do concerts of all different kinds of music—Baroque, classical, popular. One time the entire concert was Beatles music. I liked that one." Allison grinned. "After the concert, we'd go out to dinner. She lives in a really small, two-room apartment, so we really don't do anything more than pick her up there or drop her off. Since Josie moved back to Michigan, the three of them have gotten together for Christmas at either Josie's place or Daisy's." Allison shrugged. "I don't know. Dad doesn't think much of Josie. She went to California after her third husband died and apparently there was some guy who stole half her money. Then she married the guy who was twenty-some years younger than her. Dad thought that she should be declared incompetent and have her son take over all her finances."

Meg gave her nose a cute wrinkle. "Oh, come on. A lot of people marry with a greater age difference than that, and you did say she outlived him. Maybe he needed someone to care for him? You don't know." Meghan's eyes lit up. "That's it. Think how much family history you could learn, and at their ages, you may never get this kind of opportunity again. You sound like you aren't sure about doing this, but consider it a history lesson."

Meghan smiled brightly. Allison thought she saw one of her teeth glint the way they did in toothpaste commercials. "And if you leave soon, you'll avoid the summer rush. It's another few weeks before most of the schools let out. Go for it, Allie. I really think you'd just love it."

She gushes like Old Faithful, Allison thought.

After examining her toes for a few silent moments, Allison nodded. "Maybe you're right. I'll call Mom after the final tomorrow and tell her. Mom said we have to convince them to let me drive. They may not even agree."

Chapter 2

ARRIVALS

Allison paced the airport. Today, she should have been accepting the diploma she had labored four years to earn. Her parents had planned to attend her graduation; she'd chosen a dress to wear. Instead, she was waiting for a late flight in Detroit, ready to start her new job as chauffeur. Rosie's flight from Rochester was late, no arrival time listed yet. Josie's flight from Traverse City flashed on the screen as disembarking.

Alison paced, remembering the argument she'd had with her mother.

"It's not just about earning money, Mom. I need to be working with children, or children and families. I start classes for my master's degree in counseling in the fall." What she had wanted to say was she didn't want to waste her time on a pack of octogenarians.

Her mother had finally snapped. "Enough, Allison. They are family. It is your duty."

Her mother had used the same statement on her brother. There had been times when she wanted to go with him or do something with him and, of course, he didn't want his little sister tagging along. "Robert, she is family. It is your duty." Allison had been delighted that she got to go, but at the same time, she had wished that her brother wanted her to come with him.

She watched the passengers coming through the gate, wondering if she'd recognize Aunt Josie. She'd only seen a picture of Josie when she lived in California. People poured down the hall, dragging carry-ons, some confident and others looking stunned or confused. An elderly woman, white hair perfectly permed, looked anxiously in all directions. Allison slowly approached the woman. She didn't recognize her. Could that be Aunt Josie?

Before she could offer an uncertain greeting, a young man and woman with three small, look-alike children blasted past, enveloping the white-haired woman, large arms around her shoulders, small arms around her legs, and one snotty nose wiped back and forth on the waist of her dress.

Nope, not Aunt Josie.

Here came an elderly with a walker. *Hopefully that's not Aunt Josie.*

Allison felt a tap on her shoulder. She turned to face a blonde woman a couple inches taller than her height at five-foot five. Of course. She had been told the sisters dyed their hair red, blonde, and brunette.

"Aunt Josie?"

"Where's Rosie?" Josie scanned the area with a frown of consternation. "She was supposed to arrive before me."

Allison shook her head. "I'm not even sure she's left Rochester. Her flight was listed as an hour late, then the board said ninety minutes late, and now it's not even on the board."

Allison studied her aunt, who was dressed neatly in camel slacks, a chocolate-brown silky blouse, and a lightweight oatmeal jacket. She tried to remember the last time she'd seen her. Was it at her grandmother's funeral years ago? No wonder she didn't remember this woman clearly.

"I hope your flight was uneventful." *What kind of small talk do I make with an eighty-eight-year-old?*

Josie waved away her report of flight delays. "Ridiculous. This used to be a hub. Planes used to be serviced regularly. Not anymore. Now they wait for some red light to go off before making any repairs and we just hope the plane doesn't drop out of the sky before they can find out what's wrong."

Wearing a stormy frown, Josie stalked toward the airline counter, Allison tagging along feeling like a confused puppy.

"Nowadays," Josie snarled over her shoulder, "when there's a mechanical problem, the part that has to be replaced is flown in from some other airport."

Allison winced as people turned to stare at this angry, blonde octogenarian.

Aunt Josie waved a ringed hand as she spoke. "Everyone has to wait, and the staff is kept busy with a three-hour-long line of people having to rebook connecting flights. The part finally arrives, they get it installed, and then the flight crew walks off because they've timed out, and there's no crew to replace them."

Josie whirled to face Allison, who pulled up abruptly nose-to-nose with this wrinkled face of fury. "On top of it *all*, the airline has the temerity to tell you that you are on your own for overnight lodging, and they give you a measly, few-dollar meal voucher. If you are really lucky and know who to harass, they might even give you a toothbrush!" With a final huff of disgust, Aunt Josie snapped. "So who knows when Rosie will arrive."

This bundle of righteous indignation stormed up to the airline desk. "When is the flight getting in from Rochester, New York?" She snarled, leaning aggressively on the counter.

Tapping a few keys on the computer terminal, the representative looked up with a pasted-on smile. "That flight is in the air. It will arrive in just over an hour," she chirped.

"How can you stand to work for a company this incompetent?" Josie demanded.

The happy face collapsed, and the woman lowered her voice. "I'll tell ya, lady, it sure ain't the pay. If I could kick some a . . . tail, I would. Do you need to rebook a connecting flight?"

Josie shook her head, appeased by the other person's echoing frustration. "No. Thank you."

Before the next person in line made it to the counter, Josie turned back. "You should pass out bus schedules to those who have to rebook. I'm seriously considering taking a bus home."

The woman grinned widely with an eyebrow waggle. "I wouldn't blame you."

Allison glanced at the waiting line of people all staring at her aunt or nodding with frowns of agreement, wishing she could disappear.

Turning away, Josie snapped. "Have you heard from Daisy? She should be here waiting for us."

"Um—"

Aunt Josie was already striding in the direction of baggage claim.

Hurrying after Aunt Josie, Allison realized she was scuttling. "I haven't seen Daisy." It had been difficult enough trying to spot Josie, but she hadn't seen her Aunt Daisy since her grandmother's funeral when she was barely three.

"Would I recognize her?"

Aunt Josie waved her hand dismissively. "Oh, never mind. She wouldn't come in here. Daisy wouldn't pay to park her car. She'd just drive round and round waiting for us to show up." Josie continued toward the baggage-claim area. "Did you try her cell phone?"

Allison tried not to trot to keep up. Cell phone? "I don't have her number." Could it get any worse? She was not only scuttling to keep up but was starting to sound whiney.

After snagging and, with the help of a young man in long braids, hauling her mammoth suitcase off the conveyor, Josie snapped at Allison. "Where's your luggage?"

Mutely, Allison pointed to the unclaimed bags at the side of the room. "I left it with those."

"Bring it outside. I'll look for Daisy and you wait for Rosie." Allison pulled both her and her aunt's suitcases outside to the covered sidewalk.

"You go back up to where you met me. Rosie has red hair. She wears it pinned back with bobby pins." Josie pulled out her phone. "I can't believe no one gave you Daisy's number," she griped, scrolling down to call her sister.

It was an hour and twenty minutes before a Lucille-Ball-red-haired woman in a blue flowered dress came hesitantly through the gate, eyes scanning the waiting people. Bobby pins with tiny blue bows held back curls on either side. She raised her hand in a relieved wave at the same time Allison raised hers. "Aunt Rosie?"

"Allison! I'm so—"

"You're finally here."

"I'm so glad to finally make it," Rosie giggled.

Allison chuckled and offered to take Rosie's hand luggage.

"Oh, my, I am certainly late. I wasn't sure we would ever get off the ground. Are Daisy and Josie here yet, or is Josie running late, as well?" Rosie looked around, scanning for her sisters. "Josie hates it when things don't go according to her plan."

"Aunt Josie got here on time. She went out looking for Daisy. I'm not sure if she found her. She hasn't come back since I came here to wait for you."

As Allison led Rosie toward the baggage claim, Rosie gently put her hand on Allison's arm, and her voice dropped. "I need—"

Allison leaned close, trying to hear Rosie's whisper. "What?"

"*I need the lady's room*," Rosie whispered.

"Of course," Allison changed direction toward the nearest restrooms.

Rosie giggled, holding her hand to her mouth. "I'll bet Josie didn't need the bathroom."

Allison wrinkled her forehead, trying to decipher the meaning of that.

"*It's because she wears a Depends*," Rosie whispered again, then stopped abruptly, legs bent and pressed together. "Oh, dear, maybe I should have as well."

Allison stared in horror, hoping not to see a puddle appear beneath her aunt. "The bathroom is right there!" She pointed just across the hall.

Rosie hobbled crablike to her destination. So much for not wanting everyone in the waiting room to know what she needed.

At baggage claim, Rosie, comfort restored, bounced on the balls of her feet, watching intently as every bag came out of the luggage chute. Finally, a huge, hard-sided, floral bag crashed down the ramp onto the carousel. "That's it!" Rosie exclaimed, grabbing and shaking Allison's arm. "Snag it when it comes around."

As the bag made it around the carousel, Allison reached, grabbed, and nearly had her arm yanked off. Manhandling the leaden suitcase to the edge of the carousel, she hauled it with a grunt, waddling along as the belt pulled the case on around. With final mighty heave, she hoisted it onto the ground.

"What have you got in here?" she gasped, imagining that her aunt had packed a library of travel books. *And how did you ever get it into the car and airport on your own?* She wanted to ask but didn't.

Rosie giggled and picked up her carry-on. Fortunately, the suitcase had wheels, although one was broken, *most likely crushed to death*, Allison thought.

Hauling it behind her, Allison remembered her father's comment about bringing proper clothing. She'd brought comfortable travel clothes—mostly jeans, shorts, T-shirts, a couple jackets, sneakers, and sandals. Eyes wide in horror, she slowed, realizing she'd brought nothing dressy. Josie looked like a fashionable businesswoman. Rosie had on a loose dress and sensible walking shoes. Allison felt heat rising to her face.

Out on the sidewalk, Rosie scanned, then waved delightedly at a beige Buick Le Sabre waiting down the way. The car honked in return. Off Rosie toddled, with Allison dragging the heavy, wobbling case behind her. Sisters launched from the car to hug and fuss over Rosie while Allison dragged the suitcase. The sisters piled into the car, shoving two suitcases from the backseat out onto the sidewalk. Daisy popped the trunk from inside. She did not even greet Allison.

Message received, Allison thought as she hauled the three suitcases to the rear of the vehicle. Inside, the sisters gushed and exclaimed. Josie's case wasn't too bad, but Allison realized she should have spent time at the gym lifting weights to be able to manage Rosie's. After man-handling the two large cases in, she wedged her small case into a remaining corner.

Finished with her workout, Allison headed for the driver's seat. Daisy sat with her seatbelt fastened, hands firmly gripping the wheel.

"Shall I drive, Aunt Daisy?"

"Oh, you must," chirped Rosie, "Then you'd be driving Miss Daisy," she chortled.

Josie rolled her eyes. "Move, Daisy. We're *paying* her. We might as well get our money's worth."

Allison noted the vote of confidence, or whatever it was. Daisy sidled out to take the backseat, and Allison slid behind the wheel and buckled-in, once more wondering why her parents had insisted that she drive. *Isn't Daisy capable? It's her car.* She'd driven up from Toledo. She seemed to want to drive.

"Where to?" she asked.

"It's rush hour. It'll take hours to get out of the city, and it's really too late to drive back to Toledo," Daisy griped, shooting a glare at her late-arrival sister. "I am *not* going to fight rush hour traffic."

"You aren't driving. Allison is," Josie pointed out. "So, what are our options?"

Daisy shrugged dismissively. "Stay here."

Silence.

"At the airport?"

"No, at a motel," Daisy mocked.

"Obviously," Josie barked back.

"Which one? And what about dinner?" Rosie asked sweetly.

A tap on the window startled them. Allison snapped her head around to see blue with a massive black leather belt taking up most of her window. A face hove into view and made a roll-down-the-window motion. Allison complied.

"Ladies, you really—" The officer peered in at the full car.

Daisy leaned forward from the back seat. "I told you the last several times you asked us to move, Officer, that we were waiting for our sister to arrive."

He nodded. "Looks like she has, and your driver?" He looked pointedly at Allison, who blushed. "So, it's time to move on. You can't park here."

"But we don't know where to go," Rosie wailed. "It's rush hour. And it's all my fault."

The officer did a double take on the last admission. "It's your fault it's rush hour?"

"My plane was late."

"We're looking for a motel."

"And a place to eat."

Josie leaned partway across Allison. "Do you know the Henry Ford Museum, Greenfield Village?"

The officer brightened. "Sure! That place has everything."

"I was told they had Model Ts."

The officer waved his arms excitedly. "A whole fleet of them. They've got a Ford Model T bus. They give rides in them through the village."

Daisy's eyes lit. "You can ride in the Model Ts? Do they have any with rumble seats?" She squirmed in her seat. "We're going! Where can we eat?"

The change in tack threw Officer Friendly off his mark, but he recovered. "You'll need most or all of tomorrow to really see the museum. I'd say for now, go down to the waterfront, you know, on the Detroit River. Lots to do down there. My wife likes the La Palma restaurant. Do you have any idea what kind of motel you want?"

"It would be nice to be close to the museum."

A driver pulled into a tight parking spot behind the Le Sabre, nearly kissing the bumper. Allison dropped her forehead to the steering wheel, wanting to wheedle. *"Just tell me where to go."*

The officer glared at the new car's driver and kept talking. "All right. That's down in Dearborn. I think there is a hotel that might be in conjunction with the museum. It's called The Henry. I think it's on Town Center Drive. It may be a bit pricy. There is also a Comfort Inn near the museum."

Exclamations of excitement came from all except Allison who was wondering how she was going to find these places in rush hour.

. . . .

After a wonderful dinner and stroll on the waterfront, Daisy's phone GPS guided them to The Henry Hotel, where the ladies retired to the lounge, listening to a piano being tinkled. Rosie hummed along. A pert, young waitress bustled over.

"Ladies, what will you have?"

"Strawberry daiquiri."

"I'd like a pina colada."

"Make mine a Bloody Mary."

The waitress looked to Allison.

Though she didn't drink, Allison wondered if alcohol would improve the situation.

"Not her, she's our driver," Josie snapped.

Daisy countered. "We have a room right upstairs. We don't have to drive to it."

"She'll be driving tomorrow."

"But—"

Allison muttered. "I don't drink. May I have a ginger ale?"

Nodding, the waitress left.

"Well, what would you expect from Anna's granddaughter?" Daisy muttered.

Allison almost opened her mouth to ask what she meant by that but decided that at this moment she didn't care to know.

The ladies spent the next couple hours chatting and giggling over men who came to the lounge. Rosie sang along when the guy at the piano agreed to play Billy Joel's "The Piano Man." Allison had never heard it sung soprano.

Retiring to their room with two king beds, the ladies slept well.

Allison, sharing a bed with Rosie, not so much.

She stared at the ceiling tiles, feeling her fingernails. The clock read *3:17a.m.* Sleep had just been finally creeping up on Allison when Aunt Josie let out a nerve-shattering, thunderous snort. Allison felt like the cats in cartoons who end up upside down on the ceiling clinging for dear life with their claws. But she had no fingernails to speak of. Wouldn't have worked.

She sighed.

The aunts were bundled under sheets, blankets, and comforters. Allison had folded the comforter and blanket to the middle of the bed, forming a wall between her and Aunt Rosie, who was squeaking. Allison was hot with just the sheet.

Aunt Daisy sounded like she was making bombing runs. She moaned in a Doppler-like hum: *"Ehhhhhhhhhhhhhh boosh. Eeehhhhhhhhhhhhhhh boosh"* It sounded for all the world like a bomb falling from on high. Next to her, Rosie squeaked. Allison couldn't tell if it was on the intake of breath or the expelling. Josie, propped up on two pillows, was the only quiet one, until she exploded with a deafening snort, smacked her lips, shifted positions, and went back to silence.

With a despairing moan, Allison grabbed a spare pillow, threw herself onto her stomach, yanked the pillow over her head and hoped for sleep.

"Thanks, Mom!" she thought. *"How am I supposed to drive them safely if I can't sleep?"*

Chapter 3

MODEL TS

"Me first! I claim the bathroom." Rosie scrambled out of bed, scampering into the tiny bathroom as Daisy fought to free herself from the bedding.

Allison nosed out from under her pillow. "Upsidaisy, kiddo!" Daisy sang. "Could you turn on the TV? Let's check the morning weather report." She tossed the remote to Allison then called out, "Can anyone loan me underwear?" She was wearing Josie's nighty decorated with unicorns since, of course, she had no suitcase with her. They'd planned to be at her house last night.

Allison shifted out from under the pillow, pulled herself to a sitting position, and clicked on the TV. *One day down,* she sighed. *How many to go? Four weeks? Twenty-eight days?* Allison felt her stomach cramp.

"The Today Show," Josie ordered.

Allison scrolled through until they saw Al Roker giving a weather report.

"I love Al Roker. He's so cute." Daisy maneuvered around Rosie, who moved out of the bathroom to the sink.

"Undies?" she asked her younger sister.

Rosie dug into her suitcase and handed Daisy what appeared to be mint-green strings. Eyebrows raised, Daisy held the item up with one finger.

Allison nearly choked.

Josie erupted, laughing nearly as loudly as the massive snorts she gave off through the night. "A thong! You wear those?"

Daisy glared at the mint-green item. "Thong used to refer to sandals. Is this one of those things you wear up your butt crack?"

Allison blushed. Her dad was right about these ladies. Her stomach churned, and she suddenly realized she needed to—

Allison dashed to reach the bathroom before she peed herself.

"Hey!" Daisy looked from the closed bathroom door to the thong. She shrugged and scooped up the rest of her clothes.

Allison emerged sheepishly. "Sorry, Aunt Daisy."

Josie remained propped in her bed. Daisy entered the bathroom and slammed the door. Rosie headed to the tiny sink with her overnight kit.

A methane explosion erupted from the bathroom, followed by a tiny voice. "Excuse me."

"That's why they used to call some of those large chamber pots 'thunder basins,'" Josie chuckled. She peered over at Allison. "Do you need the bathroom to dress? You can go first. I'll wait for the air to clear."

Rosie peeked around the corner from the sink, toothbrush and foam spilling from her mouth. She patted her bottom, mouthed a foamy "Depends" and waggled her eyebrows.

Allison choked, trying not to laugh.

The bathroom door cracked open, and the mint green thong sailed through the air. "I am not wearing these! How on earth can anyone stand them? Don't you have any real panties?"

Toothpaste foam dripping, Rosie toddled over to her suitcase, pulled out a large pair of white cotton panties, returned to the little sink, and handed them through to her sister in the bathroom.

Josie snorted. "Granny underwear."

Allison blushed again. That was the kind she wore, except hers were in colors. Some even had flowers on them, or even stripes, which she couldn't wear if her pants had thin material, which is why she liked the white or pastel colors. Allison hid her underwear by wrapping them in her clothing as she waited for her turn to change in the bathroom.

"Okay, I've seen enough of the weather report. Which morning news do you watch?" Josie asked, propped restfully in her pile of pillows.

"None, really. I'm usually getting ready for class."

"Well, you must watch news. Which national news do you watch?" Josie persisted.

"I stream news when I have time."

Josie stared at her. Daisy, coming out of the bathroom, looked confused. "Stream?"

"On my computer." She knew immediately that wasn't enough explanation.

Rosie pulled the toothbrush from her mouth and drooled. "I have videos."

"Oh, Rosie, you can only get DVD's now."

"Huh," Josie snorted. "It's Bluetooth now."

"I think you mean Blu-ray," Allison suggested.

"I like the Blue Men." Rosie finished brushing her teeth and spat. She started wiggling her hips and moving her feet as though dancing.

Allison realized she was softly singing "Blue Suede Shoes".

Packing her pajamas into her small suitcase, Allison's hands shook. She felt ready to cry. *Not now! Not here! I like Rosie, I know I can stand being with her. But the other two? Four weeks! Stop. I need the money. This is better than stocking shelves at Walmart. I can do this. I get to travel. I will get to know relatives I've barely met. I can do this!"*

. . . .

Allison dropped the ladies off in front of the Henry Ford Museum at ten minutes to ten. They'd aimed for nine o'clock. Considering how the morning had gone, *not bad.*

Daisy snapped on a large fanny pack, Josie grabbed her tan shoulder bag, while Rosie hoisted up a worn, bulging, woven yarn purse.

"Why haven't you got a handicapped license, Daisy?" Josie demanded as they headed for the door.

"I'm not handicapped."

"But you're old."

"*Tsk, tsk.* Not as old as you."

Allison parked close to the handicap spots and found the ladies at the ticket desk discussing the various options. Rosie bounced up and down in excitement. Plastic wrist bands were placed on wrinkled arms. "Quick, Allison! These bracelets let us ride ALL the Model Ts," Rosie gushed.

Allison didn't know ladies in their eighties could scamper. Off they went, down the long hall and out the door to the outdoor part of the museum. A steam train chugged its way past as they crossed into the village. "We're riding on that, too," Daisy announced.

"Cars first!" Josie hustled over the train track and made a b-line for the building where black and hunter green Model Ts were pulling up to a covered platform to pick up passengers. Men not quite as old as the aunts drove each of the shiny, polished, clattering vehicles.

A mother and son were the only folks ahead of them in line. They got in a large town car. A black touring car pulled up next. The aunts hustled forward, excitedly piling in. Allison squeezed into the back seat with Rosie and Josie.

"Good morning, ladies!" Their whitehaired driver greeted them with a wide, white-toothed smile. He adjusted the lever on the steering column and the car puttered forward.

"He's cute," Rosie whispered. "I wonder if those are his real teeth."

Allison hoped he was hard of hearing.

"This is a 1925 town car. The prices had dropped from eight hundred and fifty in 1908 to less than three hundred by the time this model came out. As you can see," he pointed out the window at a pretty car with brass fittings heading the opposite way, "this car does not have the fancy trim of the older models. Henry Ford wanted everyone to be able to afford his cars." He tooled slowly around a corner and adjusted a control on the steering wheel. "This car has two forward gears and one for reverse. There's a brake pedal but no accelerator." He touched the bar that extended from the steering column. "This controls the spark and throttle," he shot a glance at his lady passengers. "It controls the speed of the car."

Josie waved at another car coming past them. "Does this one have a hand crank? I didn't notice when we got in."

"It certainly does, ma'am. The hand crank activates—"

He didn't get a chance to finish as Daisy took over. "—the magneto connected to the flywheel. Some had battery powered starters. In which year did those come out?"

Their driver, mouth agape, had found the love of his life. His misty eyes and parted lips said it all—or maybe it was cataracts, and he was hard of hearing. "A few of the more expensive ones had battery powered starters after 1920," he murmured, his cockiness replaced by admiration.

Daisy continued, turning to speak to Allison. "The engines are four cylinders, about twenty horsepower, with speeds of around forty miles per hour if the roads permitted such a speed. Reverse gear had more power, so on steep hills, you often had to go up backwards."

The driver gazed at Daisy with open adoration. She continued,

"Roads were pretty awful. My father-in-law carried a shovel in his car. If you had to make a turn off a rutted road, you sometimes had to shovel through the ruts to turn the wheels."

The driver nearly ran off the road.

Josie tweaked the back of his head. "Eyes on the road, sir."

He valiantly tried to resume his scripted talk. "Between 1913 and 1927, more than fifteen million Model Ts were produced."

Daisy again took over. "There were factories on nearly every continent. Not Antarctica, of course."

The driver's eyes misted. "That's why parts for these cars are so easy to come by, because there were so many made."

"Why on earth did Ford produce the Edsel?" Josie snapped.

"Nobody's perfect."

The youngest sister began humming and then softly singing:

"His little old Ford rumbled right along
and the little old Ford rumbled right along.
The gas ran out in the big machine
but the darn little Ford don't need gasoline.
The big limousine had to back down hill
but the blamed little Ford is going up still.
When it runs outta dope just fill it up with soap
and the little Ford will rumble right along."

Their driver nearly melted into the seat, sighing blissfully. "*The Little Ford Rumbled Right Along* by Billy Murray. Do you know all the verses?" The two sang on about large cars breaking down, stolen girlfriends, potholes, and angry mules. By the time they'd finished (with claps and cheers from some of the other vehicles they passed), they had arrived back at the depot. "It has been such a pleasure, ladies! Please visit us again." He took hold of Daisy's hand and gazed into her eyes. Allison thought about the song Rosie had been singing in which a preacher was picked up by the side of the road and the two in the car became wed. But Daisy extricated her hand from her admirer.

Allison hesitated at the end of the exit ramp, prepared to start walking the village. That apparently was not the plan. The aunts rushed past her and back around to the entrance line, waited impatiently for one other couple ahead of them, then Daisy hustled Allison into a cute little roadster while Josie and Rosie waited for the early model town car with the brass trim, which was tooling in behind it.

Off they went. Allison could hear Rosie singing about a bowlegged cowboy in a Model T as they puttered off through the village.

When the aunts lined up for a third ride, Allison asked to walk the town instead. She headed for Thomas Edison's laboratory, exploring many of the inventions he had developed. Down the road, she entered the boarding house that Thomas Edison first wired for lights. Many of his workers had lived there. She listened to a talk in the Wright Brothers childhood home. After reading the list of prices on the toll bridge, she didn't feel quite so bad about tolls she'd been paying.

Every so often, a Model T clattered by, with anywhere from one to three wrinkled arms waving an enthusiastic greeting. Strains of songs, in one or more voices, including "jalopy" or "tin lizzie" wafted in their wake.Allison grinned and shook her head. This trip was either going to be a hoot or drive her totally batty.

At one point, an old green bus rumbled past her, soprano strains of *The Wheels on the Bus go Round and Round* trailed merrily in its wake.

· · · · · · · · · · · ·

After wandering for over two hours, the aunts still riding in the wide variety of vehicles, Allison headed back to the Model T depot. All three aunts hauled themselves out of a station wagon as Allison arrived. "I'm thirsty. There's a café just around the corner where we could grab something to eat," Allison offered hopefully.

"Do they have lemonade?"

"I want fried onions."

"You want everything fried."

"Not oranges."

"Or men. Fried men smell terrible."

Allison felt her eyes wander in strange directions as she tried to process the last statement. She led them around the corner to a covered area with numerous picnic tables. The ladies got various flavored slushies, burgers, fries, and a chili dog and fried onions for Rosie.

"I thought you all had Buicks and hated Fords," Allison started, "but you are all delighted with these Fords."

"Oh, Honey!" Daisy waved an extra-long fry. "The Model T was built when Henry knew how to build a car. Then he made the Edsel."

"Dementia. It had to be dementia setting in," Josie growled.

"Whatever. People in Michigan knew car quality, you know, with Motor City and all. If someone drove a Ford, it was because they worked at a Ford plant. I actually ran into people who thought Ford was an acronym for 'Found on Road, Dead.'"

Rosie giggled.

"I'm not kidding," Daisy snapped at her younger sister. She slurped a brain-freezing gulp of lemon slushy and continued. "Barth, my husband," she added for Allison's benefit, "bought one. A Ford." Another slurp and a munched fry. "In 1968, he went through male menopause or mid-life crisis, I don't know, but he bought a Mercury Cougar, red with black roof and black leather interior. What a piece of dog hooey."

"Pile of dog hooey," Josie corrected.

"Whatever." Daisy waved her fry dismissively.

Rosie giggled.

"It had those headlights that powered up when the lights were turned on. By the next year, the pressure would leak out of the hoses that kept the *lids* open and the lights would drift shut. That may be okay on a city street with streetlights, but on a country road with ditches and rampaging deer, it was dangerous! I can't tell you how many times Barth nearly drove off the road frantically trying to pump the light panels back open."

She slurped hard on the now empty slushy, then waved the empty cup. Rosie jumped up to get her another.

Allison watched, slightly stunned.

"By the second winter, it refused to start when it got really cold. Barth put in one of those heaters in the engine that they use in places like Alaska. We were the only ones in Michigan with a plug hanging out from under our hood. The next winter, Barth was driving into town, took a corner, and his door flew open! Now the piece of hooey," she glared at Josie, daring her to correct her, "wouldn't start below ten degrees and the door wouldn't close and latch below twenty degrees. Barth had to rig up a pulley system so he could keep the door closed."

Josie pulled a small, point-and-shoot camera from her purse and snapped two Model Ts clattering by. Rosie returned with Daisy's new slushy and a second purple one for herself.

"Thanks. Anyway, that wasn't all. Barth drove down to New Mexico for a conference. He figured it wasn't cold there! What could go wrong? His friend made a comment wondering if the car would make it that far safely. They had just pulled into the parking garage of the conference center in Albuquerque where they would be staying, got out of the car, and there was a loud CLANG." Taking a sip, Daisy squinted and shook her head. "Cold! They looked underneath the car. The muffler had fallen off. At least the car waited until they were safely parked. After getting the muffler repaired, they wanted to see some of the sites. They drove up Sandia Peak overlooking the city. Barth should have told his friend to keep his mouth shut. 'Ya think the brakes will hold?' he asked. Well, they'd just made it back into town, turning in to the parking garage again, and the brakes got all slushy and soft. The brake line had leaked all its fluid." Daisy shook her head.

Allison was perched on the edge of her seat. "So, what happened next?"

"Barth and his friend were supposed to leave the next day. He found a garage that would take the car and have it done by noon the next day. When Barth went to pick up the car, four guys were standing around in greasy coveralls staring at the front fender. He walked up. One asked if it was his car. Barth wasn't sure he wanted to admit it but allowed that it was. 'We were wondering how you got yourself shot full of buckshot?' the guy asked. Barth looked at the rust holes on the fender and realized it did look a lot like buckshot. 'It's rust,' he snapped and went off to pay his bill."

The ladies packed up their lunch detritus, tossed it in the trash, and headed for the train depot.

"What happened to the Cougar?" Allison asked. She realized she was the only one who didn't know the end of the story.

"Barth got home safely and put the car up for sale that spring. A dad from out of state," she hissed, "bought it for his daughter to take to college. Barth was honest about the problems, but she was going to southern Ohio, and they figured it would be okay. Next summer, she must have been home on summer recess, we saw that old Cougar, left by the side of the road. A true Ford, Found on Road, Dead."

After riding the steam train, the ladies decided to head out of town before rush hour began. Allison ran to fetch the car as they toddled at a much slower pace than they had shown that morning.

With Daisy riding shotgun and giving easy-to-follow, concise directions, Allison navigated out of the city before rush hour created too much difficulty.

On the drive to Daisy's house in Toledo, Allison thought about the moral of the story of the Mercury Cougar. *Don't ever question a car's ability to get you safely to your destination.*

Chapter 4

OLD ORCHARD

After avoiding rush hour traffic in Detroit, they hit jammed roads entering Toledo. Much to Allison's relief, Daisy knew how to avoid the worst of the traffic, taking them on the way to a grocery store for dinner supplies before guiding them into the suburb of Old Orchard.

"No, all of you stay here!" Daisy ordered in the store parking lot, motioning to Allison to pop the trunk so she could get her shopping bags. "If I go alone, I'll be out in ten to fifteen minutes. If you all come, we'll be in there an hour. What is everyone's preference for some meat tonight and with breakfast tomorrow, bacon or sausage?"

Three votes were cast for bacon; Rosie abstained.

Daisy returned less than fifteen minutes later, tried to put the shopping bags in the trunk, but the suitcases took up all the room. Giving up, she put them at her feet as she took her seat to continue her job as navigator.

Ten minutes down the road, Allison pulled into the driveway of a well-maintained mustard yellow, single-story house in a tree-lined neighborhood. Every lawn was mowed, the shrubs trimmed. The front of the silver Airstream trailer poked from the rear of the house, snugged in next to the detached garage.

"Barth's truck is gone," Daisy said.

Was that a note of concern in her voice? Allison could not tell.

Thinking of all the Ford Model Ts and the story of the Mercury Cougar, Allison asked, "Is Barth's truck a Ford?"

Daisy looked shocked. "Of course not! It's a Chevy Silverado, HD 250 work truck."

Daisy grabbed her shopping bags and headed into the neat little bungalow. Allison watched Rosie and Josie head in with their bulging handbags and nothing else. She peered into the car trunk at the huge suitcases. The unspoken message was clear. With a sigh, she began the process of hauling suitcases out of the trunk and into the house, realizing with dismay that when they headed out tomorrow, there would be one more.

"Where do I put them?" she asked from the foyer.

Daisy poked out from the kitchen, "Josie and Rosie will be in the back bedroom. You'll be in the living room on the pull-out couch. Don't worry, it's pretty comfortable. Better than the floor!"

The two sisters followed Allison into the guest room to start unpacking for the night. Allison left their suitcases and went to find Daisy in the kitchen.

Daisy smiled as she entered. "Have you come to help? The pot of water is boiling. Put in that pasta." She pointed to a fistful she had laid out. "Then dice the tomatoes and summer squash. I'm about done with the zucchini." She swished some olive oil in one pan and settled several strips of bacon in another.

Allison relaxed. *This feels like home.*

Diced veggies were tossed in the olive oil.

"Dry the bacon and break it up. Usually, I mix it with the vegetables," Daisy shrugged. "Rosie didn't want any bacon. So, we'll break it up and people can add what they want. Take the bacon and this parmesan cheese into the dining room table." The directions weren't given as an order, more like a mother to her daughter, or a kindly aunt to her niece.

Five places were set at the table. Allison put the bacon and cheese in the middle and went back to the kitchen for the next load.

Daisy stood quietly at the sink, looking out the window at the driveway.

"Everything okay?" Allison asked.

Daisy shook herself. "Yes, of course. Call the girls. We're ready!" She dumped the pasta into a strainer and laid out five plates. Allison paused, looking at the five. Daisy saw her looking and hesitated. "Barth should be here." She turned back to the stove. "I'm not sure where he is." Then quietly, "I was expecting him to be home."

"Dinner's ready!" Allison called down the hall to the guest bedroom. Nothing. She approached and tapped on the partially open door. Josie and Rosie emerged, freshened up and changed into more formal clothes. Behind them, it looked like their suitcases had exploded. Clothes covered every surface. The counter in the bathroom sagged under a drug store shelf of creams, ointments, bottles, hot curlers, styling brushes and items Allison could not identify.

She hurried into the kitchen as Daisy handed Josie the spaghetti tongs. "Serve yourself. Take as much as you'd like. There's red wine on the table."

Josie peered at the pile of pasta. "Are you planning on inviting the neighborhood?" She put a small pile on her plate, then moved on to the pan of vegetables, ladling them over the pasta.

"Bacon and mozzarella cheese is on the table." Daisy waved her on into the dining room as she passed plates to Rosie and Allison.

Dinner passed with stories shared of what each of the sisters had been up to since they had last been in contact with each other. Daisy kept glancing at the door. No rumble of a truck engine yet.

"You usually take a walk after dinner, right?" Josie asked, gathering up dishes. At Daisy's nod, Josie gave Rosie's shoulder a nudge. "We'll take care of the cleanup. You show Allison the neighborhood. Take her over to where we grew up."

Josie smiled at Allison. Surprised, Allison smiled back. "I'd like that!"

Daisy chose a lightweight tan sweater from her hall closet and led the way out the door. They walked four blocks past nicely kept, mostly two-story homes, along neat sidewalks, some buckled up by tree roots. Rosie pointed to initials carved into the sidewalk at one corner. Allison frowned at the scuffed letters. "WPA?"

Daisy grinned. "Yes. Do you know what it means?"

Allison frowned and shook her head.

"These groups of young men came to put in new sidewalks all over Old Orchard when we were girls. We'd watch them after school. The guys never seemed to know quite what they were doing. They really seemed to spend more time scratching their heads, looking at charts, and discussing how to do things than actually getting any work done." Daisy grinned. "At the end of each section of sidewalk, they carved WPA. After much discussion, we decided it meant 'We Putter Around.'"

Allison nodded, with a smile of sudden understanding. "It was one of Franklin Roosevelt's Great Depression alphabet programs. What did it really stand for? Something about Work?"

"*Works Progress Administration.* They worked in towns. The CCC, Civilian Conservation Corps, worked in the countryside, planting trees and building structures in our state and national parks. We also had the FMP, Federal Music Program, come to our school. That program hired out-of-work musicians who did performances in schools."

They walked on, and Daisy pointed to a handsome, tan, two-story house. "That's where we grew up."

"I thought you grew up in Traverse City."

Daisy smiled, patting Allison's shoulder. "No, our parents grew up in Traverse City. Except for Rosie, we were all born here in Toledo and spent much of our childhood here. We went to Traverse every summer. Our grandparents were there and our aunt."

"I thought you went to the newly built high school, the one just off Peninsula Drive." Allison stared at the tan house, trying to imagine her aunts as little girls. "Where was Rosie born?"

"Rosie was born during the summer, while we were staying in Traverse City. We then moved there when I was twelve. Rosie was seven. That was when we built the house at the base of the peninsula where we grew up."

"That wasn't the summer home you went to?" Allison asked as they started walking again.

"Oh dear, no. We stayed at our grandparent's house, which is no longer there. It was on the other side of the street . . . not on the bay. Have you been to the shuffleboard courts at the park on Front Street? That park is dedicated to our grandfather."

Allison noticed her great aunt pulling the light sweater closer around her. The night was cooling. She could see televisions flickering in windows as they passed. They walked around the block, turned again, and headed back toward home.

"You see those hedges over there?" Daisy asked. "Those are behind our old house, forming the boundary of our backyard. That's where Josie and I hid to avoid the air raid warden."

Allison stopped, scanning the neatly trimmed hedgerow.

"That was during World War II. We had air raid drills in which we had to go inside and cover all the windows, no light was to show. Some old codger was hired to pace around feeling all important with himself," Daisy imitated a pot-bellied swagger, "checking to make sure everyone was complying. Josie and I would sneak out and shadow him. We were told that if we'd been caught, our parents would be in serious trouble. We might even be accused of being spies." Daisy snorted. "I guess we were supposed to be scared. We figured the enemy would have to be pretty desperate to have little girls as young as us for spies." She walked on a while remembering.

"Actually, we only did it three times. We were worried about being caught, but, my, that was exciting!"

Allison tried to picture Daisy and Josie in little print dresses, hair in braids, wearing saddle shoes (*or would they be Mary Janes?*) darting from shadow to shadow after some over-stuffed old man assigned to monitor their neighborhood for light-leakage. She smiled.

Back home, all the lights were on, but still no Chevy Silverado in the driveway.

Allison watched as Daisy checked the phone for messages. None. No sign on her face of what she was thinking or feeling.

Aunt Daisy led the way down the hall where she knocked softly on the guestroom door, then went in. Josie lay reading in one of the twin beds. Rosie sang softly from the bathroom. "I need to get a pillow for Allison's sofa bed."

Grabbing a pillow from the closet, Daisy asked, "One? Or would you prefer two pillows?"

"One is fine." Allison started to follow Daisy out the door, then hesitated and turned back to Aunt Josie. She waited until Daisy was out of hearing range. "Aunt Josie? Is Aunt Daisy worried about Barth not being home?"

Josie waved her hand dismissively. "No, he's always wandering away somewhere. She just hoped he'd be here to meet you."

Allison hesitated, unsure. Josie saw the concern and continued. "Barth has always been scattered. You know how some really intelligent people are . . . head in the clouds, can't be concerned with mundane, everyday stuff. Daisy often says if she didn't put food in front of him, he'd forget to eat." She thought for a minute. "I read an article recently about . . . asparagus. Asper—"

"Asperger's Syndrome?"

"That's it! It kind of sounds like Barth. Not everything, but the really intense way he can focus on something, poor social skills, not really paying attention to where he is or who he's with. But very smart." She shook her head. "I've always thought Daisy and Barth were more like roommates than a married couple"

Allison nodded, thoughtfully. "Well, good night, Aunt Josie."

"Nighty night. Sleep well."

Daisy got Allison settled, went once more to the door, gazing out the window to the street in front of the house, then said good night and headed for her room. Alone on her pull-out couch, Allison felt maybe Daisy wasn't so bad. It was fun learning how they had grown up as girls. Allison's roommate, Meghan, was right. She could learn about her family and its history. She wished she could meet the mysterious Barth. Maybe he'd be home by morning.

With no one nearby making night noises, Allison slept well.

Chapter 5

JOURNEY BEGINS

By morning, Barth still had not returned home. Daisy shrugged it off. "He does this sometimes. Something comes up, and off he goes!" But Allison saw her searching counters, for a note perhaps, and peering out windows whenever she thought her sisters weren't looking.

Daisy made a breakfast of blueberry pancakes and bacon. Dishes were washed, the car loaded by Allison, and Daisy packed a bag of snack foods and a cooler of drinks.

"Don't take the turnpike, Allison," Daisy directed as they pulled out of the driveway. "Go Route 2 along the lake shore. It's pretty and doesn't cost you your first-born child."

Daisy guided them out of Toledo, along streets of failing industry, and a barbeque place that Daisy swore was the best in the Toledo area, "But not for breakfast," she added. Route 2 quickly took them into farmland. Daisy pointed to the turn-off for Maumee Bay State Park.

"That is one of our favorite quick-getaway places to stay. We pick up a barbecue meal to-go at that place we passed, then pull in here for a couple days. There's a wildlife boardwalk on one side, a large camping area, a beach, and a wonderful walk along the Erie shoreline. Barth especially likes coming if there's a storm predicted for that night. It's lovely watching a tempest come in over the lake, the wind kicking up waves, and the scudding clouds racing across the sky."

She got an *"Oooo"* of appreciation from Rosie and silence from older sister, Josie.

About a half-hour further, Daisy, riding shotgun, ordered Allison to turn left into Magee Marsh in the Ottawa National Wildlife Refuge. Past the visitor center, they wound along by open meadows, along wetland marshes with herons perched in the shallow water, then on to the lakeshore. Entering the expansive, nearly empty parking area, Daisy directed Allison to the far end.

"Why are we here?" demanded Josie.

"To stretch our legs," Daisy shot back, prying herself stiffly out of the car. She led her sisters the short distance to the beach, the wide expanse of Lake Erie opening before them. Blue-gray sky reflected into blue-green water. They stopped at the edge of the beach.

"What's that smell?" Josie demanded. She was not an outdoors person.

"Smells like dead fish," Daisy answered. "Could be carp. Alewives wash ashore."

"Or maybe a shark," Rosie chimed in.

"Not in fresh water."

"Well, it could be. That movie *Jaws* was partly based on a shark that came up a river and attacked people."

Josie glared at her baby sister. "A shark would have to come all the way up the St. Lawrence River, across Lake Ontario, and then jump up Niagara Falls."

Rosie thought about it a moment. "I don't think a shark could jump that high. Salmon could."

Daisy shook her head. "I don't think even salmon can jump up Niagara Falls. Besides, Atlantic salmon don't come up rivers."

"Well, that's smart of them. If they failed to jump up the falls on the first jump, they'd get smashed on the rocks, like those silly people who go over the falls in barrels," Rosie mused. "Suppose someone wrapped himself in bubble wrap and then packed himself into the barrel with those Styrofoam things, the 'peanuts?'"

"Oh, I hate those things! When you open a box, they explode all over and stick to everything. I get them on my hands and sleeves, try to brush them off, and they just stick somewhere else."

Allison walked on down to the water's edge, away from the disintegrating conversation. She saw the remains of a large dead carp. She studied it carefully. A large carp. At least, it was the remains of a large carp. Seagulls had been eating the large carp. Most of the stomach area was gone from the seagulls eating the large carp. It smelled really bad. It definitely wasn't a salmon or a shark. It was a large carp. Allison struggled to repress a giggle. Maybe she'd be stark raving insane by the end of the trip . . . four weeks.

Snap out it! she told herself. *Yesterday was fine. Daisy is very nice, so is Rosie . . . sometimes.*

Her aunts came from behind still talking about going over the falls with packing materials.

"They make some packing stuff now out of cornstarch that dissolves in water," Rosie continued.

Daisy shook her head. "They still stick and when I try to wash them off, I get goop all over my sweater. *Ick.*"

"You can't even vacuum those little white things. Those beads they put in stuffed toys are even worse! Just try getting those off the rug and furniture."

"That's probably why no one has packed themselves into a barrel with them to go over Niagara Falls. The EPA doesn't want all those packing peanuts polluting the water."

"The cornstarch ones wouldn't pollute it."

Rosie approached closely enough to peer at the rotting carp. "Maybe that's what killed the carp."

After a moment of silence, Allison looked up from the carp. She saw the aunts mincing down the beach, walking gingerly, trying to prevent sand from piling up in their sensible shoes. Daisy glanced back at her. Allison thought she caught a slight smile and glint of the eye before Daisy staggered in the sand and turned to face forward once more. She followed, avoiding another putrid carp and the angry gulls eyeing their meal.

The ladies turned onto a path by a creek that flowed into the lake which led away from the water, then turned back toward the parking area along a ditch. Allison saw the aunts stop and form an arc around something on the grass at their feet.

Approaching, she heard a hiss.

"She's laying eggs!" Rosie breathed on a whisper. "I want to pet her. She looks soft and furry."

"I wouldn't. Her teeth aren't soft and that's seaweed, not fur."

Allison got close enough to join the arc around a very large, seaweed-covered snapping turtle who was valiantly attempting to lay her clutch of eggs. She hissed again at Allison's approach and expelled another egg.

Rosie squatted slightly; clearly her old knees didn't bend too well. "Her face isn't symmetrical. Look at her nostrils. One is higher and much larger than the other."

Her sisters bent to closely examine the mismatched nostrils. The turtle withdrew her head, hissing another warning.

"People's faces aren't symmetrical either. That's why dolls are so pretty; they all have symmetrical faces."

The sisters considered this. Josie shook her head. "I've seen some pretty ugly dolls."

"Me, too," agreed Rosie. "But not as ugly as some people."

"Nobody would buy a doll as ugly as some people."

"Oh, I don't know. Some people think if it's ugly enough, it's cute," Daisy responded.

Rosie straightened up. "I think this turtle is cute, and she's pretty ugly." She giggled. "Pretty ugly. Is that an oxymoron?"

Josie nodded, mouth pursed. "I agree, she's kind of cute, in a reptilian sorta way." She dug her little point-and-shoot camera out of her jacket pocket. Bending over as far as her old body would allow, Josie snapped a picture of the turtle's asymmetrical nostrils.

The turtle hissed.

The ladies moved on. Back in the parking area, Daisy turned right and led them to a large sign showing the many types of birds they may see in the area. Daisy led the way along a boardwalk into the woods.

"It's snowing!" Rosie crowed, holding her hands up to catch drifting specks of white.

"Can't be. Too hot. What is all this fluff?" Josie asked, fingering soft, downy puffs that stuck to the wooden railings and drifted through the air.

"Cottonwood seeds," Daisy answered. "They float like dandelion fluff."

Rosie scanned the trees around her. "It's coming from the branches, not the wood. Why is it called cottonwood? Is there cotton stuff in the bark?"

Daisy shook her head. "I don't think so."

"Can it be spun like cotton?" Josie asked.

Allison fingered some. It didn't seem strong enough to be spun, but it was certainly soft.

"I don't think so."

Josie seemed put out. "So, it really is neither cotton nor wood." And having passed her judgement, she strode on down the boardwalk.

Birds flitted among the branches. A scarlet tanager shone like a ruby among the green leaves then vanished with a flash of wings. Gold finches flitted about, adding flashes of yellow, like flowers among the treetops.

Josie, in the lead, stopped, holding out her hand to stop the others. She pointed.

Waddling hurriedly through the undergrowth appeared what looked like a very large, pale gray rat. It ran erratically around bushes and clumps of grass.

"An opossum!" Daisy and Rosie crowded closer to the handrail, watching, entranced as the opossum headed their way. It dove under the boardwalk, then emerged on the other side in a large puddle of standing water, made a sharp left, and climbed partway up a bush where it froze, seeming to notice its audience for the first time. A bead-like black eye studied them, but the creature remained still.

Josie's camera hung from her wrist. Slowly, she lifted it to snap a quick photo.

More rustling. They all turned. A second opossum scuttled along the same path as the first, making the same turns and swerves. It, too, plunged under the boardwalk and came out the other side, but instead of turning left, it continued straight.

"Over here!" Rosie called softly. "Should we call it back?"

"No!" Daisy grabbed her arm. "Look, this one is terrified of it! He's trying to hide from it."

"She."

"It."

"Maybe the one hiding is a murderer and the other is law enforcement. We should call him back."

"*Her.*"

"*It.*" Daisy shook her head. "The one hiding could be the victim trying to escape the murderer."

"He trespassed on the other's territory," Josie quickly added. "Or she or it."

"Who did?"

Josie shrugged. "One or the other."

They stood silently watching. After a few minutes, the one in the bush backed slowly down, then took off into the marsh, away from where the other opossum had gone.

Josie shook her head. "Well, I never!"

"Me, too! I've never seen opossums chasing each other!" Daisy agreed.

"A dead carp, a snapping turtle, and two opossums all in the same day. I agree. I never!" Rosie gushed.

"I've seen a dead carp and a snapping turtle before."

"Yes, but all of them in the same day?" Rosie countered.

Daisy glared at her. "I said I'd never seen opossums chasing each other, so how could I have seen them all in the same day?"

And on they went, Allison trailing behind.

· · · · · · · · · · · · ·

After their walk in the marsh, they drove on to Port Clinton where Daisy suggested they detour out to the lighthouse at Marblehead. On such a beautiful day, they agreed to break out their food supply and have a picnic at the park on the water's edge by the lighthouse.

While the ladies spread out picnic supplies on a table by the water, Allison took a walk through the cedar woods to the rescue station and then back to take a close look at the lighthouse. Across the narrow neck of water, she saw the bony spines of amusement park rides. A freighter glided by out in Lake Erie. Waves gently lapped against the massive rocks protecting the lighthouse's small rock perch.

After a lunch of ham and cheese sandwiches, pickles, sweet and dill, sliced apples, erratic conversation, and iced tea, it was time to push on.

"When we get close to Cleveland, we're going to have to get on the turnpike in order to make up some time," Daisy said. "We haven't even made a hundred miles yet today."

"But we've seen dead carp and snapping turtles and opossums chasing each other and Lake Erie and gulls and—"

"Yes, Rosie," Josie interrupted.

"And lighthouses and scarlet tanagers and cottonwood fluff and goldfinches—"

"YES, ROSIE!" Josie and Daisy chorused loudly.

Rosie giggled.

Chapter 6

JOHNSTOWN

Allison awoke bleary-eyed, forcing open her eyes after a night of desperately wishing sleep would carry her away. She must have slept briefly since the ladies were already up and puttering around, TV tuned to the *Today* show. Local news was predicting heavy rains for the day.

"Not a nice day to visit the Johnstown Flood Historic Site," Josie grumbled.

"Perfect day!" responded Daisy. "We'll get a great feeling for what it was like on the day of the flood."

Rosie chanted the children's verse, *"Rain, rain, go away, come again some other day,"* then hauled a rain slicker from the recesses of her voluminous suitcase.

Allison sighed and rubbed sleep from her eyes. "What's at Johnstown?"

Daisy perched on the side of her bed. "Your mom said you were a history buff. You don't know about Johnstown?"

Allison shook her head no, thinking, *So, it was Mom who got me in to this. I knew it wasn't Dad. He never wanted me anywhere near these three.*

Daisy began her history lesson. "Above the steel town of Johnstown, on the Conemaugh River, was the South Fork Fish and Game Club made up of the very wealthy of Pittsburgh. Their cottages surrounded a dammed lake. The old dam that created it was not properly maintained. On May 31, 1889, after days of heavy rain, the dam burst, emptying the lake in minutes. It cascaded down the narrow valley, taking out towns, railroad tracks, and even trains. When it hit Johnstown, it swept through the town, washing away homes and people until it hit the stone railroad bridge, where the crushed houses, bridges, railroad cars, and the rest of the debris was halted and started to burn, along with people trapped in the wreckage. More than two thousand people died, entire families wiped out. Many victims went unidentified."

Daisy patted Allison's leg. "Get yourself up. We agreed to hit a number of National Park historic sites on this adventure since that's your area of interest."

Allison noticed that Josie and Rosie had been listening closely as well. She wasn't the only one who didn't know about Johnstown.

. . . .

The drive to South Fork off Route 219 took them about two hours.

"That's the Conemaugh River, the one that flooded." Daisy pointed off to the side. The sky crouched dark and threatening, but only spits of rain dotted the windshield.

Following Daisy's phone GPS, they arrived at a cross street, where the device directed them one way and the sign pointed the other. "Which way?" Allison asked.

Daisy pointed right. "That way."

Josie pointed left. "That way, the sign says."

Allison sighed as the car behind them laid on the horn. She followed Josie's order, turned left and immediately saw a sign for a picnic area. Down the steep road, she found a parking lot. A path led down to the river where the original dam had held back the waters of the Conemaugh River, forming the lake that eventually crashed down the hill to take so many lives. The sisters stayed at the overlook but motioned for Allison to go down the long wooden staircase to the river.

She gratefully obeyed, following the foot path, reading each of the signs along the trail. Shaking her head, it was hard to imagine this stream causing so much damage. One sign provided details of the fish screens put in place by the wealthy folks of the South Fork Fish and Game Club to prevent the stocked fish from escaping over the spillway. Another sign contained a poem which outlined the lives lost because of the debris-clogged screens, contributing to the weakening of the dam and subsequent flood, asserting that to the rich, the fish were more important than the people of Johnstown.

Allison gazed across the shallow, rock-strewn stream to the railroad track on the far side. A farmhouse, once used by a caretaker, stood on the opposite hill. A distant rumble of thunder growled down the valley. Allison hurried along the path and back up to the parking area.

The sisters stood, huddled at the overlook where the dam had once stood. Gusts of wind riffled Rosie's flowered dress and Daisy's brunette hair. Allison joined them. In silence, they gazed at the site of so much destruction.

"I just realized that it was on *this* day in 1889 that it happened," Daisy murmured in a reverent whisper.

"What?"

Josie *tsk*ed in disgust. "She said, it was on this day, May 31 in 1889, that the dam broke."

"Oh," Rosie closed her eyes, tilting her head back, a stiffening breeze riffling her red curls.

After a moment's silence, the sisters turned. Josie put her hand on Allison's shoulder for balance as she stepped off the curb. Returning to the car, they pulled out of the picnic area. "There is a visitor center on the opposite hill. That's where we are heading," Daisy directed.

Allison turned left at the top of the drive, heading in the direction the sign had pointed.

They drove past a park that said it was a Johnstown site, then drove up a steep, narrow, dead-end road with no turnaround, to a dilapidated clubhouse. Daisy made disgusted, "I told you so" noises. She pulled out her phone, activating its GPS. "Go down that side road over the railroad track."

Over the track, past a park, and up a hill, they saw a small parking area on the left.

"Pull in there!"

Allison swerved across the road to the small parking area. A walkway led to the old spillway and the opposite side of the berm between which the dam had been built.

"This path is flat," Daisy explained. Opening the door, she hauled herself out. "We can easily walk this one."

It was a quiet walk along the wooden path past the spillway to the overlook. There, they gazed back at where they had been on the far side.

"Barth and I went to the cemetery when we visited here," Daisy informed them as they stood, overlooking the old lakebed. "There is an entire section of graves for the unidentified victims of the flood. There are monuments listing all the children of a family drowned that morning." She shook her head at the memory. "So many lives lost. It was overwhelming."

Josie dug out her camera. Drops of rain leaked from the leaden sky.

. . . .

Next stop, the visitor center, where they were just in time for the video telling of the disaster. Wealthy Pittsburgh industrialists bought a lake and aging dam. Summer homes, mansions, and club houses were built. Stocked fish filled the lake. But upkeep of the dam went unattended. In the spring of 1889, after days of heavy rain, the dam broke. Desperate telegraph messages sent to South Fork and Johnstown didn't reach them, due to broken lines. When the dam burst, a wall of water plunged down the steep river course, scouring all in its path. By the time it reached Johnstown, survivors described seeing a wall of wood and debris, no water. The video ended with a chilling litany of descriptions of unidentified dead.

Leaving the theater, the ladies walked quietly through the museum. They paused by a mock-up of a boy clinging to the side of a twisting, disintegrating barn. "That's the boy who stood on the top of the barn and saw the wall of debris coming," Rosie said.

"Victor."

"What?"

"His name was Victor. When the barn tore loose, he scrambled up the sides and along the base as it was rolled along by the water." Daisy repeated what they'd learned in the presentation.

Behind them, the rain started. All three turned to peer out the smoked-glass window. "That must have been what it looked like. Not just rain, but the sky opening up," Rosie murmured.

Allison stood mesmerized.It was easy to imagine the dam still in place, the large summer homes lining the lake, and men frantically bringing loads of straw and stones to try to shore up a failing dam. A rider had been sent to inform the railway telegraph operator that the dam was likely to go, but he had ridden away before being told that the lines were down. There was no way to reach Johnstown.

Allison shuddered.

Downstairs, photos lined the walls, showing the grim aftermath of the destruction. When the debris had piled up against the brick railroad bridge, trapping people in the rubble, coals from the foundry or from people's cooking stoves set the wood on fire. The water flowed on, leaving only twisted wood, metal, and broken people. Fires started. Dusk was filled with screams of those trapped and cries for aid by frantic people using their hands to claw the trapped victims free.

"Carnegie, Mellon," Allison read. "They had summer homes here. Is this disaster one they could have prevented, and the reason why they gave so much to philanthropic organizations? Guilt? No one was ever held responsible for this tragedy."

Her aunts nodded, "Could be. I'm sure—I hope—they were deeply affected by this. None of them ever returned."

After viewing the photos and reading the interviews of people who had lived through the flood, and finding the photo of Clara Barton and how her Red Cross had rushed forward to help the survivors, they headed out into the pounding rain. The aunts stood under the overhang of the building while Allison dashed to the car, bringing it as close to them as she could.

They left the area in subdued silence, taking a last look through the rain at the valley which once held a peaceful lake.

Allison was stuck on the image of a boy, Victor, who had seen the huge wall of debris coming and could do nothing about it. *What did he feel and see?*

Daisy directed Allison down country roads, twisting and turning through the steep hills, exclaiming how beautiful this area was in spring. Rain sheeted down. Allison leaned forward over the wheel, trying to see the road through the *flop-flop* of the speeding windshield wipers.

Allison hiccupped.

Josie and Rosie in the backseat peered out their windows. "It looks gray and wet to me," Rosie said.

"Hard to tell how beautiful it is with all this rain," griped Josie.

Daisy harrumphed. "It's beautiful on a sunny day, all green and hilly."

Allison glanced through the relentlessly pounding rain up each gully and valley they passed, imagining walls of water cascading down on them, sweeping their Buick Le Sabre into the madly rushing torrent on the other side of the road.

She hiccupped.

Rain slashed in waves, sheets sweeping down, causing streams and rivulets in the road. She slowed to avoid hydroplaning.

She hiccupped. Taking a deep breath, she tried holding it.

The road wound up and down, curving and twisting. Allison gripped the wheel tightly and hiccupped.

Finally, a straight stretch of road opened in front of her, not a car in sight, the rain letting up enough that she could see ahead more than a few feet. Flexing her fingers, Allison leaned back in the seat, relaxing slightly.

And hiccupped.

"KNOCK IT OFF!" Josie exploded from the back, slamming the back of Allison's seat.

Allison yelped, swerved, causing Rosie's head to smack the window and Daisy to grab for the handhold over her head.

Josie chortled.

"Nice one," Daisy snapped.

"She won't dare hiccup for years now!" Josie cackled.

Rosie leaned forward, rubbing her head with her other hand. "Are the hiccups gone, dear?"

Startled into a brief laugh, Allison remembered her dad doing the same thing to her brother when he was about twelve. She recalled that she'd laughed hysterically when her brother had replied, "I don't know about the hiccups being gone, but I think I wet myself."

She wasn't yet comfortable enough with these ladies to use her brother's comment, so she merely responded. "I sure hope so."

The rain had stopped. The overcast hung on. Clouds oozed down wooded hillsides, looking like smoke from damp wildfires. Traffic picked up as they got closer to the eastern cities.

Daisy asked, "Does anyone ever call you anything but Allison?"

Rosie's head came up as she roused from her nap. Daisy turned to glare at her. "All that squeaky breathing—for a minute, I thought the car needed new shocks." Then she turned her attention back to Allison. "Well?"

Having been given a moment to gather her thoughts, Allison said, "Back in fourth grade, I had a young, second year teacher who hadn't developed very good classroom control as yet. In my class, there was me, Allison, and also Alexander, Allen, Albert, and Alexis. Our teacher soon realized that if she bellowed '*AL*' she would have the full attention of twenty percent of the class. The other eighty percent would stop whatever they were doing and stare at us for the entertainment of finding out who was in trouble now. I don't think any of us ever went by Al after that year."

"What about Ally?"

Allison shook her head. "Sixth grade. I got called Ally by a young teacher who wanted to seem with-it. The class bully quickly changed it to Alley Cat and that darned teacher thought that was cute."

"Cripes." Daisy seemed satisfied.

Not Josie. "Allison . . . Sonny!"

"Bono or Corleone?" Allison deadpanned.

"Sonny Boy!" chirped Rosie.

"I see the problem," Daisy admitted. "Do you remember Gladys Wysluzski?"

Josie leaned forward. "Didn't she live over on Sixth Street near the library?"

Rosie looked from sister to sister, obviously not familiar with the person.

"When we moved to the high school."

"The one at the base of the peninsula, down from where you lived?" Allison asked.

Daisy nodded and waved a hand dismissively. "The first week we were there, Gladys kept introducing herself to students from other elementary schools and even to some of the teachers as Happy Hiney."

Josie chuckled and nodded. Allison's eyebrows shot up. "Happy Hiney? Why?"

Daisy grinned. "That's what one of our teachers wanted to know. One day, walking down the hall, Mrs. Carlson grabbed her by the arm and hissed, 'What is wrong with you, Gladys? Why are you telling people your name is Happy Hiney?' And Gladys looked her right in the face and responded, 'Well, it is. I don't see the difference between a *Happy Hiney* and a *Glad Ass*.'"

Josie guffawed, slapping the seat with her flat palm. Rosie snorted and Allison gave Daisy a shocked glance. "You've got to be kidding!"

Daisy shook her head soberly. "Honest truth. She got a week's detention, and I got one day, I guess for being caught with her when she said it. She was a hoot." Daisy turned back to Josie in the back seat. "Remember at lunch, she had perfect timing with her jokes and snide remarks. She could make any kid blow milk out her nose."

"Except Bethy, who nearly choked to death." Josie shook her head. "I'd almost forgotten how funny Gladys was."

"Why?" Allison asked. "Did something happen later?"

Both older sisters were silent for a bit. Then Daisy sighed. "We thought she might be the next Phyllis Diller or Carol Burnett. But she married. Polite society did not approve of a woman with her wicked sense of humor. She married a guy who also was a clown. Seemed like a perfect match but turns out he didn't like competition. If he wasn't the center of attention, he got mean. Gladys had two young children, and one day she disappeared. Her husband was blamed, but there was no proof of wrongdoing until her body washed up on shore two weeks later. A bottle of vodka was found on the beach, and she had alcohol in her blood. Her death was deemed an accidental drowning. Those of us who knew her knew she didn't drink, and that she was a powerful swimmer. I think she drank enough to dull her senses, then swam out until she couldn't swim anymore."

"She committed suicide?" Allison asked, her voice softening.

Daisy nodded. "You are lucky you live when you do, Allison. You can do pretty much whatever you want."

Josie leaned toward the front seats. "I have noticed how many of the intelligent, creative women of my generation became alcoholics because they could not be who they needed to be. We are not all cut out to be wives, mothers, or to put our needs to one side to serve others."

Allison glanced in the rearview mirror at Aunt Josie. "Is that why you divorced your husband and went off on your own?"

Josie flopped back against the back seat. For a long moment, the only sound in the car was that of the windshield wipers flop-flopping.

"It was either that or become an alcoholic." Her voice dropped. "The truth is, I was on my way in that direction."

Silence descended. Allison drove, pondering the restrictions women of her great aunt's generation must have faced. Also, she thought about what her father had said about these women. Did he really know enough about them, or what they'd had to live through, to judge them the way he did?

Daisy played with her iPhone and scrabbled in her bulging fanny pack, hauling out her overstuffed wallet.

As they approached Philadelphia, Daisy flicked through apps on her phone. "Up ahead, get on Route 76 and take it in to Philly. I've booked us a hotel right near Independence Hall. We can walk the area in the morning. I also got us a really good deal on a two-night stay in Atlantic City."

"Show off," Josie grumbled.

Rosie giggled. "Good job, Sis!"

Allison shot a glance at her aunt Daisy. *Atlantic City? Drinking? Gambling? Picking up men?*

Her thoughts reverted to her father's dark statements about these women. She hoped he wouldn't be proven right.

Chapter 7

CITY OF BROTHERLY LOVE

The aunts rose early, took turns in the single bathroom, repacked luggage, chatted aimlessly, and were checked out and exiting the building three hours later.

Allison sighed. She should have brought a book. No, a pile of books. Long books. She could be up, ready, and out the door in ten minutes flat. She and her roommate in college had timed themselves.

With these women, time slowed to a crawl . . . then dragged.

While the aunts performed their morning ablutions, they had breakfast brought up: a soft-boiled egg and piece of toast, rye, for Rosie; cup of fruit, no melon, and a banana for Daisy; and two eggs, two bacon strips, two sausage and two pancakes for Josie. She finished all of it. Allison watched her with awe. That was the best entertainment of her morning, along with watching Rosie put on a pair of orthopedic stockings. Of course, Allison's morning calisthenics consisted of lugging all their luggage out to pack the car.

After yesterday's relentless rain, the morning glowed, sunny and bright. Crossing the park to reach the Independence Hall visitor center, a young man holding a fistful of recently plucked tulips danced up to them. "Good morning, ladies! What a glorious day it is," he burbled, holding the flowers high, then swinging them toward the three older women. "These flowers will brighten your table at home. Only five dollars for the bunch." Reading their expressions, he changed quickly to a demure, childish pout. "Please?"

Rosie, Josie, and Daisy exchanged glances with expressions suggesting they were on the hunt. Allison shifted nervously.

Changing tactics again, the young man straightened, held the tulips out toward them, and began his story. "I came to this fine city to find a job. I'm staying with my friend. He said I could stay as long as I helped with the rent." He proudly fished under the collar of his Philadelphia Eagles T-shirt, hauling out a key on a string. "See? He gave me a key to his apartment!"

Allison nudged Josie. "I'll give him five dollars, Aunt Josie." Partly, she just wanted to get going, but the guy was kind of cute.

The young man shoved the tulips toward Allison with a day-brightening smile. Josie swatted Allison's hand. "I've got this." She scrabbled through her huge purse and peered deeply into it before extracting a crisp five-dollar bill.

Grinning broadly, the young man passed Josie the slightly drooping tulips. Waving them around hadn't done the stems much good. "Thanks, Aunt Josie," he bubbled. He darted forward to give Aunt Josie a quick kiss on the cheek.She grabbed hold of his Eagles shirt, yanked him forward, and put him in an age-wrinkled lip-lock. His eyes got huge, his hands stuck straight out, spasming.

Josie released him, smacking her lips. He staggered back, blinking rapidly. *"Mon Dieu!"* he breathed.

Allison gaped, open-mouthed. Daisy glowered. Rosie giggled and took a step back.

"Now that we're better acquainted, what's your name?" Josie shook the fistful of partially squashed tulips and passed them to Allison.

"Me? I am Antoine," he stated proudly.

"French. Are you French?" asked Daisy.

"Ah *oui*. Well, sort of. My mother came from. . . " he snapped his fingers. ". . . the island, the one with the earthquake, and the hurricanes."

"Haiti?" Josie asked.

Antoine grinned. "That's it! Opposite of Lovey." Allison found his grin infectious.

Daisy shot another glance at her older sister. "Well . . . how was it?"

Allison nearly had whiplash snapping around to look at this octogenarian sister.

Josie smacked her lips again and waggled her eyebrows. "Not bad."

Antoine huffed, hands on hips. "Excuse me? Not bad?" He raised his chin, giving a look of hauteur. "You took me by surprise, madam."

"Hmmm." Daisy eyed the young man speculatively. "Well, it's not like I'm cheating. It's just a kiss." Daisy mumbled as she hauled her fanny pack around in front and dug out her wallet. She pulled out a twenty-dollar bill. "Josie got the five-dollar treatment. I want the twenty."

Antoine looked at the bill being shoved at him, shuffled his feet, pursed his lips, glanced from under his long lashes at Aunt Daisy, then resolutely stepped forward.

"Rent money," they chorused together. He laughed. Daisy draped her arms over his shoulders and pulled him in to her iron maiden-formed ample bosom. To Allison, it sure looked like there was tongue involved.

Finally, coming up for breath, Antoine staggered back as Daisy put a hand on her heart and glowed.

"Whoa, mama! Whoa MAMA!" Antoine gulped for air and then grinned from ear to ear. "You ladies here tomorrow? I'm gonna bring

you roses. I can find roses, and . . . and, BIG white flowers, don't
know their names, but I will have them for you."

Rosie giggled and eased a step back.

Josie shook her head. "I'm afraid that's it for us. We're heading
on this afternoon."

Antoine gave her his puppy dog eyes. "Can you pack me in your
suitcase?"

Josie gave a low chuckle and patted him on his shoulder. "Honey,
I don't think our aged hearts can take much more of you. You go give
your roommate that rent money. Don't you lose it," she admonished,
sounding now like a mother rather than an aging seductress.

"Thank you, Aunt Josie, and Aunt—" He looked quizzically at
Daisy.

"Aunt Daisy," she supplied.

Blowing a kiss, Antoine bounded off across the park, skipping
and leaping over a shrub.

"So, what do we do with the flowers?" Josie asked, gazing at the
slowly wilting, half squashed tulips in Allison's clutch.

Daisy looked around then pointed to a post with a small box
on it. Stumping over in her sensible shoes, she hauled out a thick
ribbon of dark green plastic, yanked it free, ripped a section off, and
stuffed it into her fanny pack and then, fiddling with the end of it,
returned to her sisters.

"Dog-poo bag. They have them all over now. Really handy."

Josie shook her head. "Why do we need a dog-poo bag, and why
does it show two happy young people walking hand in hand? Are
you sure it's for dog poo?"

Daisy finally wet her fingers and squished the bag open. She
glanced at the picture on it of a couple walking. "Obviously, they
are walking their dog." She shook the bag open and headed for a
drinking fountain in the opposite direction. Partially filling the bag,
she took the tulips from Allison and shoved the stems into the blue
plastic bag. "Anyone have a rubber band or twist tie?" The sisters

each began deep excavations into their voluminous handbags. Rosie emerged first with a black twist tie.

With the dog poo bag securely fastened, she handed it to Allison.

Gingerly, Allison inspected the results and thought about carrying it with her throughout the rest of the day. She looked up at the sisters brightly, "I'll just run this back to the car, shall I?" She chirped and took off at a mad dash.

. . . .

Allison found the aunts in the Independence Hall Visitor Center, pawing through the brochures on a table. Daisy greeted her. "Tickets for Independence Hall are almost all gone already, the only ones available were for four o'clock. We'll be gone by then."

Rosie squealed, "Here it is. Big Bus. That's what the ranger said we should do instead." She waved open a brochure showing a map of Philadelphia with a thick blue line showing the bus route.

Daisy put her hand on Allison's shoulder. "Do you mind if we don't go into Independence Hall? Apparently, they only have so many spots on the tours, and they are all filled. The ranger suggested we go through the museum right across the street, see the Liberty Bell, then over to Carpenter Hall and then get the tourist bus for a tour of the city. He said there is a great place to get a Philly Cheesesteak sandwich just up the block from the bus stop."

"That sounds great. Whatever you want to do," Allison agreed. She saw Daisy sigh with relief. "I thought this was something you really wanted to do."

"Oh, honey, we've all been through Independence Hall, with all the old desks with their ink pots, and Washington's chair with the sun on the back that Ben Franklin said was either rising or setting. All the signers of the Declaration knew that if the colonies lost the war with Great Britain, the signers would be deemed traitors and could be hung. They were all taking a terrible risk, taking on the greatest military force in the world at that time."

Allison remembered the last history class she'd taken. "But the colonists had internal supply lines. The British had to send troops and supplies all the way across the ocean."

Daisy smiled, eyes brightening. "However, only about a third of the colonists were willing to rebel. Another third felt we should stay with our mother country, and another third didn't care."

Allison grinned. "My professor said that by 1776, when the Declaration was signed and we'd already been fighting for nearly a year, it was closer to two-fifths for, two-fifths against, and one-fifth undecided. Then the British soldiers treated all colonists poorly, and since the British army often treated their soldiers brutally, soldiers began to desert. Colonists turned against each other. Supplies were often given to the British rather than American forces because the British promised to pay. They could. Washington ordered that supplies taken from farmers had to be paid for, but with what? Military scrip and promissory notes would have no value if we lost."

"Bravo!" Daisy nodded. "Now, I am sorry you will not be able to see the inside of Independence Hall. You would have appreciated it."

The sisters and Allison joined the line that wound through the Liberty Bell Hall, carefully reading each panel and gazing at each photo or graphic.

The Liberty Bell, which was not rung until it cracked (as the myth states), hung regally before a large window, showing a bed of tulips and the face of Independence Hall.

Leaving the building, Daisy waded into the tulip garden to grab a shot of the hall with her phone. There was a worn path, but she got scolded by a docent for her indiscretion anyway.

After a brief tour through Carpenter Hall, Rosie started patting her stomach. When she was ignored, she patted louder. Soon, it sounded to Allison as though they were being trailed by a bongo drum.

Finally, Josie whirled on her sister and snapped, "Are you hungry?"

With a final slap to her muumuu covered midsection, Rosie grinned and nodded. "Those Philly Cheesesteak sandwiches sound mighty good right now."

With a huff, Josie looked for the exit. "Which way did that ranger say it was?"

"Go up to Market Street and turn right. He said it was called Sonny's," Daisy directed. As Josie led the way out, Daisy leaned toward Allison. "On our travels, Barth and me, I was the navigator. It was also me who asked directions when we needed them. You know men. They'll get lost for hours and never bother to ask for assistance. If we were lost, I'd say I needed a bathroom, then go in and ask directions."

Reaching Market Street, Rosie pointed to the left. "*Ooooh,* there's the hop-on-hop-off bus. That's what we want to ride."

Josie whirled on her again. "I thought you wanted to eat."

Rosie wilted and murmured, "I do," then giggled, and with a flounce, added, "but I'm not that kind of girl."

The ladies headed right down Market, while Allison tried to puzzle out Rosie's comment. On her visits to Aunt Rosie in Rochester, she'd never seen her act this immaturely. *She's acting like a baby! She's not the younger sister, she's the baby.* Intrigued with her new insight, Allison paid more attention to the sisters' interactions.

The cheesesteak place contained a counter like a Subway restaurant and various long tables sticking out from the wall. The ladies stood in line, requesting what they wanted on their sandwiches: Josie demanded steak sauce; Daisy wanted some greens and peppers; and Rosie asked for fried onions on hers. Allison got plain and added salt enough to make Josie wince and snatch the shaker from her. Josie ordered lemonade, and French fries rounded out the meals. Watching the interactions, Allison smiled in understanding. *Josie, the oldest, is the boss, Rosie the baby, and Daisy? Hmm. Mother?*

· · · · · · · · · · · ·

On the way to the bus stop, Daisy opened the large map of the bus route, and while examining the stops, walked into a light pole. She stumbled into Josie who grabbed Rosie for support who stepped on the foot of a gentleman headed the opposite direction, causing him to trip sideways and catch his leg on the leash of a small dog being walked. Falling hard on his hip across the leash, the small dog yelped as it was nearly squashed by his flailing arm. The frantic owner lunged to rescue her dog who promptly nipped her in panic. She sat hard on the man's shoulder as he tried to rise.

Josie smacked the map out of Daisy's hands, snapping, "You're dangerous!" as the three hurried on. Allison stopped to help the woman up first, who grabbed her dog with a huff and scurried off crooning soothing nonsense in its flattened, furry ear. Allison then held out her hand to the man. His pants were wet with who knew—or didn't want to know—what, and his mood was toxic. He batted her hand aside, rolled to his feet, rescued the phone that had shot from his pocket in a frantic bid for escape, and glared from Allison to the retreating trio of elderly ladies.

"They should be in a home," he snarled and stomped off. Allison cringed and hurried after her aunts.

. . . .

A bus at the canopied bus stop disgorged passengers as the ladies fussed over the price of their tickets. "Do you have a senior discount?" Daisy demanded.

"It's already been applied," the ticket seller answered, without looking up.

Daisy looked appalled and accusing. "You didn't even check our driver's licenses."

Rosie shuffled her feet and whispered, "I haven't got mine."

Josie glared at her. "How did you get on the plane? You need photo ID."

Scrabbling in her overstuffed purse, Rosie produced her passport. Josie rolled her eyes, shook her head, and turned away.

Hauling themselves up the steps of the bus, the three sisters came to a stop in front of the stairs leading up to the open, upper level.

"I want to be up there."

Daisy pointed to the sign. Allison read, *"One way. Exit only."* All three stared at the sign.

A young lady pushed in and started up the narrow stairs, sign ignored. She was imperiously ordered by the woman taking tickets to come back down. She straight-arm pointed to the stairway at the back of the bus.

Rosie, Josie, and Daisy followed and ascended the rear set of stairs to the rows of seats above. Wanting the best view possible, Rosie and Josie scooted down one bench to be by the rail, while Daisy and Allison took the bench seat in front of them. Soon a young man, clad in a bright yellow shirt that contrasted with his dark chocolate complexion, and sporting a radiantly bright smile, picked up a microphone clipped to the wall.

"*Kon'nichiwa! Kyō wa dono yō ni minasandesu ka?*" He gazed around the bus, eyes alight. "Oh, this isn't the Japanese tour group? *Bonne après-midi! Comment êtes-vous tous aujourd'hui?*" Again, he smiled beguilingly. "No? *Guten Tag! Wie geht es euch allen heute?*"

This time, two girls answered him—in German. Rosie giggled.

He chatted with them until the bus was ready to leave, introducing himself as multilingual, with a degree in theater. He had lived for eighteen months in Germany while touring Europe with a theater group. He launched into a rendition of something Shakespearean as the bus pulled from the curb and started its run. He had the three sisters entranced. Allison worried. After their show this morning, she wondered if any young man was safe.

The bus chugged by the US Mint, Betsy Ross' house, and Christ Church. A stop was made so people could get off and see the sites, then get back on when the next bus came by. Rosie hopped up. Her sisters pulled her back down.

"We haven't got time. We're just riding the bus, Rosie."

Daisy flipped open the map. Since they were safely seated, Josie allowed her to carefully examine the blue line on the map the bus would follow. Echoing what their tour guide was saying, Daisy read off each of the sites they passed: City Hall, Academy of Fine Arts, Logan Museum, the Rodin Museum . . . Their guide pointed out various statues of people famous to the city of Philadelphia and state of Pennsylvania. They stopped in front of the Museum of Art, where Sylvester Stallone had run up the steps in the first *Rocky* movie. The statue of him was pointed out in a copse to the right of the stairs. Their multilingual guide explained in both English and German that the art museum did not consider the Rocky statue to be a work of art, so after the movies, they did not want it at the top of the stairs, or at all. But it was now a tourist attraction, so finally it was agreed that the statue could prance, arms raised, forevermore among trees on the grounds of the museum.

The bus puttered on. At a long traffic stop, Daisy glanced up from the map at a set of golden legs. She looked up to see a statue of a proud woman carrying a banner, riding a high-stepping charger. The statue occupied a tiny island in the middle of the road, traffic streaming by on the far side. Their bus was snugged up close enough that Daisy tried to reach out and touch the leg of the horse. She couldn't. The guide identified the statue as Joan of Arc, and the bus moved on.

"Why is Joan of Arc standing in the middle of the road?" Rosie called to their guide. A blaring car horn drowned out her question. She turned around in her seat to ask her sisters, insistently, "Why is Joan standing in the middle of the road?"

Josie shook her head and shrugged. Daisy buried her nose in the map. On the swing back, they went by the Academy of Natural Sciences, back around City Hall, past the Bellevue, and down antique row. Finally, the bus paralleled the Delaware River before circling the Liberty Bell and ending where they had begun. Allison hopped up, ready to bound down the stairs after the long ride. Three very stiff ladies levered themselves out of their benches.

"*Umm-umm.*" Rosie attempted to get their guide's attention.

Josie grabbed her elbow and hustled her toward the exit stairs. "He's busy giving directions to those German girls."

"Yes, but—"

Daisy, gripping the handrail, glanced back at Rosie and at the attractive young ladies chatting in German with the guide. "They're a lot cuter than you are!"

"Yes, but—"

Daisy descended stiffly. Josie maneuvered Rosie into position to follow her.

"I want to know why Joan was standing in the middle of the road," Rosie wailed.

Stopping to wait at the bottom of the narrow stairs, Allison watched Daisy inch her way down. Allison held out her hand to steady her on the last step. She waited while Rosie and Josie came down, one careful step at a time. Offering them her hand, she pointed out the bench near the ticket kiosk.

"Why don't you three wait there? The car is all packed and ready. I'll go get it and pick you up here. It looks like I can then go right over to the boulevard by the Delaware River, cross the bridge, and we're on our way to Atlantic City."

Instead of sitting, Rosie hurried over to the two young ladies in the ticket booth. "Excuse me? Miss?"

One of the girls glanced up from her ticketing computer, raising her eyebrows.

"Why is Joan standing in the middle of the road?" she asked earnestly.

The girl continued working on her computer and gave a little shrug. "To show she's invincible."

Rosie nodded, satisfied, and turned to walk back to her sisters. Allison guessed that was as good an answer as any. Then she heard the one girl turn to the other, indicating with her chin to the three old ladies. "Which one of 'em do ya think is Joan?"

After getting the aunts settled on the bench, Allison dashed back for the car. She scanned the park as she sprinted for the hotel parking area. Their friend, Antoine, was not in sight. She grinned and shook her head at the memory.

. . . .

Leaving Philadelphia proved surprisingly easy. They crossed the bridge over the Delaware River into New Jersey and were on the Atlantic City Expressway.

Ten minutes later, Rosie started squeaking, head resting against the window. Josie snorted and gurgled. It sounded like she was choking. Daisy reached back from her seat up front and poked her. Josie snorted and let her head fall against the sidewall. Allison glanced in the rearview mirror. Josie, mouth open, drooled. Within minutes, her head cushioned by her sweater against the passenger window, Daisy started her bombing run, sounding like her aircraft had engine trouble.

Glancing down at the now-deflated tulips in the leaking dog-poo bag tucked into the cup holder, Allison thought of her octogenarian aunts' lip-locking Antoine. She shook her head. Her father would have found their behavior appalling, shocking, disgusting. Allison felt a smile emerging. She thought it was rather cute!

Chapter 8

CASINOS AND KARAOKE

Arriving at Atlantic City two-and-a-half hours later, Allison managed to find someone to help lug the aunts' massive suitcases to the elevator and down the long hall to their third-floor suite. Josie and Daisy took the first bedroom they came to, leaving Rosie and Allison the second. By the time they'd plopped Rosie's suitcase on the bed nearest the bathroom, Daisy had gotten the connecting door open with exclamations of delight. All three hustled over to the window to gaze out over the grounds and see if they could see the ocean. They couldn't. Daisy had gotten the least expensive two-bedroom suite available. But the view delighted them anyway.

Allison collapsed on the bed, watching the aunts' bustle about the two rooms, checking the bathrooms, counting the towels, oohing over the little shampoos and soaps. "Look, even plastic shower caps!" Rosie gushed.

Room service menus were scanned, and prices tut-tutted. Closets were thrown open and the little personal safes found and examined. Josie managed to get hers open. But Daisy then intervened.

"Remember what happened the last time you used one of the room safes?" she admonished. "You got your things in there, locked it, and the next morning you couldn't remember your code. It was a mess."

Josie waved her hand dismissively. "Oh, it was just some cheap junk jewelry and the rest of our itinerary. Nothing important."

"Yes, but it meant the next person who used the room couldn't open the safe."

"Well, the hotel was nice enough to return my things."

Daisy snorted. "And you gave them that lame story about being old and forgetting you'd left them in there."

Allison propped herself up on her bed. "You mean you just left your things there? Didn't you tell someone about the problem?"

Daisy rolled her eyes. "No. She was afraid they'd have to blow up the safe or something and she'd be charged for it."

Allison hesitated. "I think they have a master key that opens all of them. I'm sure it happens fairly often."

Daisy wheeled on her sister who was still hovering by the open safe. "Well, she is NOT going to put anything in this time."

Rosie giggled.

Shaking her head in amusement at her baby sister's obvious joy, Daisy turned to root around in her suitcase. She hauled out a clanking cloth bag. "All the quarters and nickels from our coin jar— I'm ready to face the one-armed bandits."

Allison starred wide-eyed at the bulging bag. No wonder Daisy's suitcase was so heavy. There must be a good ten pounds of coins in that bag.

Rosie dug and came up with a much smaller baggie of quarters. "Let's hit the slots," she crowed.

"I'm heading for the poker tables," Josie announced, strapping on a waist belt with a small wallet of money.

Allison carefully extracted a five-dollar bill from her wallet and tucked it in a front pocket.

Daisy watched. "That's all?"

Allison shrugged.

"Better grab a few dollars more. We're all on our own for supper."

Once on the casino floor, the ladies went their separate ways. Allison stuck with Rosie. Approaching one of the more colorful slot machines, quarter in hand, Rosie hesitated. "Where do I insert the coins?" she asked, looking over the front of the machine.

There was no coin slot. "What do I do with all my coins?" Rosie wailed.

A bespangled, elderly woman nearby pointed to a machine by the wall. "Dump your change in there, honey. It gives you bills that you can use in the slots." She patted Rosie's arm and went back to punching buttons and staring at spinning pictures.

Rosie slowly dumped her coins into the plastic mouth of the swirling machine. Allison heard another machine gulping coins and saw Daisy just down the way dumping entire freezer bags of coins into the open maw. Daisy's machine swirled the coins, clattered, clanged, chirped, and spit out a series of bills. Daisy grabbed the money, then noticed Allison watching. Shaking her head, she shrugged. "I should just walk out now. This is the best machine in the whole room. It entertains, makes noise, and you always break even."

She didn't heed her own advice and headed back to the casino floor.

Rosie's machine coughed out a ten, four ones, and a quarter.

It wasn't long before Allison's five dollars was gone. She drifted over to watch Rosie punch buttons and listened to the pinging and bonging. After another twenty minutes, Rosie threw her hands up, pushed one last button that produced a white slip of paper, and hopped up from the stool. "I won!" she chortled. "I won in Atlantic City."

"You did? How much?" Allison exclaimed, listening for the bells and sirens that usually announced a big win.

Eyes sparkling, Rosie announced, "I started with fourteen dollars and twenty-five cents. After using all of that, I now have twenty dollars and fifty cents! Shall we eat? My treat since I'm feeling flush!"

Allison smiled. It didn't take much to make Rosie happy. "How about if we walk a bit first, go see the ocean while there's still some light."

With a happy nod, Rosie took Allison's arm and the two headed for the main doors.

They strolled slowly to the boardwalk, Rosie still clutching Allison's arm. The wind gusted, flinging stinging grains of sand at them. Waves scoured the beach clean of footprints and left hopes of new seashells for the morning. Thick clouds shrouded the setting sun.

Rosie soon tired of the wind and sand. "Let's find something to eat," She mumbled, trying to keep from getting a mouthful of blown sand.

Ducking her head as another blast hit, Allison agreed. "Lead the way."

Rosie staggered against another wind gust, grabbing tighter for Allison's support. Heads ducked, they headed for some flashing signs. Between the buildings, the wind grew less, allowing Rosie to look carefully at each option. Singing emanated from one eatery. Not very good singing. Allison winced as a particularly sour note ricocheted out of the doorway.

Rosie giggled and hurried to the door, pointing to the sign that announced karaoke. That explained the out-of-tune singing.

Rosie chose a table to the side, near the karaoke stage, listening avidly to each person who came forward to belt out a favorite song. She and Allison ordered a cup of soup and half a sandwich. Allison found the choices good, but prices rather high.

Rosie ate slowly, sometimes humming along quietly or singing under her breath.

They'd been sitting for over an hour, Allison getting restless, though amused by Rosie's obvious enjoyment.

A young man came to the tiny stage, leading a reluctant young lady. They huddled together, coming to an agreement on what song to choose. Decision made, the young man confidently held forth his microphone. Looking adoringly at his lady, he began.

"We didn't care if people stared,

We'd make out in a crowd somewhere. . . "

Rosie started bouncing in her seat, a big grin lighting up her face. "I love this one! I know who sings it." The bouncing became more pronounced. "Oh, oh, oh... Princess Leia. Carrie Fischer. Underwear."

Frowning, Allison eyed her aunt. *Dementia?*

The bouncing increased. "Underwear? Under where? Underwood! Carrie Underwood and . . . Shawl."

The young lady's turn to join in brought a stutter and cough. All she needed to sing was *"Remind me, remind me."* She froze, face ashen.

"Colorful shawl, Nail! Brad Paisley!" Rosie's eyes were alight. Allison blinked in confusion. *Nail? Brad? Oh. A nail is like a brad, and paisley is . . . okay.* Allison would not have associated paisley with a shawl.

Backing up a step, the young lady pushed her boyfriend away. He sang his part of the duet, but she started to tear up, trying to pull free from his restraining hand as he motioned her to join him.

"So, on fire and so in love," he sang to her, looking like he really meant it.

Her remind-me response came around again, producing a look of terror on the young lady's face. A sweet soprano rang out on the second, *"Remind me!"* About twenty pairs of eyes swiveled to the old lady in the blue and orange muumuu with the ecstatically glowing face, bouncing up and down in her seat in the corner. *"Remember the airport, dropping me off?"* Rosie sang in heartfelt country tradition.

His turn again. He sang to Rosie who rose from her chair and walked around behind the couple. As he sang, Rosie whispered quickly to the woman, then pushed her forward to stand next to her man. At first the young woman looked unsure, but Rosie, the back-up singer, took up a position behind her. As the young woman lip-synced, Rosie sang the Underwood part. It wasn't long before the young lady started hamming it up with her beau, leaning into each other, hand-gesturing, and posturing.

The song ended. The couple pulled Rosie forward as people cheered and clapped. The young man went into a huddle with Rosie, his dark hair nearly touching her red curls and hair bows. She looked at a screen he showed her.She pointed, he hesitated, then nodded. Rosie giggled, as did the young lady.

Allison put her hand to her mouth as the strains of Stevie Nick's *Leather and Lace* pulsed from the sound system, astonished that seemingly innocent Rosie had chosen *this* song.

"Is love so fragile and the heart so hollow," Rosie crooned, looking skyward as though addressing the cosmos.

It was now that Allison noticed the crowd. They had been talking, eating, and drinking through the previous duet. But all that had stopped. Every eye was turned on Rosie and the young man.

When Rosie reached, *"I have my own life, and I am stronger than you know,"* she held up her skinny, droopy arms in body-builder stance.

Chuckles, guffaws, and a few hoots resounded from around the room.

While singing the verse, *"Still I carry this feeling, when you walked into my house, that you won't be walking out the door,"* Rosie motioned as if fiercely locking a door, dropping the key down her skinny chest, and holding her arms out to prevent him from leaving.

The audience howled.

She got nose-to-nose with the young man on *"Lovers forever, face to face."* He started to chuckle, almost missing his entrance.

"You in the moonlight, with your sleepy eyes."

Rosie mimed falling asleep, sagging against the man.

"But that time I saw you," he continued, miming turning on bright lights. *"I knew with you to light my nights, somehow I'd get*

by." Rosie batted her eyelashes, hands clutched at her bosom. Her partner mimed looking for a way to get by her.

Then into the duet, *"Lovers forever, face to face"* the two of them stood face to face, singing to each other. Rosie's voice became husky, smoky as she repeated the refrain. The young man struggled to keep a straight face. On the final *"Give to me your leather,"* she grabbed his belt, yanking him close, then, in a bedroom voice, *"Take from me my lace."*

The audience went wild, one person chanting, *"Cou-gar! Cou-gar!"* It was taken up by others.

The young man grinned and bowed gallantly.

The whole crowd now crowed, *"Cou-gar! Cou-gar!"* as Rosie, hand to her mouth, demurely giggled.

The young man helped the old woman down the two steps from the tiny stage. As he escorted her to their table, Allison rose to help. On the stage singing, Rosie had seemed vibrant and lively. Now, in her nearly shapeless flowered dress, she looked old and frail. Her voice had been so strong and sure. Allison helped her aunt back to her seat. Rosie's face radiated happiness, while the audience continued to cheer and chant, *"Cou-gar!"*

. . . .

It was dark as Allison and Rosie made their way slowly back to their hotel, braved the noise and bustle of the casino, and rode the elevator to their room. Allison showered as Rosie went through her pre-bed routine. Finally, Rosie nestled herself under her blanket and comforter. Allison turned off the light. She heard Rosie murmur, *"Cou-gar!"* and giggle.

Shortly, Rosie started her nighttime squeaking.

Allison smiled as she stretched out under her coverlet. *What a day.* She found herself actually enjoying the antics of these old ladies. Was this, this innocent fun, what her father meant when he said the aunts "picked up men?"

Chapter 9

ATLANTIC CITY

"You go ahead and take a walk." Daisy flapped her hand at Allison.

The aunts shuffle around the suite. Allison had been ready within twenty minutes. Having two bathrooms really did speed up getting ready, at least for Allison.

"Okay," she agreed, shoving up off the bed. "Where will you go when you leave here? Where can I find you?"

"Breakfast first," Daisy began.

"No. We want room for a buffet, and the lunch buffet is less than the dinner," Rosie interrupted.

Josie added her two cents. "I agree with Rosie. Let's have a cup of coffee." She pointed to the coffee maker in the room. "Then pick up a pastry or something light. We'll do the lunch buffet. So, Allison, if we are not here, we will be on the floor, probably slots and poker tables."

No one saw her wave as she headed out the door, their attention back on the long process of getting ready for the day. No one accompanied Allison in the elevator to the lobby floor.

Emptying out into the casino, a few people at the slot machines poked buttons and swiped cards. Bells bonged and lights flickered and flashed. It was too early for most people. Allison made a b-line for the wall of glass doors, eager to be away from the battering sensory stimulus.

The sun sparkled off the waves as they lapped gently at the sand. A salty breeze ruffled Allison's light brown hair as she strolled along the boardwalk, listening to gulls and watching the sandpipers hurrying along the wave line. No sound emanated from the massive casinos, except when the doors opened to let chattering groups of people in or out. Way out in the waves, she saw a dark form rise out of the water, a rounded back, a triangular fin.

A dolphin? She stood, watching, relaxing.

There it was again, the dark mound rising out of the waves, and a second one. She smiled. *Two dolphins!* She wished they would come in closer. Allison found a bench and sat in the sun with arm across the back, legs outstretched.

Pulling out her cell phone, she used the quiet time to call her mother with an update of the trip so far, describing the young man in Philadelphia and Rosie singing a duet the night before and being called a cougar. She heard the relief in her mother's voice that there had been no disasters, no major embarrassments, and no disappearing aunts.

With a deep sigh, Allison roused out of her daydreaming. *Back to work.* Checking her watch, she headed back to the clamor and commotion of the casino. Entering by a different door, Allison rode the elevator back to their floor, striding down the startlingly loud, busy hallway rug. Swiping her card, she pushed open the door and came to a horrified halt, hand to her mouth.

Her room had been tossed! She could see through the open door into the second bedroom. Clothes strewn everywhere, on the floor, covering every surface. It looked as though the suitcases had exploded.

Every surface groaned under the loads covering them. Clothes draped every chair, open drawer, every inch of the beds.

Draped, not thrown. Allison let out her breath. She did a walk-through of both bedrooms, shaking her head. Every surface was covered with creams, bottles, brushes, curling irons, and items Allison could not identify. She daintily picked up one such item. An undergarment, apparently. Holding it up and turning it back and forth, she studied it, trying to decide what it was for and how on earth one put it on. Gently, she placed it back on the seat of the chair where she'd found it. Slips, orthopedic stockings, shoe inserts, brassieres and things that could be inserted into the brassieres. She shook her head and returned to the bank of elevators.

On the casino floor, Allison found Josie at the poker tables, a small pile of chips in front of her. At least she hadn't gone broke. Unsurprisingly, she found Rosie listening to a band in one of the bars, humming and bouncing to the beat. Walking down the aisles of bonging, whirring slot machines, she spotted Daisy holding her cell phone to her ear. She wasn't speaking. With a shake of her head and pursed lips, she held the phone in front of her, tapping a couple buttons. Her expression was what? *Concerned? Worried? Annoyed?* Tapping one last time, Daisy slid the phone back in her waist pouch.

Allison approached and perched on a stool next to her. "Hi, Aunt Daisy." Daisy smiled and nodded. "Is everything all right?"

Daisy quirked her lips. "I've lost eighteen dollars." They sat silently while Daisy punched buttons and watched wheels spin and pictures click to a stop across the screen. "Yes!" Bells bonged as Daisy's spin count increased by five.

Message received. Mind your own business. Allison gazed around at the glitz and lights, mirrors reflecting it all, increasing the spectacle. She got up and walked among the machines, wait staff hurrying by carrying trays of pretty drinks.

While watching one bejeweled, overweight lady stuffed into bright pink-camouflage yoga pants which clashed with her violet-purple hair, she felt someone come up behind her. Turning, she came nose to chest with a man peering down at her. He grinned, showing a gap between his two prominent front teeth. Allison fell back a step.

"Hey, cutie. You here alone?"

Allison glanced at his slick-backed hair and synthetic green and orange sport coat. She nearly blurted out, "I didn't know you could still buy Brylcreem." It brought back images of the old TV shows she watched and her mother's stories of guys in the 1970s. Take him back fifty years and he'd be in a broad-collared, shiny polyester shirt, unbuttoned to the navel, with gold chains tangling in his chest hairs. She stifled a laugh.

He took it as a positive response and moved in closer, waggling his single, long, bushy unibrow.

Allison felt her belly clench as she struggled to refrain from yelling, *"Oh my gosh! There's something crawling across your forehead! Don't worry, I'll kill it!"* and smack him.

"Uh, no. I'm not alone."

His smile faded. Then he tried to fire it up again, obviously thinking that maybe she had other women with her.

"I'm here with my aunt!" Allison blurted, thinking, *Daisy? No. Rosie? Definitely not. Josie!* With a forced smile, Allison trucked off across the casino floor toward the poker tables. Of course, he followed. Fortunately, as she approached the gaming table, she saw Josie was between hands.

As her unwanted admirer's hand brushed her shoulder, she shuddered, and called out, "Aunt Josie!" As soon as Josie looked up at her, she mouthed "HELP."

With his sweaty, unwanted palm resting on her shoulder, Allison loudly introduced her aunt. "This is my Aunt Josie," Allison said, shifting sideways out from under his hand.

Josie scanned him slowly up and down, gaze stopping about at belt buckle level. "Oh, you're a big boy, aren't you?" she purred, sliding slowly from her seat.

Others at the gaming table froze, intrigued.

Josie moved into the man's personal space. He fell back a step. She languidly reached a wrinkled, be-ringed hand toward his belt. "Yum!"

Allison's eyebrows shot up. He fell back further, a look of horror dawning.

He turned and fled.

Allison grinned. Josie smirked and held up her hand for a high-five. The other players at the poker table clapped appreciatively.

"Now that you're back from your walk, let's gather the others for lunch." Josie turned to the players at the table, nodded to them, and gathered her chips. Several congratulated her, others looked relieved that she was leaving.

"Have you seen Daisy or Rosie, or do we need to search?" she asked Allison.

Allison led her eldest aunt to Daisy first, who punched out of her machine, taking what little was left. Then into the bar to gather Rosie, who was finishing her fish-bowl size Pina Colada. She picked up the little umbrella, twirling it between her fingers. "They sure skimp on the rum on these drinks," she chirped, before taking Allison's arm to steady herself.

They all trooped off to the buffet, happily paying the hefty price to paw through piles of various foods spread over myriad counters.

Daisy nudged Allison and told her conspiratorially, "You have to get in early or all the crab legs get taken."

Rosie nudged Allison on the other side and told her in whisper, "Just wait until you see the dessert table."

Josie, taking her turn to give advice, nudged Allison and commanded, "Eat the most expensive things. Look for oysters and calamari. Gotta get your money's worth."

The ladies took small amounts of many items, then toddled off to find the closest table. Allison piled her plate high, taking Josie's advice about what to choose.

Allison ate heartily, while the aunts chatted, snacked, people-watched, and ambled back for a taste of something else.

"You haven't had clams," Daisy commented to her elder sister.

"Nope, not since a few years ago."

Daisy chewed her mouthful of bacon-wrapped scallop. "Why?"

Josie shook her head. "It was after a clam bake, so I assume it was seafood poisoning. Those little gut minions decided I'd eaten something I shouldn't. They emptied me out pretty violently from both ends. Twenty-four hours later, my innards were squeaky clean from tummy to tail!"

There was silence. Daisy closed her open mouth. "Thank you for sharing," she dead-panned.

Rosie giggled.

Allison looked down at the remains on her plate and decided she was no longer hungry. Daisy saw her push it away and waved her off to go entertain herself. "We'll be here awhile, dear. You go have fun."

Allison checked all the glitzy shops, wandered the town, checked out other casinos, then headed back two hours later. It took a half hour to scan the entire casino. No aunts. Passing back in front of the buffet dining area, she spotted them, still sitting with plates of goodies in front of them. It looked like they had finally made it to dessert. Allison checked her watch. They'd been in there for three hours.

Daisy spotted her outside the restaurant and waved. Finishing a few last bites, they folded up napkins, pushed away nearly empty plates and slowly levered themselves to their feet. Walking very slowly, arm-in-arm for support, they came with bleary, blissful smiles.

"Nap time," was all that was said, as they lumbered toward the elevators. Allison shrugged and headed back outside. It was a beautiful day for a walk.

She returned when the sun hung low over the casinos and hotels. Rays sparkled off lapping ocean waves, casting a warm yellow glow on the people taking an early evening stroll on the beach. The flashing lights, noise, and odors of the casino floor assaulted her senses as she made her way through rows of slot machines. The wait staff wove deftly around machines and people, delivering drinks to ladies in bead-encrusted sweatsuits and rhinestone-sparkled T-shirts.

The swooshing elevator doors had nearly closed out the noise of the floor when three loud men in striped shorts, Hawaiian shirts, with varicose-veined legs, grabbed the edges of the closing doors. High fiving each other and cheering their masculine prowess at getting the elevator doors to open, they piled in. Allison sagged against the back wall. The men merrily punched buttons to every floor, laughing uproariously.

Dancing in and out of the door on the second floor, the men pushed Allison back in as she tried to leave, figuring it would be faster to take the stairs. "Hey, hey, hey," one waved his mates back onto the elevator. "What floor is yours, little lady?" Alcohol wafted in waves as he spoke.

"Third," Allison replied.

He nodded, waved at the bank of lit-up numbers by the door. "Third. Wow! That's easy! That's the next floor." He turned to his two friends as the door bumped over and over on one bent-over guy's extended butt. "The little lady needs to get off on the third floor."

His two friends cheered. He hauled his friend the rest of the way into the elevator and banged on button three.

Confusion erupted when the door opened. A couple barged forward to get on as Allison tried to push her way through the alcohol-fueled men to get off. The three men couldn't remember which floor was theirs and couldn't decide whether to get off or stay on.

Allison shoved her way through, escaping down the hall. Heaving a relieved sigh, she thought, *Geez, this is worse than the dorm on a Friday night.*

Her key card worked on the second try. Easing the door open so as not to hit one of her aunts coming out of the bathroom, she heard dice being shaken, lots of dice being shaken. Frowning, she entered the rest of the way. Rosie sat on a bed, Josie at the desk and Daisy in a chair by the little table. All three had a pile or large baggie of pill bottles. Each one filled one or more small, rectangular daily pill dispensers.

Daisy looked up with a big smile. "How was your afternoon walk?"

Allison flopped down on her bed, laying across the tan bedspread. "Nice. It was a really enjoyable walk. I think I saw a dolphin swimming offshore. I love watching the seagulls against the evening sky and the sandpipers skittering along at the water's edge."

All sound of dice had stopped. Josie starred at her. "Watching birds is what you find enjoyable?"

Looking down at the threads in the bedspread, Allison replied softly, "Mmm, yes."

"I think that's sweet," Rosie crooned.

"I've always enjoyed listening to frogs," Daisy stated and turned back to separating out her pills.

Josie laughed.

Silence descended, except for the sounds of bottles being popped open, pills rattling, and plastic lids clicking shut. Daisy glanced at Allison. "This one is for hypertension, this for low thyroid, this for arthritis inflammation, and the garlic tablets for everything else."

"Huh," Josie responded. "I'm on two pills for hypertension. This one is to make me whizz less."

Rosie giggled and held up a pale purple pill. "This one makes me whizz more."

With a frown, Josie continued. "This one is for migraines, and it also helps with my heart arrhythmia. This pretty one is for high cholesterol and finally a once-daily multivitamin."

"I was told by *my* doctor not to take a daily vitamin," Rosie chimed, snapping shut her last plastic case.

Daisy frowned. "Why ever not?"

"He said I was getting too much of several things and that I was better off eating right."

"I asked my doctor if Cialis was right for me," Josie announced, batting her eyes seductively. "I want to be like that lady drifting around in the diaphanous blue dress, the one who thinks about men all the time."

Rosie giggled. "Cialis is for men!"

"Yeah, so when a man *sees Alice*, he knows what to do," Josie chortled.

"I asked if Zoloft was right for me," Daisy announced with enthusiasm.

Allison looked at her wide-eyed.

Josie snorted. "You don't suffer from depression."

"They're Happy Pills. I like being happy," she sparkled, bouncing in her fake leather chair.

Heaving a wistful sigh, Rosie shared, "I want Lunestra."

"Do you have trouble sleeping?" Allison asked.

"Oh, no. I sleep just fine. I like the butterflies on the commercial."

"They're moths. Moths come out at night. You know, Luna moths," Daisy corrected.

Josie added, "You definitely don't want Lunestra. It's been taken off the market. It had so many bad side effects. It makes you eat in the middle of the night and go driving without knowing where you're going."

Rosie looked stunned. "But I do that anyway. That's why I don't drive much anymore. I forget where I'm going. And as far as eating during the night, when I wake up during the wee hours and can't sleep, I make popcorn," Rosie finished happily, making loud lip-smacking sounds.

Josie shook her head. "No, I mean, I have a friend. She got up one morning and told her family to make their own breakfast, because she wasn't hungry. Her husband asked why she had spaghetti sauce dripped down her nightgown and around her mouth. It seems she'd gotten up without knowing it. She had warmed up the spaghetti and eaten it without even being aware that she had done so."

"Speaking of spaghetti, what are we doing for dinner?" Allison asked.

All three froze. "Dinner?"

Rosie moaned.

Silence.

"You're hungry?"

Allison remembered finding the aunts still eating after three hours. "Uh, well, kind of."

"Ice cream!" Daisy blurted. "There's always room for ice cream, or sherbet. That always tastes good. And we can get it from room service."

It was agreed—ice cream and sherbet for dinner.

Figuring she needed some healthy food, Allison got a banana split. The evening's entertainment consisted of an old movie with Fred Astaire. Rosie sang along and Daisy tried dancing. Allison laughed.

Chapter 10

OUTER BANKS

Allison realized her hope for an early start was a pipe dream, utterly laughable. First the suitcases had to unexplode. Even with Allison's help, repacking took most of the morning. With an 11a.m. checkout, the pressure was on.

The aunts made use of the in-room coffee and light breakfast from room service. Allison hauled her suitcase and the aunts' bags of purchases that would not fit in overstuffed suitcases out to the car. The aunts took turns leaning on suitcases to get them zipped.

Finally packed, Allison found Daisy's suitcase noticeably lighter. The coins were gone, eaten by hungry slot machines. By noon, they were out of the city. Daisy, once more riding shotgun, dinked away on her cell phone, chatted with Siri, and directed Allison west by way of Route 40.

Cruising through a bustling hamlet, Josie spotted a grocery store. "Stop. Pull in," she demanded. "Snack run."

Allison wheeled in. The aunts piled out, grunting and manually lifting legs and dragging free purses and fanny packs. "Stay here."

"Pull in closer if a spot opens up."

"Listen to the radio. The news is about to come on. And roll down the windows, we don't want it getting too hot in the car."

Daisy popped the trunk using her key fob, grabbed a couple reusable grocery bags, and off they went.

After about twenty minutes, the car doors yanked opened. Grocery bags rustled, waking her from a gentle doze.

"So, what's the weather report?" Josie demanded.

Allison pulled herself upright, looking guiltily at the silent radio. "Weather?"

"You were supposed to listen to the weather report."

"Now, now. You heard the report this morning. Mostly sunny and breezy, seasonally warm today and tomorrow, then rain moving in tomorrow night," Daisy chided her sister.

Hands on hips, Josie snapped back. "That report was for Atlantic City."

"We're not going that far south. It won't be much different, and maybe even a little warmer." Daisy resumed her spot in the front and unloaded snacks, passing out children's squeezable yogurt tubes, granola bars, bananas, and apple-flavored juice boxes. Rosie hauled out a four-pack of strawberry flavored Ensure.

Allison accepted her banana and yogurt tube. "Is this lunch?" she asked, sounding a bit feeble.

"For us." Daisy scrabbled at the bottom of her shopping bag, carefully withdrawing a chicken wrap sandwich from the deli department and a can of Coke. Smiling, she unwrapped the sandwich and popped the Coke open before handing them to Allison. "Sustenance and caffeine to keep you going."

With a grateful sigh, Allison chomped into the wrap, savoring the mayonnaise and touch of mustard added to the crunch of lettuce and chunks of fried chicken. She took a long guzzle of Coke and felt ready to hit the highway. While Allison finished her sandwich, Daisy asked her to switch on the engine so she could power up the windows and adjust the car's climate controls.

Finished and with a satisfied grin, Allison pulled out of the parking lot, heading for the New Jersey border and Route 95 to Delaware.

. . . .

Allison had covered most of the drive through Delaware on Route 1 while the aunts napped. Rosie still lay head back, squeaking.

Daisy peeled her second banana. Taking a large bite, she masticated blissfully, eyes half closed. A chunk of the remaining banana slowly came loose and fell onto her lap. Daisy watched with amusement as it slid off her lap onto the seat next to her leg. She delicately picked it up with two fingers, examined it carefully for dust or dirt, and prepared to pop it in her mouth.

"I wouldn't eat that," Josie cautioned from behind her.

"Why not? It's not dirty."

"You don't know who's been sitting in that seat."

"Yes, I do. It's my car." Daisy popped the piece of banana into her mouth.

"I farted in that seat," Josie snapped.

Daisy's chewing paused. "You had your pants on. Besides, you wear Depends. I doubt anything escaped."

Josie harrumphed. Daisy, wearing a smug expression, finished her banana.

Allison gripped the wheel and kept her eyes on the road, wondering who may have farted in her seat.

They continued south along Route 113 on the Delmarva Peninsula with Allison hugging the right lane as cars raced past her or charged up behind her and peeled out to pass only to swing in front of her to blow exhaust in her face.

"Here!" Daisy yelled, pointing to a gravel parking area. "Turn! Now!"

Hitting the turn signal, Allison barely tapped the brake before yanking them off the road onto the lot. Gravel flew. Rosie's head banged off the side window, and she awoke with a squawk.

"Sorry."

Josie, hanging on for dear life to the handle over the door, glared and spit imprecations under her breath, then snarled. "What on earth?"

"This is the restaurant where Barth and I always stop on our way down the Delmarva. It has absolutely wonderful seafood." Daisy had already unbuckled her seat belt and clipped on her fanny pack. Wearing a stunned expression, Allison scanned for a parking spot.

"Pull around in front," Daisy ordered. "Park near that anchor."

Allison wheeled around the building to where she'd seen that massive anchor. "Why are we stopping?" Rosie asked, rubbing her clonked noggin.

"Meding's Seafood was a must stop for Barth and me whenever we came this way." Daisy had her door open before Allison had fully brought the car to a halt.

Rosie glanced at her watch. "It's four-thirty. I thought we had lunch, and it's far too early for supper."

Daisy was out of the car and bustling across the parking lot. "We had snacks, not lunch. Consider it a late lunch or early dinner."

Josie unbuckled, hauled her purse off the floor at her feet, and levered herself out the door. "I'm hungry." And off she went in pursuit of her sister.

Allison got out, opened the door for Rosie, and escorted her grumbling aunt into the restaurant.

Inside, a glass case filled with fish and shellfish on ice stretched across the room. Fish batter and spices lined the shelves in front of the cases.

Daisy and Josie were already being shown into the main dining room.

Rosie sighed loudly.

"Oh, knock it off," Daisy snapped. "Wait until you taste their she-crab soup. You can get a pile of fried oysters, or the fried or blackened fresh fish of your choice."

"Scallops?" Rosie asked hopefully.

"Absolutely."

"Raw oysters?"

"Uh, I'm not sure about raw, but probably."

Their hostess smiled and nodded confirmation that they most certainly could have raw oysters.

"Henry the Eighth ate raw oysters by the dozen," Josie shared.

"Is that why he was so fat?" Daisy asked, sidling into the booth.

"I don't know. He thought they improved his virility. You know, all those young girls he married, trying to produce an heir."

"They weren't all young."

"He still wanted to produce male heirs."

"He had Edward."

"Who was sickly. He wanted a second just in case."

"Raw oysters make you horny?" Rosie piped. "I'd heard that before but didn't know if it was true."

"Rosie," scolded Josie, "they increase virility, not make you horny."

"Does virulent come from the same root word?" Daisy asked, scanning the menu.

There was silence as the sisters pondered the implications.

Allison felt her eyes wander around the room, as frown lines writhed across her brow. *Virile? Virulent?* With a shake of her head she ventured, "No. I don't think so. Virile has an IL and Virulent is a UL. I think they have two different roots."

Josie nodded, "She's likely right."

"Darn."

"Does that mean raw oysters don't work?"

"Read your menu, Rosie."

Rosie giggled.

They feasted. Piles of fried oysters, she-crab soup, clam chowder, scallops, crab cakes, flounder, steamed clams, and a half-dozen oysters on the half shell were ordered separately and shared family style.

Allison couldn't believe how much these three elderly sisters could put away. They left an hour later, sated and staggering. Allison brought the car right up to the door to pick them up.

"Where to now?" She asked Daisy, the designated navigator, as she carefully peeled out into even heavier evening-rush traffic.

"We stay on 113 to Berlin, which is about ten miles into Maryland, then turn left on Route 376. We'll see a place called Frontier Town. The small motel I found is near there."

Rosie bounced in her seat. "We're going to see the Chincoteague ponies! We're going to see Misty!"

"No," responded Daisy, "we'll be seeing the Banker Ponies of Assateague Island. Chincoteague is where the ponies that are privately owned on the southern part of Assateague Island are driven over each year to be sold."

"We won't be seeing Misty?" Rosie asked quietly.

Allison flicked her eyes to the rearview mirror, checking Rosie's worried expression. *Baby sister. She sure acts the part with her older siblings.*

Daisy glanced at her baby sister in the rearview mirror. "That book was written over fifty years ago. Horses don't live that long," she responded gently.

Allison nodded. *Yup, mother. Nurturer.*

"I know," Rosie sighed, head resting against the window. "Will there be any pintos?"

Daisy smiled. "Yes, I am pretty sure we'll see some pintos." After a few moments of quiet, Daisy gave them a brief history of the ponies.

She explained that Assateague National Seashore in Maryland, an island, extends down into Virginia where it becomes a wildlife refuge. That's where you find the private herd that is taken across the channel each year to Chincoteague. There the herd is culled and many of the younger horses are sold. Some at a very young age. Those horses have been there for over a hundred years, left behind when their owners moved to the mainland. Over the years, since Marguerite Henry wrote the story, *Misty, of Chincoteague*, domestic horses and mustangs had been added to the private herds. Those introduced horses didn't do well in the salt grass and limited water, and usually didn't survive long. But they, well, changed the bloodlines, made horses more adaptable for domestic life.

"Now, the horses in the National Seashore and farther down on the Outer Banks of North Carolina are carefully monitored," Daisy said. "The Park Service uses contraceptive darts to keep the size of the herds down. Each mare has at least one foal to keep variation in the bloodlines. Because the Assateague mares don't foal every year, they are healthier and live longer."

Daisy turned around in the front seat to face her sister. "We can drive on into the National Seashore after we check into the motel."

Rosie's face brightened. She started rocking and bouncing. "We'll see wild horses galloping on the beach! Sparring at sunrise! Foals frisking by their mothers!"

Daisy laughed. "More like we'll see ponies grazing in the salt marsh and wandering through the campgrounds, leaving road apples as they go. And these are not wild horses. They are feral horses that are descended from domestic stock. So, they are not afraid of people." Daisy's admonitory finger came up before Rosie could say anything. "But you are NOT allowed to pet them!"

Rosie giggled. "Okay." Soon, she was again rocking in her seat.

"What are you singing?" Josie asked, pulling a bag of munchies out of the way of Rosie's bouncing butt.

Rosie blasted out in a folk song voice Allison hadn't heard before: "*Here comes Brumby Jack, Bringin' the horses down the track...*"

And on she went, happily bouncing her way through two verses.

"What are *brumbies*?" Allison asked when Rosie paused for breath.

"Brumbies are the feral horses of Australia," Rosie answered breathlessly, then burst out with more verses about herding wild bush brumbies to safety.

"You said the song is from Australia," Josie said. "When did you pick it up?"

"Remember back in 1971, I was in that band that went to Australia for several months. In this country, we had Wild Horse Annie, fighting to keep our mustangs from being rounded up on the western plains and sold for dog meat."

"You were in Australia with your band?" Allison interrupted, impressed.

"Oh, not my band. I was in several bands over the years, and we traveled all over," Rosie responded modestly.

"That must have been awesome."

Rosie shrugged. "We were young and had energy then. Fun? Yes. Especially when we had time to explore the country we were in."

Daisy proudly added, "and Rosie has always been able to memorize any song she heard."

Allison saw the sign for Assateague Island National Seashore. "Are we going there or to the motel first?"

Josie tapped Daisy on the shoulder. "Your choice, you know the hours and such. What do you think?"

Daisy checked her watch. "Let's go on in. The visitor center will be closed by now, but let's go watch sunset over the bay."

"I want to see sunset over the ocean," Rosie chirped.

"You've got a long way to go for that. The sun sets in the west, remember. If we stand on this beach looking over the ocean, we'll be facing east. We'd have to wait for sunrise."

Rosie clapped her hands excitedly. "Then we'll come back for sunrise. Let's go see some ponies and watch sunset over the bay, then come back and see sunrise over the ocean."

Allison laughed aloud at Rosie's contagious joy. Daisy and Josie smiled.

. . . .

Driving over the bridge onto Assateague Island, they saw banker ponies immediately. A thrilled Rosie rose on her knees to hang out her open window. An older couple rode their bikes along the bike path by the road and headed for the bridge over the channel that separated the island from the mainland. A chestnut yearling watched the lady bike past, then pricked his ears as the man rode by. Rosie laughed delightedly when the yearling gave a head shake and little buck as though to object to being ignored, then chased after the man on the bike. The expression on the man's face as clattering hooves closed in on him had the sisters chuckling.

Rosie bounced in delight and nearly tumbled out of the open window as she leaned out to watch the receding bicyclist peddling hard.

They drove past the gatehouse. Daisy pulled her National Park Pass and a plastic holder out of the glove compartment and hung it on the rearview mirror. Daisy had Allison drive past the parking lots that gave access to the beach. She pointed to the one-way road coming out of the Ocean Side Campground, then had Allison turn right onto Bayside Drive. They cruised through the campground. An elderly sorrel lay between an RV and the bathroom.

"Stop!" Rosie crowed, "I want to go see that pony. Take a picture, Josie."

Allison pulled into the parking area near the bathroom, barely coming to a halt before both Rosie and Josie bounded out of the car. Josie walked at an angle around the resting pony, little camera held at the ready, as Rosie approached slowly, crooning softly.

Daisy snapped a couple pictures with her phone, shook her head at her baby sister, and headed into the bathroom. She popped right back out again, "Rosie! Come and take a look at this."

With a frown of annoyance, Josie stopped walking around the pony. Rosie hesitated, but turned anyway, looking wistfully over her shoulder at the calmly resting pony.

"What is so important?" Josie raised her eyebrows, as Daisy waved them into the bathroom.

She ushered her three travel companions into the small bathroom and pointed to a poster on the wall showing a pony lunging forward to bite a woman who had approached too closely. The poster warned: *Do not approach the ponies!*

"Oh my gosh! That horse is about to bite her boob," Josie exclaimed.

Rosie giggled.

Allison put her hand protectively over her chest.

Daisy guffawed.

After everyone had relieved herself, they trooped back outside in time to see the pony heave to its hooves, shake, and wander placidly across the middle of the campground causing a tiny dog on a long leash to bark so hard it bounced across the blacktop. Rosie stood, watching with longing.

Daisy herded them back to the car and had Allison drive out of the camping area to a parking lot on the opposite side of the road. A boardwalk led out over the marsh. Walking slowly, they saw various egrets, herons, and gulls. Out over the salt marsh, Daisy pointed to a small herd, three mares and a young foal. Hand to her mouth, Rosie stood at the railing of the walkway and stared at the small herd. Two of the mares were solid color. One mare and the foal were pinto. Up came Josie's camera.

"If we drive down to the old ferry landing, the next road over, we'll be closer to them."

Rosie whimpered with joy and started at a near jog the rest of the way around the boardwalk, looking back every few steps to make sure the little herd had not vanished.

As they pulled out of the parking lot, Daisy pointed ahead at a small deer bounding across the road, leaping almost like a kangaroo. "Look."

"That's not moving like a deer. It looks smaller than a white tail," Josie commented, leaning forward from the backseat.

"It's a sika deer," Daisy whispered. "They're related to elk." She turned around facing her sisters in the rear. "Barth and I have been here in late fall when they are mating. They scream. It's the most eerie sound. Sika aren't native. They were introduced a number of years ago to the islands . . . for hunting."

Rosie began bouncing. "It's gone, let's go."

Allison drove slowly back to the entry road, turning toward the old ferry landing. Pulling into a nearly empty parking area, the ladies got out. Two men hauled in a crab pot, silhouetted by the sun sinking to the horizon over the bay and several islands. A wooden bridge arched over a waterway to another island of salt grass and mud flats. Daisy led the way, taking her silent entourage over the bridge and along the bay. Ahead, the little herd of mares grazed peacefully.

"Where's the foal?" Rosie asked.

Daisy stopped and scanned the sedges and grasses, then pointed. A small head and ears appeared for a few seconds then disappeared again. "There. It's lying down, napping."

Rosie clasped her hands, smiling. The four stood quietly as the orange sun became a hemisphere on the horizon, lighting the clouds yellow and orange. Josie walked slowly around to take a photo of the small herd with the setting sun behind them. Rosie found a small mound on which to stand so she could better see the resting foal.

A bobwhite called out over the salt marsh. Daisy slowly walked back, cocking her head toward what sounded like a large insect. She held up her hand as a sign to quiet. "Listen."

A twittering and whirring, followed by a whistle of wings and wild chittering as a speck of a bird spiraled downward in a dizzying dive made Daisy grin. "That's a male woodcock in his mating flight."

The whirring, whistling, and chittering erupted again over the salt flats. Allison smiled in delight, "Aren't woodcocks rather rare?"

Daisy nodded. "Their numbers are declining due to environmental stresses."

Josie, looking amused, said, "I thought you always said you hated traveling all the time in that tin can camper."

Shrugging, Daisy admitted, "Well, I didn't like the camper. The big ones are like small homes; they have everything. I didn't like the constant driving, but, thinking back, I did enjoy all the places we went, the people we met, and all the animals and wonderful places we visited." She smiled ruefully. "Doesn't it seem like we often complain about something while it's going on, and then later look back on it with fond memories?"

On that note, the ladies and Allison trudged back to the car.

· · · · · · · · · · · ·

The motel outside Ocean City was one story and small, the rooms plain and unadorned. Allison would again be sharing a bed with Rosie. She headed out for a mild evening walk, down the road and by a woodlot in which she stopped to watch an owl perched high on the branch of a dead tree.

After nearly an hour of leisurely wandering, she came around the corner of their little motel and heard a sniff that sounded like someone in quiet distress.

Daisy stepped out of the alcove that sheltered the soda and ice machines. She held a hanky to her nose, gave it a wipe, then tucked the hanky in her sleeve, straightened her back, and headed for their room. Turning back suddenly, she saw Allison.

"Oh, I didn't hear you." Daisy held her chin up and took the couple of steps back to the ice machine. "I came to fill the ice bucket. Silly me, I almost forget it." She snatched the white plastic bucket from on top of the ice machine, shoved open the silver cover, and raked up a half bucket of cubes.

"Aunt Daisy? Are you alright?"

Daisy tearfully looked up at her niece. In a voice that quavered, Daisy blurted, "I haven't been able to reach him! I've tried the house phone and his cell phone. Barth hasn't answered."

"You expected him home on the evening we were there. Was he supposed to go somewhere? Could he have gotten into an accident?"

Daisy shook her head, tears leaking down her cheeks. "I don't know. I would have heard, wouldn't I? I just don't know."

"Can you call a neighbor?"

"I did." Daisy wailed, sniffed again, then turned away, mumbling something Allison didn't catch.

"What?" Allison asked.

Daisy wheeled around. "Barth has Alzheimer's!" She choked on tears, turning her shoulder to Allison.

Frozen, stunned, Allison wasn't sure what to do.

"He lost things, forgot things, but he has always been scattered and disorganized. But it was getting worse; he'd get lost in places he knew well." Daisy held a hanky to her nose. "We went to the doctor three months ago. After numerous tests, we were told it's Alzheimer's." Shaking her head she said, "I've tried to call him every day since we left, both phones, but I can't reach him."

Allison put her arm around her octogenarian aunt. Comforting an adult was new to her. "Is it time to call the police?"

Choked with tears, Daisy leaned into her niece, "I don't know. I just don't know. I've called his best friend, but he hasn't answered either. I don't know. Maybe they are together. I just don't know."

"Okay," Allison sighed. He's an adult. Allison wondered, *should he be treated the same way you would a child who had gone missing?* She suggested, "Call neighbors and alert them. Give them your cell number. Call and leave messages with all his friends and anyone he may call or visit. Spread the word."

Daisy squared her shoulders and keyed up her phone, scrolling through it for contact numbers. "I don't have all his friends on here. I will call everyone I can and have them pass on the word and my contact number."

"Would you like me to stay with you?"

Daisy waved the ice bucket, which she'd been cradling like a cold baby. "You take this back. Don't tell the girls what I'm doing. They don't know yet and I'm not ready to tell them. Go! Take the ice back."

Back in the room, Allison found Josie and Rosie propped up on pillows in the two beds watching a Marx Brothers movie on AMC. "I brought the ice."

Josie nodded. Rosie smiled. Neither asked where Daisy was.

Allison half listened as Groucho tried to explain to a confused Chico about fording the river at the viaduct. Chico didn't understand why you'd need a Ford if you had a duck.

It seemed like forever before Daisy barged into the room, "I could kill him! The frickin' patoot went off with his friend to the military antiques show in Kentucky that they go to every year. He didn't even tell me. Why the bloody blazes is he not answering is goll darn phone?"

Josie looked up. "Are we talking about Barth, perhaps?"

Daisy let out a big sigh. "I've been worried. I haven't been able to reach him." She shook her upper body as though shaking off the weight she'd been carrying. "You know how he is, forget his own underwear if I didn't put it on for him." She turned, catching Allison's look of concern. With her back to her sisters, she closed her eyes in a combined expression of anguish and relief.

Chapter 11

DELMARVA

T he bed shook.
Earthquake!

Allison shot up, shoving off the sheet, and bounding to her feet to see Rosie bouncing up and down on her knees on their bed.

"Wakie Wakie!" she crowed. "We're going to go see ponies silhouetted against the rising sun, frisking in the waves, and galloping on the beach."

Allison glanced at the split in the curtains. "It's still dark," she moaned.

"Of course! We can't go to the beach to watch sunrise if the sun has already . . . rised." Rosie broke into song, *Here Comes the Sun.*

Someone pounded on the wall.

"Oops." Rosie grinned with her hand over her mouth.

Daisy came out of the bathroom, zipping up her turquoise, velour jogging suit. Josie staggered into the bathroom, dragging her clothes with her. Rosie jumped up to brush her teeth.

Allison sighed. She pulled out her clothes, glanced at the bathroom, and crawled under the sheet to start changing.

Unbelievably, they were out the door in twenty minutes. Allison drove them back into the park into the first parking area and right up to the pathway that led up over the dune to the beach. Standing there on top of the dune, backlit by a pale orange glow painting the sky, was a pinto pony posed with head up, alert, gazing down the beach.

Rosie froze, hand to her mouth. Josie hauled out her camera and clicked away. Daisy smiled and Allison glanced over to see tears of happiness in her Aunt Rosie's eyes.

The pinto whinnied and trotted down the far side of the dune. The ladies slogged through the sand to the boardwalk over the dune. Rosie stopped and looked accusingly at her footwear. Allison smiled as Rosie tried to hop on one foot to remove her fluffy yellow slippers. She was still in her nightgown and had simply put her jacket over her night clothes.

"Aunt Rosie, shall I run those back to the car?" Allison offered.

At first, Rosie didn't seem to hear. Her attention was on the dune and what might await her on the far side. Allison tapped her shoulder. With a look of delight, Rosie handed her the sandy slippers.

Tossing the slippers on the back-seat floor, Allison turned to see all three aunts silhouetted on top of the dune, Rosie with a hand to her mouth in awe, Daisy holding her camera phone, grinning broadly, and Josie clicking away with her point-and-shoot.

Jogging up to join them, Allison halted, eyes wide, mouth agape. There on the beach were two small herds of ponies.

Silently acknowledging Allison, the four women made their way on down to the beach. One young pinto stallion tried to rough-house with a dark bay male. The pinto pushed the other around, attempting to start some action. Rosie froze, watching the pinto, feeling great in the cool of morning, buck and charge a chestnut mare. She took off, racing up the dune, into the early light. The pinto followed, landing a nip on her flank. She raced back to the herd, past the young male the pinto had originally been trying to get to play. She dove in among the other horses, leaving the pinto on the outside.

He skidded to a stop, spinning and bucking in frustration. But that did it for the dark, young stallion. He wheeled on the pinto, chasing him to the water's edge. Then much to Rosie's delight, the two reared up against the rising sun, just as Rosie had dreamed they would.

Allison heard a little sob. Tears of joy streamed down Rosie's wrinkled cheeks. Josie shot photos and smiled at her little sister's reaction. Daisy shook her head and whispered, "It's all for you, Rosie. In all the times we've come here, we've never seen anything like this." Allison felt tears gathering, as well.

The sun rose over the blue waters and softly lapping ocean waves. A breeze picked up. The horses roused and headed right toward the aunts, heading for the path over the dunes to the parking area.

Stepping back to let them pass, the ladies watched in silence as first one herd, then the second trooped past. They followed. At the top of the dune, watching the small herds separate, each taking a different direction, a gust of wind kicked sand into a swirling gust. Josie ducked and Rosie yelped, covering and rubbing her eyes.

"Don't rub, Rosie." Daisy solicitously pulled Rosie's hand from her face and lead her toward the car. "Go ahead and cry now, it was beautiful, and the tears will wash out the sand."

Rosie obliged, tears streaming down the wrinkles along her nose. "It was all I could have possibly hoped for! They were stunning, weren't they? I'm so glad we did this."

"Me, too, Rosie." Daisy shook her head in wonder. "They did it for you, Rosie. I've been here many times, and I've never seen anything so beautiful."

. . . .

Slowly, they drove around checking where the two herds had gone, finding one grazing in a water meadow near the walk-in campsites, the others across on the bay side, grazing in the salt marsh as Daisy predicted they'd see them.

Few cars were in the parking lot of the visitor center. Rosie wiped her face and pulled on her yellow slippers. "Let's go in."

The ladies pored over the photos and stories of the ponies in the park, trying to identify the ones they had seen. Daisy checked out the gift shop and grabbed a copy of *Misty* and a stuffed animal, a pinto pony. Walking back to the car, Daisy handed the bag containing her purchases to Rosie, and smiled.

They drove back to the motel in silence.

Rosie changed out of her night clothes as the others packed. Allison loaded the car.

"Back out to 13," Daisy directed. "We continue south along 13 to the Chesapeake Bay Bridge Tunnel. I know of a good place to eat along the way."

They left in a comfortable silence.

. . . .

Lunch relaxed the aunts. Daisy had her phone fired up, scanning through various posts. Josie, riding shotgun, gazed quietly out the window. Rosie hummed quietly. The silence finally got to Allison.

"Aunt Rosie?"

Rosie leaned forward, placing her hands on the back of Allison's seat. "Yes, dear?"

Allison hesitated, then blurted, "When you were trying to remember Carrie Underwood, you were saying Carrie Fisher and underwear."

"No, I was saying Princess Leia and underwear."

Josie's head snapped around toward her sister. "You pictured Princess Leia in her underwear?" Allison glanced at the rearview mirror, checking Aunt Rosie's sparkling grin. "What was she wearing?"

Allison choked. Daisy looked up from her phone, her interest piqued.

Rosie giggled. "Well, I tried picturing her in that little dancing girl garment that Jabba the Hutt made her wear, but I found I kept picturing Jabba the giant slug or that toothy sand monster. It didn't work. So, the iconic Princess Leia is wearing that white robe. Under that . . . well, it had to be something like a chemise." Rosie shrugged.

"Princess Leia wearing a chemise." Daisy repeated. "Wouldn't it be more interesting to imagine her in something from like, oh, Frederick's of Hollywood?"

Allison swerved.

Rosie giggled. "I remember when Gloria and I first came across a Frederick's of Hollywood at a new mall."

Daisy snorted. "They say the best test of a man is to get something from these ladies' lingerie stores, you know, with the pink bags and names on them, and make the man carry it. I tried that."

Waiting silence.

Josie demanded, "Well?"

Daisy shrugged. "I bought a sexy brassiere, handed the bag to

Barth. Barth took it and wandered off. Didn't even notice what he was carrying. Total oblivion."

"That was no fun."

Ignoring her sisters, Rosie continued her story. "It was a new store, and they had this big table near the door with all these skimpy little . . . things on it. With feathers on them and holes in them. *Soooo*, we started picking them up."

"Picking up what?" Daisy had her phone out again.

"The things off the Frederick's of Hollywood table. In the new store. In the mall. Gloria and me," Rosie recapped. "Anyway, Gloria picked up one of these red things, with two larger holes in it, feathers, and another smaller hole right in the middle. Gloria put it on her head! She tried to stretch the sides over her ears. The hole and feather were on top of her head. She pulled a ponytail of hair through the hole."

Daisy howled with laughter.

Allison choked. *Leg holes and . . . oh my gosh! She put it on her head?*

"It didn't look right, so I tried it as a mask. The two larger holes still didn't fit very comfortably over my ears, and with just one hole in the middle, either you had to be a cyclops or it was for my nose, so I stuck my nose through the hole!"

If Josie had been wearing false teeth, they would have flown out the window. Allison spat out a laugh, swerved, and managed to bang her head on the steering wheel.

"The feather tickled my nose, so I put that one back and tried to find one with no feathers. There was a teal blue one with really thin strips of fabric and pretty lace connecting them."

Daisy interjected, "That's the crotch."

A semi blew past. Allison realized she had slowed well below the speed limit.

Rosie went on ignoring the interruption. "I tried it as a hairband, but that lacy part didn't fit very well."

Allison hit her turn signal and pulled to the side of the road before she caused an accident. Hands still on the wheel, she struggled with the image of a younger Rosie posing provocatively with a pair of sexy, lacy panties, sporting feathers, perched on her head.

"Gloria snatched that one. It fit her better than it did me. I found a really big pair that had feathers on both sides but none on the larger hole down the middle. I put my arm through the arm hole, but it wouldn't quite fit me as a vest."

With shoulders shaking with laughter, Daisy sagged against her door.

"Gloria and I noticed the salesgirls glaring at us. Must be that we were doing something wrong. But, I mean, where did that little hole go? There were also these bra things, except they had little feathers as well. Gloria and I thought they looked great as earmuffs, though the material was a bit too thin to be very warm."

Daisy hooted. Josie grinned, shaking her head. Allison leaned her bruised forehead against the steering wheel, clutching her stomach with laughter.

"I tried another set as earmuffs. It was emerald-green with three little yellow feathers sticking out of each ear. I thought I must look really cute and was posing, pulling at the elastic clasp under my chin, and it popped off. The earmuffs shot sideways and hit an elderly gentleman walking by right in the chest."

Daisy howling with laughter, wiping tears from her eyes. Josie held her hands over her chest as though the 'earmuffs' had landed on her and guffawed. Allison picked her head up, tears streaming, to try to catch her breath and saw the state trooper car slide slowly by.

"Oh, crap!"

Rosie corrected. "No, he stretched the, uh, earmuffs across his chest. Actually, they fit pretty well. His wife snatched them off him, held them up, and then held them to her own chest, grinning."

Allison sobered up as the trooper car pulled off in front of them and turned on his red and blue trooper lights.

"When the lady dragged her husband over to see what else they had at the Fredericks of Hollywood table, Gloria tossed back the earmuffs she was trying on and we scooted out of there!"

Allison powered down her window as the trooper slowly got out of his car and made his way back to the Buick, checking out the license plate, taking note of who was in the car.

He peered in the opened window at Allison and the three aunts. Allison did a quick survey. None looked entirely sober or sane.

"Everything all right here, ladies?"

Josie leaned across. "Our driver here," indicating Allison, "swallowed wrong and was choking. In the sake of safety, she pulled over."

The trooper's gaze slid once more over the ladies. "Driver's license, please, miss. And could I see your registration?"

Daisy waved her hand to the glovebox. Josie popped it open and dug out the leather folder that held the registration and insurance papers.

Waiting for the trooper to run them through the system in his squad car, Rosie asked hesitatingly, "Bad time to tell that story?"

They waited in silence.

"He's kind of cute," Daisy offered.

"Too young for me," Josie deadpanned.

Rosie giggled. "What? You're not a cougar!"

The trooper sauntered back and leaned in the window. "You're Allison Robinson?"

She nodded.

"The registration is not in your name."

Daisy leaned forward, hand up. "It's mine, officer." She hauled out her fanny pack to dig out her wallet and license.

"Any reason why you aren't driving, ma'am?"

Daisy pulled out her license, hand shaking like an aspen leaf in a stiff breeze, and handed it across to the officer. As he turned to take it to his vehicle, Daisy stopped him. "Don't bother. You'll find that I have so many speeding tickets that if I get one more, I could lose my license."

The officer's eyebrows shot up.

"I get daydreaming and go lead foot." Daisy smiled sweetly and waved at her sisters. "Take a look at us. Tell us honestly who you would prefer to see driving."

The trooper looked at the other two ladies. Rosie, with her red, puffy eyes from crying over the ponies and getting sand blasted, gave him a two-finger wave. Josie, up front, tried to look old and feeble.

The trooper handed back Allison's license and the registration. He tipped his hat. "Drive safely, miss."

Allison waited for him to pull back into traffic, then collapsed against the steering wheel.

Rosie giggled. Josie turned accusingly to Daisy. "You don't shake that badly."

Daisy grinned. "I do when I've had a double coffee at lunch. They were out of decaf. Caffeine makes me shake like I'm palsied."

"And those speeding tickets?" Josie continued accusingly.

Daisy shrugged. "Call me lead foot. I get on a thruway or straight stretch in the country, start daydreaming, and," she shrugged again with a quirked smile, "*zoom!*"

Rosie giggled. "I cry."

"What?"

"Sure. When I get pulled over, I start to weep. 'I'm an old lady! I'm eighty-two, or whatever, and I've NEVER gotten a speeding ticket!' I've never been given a speeding ticket." Rosie finished with a satisfied grin.

Josie frowned. "How many times *have* you been stopped?"

Allison peered in the rearview mirror at her sweet elderly aunts and fully understood why her mother had insisted she drive.

"Only five times."

Daisy's eyebrows shot up. "This year?"

Rosie giggled. "No, silly. Five times in my life."

"You haven't been an old lady all your life!"

"Well, most of it. I guess I've been stopped five times in the last twenty years. But anyway, I've never gotten a ticket, that's the important thing."

Josie shook her head and waved her hand in a *let's-go* gesture. "Drive."

Gripping the wheel with one hand, Allison shifted into drive, looked over her shoulder, and eased the car carefully out into traffic.

It took another hour to reach the Chesapeake Bay Bridge.

· · · · · · · · · · · · ·

"The bridge is 17.6 miles long from shore to shore, two lanes going north and south bound most of the way," Daisy, the tour director, informed her crew.

"Most of the way?" demanded Josie.

Daisy nodded. "Except where it goes through the two tunnels, where it's still single lane."

Rosie's eyebrows shot up. "Tunnels? I thought this was a bridge."

"The Chesapeake Bay is a major shipping channel. Ships have to get in and out."

Rosie shifted around to face Daisy in the backseat next to her. "Can't they go under the bridge? You didn't say anything about tunnels! How can a bridge have tunnels?"

Allison wondered the same thing. She kept glancing in the rearview mirror at Daisy, curious for the answer.

"The bridge goes over several islands on this end, then on pylons for a stretch. It then ducks down under the bay."

"*Under?*" squeaked Rosie.

Daisy put on her exasperated older sister look. "Yes, under. There are tunnels so that the shipping traffic can pass overhead."

Hands to her wrinkled breast, Rosie started hyperventilating.

Tsk-ing, Daisy slapped her sister's hands. "Stop being such a baby! It's perfectly safe. Barth and I have done it in our big RVs numerous times. There's a pull-off midway along where you can stop to look at where the tunnels go under the water. We can get snacks, and there's a gift store!" She put on an excited smile.

"Can we get postcards?" Rosie was hooked.

"Absolutely."

"And take pictures? Josie, you'll take some photos?"

"Absolutely," Josie mimicked Daisy's answer.

Arriving at the bridge, Daisy handed Allison money for the toll. Rosie squealed in delight when the road dipped down into the first tunnel. Both Rosie and Allison kept close eyes on the white tiled walls of the tunnel, looking for leaks. Huge fans kept the air and exhaust moving, and signs admonished drivers to remain in their lane. Finally, they popped back up into daylight.

And there was the sign for the rest area in the center of the bridge. Pulling in, the ladies piled out, Rosie hustling over to the railing to look at the pile of rocks that marked the entrance of the tunnel. Several small pleasure boats motored by. A large tanker approached from the open ocean. Josie clicked photos of each. Rosie bounced and started singing about barges passing in the night.

A thorough inspection was made of the gift shop. Two candy bars, a bag of sugar-free Gummi Bears, and ten postcards later, they piled back in the Le Sabre and finished the drive over the bridge.

"Hotels are booked up. I was hoping to head down to Fort Story military base and go to the Old Cape Henry Lighthouse. You have to drive on to the base to get to the lighthouse, through security. They bring this big mirror on a long pole to look under the vehicle. But I can't find any motel vacancies in that direction." Daisy waved her hand at Allison. "Get on Route 60 and take it across the bridge to I-64. We'll find something northwest of here. Lots of motels up around Colonial Williamsburg."

Allison wheeled into the parking lot of the first motel they'd seen with a vacancy sign. Pulling up to the entryway, the aunts piled out, grabbing handbags, patting hair into place, adjusting undergarment straps. Allison pulled forward to a parking spot, hit the door lock, and was at the motel door before them to hold it open. They heard a television broadcasting the next day's weather report from a room hidden behind the front desk. Trooping forward with hands on overstuffed purses or on a bulging fanny pack, Josie reached the desk first and banged the little bell just as a woman half the age of the aunts wandered out from the small room from which the television chattered.

"Evening, ladies," she drawled with a welcoming smile. "We've only got one room left."

"Room for four?" Josie countered.

The woman gave a brief, half head shake. "It has two queen beds."

"Well, that's room for four," Josie snapped. Turning to include her sisters, she continued. "We grew up when not every child had his or her own room, much less her own bed! Of course, we can share. That's what double beds are for, they're for two people."

The woman smiled, enjoying Josie's attitude. "You'all here for the Music Festival? That's why all the motels are full."

Rosie's eyes lit up. "*Oooh*, what kind of music?"

"Country, honey." Glancing at the other two sisters, she added, "And it's being combined with a beer fest held by the local microbreweries. That's really why most people are here. Microbreweries from a hundred miles around are here."

That got the full attention of Josie and Daisy. "Where? When does it start?" Josie demanded.

The lady laughed as she tapped on her computer, registering the ladies for their room-for-four. Daisy, whose turn it was to pay, handed over her VISA card. "It's in the town just up the way, about ten miles. It started at four so it should be well under way by now."

Three elderly ladies checked their colorful, bejeweled watches, 5:35p.m. "Maybe we'd better eat first," Daisy suggested.

Josie nodded. "If there's beer, we need to eat first."

The lady handed back Daisy's credit card. "There's a Cracker Barrel straight across the street and a Denny's just down the way. Now, are two key cards enough?"

"Cracker Barrel!" chirped Rosie.

"How do we get to the festival?" Daisy asked.

The lady rummaged under the counter, coming out with a Xeroxed local map. She marked in orange marker the route they should take. "Just go right out of here to the east on Interstate 64, go three exits, then at the base of the ramp, turn left. You get to the bridge; you've gone too far. They'll be signs, plenty of signs. Y'all may have trouble finding parking."

Rosie bounced up and down in excitement. Daisy took the two key cards, tucking one in the outer zippered pocket of her fanny pack; the second one she passed to Allison. "Cracker Barrel then. I'm getting the special, whatever it is." She announced as she headed for the door.

"Country fried steak and turnip greens!" from Josie.

"Catfish and baked apples, and beer at the festival!" crowed Rosie.

Daisy walked while examining the map she'd been handed.

Stopping suddenly, the sisters banged into her. Allison pulled up, nearly giggling. They looked like something out of an old comedy film.

"What?" Josie demanded.

"We're getting takeout," Daisy stated firmly.

"Why?" Josie used her elder sister, in-command voice.

Daisy wheeled, thrusting the map in her face. "We can take the Colonial Parkway along the York River. We are getting take-out then driving out to an overlook of the York River." Grabbing Allison's arm, Daisy continued out the door. "I'll give you directions."

"Room first. We need to freshen up."

Allison clicked the car door locks open and said nothing. Josie and Daisy strode off toward the room, heatedly debating Daisy's ultimatum. Allison pulled in as the aunts opened the door to their room, ground floor, facing the parking lot. She hauled Rosie's suitcase in first. Daisy had already claimed the bathroom. Rosie bounced as she unzipped her suitcase and hauled out her outfit for the evening.

Next suitcase Allison dragged in belonged to Josie. Rosie had taken over the bathroom. Allison was then able to haul both hers and Daisy's in and kicked the door shut. Rosie stood before the mirror carefully brushing her red hair and repositioning her two hairpins with their bright blue bows. Her evening wear consisted of a white muumuu with loud flowers in primary colors and sensible blue leather sandals.

Josie came out wearing pull-on khakis with a black T-shirt sporting a picture of a tipping wine glass in sparkling beads and rhinestones.

"It's a beerfest, not wine tasting," Daisy snarked as she unbuttoned her blouse revealing a silky camisole, which covered her iron-maiden brassiere. She pulled from her suitcase a tiny turquoise crinkly blouse covered with peaks and dips. Allison frowned. It looked like doll clothes. Daisy pulled it over her head. The crinkles opened out and it seemed to magically grow to fit!

"Cool!" Allison commented, feeling the soft, light-weight material.

"You haven't seen one of these?" Daisy rummaged and came up with another in bright red. This one had raised circles instead of peaks. "This would go with your jeans. Try it on."

Shaking her head at how small it looked, Allison took her turn in the bathroom. Daisy clapped in delight when Allison came out wearing a gently clinging, soft red blouse.

"Enough with the fashion show. Let's go drink beer!" Josie said.

"And listen to music!" Rosie crowed.

"After we have dinner and sunset on the York River."

. . . .

Allison had to admit, having fast food burgers and fries at a parking area on the York River was gorgeous. The sky turned from blue to pastels to what Josie described as boudoir pink. Then it was on to the music/beer fest!

The aunts spent the drive to the music fest in a state of giddy anticipation. Allison glanced at Josie and Daisy in the back seat, grinning and whispering, giggling and poking each other, obviously sharing memories from their pasts. For the first time on the trip, Rosie sat up front, humming, singing, and bouncing in her seat. Allison recognized some lyrics; others she didn't. She felt like she was traveling with a bunch of her college friends.

Closed streets and bright orange plastic fencing marked the perimeter of the festival. Allison dropped the aunts off near the entry booth and went in search of a parking space. As soon as the aunts saw her returning, they headed for the booth.

"Three seniors and one chaperone," Josie announced. Green wristbands had been strapped on three wrinkled wrists when Allison finally made her way to them. She was given an orange wrist band.

Rosie, first through the gate, followed by Daisy and Josie, paused when Allison was stopped by the gate monitor. "ID, please." She searched for her driver's license, which was carefully examined.

"Hold on a minute!" Josie barked, stomping back to the monitor. "That's age discrimination! You didn't ask for OUR ID's!"

The burly young man gave her a small smile and pointed to her wristband. "You told them you were a senior. That means you are well over twenty-one." He cocked an eyebrow at the elderly ladies. "Were you lying?"

Josie huffed, and the young man winked at Allison and let her through.

Crowds of mostly young folks stood in groups yelling above the music. Beer stalls flanked both sides of the sound stage on which a band of five musicians belted out twangy rock-a-billy. A few couples danced in front of the stage, and a straggly line of line-dancers laughed and stumbled into each other as they tried to keep their footwork in sync.

Allison missed the discussion that determined which beer stall to visit first but followed as the aunts approached one. Each aunt ordered a different brew, accepted their plastic cups of beer, and took delicate lip-smacking sips before passing their cups off to each other so they all got a sample.

Over the next two hours, Josie and Daisy shared beers from several of the vendors. Every half hour, a new band played modern country and, much to Daisy and Josie's delight, Rosie found someone to dance country swing with. She also joined in for several line dances.

Rosie came back to join them during a break when one band had finished their set and a new one had started. With a smile as wide as the ocean, out of breath, flushed, and eyes shining, she was handed a fresh beer by Daisy. But her mind was elsewhere. Rosie threw her hands out, exclaiming her happiness, knocking the offered beer which splashed Daisy full in the chest, dousing her thin, light-weight blouse. Rosie froze in horror; Allison ran to get some napkins to sop it up, and Josie hooted and yelled, "Wet T-Shirt Contest!"

Daisy looked up from her wet front, the clinging shirt clearly exposing the lace and straps of her camisole as well as hints of the foundation garments beneath that. "Oh, now, a wet T-shirt contest with me is likely to drive folks away!"

Josie laughed. Rosie grinned and relaxed.

The young man behind had seen and heard the exchange and, having imbibed a few too many beers himself, tossed his cup of beer on his young woman companion, echoing Josie's cry of "Wet T-shirt Contest!" She screeched and threw her half a beer in his face. The young lady behind them dumped her cup of beer down her own front and laughed loudly.

It spread.

Looking around, Allison saw people running to the beer stalls grabbing fresh cups of beer. Ladies and a few men got doused. Laughter and shouts and shrieks of dismay and delight drowned out the band. Beer flew freely, causing stagehands to race to protect sound equipment. As the band crooned that they loved God and liked beer, the power to the sound equipment shut down to prevent electric shocks. The equipment itself was then whisked out of the danger zone.

Josie started moving her small group toward an entry gate. The melee intensified. Beer sellers were no longer taking orders, just filling cups and passing them out, taking in bills in turn. They were making a killing. Some people chugged the beer, some tossed it, some did both.

Once out, the ladies looked at Allison. "Which way to the car?"

Allison led.The ladies followed arm in arm. The yelling, hooting, laughing, and screaming continued to escalate behind them.

"That was fun."

Chapter 12

COLONIAL WILLIAMSBURG

D aisy came back from the motel office after dropping off the key card and gathering information for their day's visit to Colonial Williamsburg.

In deadpan, she announced, "It seems there was some kind of riot or something at that music fest we attended yesterday evening. Guess we missed it."

"Um, didn't we kind of start it?"

"Start what, Allison?" Daisy quipped.

Catching Allison's eye, Rosie giggled.

Breakfast at Denny's involved agreeing on two massive breakfasts then splitting them four ways. It was 10:30 when they arrived at Colonial Williamsburg. Josie made a dramatic show of hyperventilating when she was told the cost for the four of them.

"Oh, stop!" Daisy shoved her out of the way, showed her Williamsburg membership card and paid their discounted price.

Collecting the map of the village and checking the list of events, the four headed for the Door into History.

"You're a member?" Josie asked.

"Yes."

Josie frowned. "How often do you come here?"

Daisy shrugged. "Barth and I have been here four or five times."

They walked in silence under a stone arch with a small stream flowing alongside.

"So why do you maintain a membership? Isn't that costly?" Josie inquired.

"They keep sending us note cards and address labels."

Josie nodded. "Oh."

"And a calendar every year."

"Really?"

Rosie hurried to come abreast of her sisters. "How do I get one? Do I have to become a member?"

Josie snorted. "Rosie, you give me one of those free calendars you get every year. You said you get around ten from various organizations . . . every year!"

Rosie fell back a step, looking slightly crushed. "I like choices. Besides, I don't ask for them, the places who want me to donate just send them to me."

Daisy laughed. "I'll send you mine. I get too many each year as well."

A large windmill came into view. The mill building perched upon a wood-frame pedestal with a long, log handle attached. At the end of the log was a wheel. As they watched, a group of five- or six-year-old children ganged together under the direction of a man clad in knee britches and a muslin blouse and started pushing on the long, white-washed log handle. Slowly, the entire building began to pivot on its base.

Daisy pointed to the furled shrouds on the windmill blades. "The whole building can be turned so that the windmill blades can catch the most wind."

The children *whooped* and high-fived each other at their success in moving an entire building.

The ladies moved closer to hear the interpreter explain the milling process to the children. What they heard was general agreement that the children preferred pancakes to oatmeal for breakfast. The ladies moved on to a farmhouse. Various fowl clucked, quacked, and squawked through the crops. Once more, Daisy filled in for one of the Williamsburg interpreters. "Ducks eat the grubs off the tobacco plants, chickens eat various insects that infest the garden plants, and Guinea fowl eat ticks."

"Do they keep ladybugs to eat the aphids?" Rosie asked.

Daisy laughed. Josie explained with mock patience, "Chickens, ducks, and Guinea fowl also lay eggs that you can eat. Ladybugs don't lay eggs, not ones you can see and eat. And you can't eat a ladybug that gets nasty with you."

"I want a chicken," Rosie sighed.

"You live in an apartment in Rochester."

With a mischievous grin, Rosie suggested, "I could say it's an emotional support pet."

Daisy snapped her fingers. "Yes! Explain that when you get really angry about something, you can strangle the chicken and eat it!"

Josie burst out laughing. Rosie feigned horror, then giggled.

Entering the cabin, Josie nudged Rosie. "Just like where we grew up."

Allison blinked in surprise until she heard Rosie's joking riposte. After looking around at the open fireplace, trestle table and hollowed-out wooden bowls, Rosie giggled. "Putting one of those bowls on Daddy's head was how Mama cut his hair."

Progress through the historical community was conducted slowly, with numerous rest breaks. At a visit to the tavern, Founding Fathers discussed politics. Next up, the House of Burgesses where Patrick Henry issued his famous *Give me Liberty or Give me Death* speech, and the armory where weapons of war, such as pikes, spears, and drums, were kept in case of attack.

Allison saw Josie's frown as they exited the armory. "They show the . . . oh, romance of the period." Shaking her head, Josie strode on, saying no more.

Further on, they learned that shoemakers could make shoes on Sunday, but only for charity to give to the indigent. Wig makers preferred the hair of young women who drank goodly amounts of beer and hadn't washed their hair in six months. To have articles made of silver, one had to give the silversmith enough silver coins to be melted down for the project as well for payment. Men could beat their wives with a "rod no bigger around than a thumb" and could even be ordered by the town justice to do so.

Heading slowly back down the main street, Josie and Daisy holding on to each other and Rosie clutching Allison's arm and hobbling as though her feet hurt, they saw a group of school children with their teachers at the stocks in the village center. One boy sat laughing with his ankles clamped in the ankle stocks. A giggling girl stuck her head and wrists in the pillory and asked her friend to take a picture of her.

Allison glanced at Aunt Josie then did a double take at her stormy continence.

"Aunt Josie?" she ventured.

"When you come to places like this, it's all so lovely looking. Tourists—like us—we like that. But it doesn't tell the full truth. Not at all. People leave with picture-postcard ideas about the past."

"What do you mean?"

"People come here and think they know about the past, but they know almost nothing." Allison had never heard her aunt sound, not angry, but forceful.

The ladies had stopped to watch the group of young students. The teachers paid little attention as the young people enjoyed themselves, pushing classmates toward the stocks, laughing as they took their turns. Allison realized that Josie, standing next to her, seemed to be vibrating. Josie shook off Daisy's hand and marched forward.

"Think it's funny?" she demanded, her voice soft but with a force that stopped most of the laughing and even got the attention of the teachers and parent aids. The girl in the standing pillory craned her neck up to see who was speaking.

Josie motioned toward her. "What will you do when someone throws things at you? You can't block; you can't dodge to avoid. Yes, most of what is thrown will be rotten food, things that are soft. But someone may throw a clod of dirt, or a rock." She rounded on the other children, "I'm sure all of you could think of some very interesting things you could throw at someone who was being publicly humiliated."

"Like poop!" yelled one, followed by laughter.

Teachers and parents glared.

Josie nodded, turning her attention back to the children in the stocks and pillory. "What will you do after several hours when you have to go to the bathroom? What if you are sentenced to the stocks for a full day or more? You'd better have someone who cares enough to bring you water. You'd better have someone here who brings you a bit of food."

She paused and looked up at the sun, and at the boy watching her from the ankle stocks. "How sunburned are you going to get? There's no shade here. What if it rains? How cold will it get at night? Anyone here willing to bring them a blanket or do anything to cover them if it rains?" She turned back to the children, now wearing serious expressions. "You have a friend willing to bring you a blanket, but can you prevent someone from then snatching it away from you?"

The boy squirmed.

"Getting uncomfortable?" Josie asked him. "How long have you been there? Minutes? You are standing and sitting on narrow pieces of wood. In another hour or less, you are going to be in real pain." The girl started squirming to get free. She couldn't lift the bar holding her in place even though it wasn't latched down.

"Getting stiff yet?" Josie asked her. "After a few hours in there, you'll be stiff for days."

One child raised his hand. Josie raised her eyebrows at him.

"Why did they use these then? Is it better to be put in the jail?"

"Good question. Were you shown through the prison?" The children nodded. "Who were the people usually kept in the prison?"

A girl stepped forward half a step. "People waiting for the circuit judge to come around, ma'am."

Josie nodded. "Most people held there were being held for serious crimes. People put in the stocks or the pillory were usually here for minor crimes, like being drunk in public, stealing something small, or saying bad things about the king of England or about the governor."

"But what about freedom of speech?" a child demanded.

Josie shook her head. "There was no freedom of speech then. You could be punished for speaking out against those in power. You could even be punished for not attending church."

"I want to get out!" The girl in the stocks tried to buck and pull her way free. A parent stepped forward to help her. Josie put her hand out and moved right next to the girl. "Not funny now, is it? You know what else isn't funny? You may be in there because you weren't obedient enough."

The girl tilted her head as much as she could and snapped, "Because I'm a Negro?"

"No!" Josie shot back, "not because you are Black. Because you are female. As a female, not just an enslaved female, you are owned first by your father, then by your husband. In most colonies and later in the states, you had almost no rights. Anything you had belonged to your husband. Anything you earned belonged to your husband. He had the right to beat you."

A girl yelled, "I'd divorce him!"

Josie nodded. "In most cases, you could, especially in the New England colonies." She saw surprise among the adults. "However," she addressed the girl who wanted a divorce, "if you had children, they are your husband's property, by law. If you divorce, you might never see your children again. Would you be willing to make that sacrifice? Would you be willing to abandon your children if you think your husband is so bad?"

"I'd call the police," another girl tried.

"If your husband beats you, it's your fault. You even see that at times now. Spousal abuse was still treated that way when I was young. If a woman complained that her husband beat her, she was asked what she'd done wrong. The wife was blamed if she got beaten. She was told she wasn't keeping the house clean enough or making meals on time or being obedient enough. Her fault."

Two of the boys giggled and shoved each other. Josie rounded on them, bringing a *you-go-girl* grin and nod from a teacher.

"Funny? You think getting beaten is funny? Remember you were property, as well. Your parents, both of them, could beat you, prevent you from going to school, lock you in the attic or basement. Read some of the cases of children killed by their parents. A boy's body was found mummified in an attic wall. He couldn't write in a neat enough hand, so his parents left him in a freezing cold attic, feeding him very little and making him practice and practice. He died there, surrounded by all the paper on which he'd tried so hard to write neatly enough to please his parents. There was a girl whose mother died, and she had to take over all her duties." Josie shot a glance at Allison and the adults to make sure they understood what all her duties would include. "Her father beat her when she could not handle all her mother's duties: taking care of several younger children, cooking for them, cleaning, washing all the clothes, mending the clothes, keeping a garden, and anything else he demanded of her. She died of the beatings and exhaustion. Then there was an orphaned boy, who was treated like an animal, kept in a cold barn where he was finally found frozen to death with shredded clothes. He'd buried himself in a pile of manure in a desperate attempt to stay warm. NONE of these were prosecuted as crimes." She rounded on the boys again. "You were OWNED. You were PROPERTY."

She stalked menacingly among the children.

A quiet voice asked, "Can I get up?"

Josie rounded on the boy in the ankle stocks, "No!"

The boy bowed his head, tears spilling down his cheeks. Softly he exclaimed, "It hurts."

"Even Abe Lincoln could not earn money for himself, as a young man, until he had paid off his father's debts. His father was a good man, who loaned money to people who needed it, but then the people didn't pay him back. He had no money to pay his taxes and bills. His son was held responsible for his father's debts because Abe was his father's property." She stressed the last part of that sentence. "Anything young Abe Lincoln earned was not his, it belonged to his father." She scowled at the now silent boys. "You want to be held responsible for your parent's debts, for your parent's mismanagement of money?"

Children shook their heads, some looking at the ground, others meeting the gaze of this angry, demanding woman.

"Your father could even sell you if he needed money," she continued, glaring and stalking among the silent children.

One hesitantly asked, "You mean, like a slave?"

Josie looked at the child's earnest look and addressed him more softly. "No, as an indentured servant. You would be sold to someone for a period of years. Up to seven years, in most cases. You had to obey and labor for that person. As a child, you really had no rights."

She sighed, looking around at all the now mostly quiet, concerned faces. "You don't know how good you have it. You don't know how much WE have fought to give it to you. People fought and died to give you the right to free speech." She glanced at the child who had cited that right. "We fought for your right to be free, to have the right to vote. My mother was born when women did not have the right to vote. It was after women fought so hard to be allowed to vote, that YOU, you children, started getting more rights, more protections. Have you studied the Civil Rights Movement?"

She got nods and some kids looking at others in question. "People, Black and White, male and female, worked to get voting rights for all people. The people fighting for your rights were harassed, imprisoned, beaten, even killed. Black families who dared to register to vote were kicked out of the homes where they had lived for generations. They were fired. They were beaten. They were shot at. It took courage and heart and even people's lives to give you all that you have."

Josie went over to the girl in the pillory. By now, she was struggling to keep her feet on the narrow piece of wood, craning to find a more comfortable position for her neck and wrists. Josie shoved the bar up that held her in place. She turned and freed the weeping boy as well. She offered him a hand, knowing he would be stiff.

Standing next to Rosie, Allison realized her youngest aunt was clutching her hands together, shaking. Her chest heaved. Her breathing was harsh, ragged. Looking more closely, she saw unshed tears. "Are you all right?" Allison asked quietly.

Rosie nodded slightly, dropping her head and backing up a step. Allison respected her need not to tell her what was wrong—at least not now, not here.

The teachers and parents gently gathered their now subdued students. Allison heard Josie tell the girl she'd freed from the stocks, who was still standing beside her, waiting for her classmate to get steady on his feet, "Go forth. Learn our history. Pay attention. Vote. Be proud of all you have."

Both children nodded solemnly, the girl murmuring, "Yes, ma'am," the boy echoing, "Yes, ma'am."

One of the parents touched Josie gently on the shoulder and quietly thanked her.

Allison took a deep breath. She heard Rosie take one too. Daisy looked over at them and shook her head. "She should have been a professor."

The four once more started their slow slog back to the car.

"Impressive," Daisy told her sister. Josie nodded in acceptance.

. . . .

"Where to?" Allison asked when they returned to the car.

Daisy had already pulled out her smartphone and was busy tapping. "Head out Route 5 toward Charles City. Would anyone like to visit Berkeley Plantation?"

"Why? What's there?"

"It's the site of the actual first Thanksgiving. Settlers landed at the Berkeley Hundred, as it was called then, in 1619, one year before the Mayflower landed in Plimoth Plantation. The group's London Company Charter insisted that they hold a Thanksgiving to God on the day of their arrival and to celebrate that day every year, perpetually. The 1726 Georgian Mansion was the birthplace of Benjamin Harrison the Fifth. He was a signer of the Declaration of Independence as well as governor of the Virginia colony."

Allison glanced at Daisy who was reading off her phone. "I thought Benjamin Harrison was president in the late 1800s."

Daisy nodded. "He was, and though it says this was the home of two presidents, it wasn't the birthplace of two. President Benjamin

Harrison, our twenty-third president, was born in North Bend, Ohio. His grandfather, William Henry Harrison, who was our ninth president, was born at Berkeley. The one who was signer of the Declaration of Independence was Benjamin Harrison the Fifth." Daisy went back to summarizing what was on her phone. "There was a massacre at the settlement there in 1622. The first brick mansion was built by BH Five in 1726. His son was Willian Henry Harrison. He's the guy who fought at the Battle of Tippecanoe."

"Tip the Canoe and Tyler too!" Rosie sang out.

Allison added, "The Harrison slogan was 'Tippecanoe and Tyler, too', since Harrison's chosen running mate was John Tyler. Wasn't 'tip the canoe and Tyler too' used by the opposition party?"

Josie snorted. "Either that or it came from a Walt Kelly 'Pogo' cartoon."

Allison glanced in the rearview mirror. "Who were Walt Kelly and Pogo?"

"You're kidding! How can you not know Pogo?"

"We have met the enemy, and he is us!" Rosie proclaimed, thrusting her forefinger in the air.

"Pogo poetry was some of my favorite!" Daisy gushed, momentarily forgetting her smart phone. "*Once you were two, dear birthday friend...*"

"*In spite of purple weather,*" Josie continued. "*But now you are three and near the end, as we grewsome together.*"

Daisy took it again. "*How forthful thou, forsooth for you, for soon you will be more!*"

"*But 'fore one can be three be two, before be five be four!*"

All three sisters broke into peals of giggles. "Okefenokee Swamp! We have to visit the Okefenokee Swamp!"

"Where is it? Is that where Pogo and Albert the Alligator and Howland Owl live? Is it on our way?" Rosie asked excitedly.

"It's in southern Georgia, on the Florida border," Daisy said. "I'll put it on the list of Must-See List."

"Geez," Daisy sighed and got back to her description of Berkeley, shortening her narration a bit. "Anyway, due to poor farming techniques, Ben Harrison the Seventh went bankrupt, the bank foreclosed, and they were evicted."

"Oops."

"Fast forward to the Civil War; it was known as Harrison's Landing. Union troops stayed there and it's where General Danial Butterfield wrote *Taps*. It was first played there by his bugler. After the war, it was rented out by the bank to tenant farmers, used as a barn, and eventually trashed. It says here there is still a cannon ball lodged in a wall."

"I want to see that!" Rosie bounced in the rear seat. "How far is it? Will we get there in time?"

Daisy dinked on her smart phone. "Yup, it's open, and the last tickets are sold at four-thirty. We should make it just fine!"

. . . .

They pulled into the parking lot of Berkeley Plantation where Allison dropped the aunts off at the two brick gate posts marking the path to the entrance door. She made the mistake of calling it the front of the mansion.

"This is the rear," Daisy corrected. "The front of these mansions face the river since most traffic came by boat or barge."

Allison let them out and sighed.

After parking, she entered in time to hear Josie asking for three senior tickets and one student ticket.

The woman glanced up at Allison and raised an eyebrow.

"Uh," Allison began.

"You are a student," Josie snapped. "You are going back to college in the fall." Josie took the tickets and grabbed Allison's arm.

A guide met them and asked them to join the four guests already waiting. They were led through an arched doorway into the first room, surrounded by opulent furnishings and heavy brocade draperies.

Rosie sidled up to Daisy. "Where is the cannon ball in the wall?" Daisy shushed her.

In to the dining room, a chandelier hovered beautifully over the table, a ready-laid fireplace next to it with silver candlesticks. Rosie peered all around the room, then she sidled up to Josie. "Where's the cannon ball in the wall?"

The guide started giving Rosie concerned looks. Through the next arch into a living room was a fireplace, an oriental carpet, and a wooden-legged soft green sofa. Rosie scanned the walls, trying to peer behind the portrait over the fireplace. Allison saw the guide frown slightly as he watched her aunt.

Rosie shuffled over to Allison. "Have you spotted the cannon ball in the wall?" Allison wanted to announce loudly, *She's not with me! I've no idea who she is!*

They were eventually left in a lower floor room with paintings showing the history of the property hung on the brick walls. The guide, addressing the three elderly sisters, asked sweetly, "Does anyone have any questions?"

Rosie's hand shot up. "Where's the cannon ball in the wall?"

Their guide laughed in relief. "The cannon ball is embedded in an *outside* wall. When you finish in here, leave through that door into the garden, and turn to your left. It is in the side of the wall with a large sign pointing it out."

Rosie fidgeted while her sisters studied the painting, which portrayed the attack by Powhattan's son during which the early settlement was burned and settlers were killed or fled down river. She sighed loudly as they examined the painting of wealthy planters visiting the brick mansion.She stomped her foot in frustration as her sisters paused by a painting of Benedict Arnold ransacking and burning the house during the Revolution. At the final painting, she sidled toward the door as her sisters pointedly ignored her, all gazing at the painting which showed the housing and work of the enslaved population.

Allison noticed that Rosie wasn't the only one who seemed short on patience and footsore after their long day. Rosie excitedly led the way out the door and to the left, where she pointed delightedly at the sign on the outside wall marking where a cannon ball punched into the brick wall during an attack by General Stuart in 1862. Rosie clapped in delight as Josie clicked a photo for her.

Daisy took Allison's arm. "Why don't you take a look around while we take a rest here, and then tell us what you see." She pointed to a bench near a pink-flowered dogwood tree. Most of the petals had fallen, scattering pink across the grass and brick walkway.

Allison left the three resting, massaging feet, rubbing sore legs, or just wilting into the hard bench. She went down toward the James River, seeing the front of the mansion, boxwood hedges, gardens, and a path from the gardens down to the river. On the walk, Allison stopped to read the sign that outlined the plantation's history. Another sign told of Benedict Arnold who had encamped there toward the end of the Revolutionary War, during which he pillaged the house, stole cattle, and kidnapped forty enslaved people. Up closer to the house, she saw the sign detailing the Civil War encampment during which Brigadier General Butterfield worked with a young bugler on the tune that became *Taps*.

Returning to the bench, she found Daisy barefoot, her pink, New Balance walking shoes kicked off in front of her. Rosie's ankles looked swollen above her blue and gray orthopedic Propets. Josie stood as Allison approached. "Daisy has found us a motel near Hopewell, which is right off Route 295. We'll pick up some food along the way." She looked back at Rosie who remained slumped on the bench.

After getting on her shoes, Daisy stood and helped Rosie to her feet. They slowly made their way around the side of the plantation house. Allison hurried ahead to bring the car around. She shook her head. It was obvious they'd done too much today.

. . . .

After checking into their motel, the ladies had Allison take them back to Fast Food Row. After several stops, the ladies carried in two cheeseburgers with a plastic knife to cut them in half, a medium pizza, one side with sausage and black olives, the other mushrooms and spinach, a plain salad, Caesar salad, cobb salad, a salad with strips of grilled chicken, and an antipasto.

And two large orders of French fries.

And a six-pack of beer, after a heated debate over Sam Adams or Yuengling.

And a milkshake for Allison, after she lugged in all the luggage.

Daisy found a Jimmy Stewart movie on AMC, and the ladies settled in for the night.

Allison lay back to enjoy the movie. Seeing the women in their tight-waisted dresses and high heels, she remembered Josie's tirade. *She's right. We have come a long way. I need to remember and be grateful for that.*

Chapter 13

KITTY HAWK

After numerous nocturnal bathroom runs, the ladies were up and preparing for the day by 7:30. Stiffness greatly affected the morning preparations. Allison cleaned up the dinner detritus, rinsing and then setting the beer bottles by the door to take out.

"Those can go by the trash, dear." Josie waved an imperial finger.

Allison sighed. Imperial fingers now directed her morning and evening. Every time she felt herself resenting or balking, she heard her mother's stern admonition, *"It's your duty!"*

. . . .

With, suitcases heaved in the trunk, bag of snacks at Daisy's feet, and large handbags at Josie and Rosie's feet, they were ready to begin the day.

"Where are we going?" Josie asked as Allison pulled out of the hotel parking lot. "Which way?"

Allison realized that she had simply planned to turn the opposite way from where they'd come in the evening before. Daisy was so good at giving directions that she just assumed she'd be told which way to go.

Daisy looked startled. "Oh . . . we didn't plan a route last night." She scrabbled under the seat, unclipping her seatbelt to lean far enough forward.

"How close are we to Kitty Hawk? I've always wanted to see where the Wright Brothers made their first flight." Allison wasn't sure she had a say in where they went, but that was a place she'd wanted to visit since she'd read a biography about the Wright Brothers in sixth grade. "I've been to the Huffman Prairie site in Dayton where they perfected their aircraft. I've always wanted to see Kitty Hawk."

"Done," Daisy replied, gladly abandoning her fruitless effort to reach the map book under the seat. She switched to her phone GPS and within minutes was directing Allison down Route 460 toward Chesapeake, Virginia, then 168 to Currituck, North Carolina.

Traffic being light, Allison let her mind wander. *Is this at all what I expected? Are the aunts anything like how my dad described them?* Glancing in the rearview mirror at Rosie looking pensively out the window and Josie fiddling in her handbag, then tapping the armrest, Allison thought about what she'd seen yesterday. Daisy had visited many of these places with her husband, Barth, so she knew her way around. Where had Josie gained so much knowledge about history? Then there was the strange, upset look Rosie had when Josie was talking about the Civil Rights time period.

. . . .

Stopping at a rest area for bathroom break and snacks, the ladies tottered stiffly after levering themselves from their seats. "I think today is going to be your day," Daisy informed Allison as she paused, keeping a steadying hand on the car door.

"Don't get old," Josie joked.

"The Golden Years," Rosie huffed. "Whoever came up with that name? It's the stiff years. Everything gets stiff, even parts you didn't know you had get stiff."

Daisy chuckled and pushed off from the car, starting the long, stiff march to the beckoning restrooms.

By the time they left the rest area, Allison was relieved to see that her stiff aunts had loosened up some. "Is there someplace else you'd rather go?" she asked them. "We don't have to go to Kitty Hawk."

"Honey, you've been following us around without complaint. They have a nice museum where we can totter around, watch some videos, read all the signs, and you can go out on the grounds. Don't you worry about us. We'll find things to do."

"Should we have lunch first or after?" Josie turned to Allison. "How long do you intend to wander around?"

Daisy tutted. "If that's your attitude, we'd better have lunch first, so you don't get grumpy."

Josie rolled her eyes. Rosie giggled.

After a seafood meal overlooking the ocean in Currituck, Allison drove south along the peninsula to Kill Devil Hills and the Wright Brothers National Memorial. Once more, Allison drove her stiff aunts as close to the visitor center as she could.

Daisy paused before shutting her door. "If you want, go walk the grounds first. The monument is up on that hill." She pointed toward a granite obelisk. "Then you can go to the hangars and airstrip where their first flights got off the ground."

Allison parked in the shade of a tree, then headed off to walk the grounds, up to the monument, then to the hangars. She walked to each of the markers that showed how long and how far each flight had taken. Flight one: twelve seconds, 120 feet flown by Orville. Flight two: twelve seconds, 175 feet, Wilbur. Flight three: fifteen seconds, 200 feet, and finally the fourth flight, when Wilbur really got some air time, fifty-nine seconds and 852 feet!

Allison stood grinning, looking back to where the plane had left the ground. That far, she thought, only to have a gust of wind pick up and smash their safely landed aircraft as they celebrated and hugged each other.

She went in and found her aunts. She saw Josie in front of a timeline display and Daisy reading the history of the brothers' four years of effort. Rosie stood in front of the replica of the Wright flyer, quietly singing *"Up, Up, and Away,"* except she substituted *"in my beautiful machine"* instead of balloon. Allison smiled and moved to stand with her. The two pointed and marveled at the system the brothers had rigged to change the pitch, roll and yaw of the craft, the cradle in which they lay on the lower wing.

Daisy wandered over to join them as Allison was explaining, "The brothers understood pitch and roll by watching birds. They saw that birds' tails controlled pitch, which is whether the nose was pointed up or down. Roll could be controlled by warping the wings, changing the amount of lift on the wings. But when the roll was changed, they found the nose of the glider they were using would turn toward the low wing sometimes leading to stalling."

"At which point, the craft would *well-dig*, meaning it would smash nose-first into the ground," Daisy added.

Allison smiled, delighted that her aunt also shared her interest. "It took the brothers about two years to figure out the third control they needed. They started with a stationary rudder to try to prevent yaw, the nose turning side to side. It helped a little but not much."

"But why did it take so long?" Rosie asked. "They wouldn't be able to turn the glider if it crashed every time."

Allison shook her head. "At first, they were only trying to fly straight, always into the wind. At this point, they were trying to stop the glider or plane from turning. Turning, flying in an oval would come later at Huffman Field, back in Ohio."

"So how did they solve this last problem?" Rosie gazed at the upright rudders on the back of the Wright flyer, and the movable parallel elevators in front that were controlled by a wooden control bar.

"They realized that the stationary rudder wouldn't work. Then they realized that they needed three motions to control and only two hands. So, the pitch was controlled by the elevator control. The cradle, where the pilot laid along the wing, controlled both the yaw and roll by moving your hips back and forth. In other words, the cradle controlled both the warping of the wings and the movement of the rudder." Allison pointed to each part of the plane as she explained.

"But the propellers are behind the plane. Shouldn't they be in front?" Rosie pointed to the two propellers mounted to the rear of the wings.

"The airfoil design of the wings was a Wright discovery. Propellers also use that design. I guess the brothers thought the propellers pushed the plane forward, but actually the propellers pull a plane forward, which is why they are usually on the front of the craft."

"You certainly seem to know a lot about planes," Daisy said.

Allison looked abashed. "I'd really love to be able to fly. It's one of my dreams, to learn to fly."

"Why don't you?"

Allison shook her head. "It's so expensive. There's no way I could afford it."

Daisy patted her arm. "Then keep it as a dream. But make it come true! Start now, setting aside some money to make it happen."

"All my money has to go for college, then I'll have loans to pay off," Allison muttered, shaking her head.

"Stop it. Hold on to your dreams, then make them come true. Even if you only put aside pennies until you are out of college, then work up to nickels, dimes. Just make it come true, somehow."

Allison nodded. Thoughtful. *Start small but do something.* "I will, Aunt Daisy."

The three continued their tour through the museum, reading panels and histories. Josie joined them to watch a video showing work done by the Wright Brothers at Kitty Hawk.

Heading to the car, Josie asked, "Should we go on down the Outer Banks to Hatteras Island and Ocracoke or turn back to the mainland to Manteo and go to the Fort Raleigh historic site?"

"I'm not sure we can go all the way," Daisy said. "There was a hurricane that destroyed the ferry landings on Ocracoke. I'm not sure that they are up and running yet. If we went that way, we may have to turn around and come back."

Josie nodded. "Manteo it is." Turning to Allison, she asked, "Any desire to visit Fort Raleigh?"

Allison shrugged. "What's there?"

"It's a National Park site that shows the 1585 settlement on Roanoke Island. There isn't a lot there to wander around and see, but I wouldn't mind spending an hour or so if you want to stop."

"Sure," Rosie chirped, adding a little skip to her step.

· · · · · · · · · · · · ·

After a short but slow drive through the heavy traffic of Nag's Head, they turned inland to Manteo and followed the signs to Fort Raleigh.

Earthworks remained of the original Roanoke settlement. The ladies strolled into the small outdoor work area manned by re-enactors showing the puffy-pants dress and daily chores of the late 1500s.

Rosie and Daisy stopped to peer at a metal rod with wire wrapped around it. A section of interwoven chain links lay on the rough, wooden table nearby.

One of the men in old English dress approached, "Gentle ladies," he greeted, with a slight bow.

"Why do you have a screen door spring here?" Rosie blurted, pointing at the wire-wrapped metal cylinder.

He gave a slight smile and headshake. "That is wire that will be cut and used to make chain mail." He held up the few inches of interlocked mesh. "The wire is wrapped then cut in rings. Those rings are then fitted together to make the chain mail."

Rosie examined it carefully, feeling the separate links. She looked up brightly. "You could have one of those bins at the Redemption centers and have it marked for used screen door springs. Then you wouldn't have to waste all this time wrapping wire, and you could recycle old springs!"

Allison watched as the man's polite smile drifted south. He must have heard a lot of dumb ideas from people who visited. He made a valiant effort to look politely interested.

"You could make a lot of them from old springs, then use them like those bulletproof, Velcro vests the police wear."

Daisy corrected her sister. "I think you mean Kevlar. Bulletproof vests are made of Kevlar."

"But they're held together with Velcro," Rosie said.

A re-enactor intervened, possibly concerned that these two possibly senile elderlies might possibly get into an argument, possibly with violence, right here, and cause a scene. "Ahh, ladies, the reason chain mail went out of use was because chain mail did not stop bullets. It became useless when firearms became commonly used."

Nodding, Rosie and Daisy moved off to look at other work areas. "Really," Rosie continued, "it would save a lot of time to just use old screen door springs to make chain mail."

Daisy nodded. "It would have helped even more if those could have been used back in the 1400s or 1500s when people still needed the chain mail."

"So, old screen door springs need to be collected, and then figure out a way to send them back in time so people can recycle them into chain mail!"

Daisy patted Rosie's arm. "Yes, Rosie. But who would they be given to? Suppose you gave them to London armorers who made lots of chain mail and then it turns out the wrong side won in one of England's battles for the throne?"

Rosie giggled. "Like when Henry of the Lancasters invaded from Brittany at the end of the Wars of the Roses? If he'd lost to Richard III—"

Daisy took over. "—then Henry would not have become Henry VII, he would not have wed Elizabeth of York, and there would be no Tudor line of succession."

Rosie put a hand-to-mouth look of despair. "Then no Queen Elizabeth II, no Princess Diana! We cannot change history. I guess we'd better not send screen door springs back in time."

Daisy shrugged. "Besides, most screen doors no longer have springs. They have those aluminum tube things instead." She glanced back at Allison following closely behind them with a look of confused bemusement. Poking her sister, Daisy pointed back at Allison and grinned.

"This is something we did with Daddy," Daisy explained. "He was so good at it. We'd get on a topic and just, I guess you'd call it, *free association*. Mama didn't join in, but we'd look over at her and she'd be collapsed in silent laughter. It was such fun." Daisy's voice drifted off into her fond memories of childhood.

"Did Grandma Anna join in?" Allison asked, seeing both her aunts' faces go from fond memory to disgust.

"No," Daisy snapped.

Rosie took over. "She'd call us all stupid or dumb and flounce out."

"We tried to ignore her, but Mama would stop laughing. Even if we were able to get back into the rhythm of our game, Mama would no longer laugh."

Rosie sighed. "It really hurt her."

A feeling of sadness and disappointment washed over Allison as she heard such things about her grandmother. Then she thought about that day on the beach with the carp. "That first day out from your house, Aunt Daisy, on the beach with the carp. That's what you were doing!"

Daisy beamed. "And you handled it fine. Oh, but the look you had on your face!"

Rosie mimicked hands-in-the-air terror. "They're crazy! Flee! Hide! I'm with a bunch of crazy old ladies!"

Josie stomped up. "Who's a bunch of crazy old ladies?"

Allison chuckled at Rosie's antics and the expression she realized she must have had that morning on the beach. She really had wondered if they were crazy.

"We were talking about a time Allison probably thought we were a bunch of crazy old ladies," Daisy explained.

"Oh, you mean at least once a day!" Josie cackled, then turned to lead them back to the car.

· · · · · · · · · · · ·

An hour into the drive to Williamston and feeling pleased about the way the day was going, Allison was startled when she heard an insistent, "Pull over! Pull over!"

The car slewed on gravel as Allison wrenched the car onto the shoulder, trying to miss the gang of men in brightly colored coveralls picking up trash by the roadside. "What? What is it?" She demanded, checking the dashboard for idiot lights, then turning to check her passengers for signs of distress.

Too late. All three aunts had barreled out of the car. Daisy called over her shoulder, "It's an Adopt a Highway group! I've always wanted to ask about that!" And off she hustled.

In the rearview mirror, Allison saw an armed sheriff's deputy hurrying forward, his shotgun across his chest. "Get back in the car!" he bellowed.

The aunts were spreading out.

Allison opened her door, yelling to the scattering aunts. "It's a prison gang, not an Adopt a Highway group!"

"Get back in the car, NOW!" shouted the growing-flustered officer.

Allison slammed her door shut from inside, hands tight on the wheel. In the rearview mirror, she saw a young convict scrambling up the embankment to the overpass. Another leaned on his paper-gripper claw and grinned.

Rosie stopped right in front of the deputy as Daisy whipped out her cell phone to take photos. "Is picking up trash dangerous work? Shouldn't you be wearing bright colored clothing as well?"

"Ma'am—"

"*Ooo*, there must be more trash up there, that man is certainly dedicated to scramble up to that other road."

"Johnson! You get back here, now! You hear me?" The deputy turned, bellowing at the orange-clad escapee.

"Yes, boss." He whined, sliding back down the slope. "I just want to go home for a while."

"I know, kid, but it ain't worth it. You only got a few weeks to go. Now get back to work."

Josie strode up, chin out. "I see no point in bullying that young man. Since Adopt a Highway is a volunteer program, he should certainly be allowed to go home if he wishes."

Behind the officer, Allison watched as a man unzipped his fly and started making very rude gestures. Rosie looked his way and froze, transfixed. She tapped Daisy's arm. When ignored, she yanked Daisy's sleeve.

"What is it?" her sister demanded. Rosie pointed. Daisy's cell phone came up.

Allison screamed from inside the closed car. "It's a prison work gang! Get in the car *NOW* or I'm leaving without you!"

The deputy hustled them toward the car. Another officer came rushing from down the road, calling for back-up on his radio. The man making naughty gestures really started getting naughty, thrusting his pelvis and making unsavory noises. Allison was glad for the competing noises of traffic and deputies yelling.

"You don't have to be pushy, young man. We were merely curious about that Adopt a Highway program. It's on all the roads, you know."

"Didn't anyone adopt this stretch? Is that why you have to get people out of prison to do it?"

The deputy was struggling to remain calm. "They're from the local jail, ma'am, not prison. They aren't a danger to you."

Allison glanced again at the guy doing naughty gyrations.

One by one, slowly as only women in their eighties can be, the aunts maneuvered themselves back into the car.

Not wanting a speeding ticket on top of whatever other offense they may have committed, Allison pulled very gently back on to the road after very carefully checking all her mirrors, including the one in which she could see the naughty man bending over with his behind to her and his hands on the waistband of his pants. Allison stopped checking the mirrors and got out of there.

"Well, that was enlightening." Josie adjusted her seatbelt and fidgeted with her massive purse on the floor at her feet.

"I thought that man doing things with his crotch was, well, getting interesting. Did you get any photos of him, Daisy?"

Daisy powered up her phone to check the photos, passing it over for Rosie to see. Heads together, the two pointed and giggled.

Josie ignored them. "I do find those Adopt a Highway signs to be interesting. Sometimes it's local businesses or organizations and sometimes it's families or in memory of someone." She paused. "I'm not sure I'd be too flattered to have trash picked up in my name. But maybe that would be a nice gesture."

"Barth and I saw Adopt a Highway signs in Utah that were adopted by the Freedom from Religion Society and another section adopted by The Latter-Day Druids," Daisy shared, shutting down the photos on her phone.

From the front, Josie asked, "Are Wiccans associated with Druids? Do you think they really dance around in their birthday suits?"

Rosie snorted. "Wiccans and Druids lived in England. Dance around with nothing on, you'll get gorse in your feet and catch your death of cold!"

"And how would you know?" demanded Josie.

"I was a Wiccan."

"What!?"

"I had an ivy plant in the window, a collection of leaves in the bathroom, and herbs growing in the kitchen," Rosie explained.

Silence.

"And I never danced around naked."

"I had an ivy plant once," contributed a thoughtful Daisy.

"Well, I'm sure Wiccans could dance nude in this country, especially here in the south, without catching their death." Josie stated sternly.

Daisy tucked her phone back in her purse, "Oh dancing nude isn't all it's cracked up to be."

"And how would you know?" Josie again.

Daisy shrugged nonchalantly. "Barth and I went to nudist camps. We danced on the beach and such."

Allison tried not to swerve off the road.

Rosie's eyes lit up. "Was it. . . interesting?"

"That's what Barth had hoped. You know the beauty of Greek statues? Imagine that they are made of wax and have been in the hot sun too long. That's how most of the people there looked. Sculpted muscles sunk into pot bellies, wrinkles and sagging all over. I wasn't impressed. I got sand where it wasn't wanted, sunburned on parts that had never seen the sun, then the mosquitoes came out."

Rosie giggled. Josie snorted.

Allison tried very hard to concentrate on driving and not picture Daisy dancing nude and swatting mosquitos.

Josie shot a side-ways glance at Allison and muttered with a cheeky grin. "Bunch of crazy old ladies."

Chapter 14

CAPE FEAR

Routine.
 Try to sleep through a night of squeaking, snoring, snorting, and things getting knocked over during nocturnal bathroom runs. Get up and fight for the bathroom. It was so much easier when they got two motel rooms as they had the night before. Allison found that they generally got started an hour sooner with two rooms. After watching Daisy struggle to help Rosie get her orthopedic stockings on, Allison had sped up the morning routine by taking over that task.

Next phase of routine.

Have a breakfast from Daisy's snack bag of yogurt, fruit, and granola accompanied by complaints from Josie that she wanted bacon and eggs, or a ham and cheese omelet or eggs Benedict. Clean up and repack the snack bag. Repack exploded suitcases, which was getting faster since dirty clothes were shoved to the bottom of the suitcases, and there were a lot of dirty clothes. Haul suitcases out and shove them into the Buick's amazingly large trunk. Decide who was to ride shotgun that day (Daisy or Josie; Rosie always sat behind the driver). Pack the ladies into the car. Search the room for anything left behind: favorite lipstick, medications, cell phone (Daisy), lacy underwear (it was already packed), and raincoat.

Head out of the motel parking lot and let Daisy direct the route. It wasn't so bad.

Daisy directed them on to Route 17 south to New Bern.

"There. We should stop there." Daisy pointed to a sign that announced Tryon Palace. "New Bern was the colonial capital before the Revolution. This was the governor's palace. After the war, this remained the capital until 1794, when it moved to Raleigh."

"How do you remember all this?" Josie demanded, frowning toward her know-it-all sister.

Daisy waved her smart phone dismissively at her sister in the back seat. "I don't, my phone does."

Rosie giggled.

Daisy pointed to a sign for Tryon Palace by the roadside. "Shall we go?"

The silence was deafening.

"Or not." She shrugged.

Allison glanced in the rearview mirror at Josie and Rosie in the back seat. Josie stared out the window, frowning pensively.

Rosie hummed quietly. "I'm hungry, and my feet say they want to rest."

Daisy held her phone aloft like a saber and commanded, "Onward! I remember a Golden Corral along this road somewhere."

Rosie and Josie cheered.

Allison watched the road and drove, wondering how many pounds she'd gain during this trip and how her aunts could put away so much food.

During another free-for-all feed, including several trips to the chocolate fountain, the sisters went over a map of North Carolina and decided to head south along the coast toward Wilmington and Cape Fear. Daisy used her free-stay options and found a hotel within an easy walk of the beach. Allison sighed in disappointment when only one room was booked.

Allison continued driving on Route 17 through Jacksonville and following Daisy's barked directions, through Wilmington. After finding their motel in Seabreeze, checking in, hauling in luggage, and using the facilities, they headed on down the peninsula. Their chosen destinations included the North Carolina Aquarium and Fort Fisher at the very end of the peninsula.

"I like the jellyfish," Rosie enthused.

"Octopus and sharks," Josie added.

"Hmm, I guess my favorites are sting rays and horseshoe crabs. How about you, Allison?" Daisy asked.

Thinking a minute, Allison answered, "I like the filter feeders like barnacles and corals. I always thought they were just, you know, coral and the empty barnacles you see on rocks on the shore. But they have little fronds that come out and scoop plankton out of the water." She turned to grin at Daisy, who lifted an amused eyebrow.

The first tank they came to in the aquarium held a large albino alligator. "*Oooh*," Rosie breathed.

Then turtles. "Sweet!" cheered Daisy.

Poison dart frogs came next. "Lovely," crooned Josie.

Allison felt her heart rate increase. This was going too well. She had a sinking feeling in the pit of her stomach that disaster was right around the corner, as it so often was with the aunts. What would it be today? Releasing the alligator? Falling into a shark tank? Inadvertently smashing one of the massive glass walls of the aquarium?

Stingrays, horseshoe crabs, big silver-sided fish, small brightly colored coral reef fish, starfish, jelly fish, anemones, eels, filter feeders of various types and no disasters.

Allison felt nearly dizzy with relief. One and a half hours of totally normal behavior, not even any snarky comments. A smile of delight tentatively inched across her face, until a tiny mite in her head scuffed its feet and complained, *how boring.*

She glanced at the rapt expressions on all three aunts as they gazed mesmerized at a ceiling-tall tank filled with large fish sculling and swishing back and forth, up and down, as a diver, blowing shiny bubbles from her regulator, wafted handfuls of fish guts through the water.

They seem so normal. Allison shook her head. *But they're not! Don't let your guard down.*

. . . .

Allison drove the ladies down to the old fort at the end of the peninsula, groves of twisted, bent trees lined the road on the approach to the parking area. She let the aunts off right in front of the red brick entranceway to the visitor center. After parking, she joined them in the cool of the building.

The exhibits explained that the construction of the fort started in 1861 to protect the entrance to the Wilmington harbor. The ladies trooped into the auditorium to watch the video. For four years, the massive earthworks and seacoast guns protected blockade runners bringing supplies to the Confederate positions. It wasn't until the end of 1864 and early 1865 that the Northern Army launched an amphibious attack and finally took the fort.

After looking through the museum exhibits and shopping in the gift shop, Allison ran the small purchases back to the car while the aunts started their slow walk on the boardwalk around the fort and earthworks.

Allison sprinted to catch up. *They're out of my sight. Who knows what they'll get into?* Breathing hard, she found the three making their way slowly along the wooden walkway, stopping to read signs, snapping an occasional photo. Allison frowned and shook her head. Anyone watching would think they were normal old ladies.

The ladies crossed the street, through a row of twisted, gnarled live oaks to the oceanfront walkway. They walked the length, slowing until they finally found a bench, heaving sighs as they gazed out over the ocean. Daisy removed a sandal and rubbed her foot. Rosie rubbed a sore knee. Josie leaned her head back, eyes closed.

"I'll bring the car over," Allison offered gently.

Josie nodded without opening her eyes.

Daisy looked up with a smile of relief.

Allison jogged back to the parking area. *This is more like it, just three elderly women enjoying a road trip.*

The rest of the afternoon and evening went just as smoothly. Two hours spent relaxing on the beach. Daisy checking emails on her phone, Josie reading a book, and Rosie sifting the sand for seashells and watching, mesmerized, as sandpipers ran back and forth on the waterline.

That evening, Daisy chose a nightclub for dinner and relaxation. Rosie inched her chair closer to the man playing piano. When *Someone to Watch Over Me* was requested, she started singing softly until the piano player glanced her way. She stood, moved to stand by the piano, and sang beautifully. More songs followed.

Allison smiled.

Back at the hotel room, the ladies prepared for bed, softly bantering.

For the first time on the trip, Allison was the first to fall into a sound, blissful sleep.

Daisy driving, speeding, laughing maniacally. A line of police, sheriff, and trooper cars wailing along behind, red and blue lights strobing. Rosie perched on her knees in the back seat, throwing cup after cup of beer at each car that sped past. Daisy weaving in and out, cutting off cars, causing them to swerve and spin out of control. Josie screaming "Wet T-shirt contest!" and "Faster, faster!" as she pounded the dashboard in excitement.

Allison shot up in bed, heart pounding, gasping.

Quiet surrounded her, except for Daisy's bombing-run snores, which sounded rather like the sirens in Allison's nightmare. She fell back on her pillow, fighting down feelings of dread.

She felt it in her gut. *Tomorrow is going to be a disaster.*

Chapter 15

Biker Bar

"That one! That looks like a good place to eat."

Allison pulled slowly into the parking lot between the many vehicles clogging the place. "They're all motorcycles," she said, sounding apprehensive.

"You can tell how good a restaurant is by how many vehicles are parked there," Josie said.

"But . . . they're all motorcycles."

Rosie leaned forward, examining the bikes as they eased carefully past them. "This looks like a really popular place."

"For bikers." Allison wove between the scattered bikes, aiming for the one empty parking place near the building's front porch.

"I'll bet they have good beer." Josie scooped her bulging purse off the floor.

"They shouldn't drink and drive." Allison pulled into the parking spot. "Are you *sure* you want to eat here?"

Three car doors were already open. "Don't be such a wuss," Daisy snapped as she pried herself out of the back seat.

Rosie stopped to admire a Harley with flame designs covering its tank. "Oh, look!" she exclaimed in delight, "that one has streamers on the handlebars just like my first bicycle!" She turned to Daisy. "Remember, it was pink, and the streamers were pink and white. You were jealous because the bike you got was second-hand and the streamers had been ripped off."

"Yes, but then I made *you* jealous by using birthday ribbon and making mine even longer and multicolored!"

Rosie stroked the black streamers on the motorcycle's handles. "Those were pretty. I'm sorry I cut them off."

The ladies filed up onto the porch, Allison bringing up a cautious rear.

Their entrance into the murky interior of the restaurant/bar brought a spreading silence except for the '60s oldies blaring from a colorfully lit up jukebox. Heads turned, beards waggled, leather creaked, and chains rattled as twenty or more pairs of eyes swiveled to take in the new arrivals.

All male, Allison noted.

The bartender broke the silence. "What'll ya have, ladies?"

Josie strode forward. "We're here for lunch. It looks like such a popular place. The food must be excellent."

Smirks all around, though the bartender looked almost pleased.

"I'll have your house beer," Josie finished, mounting one of the free stools at the bar.

Now it was the bartender's turn to smirk. "House beer, huh? Well, that would be our Black Devil, produced at a local microbrewery. It's a dark beer."

Josie nodded. "Perfect."

Daisy was next to choose a stool. "What have you in wine? I'd prefer a dry red if you have one."

Snickers.

"No wine, lady. Beer, ale, lager, schnapps, whisky, vodka. . . " His list trailed off.

"A light beer, then."

Another smirk. "Watching your girlish figure, are you?"

"I stopped watching that years ago," Daisy smirked in return. "I'm watching my matronly sprawl at this point."

The bartender chuckled and turned his attention to Rosie, who was scanning the room. "And you, missy?"

Allison jumped, but the bartender was focused on Rosie.

"Butter beer, please."

Thundering silence.

Then a beard parted, and laughter boomed out. "Butter beer? Like in Harry Potter. She must be a witch!"

Daisy swiveled on her stool toward the voice and announced with pride, "No, she's a Wiccan. She has an ivy plant and everything."

Deepening silence, punctuated by unsure creaking leather.

Again, the bartender came to the rescue. "How about root beer?"

"Sure."

Hugging the last empty stool to her, Allison strove to wrap Harry's Cloak of Invisibility about her. A light touch brushed across her shoulders. She froze, clutching the stool harder. The brush became steady pressure. She yelped and leaped forward, swinging the stool around, holding it in front like a lion tamer, and found herself looking up into the face of a great, mountain of a man, clad all in black and chains, much like the rest of the patrons. Some decorated it or themselves with embroidered patches (on the jackets) or tattoos (on every part of themselves).

The bartender glared at her. "Well, what'll you have? And put down my stool."

"Cheeseburger and ginger ale, please," she blurted, carefully setting the stool down between her and Mountain Man.

"I'll have hot wings."

"Make mine mild."

Josie examined the board behind the bar. "I'll have a cheeseburger, medium rare, and a green salad."

The bartender came to a halt. "Lady, no salads."

"It says right there, lettuce and tomatoes are put on the burgers. Cut them up, and put them in a bowl. There is bleu cheese that comes with the wings. I'll have that on the side as the dressing."

With a shrug, the bartender drew their drinks and called their orders to some invisible cook back in the dim recesses of the building.

Allison realized that she and the aunts were providing high entertainment for the assembled crowd, most of whom were still watching them in enthralled and leering silence.

Mountain Man grunted his way onto the empty stool Allison had been clutching, forcing her to sidle around him and flee to the other side of her aunts. He leered in amusement as Allison tried to ignore him.

Other men began to move, some to talk quietly among themselves. Balls on the pool table started clicking and smacking. Someone slapped down a twenty-dollar bill on the bar and announced he was paying for the ladies' drinks. Two more ordered wings, as well, and shifted their stools closer to Rosie and Daisy.

Rosie giggled.

"You ever ridden on a bike?" growled the man closest to Rosie.

"Oh, sure, I had a Schwinn when I was a girl," she burbled. "It was pink, with white racing stripes."

"I mean a *real* bike, a motorcycle."

Rosie nodded. "I rented a moped when I was in Bermuda. I traveled all over the island on it."

"Moped," he repeated, and chuckles circulated through the dark room.

Wings, burgers, and a grudging salad arrived.

Josie decided to show what she knew about motorcycles. "I've always wanted a ride on a Hog."

Smugly, Daisy contributed, "Barth and I toured the country on our motorcycle."

The man next to Rosie whispered in her ear. Rosie's eyes opened wide. She swung around to her sister. "Can you really get an orgasm while riding pillion on a Harley?"

Daisy shrugged, but her face lit up. "I don't know about a Harley, but it works on a Goldwing."

Rosie swung back around to her paramour, radiating awe and wonder. He grinned and sucked the meat off another wing. "Finish up, sweet thing, and I'll take you for a ride."

"I haven't got a Goldwing, but my Yamaha V Star gives a good ride," Daisy's partner informed.

The clean-shaven biker who eased in next to Josie wasn't wearing black or chains. His jacket was brown leather, Western with fringe. "My Hog's just waitin' for you, honey bunch."

Allison blanched. "Wait, you're not serious."

But they were. She watched in horror as her three aunts quickly polished off their meals, and the men slapped down payment; only her Mountain Man kept his wallet in his pocket, and they all headed for the door.

"Wait!" Allison yelped as she pelted after them, grabbing Josie's arm. "You're not actually going to go with these guys. You don't know them."

Josie halted. "She's right, young man. You are—"

"Scab . . . Antonin Scabitini, at your service, my good lady." He flourished a bow and took her elbow like an overgrown Boy Scout escorting an old lady across the street, then he led her outside to his waiting Hog.

Daisy eyed her escort.

Without the flourish but with an evil twinkle, he grinned. "They call me Roach." Daisy crossed her hands primly and waited. "Reginald Dupres," he muttered.

Daisy nodded curtly. "Thank you, Mr. Dupres. You may lead me to our ride."

Allison stood dumbstruck. She wheeled toward Rosie who stood admiring the Harley with the flames decorating its fuel tank.

Helmets were tossed to the ladies amid good-natured ribbing.

"Aunt Rosie?" Allison hoped that at least one aunt would come to her senses.

Rosie looked up, wonder and longing in her wrinkled face. Her paramour placed the helmet gently on her head, careful of her bobby-pinned curls. "Hammer," he told her. "Sal Hammerschmidt."

No one offered Allison a ride. Mountain Man just stood there, meaty hands dangling at his sides.

Off roared the aunts.

Off growled an escort of riders.

Only three motorcycles leaned on their kickstands in the parking lot.

Allison whimpered as she waited on the porch, scanning the road, listening for the roar of returning motorcycles.

Nothing.

Mountain Man came out a couple times, staring at her. The aunts had been gone about forty-five minutes when Mountain Man finally approached her. Allison tried to ignore him, once again wishing for that Cloak of Invisibility.

He sidled up behind her, too close. Then she felt him take a strand of her hair, rubbing it between his fingers. With a gasp, Allison shot off the porch. Pawing the car keys from her pocket, she punched the unlock button, jumped in the car, and locked all the doors.

Mountain Man circled the car twice, looking in at her. Then went back inside. Who knew for how long, though?

And *now* what?

An hour crawled by.

Fifteen more minutes.

At an hour-and-a-half, Allison fingered her phone. Should she call the police? What would she say? *My aunts went for a ride with a bunch of motorcyclists.* So?

She called her mom.

No answer.

"I'm not available. Please leave a message," came across the line in her mother's voice.

"Mom! I've lost them. I've lost the aunts." Allison choked up, all the emotion she'd been holding in burbling up as soon as she heard her mother's voice. "They took off with a bunch of bikers—*motorcycle* bikers. They haven't come back. I don't know what to do!" Sobs wracked Allison as she tried through blurry tears to find the phone's *End* button.

She leaned back in the seat. With the windows up, the car had become steaming hot. She struggled to jam the keys in the ignition, turned them enough to power the window down, just a bit, not enough for someone with a ham fist to get his hand in. But what about his fingers? Could he pop the window out if he could get his fingers in the slight opening?

Allison moaned and closed her stinging eyes.

A gentle tapping on the window caused Allison to leap forward and sideways, bashing her arm on the wheel.

Black leather, fringe, and lots of silver studs filled her view. A face appeared—not the Mountain Man—looking concerned. "Roll down the window," making a rolling motion with his hand.

Allison hesitated.

He made an exasperated face. "Then come on out. The ladies are fine." He turned and walked back to the porch where he plunked down on the top step.

"You've heard from them? Do you know where they are?" Allison shouted from the car.

The man held his hand to his ear as though he couldn't hear.

"Oh, bother." Allison wrenched the keys from the ignition,

unlocked the doors, and stomped over to the man on the porch. He patted the porch boards next to him.

"Have a seat."

Exhausted, unnerved, and shaken, she sank down next to him. The sun touched the treetops. She checked her watch. Had it really been more than three hours since they all took off?

"They're your aunts?"

Allison nodded. "My great aunts. I'm driving them on a road trip."

He smiled. "They're fine. Really. They're in good hands."

"But they've been gone for hours!" Allison wailed. "Can you call them?"

"I can call, but if they are on the road, they won't answer. It isn't safe to be on a phone while driving."

They sat in silence as Allison watched the shadows slowly lengthened.

Mountain Man came out again. "Hey, Full Monty! You gettin' a little, huh?" He chortled like an adolescent who'd just told a bathroom joke.

Allison scooted farther away. Mountain Man grabbed his crotch, grinned, and headed back in.

Head down in embarrassment, the other biker mumbled, "Sorry. My name here, today, is Full Monty." Then he smiled and extended his hand. "Monday morning, I go back to being Montgomery Roberts, computer programmer and trouble shooter. And you are ... Allison?"

Allison nodded and accepted the handshake.

Full Monty pulled out his phone, dialed, and waited. "Hey, Scab, the kid's worried about her aunties. Check in when you can." He put the phone away. "He'll call when he's able."

He reached over, patting Allison on the shoulder. "Come on in. I'll buy you dinner."

"Oh my gosh!"

Full Monty hesitated. "Yes?"

"Their purses. They left their purses inside."

Allison bolted in, searching around the stools where her aunts had been sitting.

"Looking for these?" The bartender pointed to two overstuffed purses perched side-by-side on the shelf behind his cash register.

Allison heaved a deep sigh. Of course, Daisy would not have taken off her fanny pack. "Thank you so much." She took charge of purses, and returned them to the car, stashing them on the floor where each aunt usually sat. It seemed more like they'd return if their big purses were in their proper places.

Dinner hour arrived. The lowering sun painted the gathering clouds pink and mauve. Full Monty ordered a couple pizzas for the four who remained in the bar. In the middle of their meal, his phone squawked like a parrot. Scab was calling to say everyone was fine and they would return after watching sunset.

A half-hour after sunset, the roar of returning bikes silenced the chorus of frogs and a pair of barred owls.

Allison ran out, watching as bikes sprayed gravel before coming to a stop in front of the steps. Full Monty headed over to help Rosie from her perch on the rear of her flame-decorated Harley. That freed her escort up to help the next aunt. Each woman was carefully assisted from her ride.

"Oh, Allison, it was wonderful!" Rosie gushed. "We rode all over the back hills. I've never seen such beauty, with the wind whipping and a powerful machine between my legs. We stopped at the guys' favorite watering hole for salsa and beer."

"There was peach and cherry salsa. The peach salsa was awesome!" Daisy chimed.

"We stopped at a roadside stand and got fresh-roasted pecans."

Daisy exclaimed, "Oh!" and unzipped her fanny pack. She worked loose a four-ounce baggie of pecans, handing them proudly to Allison.

Rosie continued, "Then we picked up pizza and beer and went up to a reservoir, where we sat on the embankment and watched the sunset. An eagle flew over, and deer came down from the woods to graze. There was even a pair of muskrats playing in the water. It was lovely," she enthused, hands clutched at her chest.

"I'm so glad you had a good time, Aunt Rosie."

What Allison wanted to scream was that she had been scared to death and why didn't they come back sooner?

Scab sauntered over, arm protectively around Josie's waist. "Got a place to stay tonight? It's quite a drive to the next town of any size."

Josie looked at Allison. "We'd intended to get at least a hundred miles farther today." Looking at Scab. "Can you recommend a place nearby?"

Allison felt her stomach clench.

Scab pulled out his phone, dialed, and waited with a smile. "Maggie! Hey, it's Scab. Got any rooms left?" He waited a beat. "That's it? Four ladies. Yeah, I'll ask." He covered the phone and turned to Josie. "There's a motel we use a couple miles from here. It's clean and quiet, at least when we're not revving our machines." He grinned. "Anyway, she only has one room left with two queen beds."

"Some of us can double up. We can free up another room for you all," Roach offered.

"We'll take the room. Thank you for the offer, Roach, that's sweet. We're fine with one room." Daisy took Roach's arm, causing him to blush. "Can you guide us to it?"

Everyone split up, hopping on bikes, climbing slowly and stiffly into cars, and revving up engines. Just before heading out, Allison gulped, then choked on a sob. "I was so worried." Her hands on the wheel were shaking.

"Oh, honey." Josie turned to her. From behind, Rosie leaned forward, wrapping her arms around both the seat and Allison. Daisy, sharing the back seat, reached forward, rubbing Allison's shoulder. Josie continued, "We should have realized you would worry. You don't need to, really. Please don't worry about us. We have all three lived past the average life span. We're grabbing all the fun and experiences we can cram in.

"You don't remember your grandmother—our sister, Anna. She was the *good* one. She married at twenty, had four children, and spent her life caring for her husband and her children. She had everything that we'd always been told should make us happy. Rosie never married . . . our old maid. I married and had a child, but I wasn't happy. As soon as Clayton headed for college, I got a divorce and took off. Broke my husband's heart. He was a good father and provider, and so boring I felt I was suffocating. I thought there was something terribly wrong with me that I could not be happy with him."

Daisy took over. "I married, but couldn't have children. We tried for a while, then considered adopting. Everyone said that we were not *a family,* not complete without children. But we realized a child would only get in the way. We did what we wanted. Barth made good money and was able to take time off when we needed to get away. He went to conferences all over and I was able to go with him. We weren't saddled with children. I also felt there was something wrong with me for feeling that way. As your Grandma Anna's children got older, she went to work, not to please herself, but to put away money so her children could go to college. When her children turned sixteen, they had to work over the summer to earn money. They never got to travel, to explore, or just *do* something because they wanted to. On the rare occasions we got together over the years, we realized that we were happier than Anna. I remember being shocked to find that she was not happy. Content, yes. She loved her husband, she adored her children, but she disliked her life."

Josie's voice was quiet. "Then she got cancer and died. The three of us swore at her funeral that we would not live our lives dying. We would not sit around waiting for cancer or heart disease to take us. We would die living. Allison, if any of us die for any reason on this trip, we have died living."

From behind, Rosie snuggled her chin next to Allison's ear. "We had fun. That's what it's all about. We had fun. I want that on my tomb stone. I enjoyed my life. Please forgive us for scaring you, though."

"We were a bit thoughtless," Josie murmured. And Daisy nodded.

Two motorcycles waited for them in the parking lot, but the rest had left. Allison nodded and sniffled, not yet able to respond to her aunts.

"You're young, sweetie. You have some cause to fear the unknown. We don't." Josie patted her shoulder again. "Now, drive," her commanding tone back. "I'm ready to fall into bed."

Chapter 16

HELMET HAIR

Allison stared at the streetlight-illuminated ceiling, listening to the snoring, whistling, moaning of her aunts. Her mother's phone call played through her mind again.

She'd laughed.

That's all Allison remembered—her mother's laughter.

Her mother had called back soon after the motorcyclists had escorted them to the small, roadside motel. It was cute and clean; they'd been given a tiny room with a tiny bathroom. There wasn't room for their four huge suitcases. The ladies had unpacked what they'd needed then had Allison lug the suitcases back out to the Le Sabre. While hefting the suitcases back into the trunk, her mother had called.

"What happened? Did you find them?"

Allison told her mother all that had happened and her mother had laughed.

Allison pulled the sheet up over her head, turning into her pillow, trying to silence the memory of her mother's laughter. She bet her father would have been disgusted. Sighing and shifting again, trying not to awaken Rosie, Allison realized she was glad she'd told her mother and not her father. She'd rather hear her mother laughing at their antics than hear her father's scorn.

· · · · · · · · · · · · ·

Sunlight peeked between the curtains, seeking someone to awaken. Allison blinked and stretched, checking her watch. Almost seven. Rosie would want to see the *Today Show*. Daisy would want to check the day's weather. She scrabbled on the bedside table and found the TV remote, quickly lowering the sound so as not to wake the aunts.

Two very serious commentators shook their heads, repeating the local headlines from the capital city. Motorcycle gang members had beaten and raped an old lady. She was in critical condition in the hospital. Allison felt her chest constrict. She heard a cluck from the other bed. Josie looked at her.

"That could have been you," Allison whispered, feeling shaky.

Josie shook her head seriously. "No, it couldn't. But, I promise, if we pull that again, we'll take you with us."

Allison stared at her aunt, noticed her expression, then burst out laughing, not because it was funny, but because of the ridiculousness of her statement. Josie winked and chuckled.

Allison shook her head. "You're right, I was obsessing."

"I take it you were too busy in fear mode to notice the bikes." Allison lifted a questioning eyebrow. "They were too clean to be motorcycles that were on the road all the time. Then when we got inside; no women."

Daisy snorted loudly, shoving the covers down far enough to see over them. "Oh, my poor bones!"

"Good morning to you as well," Josie replied.

Daisy continued, having been following the conversation. "No women meant these were 'weekend warriors'. They were guys out for a weekend of *male bonding*. A biker gang would have had women."

"But the tattoos," Allison began.

"I have a tattoo." Daisy pulled down the neck of her nightgown, exposing a small blue and yellow butterfly high on her left shoulder blade.

Rosie, next to Allison, thrashed sideways kicking Allison in the leg then moaned loudly.

"Are you all right?" Allison asked in concern.

"I want to see the tattoo!" Rosie peered over at her sister and giggled. "I have one on my right butt, a little gray kitty playing drums." She giggled again.

Josie looked from sister to sister. "Dang! I need to get me a tattoo."

Rosie shifted and moaned as she tried to push herself up. "Could you hand me that bottle of Excedrin?"

Shoving herself into a sitting position against her pillow, Daisy groaned. "Oh my, I am so stiff! Riding a bike didn't used to make me this stiff."

"Surprise, surprise." Josie waved her imperial finger toward the tiny sink in the bathroom. "Allison, could you bring me my overnight bag, or just grab the bottle of Aleve out if it?"

"I can't take Aleve." Daisy shifted uncomfortably. "I'd be in even more pain. Aleve tears up my stomach. You really shouldn't take it on an empty stomach."

Josie nodded to Allison, who had the bottle of Aleve and stood waiting for further directions. "One of the yogurts."

"Please," Daisy added pointedly.

Allison handed her aunt the bottle and a strawberry yogurt tube. "I'd prefer the—" Josie began.

"AHH!" Daisy held up a stop-sign hand. "Beggars can't be choosers. You want something else, you get it yourself."

Frowning, but with a small smile, Josie accused, "You sound

just like Mother. Ee gads! I remember telling Clayton the exact same thing." She finished by squirting the tube of yogurt into her upturned mouth.

Rosie held the bottle of aspirin and waved a finger at Allison. Reading her sign language, she filled a glass of water for her, then one for Daisy as well. Taking them over, she handed one to Rosie, then handed both the bottle of aspirin and glass of water to Daisy in the other bed.

The three aunts rested while watching the morning news and weather, waiting for their various pain relievers to take effect and to sort out the weeks' worth of medications. Each had her baggie of pill bottles and daily dispensers, shaking, rattling, and counting out various colored pills. Out in the parking area, engines revved, but, to Allison's amusement, the one that roared was quickly throttled down. The bikers didn't wish to awaken or disturb the ladies.

Waiting for pain relief to kick in and motorcycles to leave gave Allison time to grab a shower, quickly dress, and dash out to haul in suitcases for repacking.

It also gave her time to think. *I felt so grown up when I headed off to college. After four years, I thought I knew a lot. But Aunt Josie just proved to me how naive I am. I didn't notice anything that they did. All I saw were motorcycles, a dark bar, and lots of scroungy looking men. How depressing.*

She remembered a quote she'd once read: *When you are not afraid to die, you are free to live.* She remembered reading that in her teens and thinking how powerful it would make you feel, how free. That's what they were trying to tell her.

Thinking about her grandmother, their sister, she thought about Anna's hardships. That explained some things about her father. He had also insisted that she and her brother start getting summer jobs when they turned sixteen. The only travel they had done when she was young had been for a weekend, usually to a historic site or outdoor museum. It was why she had an interest in history.

It was also why her mother had been eager for her to drive her aunts on this trip. She knew how desperately Allison wanted to travel.

"This bathroom is too small!" Josie hip-checked Rosie who staggered backward into Daisy causing her to smear lipstick across her cheek.

"Dadgum! Knock it off!" Daisy snapped, shoving Rosie back into Josie. Josie staggered against the toilet, arms flailing, causing Rosie to squeal and duck.

Allison cowered on the far side of the room, watching the struggle for position in front of the tiny sink and mirror.

Daisy hooted, "Alphabetically! Line up alphabetically!"

At that, Allison stood up. "That means I'm first." She approached tentatively, snagging her toiletries case from the small table on the way.

Daisy stood, mouth open. Josie sputtered, glared at Daisy, and backed away. Rosie giggled and gave Allison a high-five.

While her aunts fidgeted impatiently, Allison again thought how much this was like her college dorm. Another two years of college, and she still wasn't sure if counseling was what she really wanted. *Maybe I should take a year off. And do what?*

Allison finished her morning ablutions while the aunts glared, Daisy tapping her foot in annoyance. Rosie tried to glare, but kept breaking into giggles. After finishing, wiping her mouth on the thin towels, Allison assisted each aunt in her packing, and in Rosie's case, dressing, as they took their alphabetical turns at the tiny sink. As each finished, she lugged that suitcase back out to the car.

While Rosie finished her turn at the sink, Josie stood behind her, brush in hand, attempting to fluff her blonde hair. Huffing a sigh, Josie tipped her head forward to see her part. "Enough. We all need a hair dresser. Those helmets yesterday left my hair flat and I need a touch-up on the color."

Rosie tried to twang a flat curl. "I second that." She shoved a bobby pin decorated with a lemon-yellow bow into what was left of her drooping curls.

Daisy turned to Allison as she struggled to close Josie's suitcase. "It's Sunday and may be hard to find anything open. So your assignment, if you chose to accept it, is to find us a beauty parlor."

"There is no choice involved," Josie snapped. "I insist on finding someone to do something with this rat's nest." She tried again in vain to fluff her hair. "Looks like a bleedin' elephant sat on my head."

· · · · · · · · · · · · ·

Allison accepted the challenge. Leaving the motel after ten, Daisy directed her on a route that would take them through a couple large towns, hoping that after Sunday services someone may be open. After finding lunch in the nearest large town, she found a strip mall in the second with a sign for Mazie's Color and Cuts. It was open. Parking as close as she could get to the salon, the aunts piled out, dragging handbags and buckling on fanny packs. Josie shoved open the salon door.

"We need help," she nearly shouted. Startled older ladies in beehives and smart-looking businesswomen looked up. Two hairdressers. One open seat, the occupant having just moved to sit under the drier.

"Yes, Ma'am, how can we help?" The platinum blonde hairdresser's voice dripped with Southern sarcasm and exuded the unspoken accusation "Pushy Yankees."

Daisy elbowed to the fore, "We were riding motorcycles yesterday. We have helmet hair."

There were gasps from two of the older-looking ladies. A flustered Rosie added helpfully, "I don't think any of us had an orgasm." Then put her hand to her mouth and turned a shocking red that clashed with her hair.

One of the gaspers got up and flounced out.

One smartly dressed woman with a head of brassy-tinted tight curls waved her ring-bejeweled hand. "Oh, sweety, I get that!" which caused a few embarrassed giggles, but broke the ice.

The one hairdresser with the open chair stood hand on ample hip and surveyed the damage to the aunts' hair. With a cluck of her tongue and a head shake, she announced, "I can fit in two of you, not all three."

Rosie whimpered. Josie frowned, and Daisy blew a sigh of exasperation.

The woman under the drier raised her hand and wiggled her fingers for attention. "Um, there is another salon just down the way." She indicated to go to the right outside the door.

Daisy nodded. "I'll check. If I am not back immediately, then I'm in." She ignored the whispering among the other women and strode out the door and turned right. On the opposite end of the strip mall, she found Shania's Hair and Nails. The sign on the door listed that it was open Sunday from one to five-thirty. Pushing the door open, all the chatter stopped, and nine Black ladies turned their attention to Daisy.

The silence was broken by the manicurist who pointed back the way Daisy had come. "I think you'd be more comfortable in the salon down the way."

Daisy ignored her, all her attention on one of the ladies occupying a salon chair. Long burnt-orange extensions were being added to her straightened hair. "Those are lovely!" she breathed in admiration. "I want some."

One lady shrieked in delight, another clapped her hands and the woman in the chair with the extensions turned a 100-watt beaming smile on the mesmerized Daisy. The young woman in the middle chair hopped up. "We finished! Here," she tapped her chair, "I'm done. We were just shootin' the breeze."

Daisy thanked her then went to examine the extensions more closely. "May I touch them?"

She was handed a handful of the long, orange-tinged braids. Daisy's smile widened. She turned to the stylist in charge of the chair she'd been offered. "My color is golden brown, and I need a touch-up, but—" She looked back at the long braids. "I'd love to have some braids? Is that—" she looked longingly at the mass of extensions.

Nodding, her stylist flipped open a new cape, motioning for Daisy to take the vacant seat. With a pat on her shoulder, she assured Daisy, "I can certainly do that. I'll get you a book and you take a look through while I clean up here and get ready for you."

Daisy beamed.

Two hours later, Josie and Rosie left Mazie's, helmet heads healed, newly washed, colored, and set. Allison pulled the car up closer to pick them up. "No Daisy yet?" Josie asked.

Allison shook her head. They drove down to Shania's, pulled up to a parking space in front, and waited.

The car got hot. Josie sighed. Allison rolled down the window. Rosie hummed.

No one came out of Shania's.

Josie fell asleep, snoring. Allison got out and paced up and down the sidewalk of the strip-mall. Rosie dumped the contents of her purse and rearranged it all.

No one came out of Shania's.

Cheering from Shania's awoke Josie. Rosie had her door open to get some air. Allison stopped her pacing and watched the door of Shania's Hair and Nails.

The door was thrown open. Daisy strode out side-by-side with a woman with waist-length burnt-orange braids, flanked by several other Black ladies with wonderful hair and flashing awesome nails. Josie eased out of the car, mouth agape. Rosie's eyes widened in amazement as she pulled herself from her seat, riveted on the mass of braids intricately wound about Daisy's head. She started quietly singing *Hair*, swaying her hips, causing her yellow muumuu to sway.

Josie walked right up to her sister, gazing in awe at the mound of brunette tresses, highlighted with tints of warm honey and twined with intricate braids. "Where did you get all that hair?"

The woman with the orange extensions grinned and raised one carefully shaped eyebrow. Daisy touched her 'crowning glory' proudly. "Extensions. You like?"

Josie looked around at the other ladies, then back at Daisy. "Glory be. Can I get some?"

Rosie hurried forward, "Me, too!"

Amidst laughter and the showing off of painted, spangled, and dangerous looking fingernails, all the ladies, except one who insisted she must get home, trooped back in to Shania's Hair and Nails. The next hour was spent with Josie deciding on a fish tail (five strand) crowning braid. Meanwhile, Rosie and Daisy got their nails done. Rosie got a different brightly colored flower on each pasted-on nail. Daisy got dark blue with glittering stars to go with her light blue T-shirt with rhinestone yoke. When it was Rosie's turn for a braid, she giggled and asked for a long, thin braid like Obi Wan Kenobi had in his younger version on *Star Wars*. "But I don't think I have enough hair to braid it in!"

Daisy's stylist smiled and brought out a book full of different colored single braids with tiny clips on the ends. She chose the one closest in color to Rosie's newly dyed red hair and gently eased the clip up under her newly-minted curls. She looked at the two yellow bows on the bobby pins holding back her side curls and finished off the long, skinny braid with a tiny yellow bow.

Rosie beamed.

Josie delightedly examined her new fire-engine red fingernails, each with a rhinestone in the center, except for her right index finger, on which a set of sharp, white teeth topped off the dangerously pointed tip. Josie grinned.

Allison huddled out of the way, watching. Touching her own straight brown hair, she realized she'd been wearing it the same way most of her life. *Daisy looks fantastic! I wish I had the nerve to try new styles.*

Daisy stood and announced, "This has been a very long and very fruitful afternoon. Dinner is on me," which was met with cheers, shouts of approval, and one dissenter.

"We have families to get to. We can't stay too long." Shania looked crestfallen.

"Take out, with left-overs to take home. What kind of takeout would we all like?" Menus were pulled from drawers and pored over. Three different calls were made for pizza, Chinese, and a combination of fried chicken and fried catfish with hushpuppies. As they waited, Allison, sitting unnoticed in a corner, realized that the ladies were looking at her.

She squirmed.

"Lordy, we forgot one."

"Look at that poor child."

"Now what can we do with that hair?"

"Don't you worry, honey, we got this."

"Poor darlin' looks terrified!"

One of the stylists appraisingly approached Allison and felt her hair. "Healthy and fine." She nodded, a chair was readied, and Allison felt panic bubbling as she was hauled to her feet and parked in the swivel, tippy chair with a plastic cape draped around her. The manicurist grabbed her hand, looking at the short but healthy nails.

The aunts grinned. Allison knew there was no rescue coming from them.

Two young ladies who stayed after having their own hair done and one stylist started to work on Allison's straight, light brown hair. Another set to work on Allison's nails.

Allison watched in fascination in the mirror as her hair was braided, piled, fluffed, spritzed, pinned, and teased. Strands came loose from the styles each time and hung limply.

"I've never done anything with hair like this," muttered one of the young women in consternation as another strand escaped and played dead.

Realizing she hadn't been paying attention to the whispers and giggles going on between her aunts and the manicurist, Allison glanced at her hand.

She jerked, yanking her right hand up to take a closer look. Each finger now sported a pastel nail decorated with a *My Little Pony*. "You've got to be kidding!" she blurted.

Josie replied, deadpan, "It was that or roosters."

"We could put rooster nails on your other hand," Rosie offered helpfully.

Daisy grinned wickedly. "Get over it. They're fun."

Gritting her teeth and ignoring the tension in her stomach, Allison held up her other hand. "Go for it. More ponies. I always liked Rainbow Dash."

Amidst general clapping and cheering, she saw Josie nod her approval. Allison knew she'd passed some sort of test. Gazing again at the cartoon ponies on her fingertips, she flicked each finger while announcing the ponies' names, "Pinky Pie, on my pinkie, Sweetie Belle, this one I'm not sure of, but the next are Princess Celestia, one of my favorites, and Apple Jack."

More clapping and cheering.

Allison smiled contentedly and leaned back in the chair. A few other costumers came and went or stayed for food and conversation.

In the end, Allison's hair was cut, shaped, and cupped, framing her face nicely and adding volume that she didn't think was possible. On her left hand, Rainbow Dash decorated Allison's index finger flanked by her pastel herd of friends.

Daisy got instructions on how to use the blower and styling brush to maintain Allison's new do. The last of the pizza, Chinese, chicken, fish, and hush puppies were eaten or packed up by ladies to take home and share with family. It had been quite a spread.

Three spent elderlies, and Allison, collapsed into their car. "Guess we're not going to make much more headway today."

"We made excellent headway today, just not in miles."

Allison looked at her pastel nails and grinned. What the heck, she could always pop them off.

Josie grinned. "You like them, don't you?"

Allison grinned broadly, nodded, flicked her new hair, and started the car. "Where to?"

JOSIE'S STORY

A blast of thunder shook the room. Rosie yelped. Daisy shot straight up in bed. Josie muttered and turned over.

Allison looked at the clock; just after 5a.m. She heard the rain slam into the window, sheets of hard rain. The aunts sighed, burrowed deeper into their covers, and went back to sleep. Allison lay on her back, listening to the sweep of wind-driven rain and the decreasing boom and mutter of thunder.

She thought about growing old. *What must it be like to have more than eighty years' worth of life experiences? What do they look forward to? What is there to look forward to?*

"Do you know what you're doing?" Josie asked.

"Of course, I do."

Daisy had Allison seated at the small dressing table chair in front of the mirror. Wielding her styling brush and blow dryer,

Daisy played with Allison's hair, attempting to bring back the fluff and shape of the day before.

Josie *humphed*. "With only a son, I never got to play with anyone's hair. You don't have any children."

"What has that got to do with it? We went through the '80s. Remember? The Big Hair, the Farrah Fawcett look? I had longer hair then and totally went for that Big Hair thing. That took a lot of blowing and fluffing." Daisy patted Allison's shoulder. "Don't you worry, I won't go overboard with your hair, just a little body." She directed her question to Josie. "What were you doing in the '80s? I don't know much about your years after you left your first husband."

Allison perked up. Her father had told her Josie was a hussy who slept around, married frequently, was a gold digger, nearly lost all her money, should have been declared mentally incompetent, but he never had the information to back up the claims.

Josie leaned back in one of the two overstuffed chairs in the room. Rosie sat in the other by the window, gazing out at the steady rain and humming quietly.

"After the divorce, I was trying to find myself, along with everyone else in the '70s. I'd found a job pushing papers at a small medical clinic in central Montana."

"Montana?" Allison asked. She realized the other two aunts already knew.

"*Mmm*, yes, escaping, you know. There was not much around. The heat was unbearable in the summer. But the hospital had air conditioning, unlike my tiny apartment, so I did overtime whenever I could that summer. One day a rancher came in, handsome in a rugged way. He had gashed his arm pretty badly. When he was checked out, he was told he couldn't drive. He was furious, stomping around, swearing and insisting there was no one who could drive so far to pick him up. But the discharge nurse would not give him his truck keys and insisted he find someone to drive him home. He got riled up and was yelling.

"He was yelling and threatening everyone, and it was near the end of my shift, so I offered to drive him . . . just to get him out of there. His ranch was a good forty miles away and down a long dirt road. Jack had to come back into the clinic several times to get his arm checked, because a mild infection had set in. So, he'd aim to get there toward the end of my shift, and we'd go out for dinner. Jack wasn't much of a talker, but he was a gentleman, and I was pretty lonely." Josie sighed and became silent. Daisy said nothing, just waited. "I got laid off that fall. Some administrator wanted his daughter to have my position. 'Nothing personal,' I was told. 'We'll give you a good recommendation.' I had enough money saved to last me maybe a month. When next I saw Jack, I told him. Three days later, he called me with a proposition . . . or should I say a job offer?"

Daisy chuckled. Josie glared.

"In exchange for cooking for himself and his two hired men and getting his books caught up, I could live on the ranch and have a small salary. I took it." She glared at Daisy, daring her to ask for personal details.

"By spring, I'd realized that I was treated much like his livestock. He talked to his dog more than he talked to me. For that matter, I talked to his dog more than I talked to him. The winter was brutal, the ranch house old and drafty, and the hired hands gave me the heebie-jeebies. So, in May, when the roads finally cleared, I got my little car working again. It had been parked in a barn all winter. I cleaned out my bank account and headed south to Colorado. I spent a year here and a year there, then met my second husband, Arnie. He owned a bookstore I frequented. I'd gotten a job there and was making suggestions of things we could do to draw in more people—have a children's play area, have a reading corner with a coffee machine, places for people to meet. Arnie started calling me in to talk about my ideas, and one thing led to another. He and I were together for over twenty years." Josie sighed. "God, I loved him. He was my soulmate."

Allison watched Josie in the mirror, trying to imagine her aunt in her younger days. Josie's pain of the loss showed clearly on her face as she continued.

"We traveled every year. He'd take two weeks off three times a year and we'd take a road trip or a cruise or a trip to Europe. He knew he was getting too old to keep up the pace of running the bookstores on his own, which were very successful by this time. He had expanded, setting up two more satellite stores in smaller communities. After selling one of the smaller ones, he sold half-ownership of the main store to a manager who showed real promise. We used some of that money to take an around-the-world cruise. It wasn't one single excursion; we jumped from cruise to cruise leaving from California to Hawaii, Pacific Islands, New Zealand, Australia, China, Thailand, India, then down around Africa . . . well, you get the idea. It was a blast! We had two more good years of travel and part time work at the bookstores. I loved working there, no matter what I found myself doing. I'd go in and just take over whatever job needed doing."

Allison saw tears swimming in her aunt's eyes. Daisy stopped working on Allison's hair, put her hip against the dressing table, and turned to face her sister. When Josie took up the tale, her voice was husky, nearly choked.

"Arnie started coughing. Kept saying it was nothing. When we finally went to the doctor, it was too late. He had advanced lung cancer."

Daisy handed her sister a tissue as the tears escaped and wove slowly down the creases in the elder woman's face. "He lasted less than three months. After he passed, I found he'd finished the sale of the bookstores and put all his money in my name. He had no children, and his first wife was long out of the picture."

Rosie had stopped humming long ago and listened from across the room.

Josie shook her head. "I felt totally cast adrift. Luckily, I'd gone to a financial advisor about the money Arnie had left me. It wasn't the advisor he'd used. I didn't really like him. Actually, I contacted AARP and got connected with someone in the area who could advise a senior. I am so glad I did." Daisy handed her the box of tissues and she blew her nose. "I met a guy, Bryan, very nice, very sympathetic. He was the shoulder I desperately needed to lean on. Eighteen months after Arnie passed, Bryan asked me to marry him. I said yes. I had a regularly scheduled meeting with my advisor before the wedding. I think he saw that I was on the rebound and maybe not making the best decision. He told me under no circumstances was I to put my money in both our names. He even advised that I keep Arnie's surname. He pointed out that it's done all the time now. There's no need to change it." Josie sighed again, this time not in sadness but in an emotion Allison could not yet read. Josie shook her head. "I'm so glad I had that advisor. As soon as we were married, Bryan wanted all our accounts put in both our names. He moved into my house, Arnie's house. Anyway, I followed my advisor's advice and refused to put anything in both names. That's when Bryan insisted on buying life insurance. He said he wanted to get me covered. I insisted that we both should get life insurance."

Josie paused, tissue to her nose, then resumed, with subtle anger resonating. "We'd been paying on the insurance—no, amend that—*I* had been paying on that for seven months when I finally saw a copy of the life insurance policies. I was paying a pretty high premium. Bryan had coverage of ten thousand. My coverage was for a million."

Daisy sucked in her breath. Eyes snapping. "Yes. Exactly what I thought. Maybe I'd read too many mystery and thriller books at Arnie's bookstore. News at the time was all about a trial going on of a woman who slowly poisoned her husband to get his large life insurance policy. My first thought was that he means to kill me. So, I made a copy of the life insurance policy and went right to my financial advisor. By the next day, he had an appointment for me to see an attorney, also recommended by AARP. She told me we'd have to play this carefully or Bryan could take me for a large chunk of money since I would be the one filing for divorce. We'd been married just over a year. It took about three months of me walking on eggshells, not eating anything Bryan gave me, and watching my back. Because I hadn't used Bryan's surname, I was told it would be easiest to simply get the marriage annulled, which is what happened."

Both Daisy and Rosie made *Oh my!* comments. Allison realized she'd been holding her breath. This was as riveting as any epic family saga she'd read.

"As soon as the marriage was annulled, I got out of Dodge. I wandered and traveled for a couple of years. It was during that time that I came to visit you, Daisy."

Daisy nodded. "Here I was thinking you were some happy-go-lucky jetsetter out for a lark. You never told me all that had happened."

Josie shook her head. "I felt like a stupid old woman. How could I have let that guy sucker me like that?"

Allison frowned. Her father had made it sound like Josie had actually been suckered. He'd said she should have been declared incompetent and her money put in a trust. But it sounded like she had sought appropriate help and followed the advice she'd been given. She turned her chair to face her aunt.

"Aunt Josie, did you tell anyone in your family about this guy?"

Josie nodded. "Of course. My son, Clayton, was an assistant district attorney. He was instrumental in gathering information we needed to get the annulment. He found out Bryan had a shady background and had changed his name at one point. We used that information to get the annulment."

Allison nodded. So, her father had gotten the information from Clayton. She wondered what he had actually been told. She frowned. "Aunt Josie, I was told . . . I mean weren't you married to a guy who fell into Boardman Lake?"

Josie snorted a laugh. "No, definitely not married. We were engaged, sort of."

"Sort of engaged?"

"I was eighteen. Allan, with whom I was *friends*, and I got drunk during a high school graduation party. Really drunk. We ended up in the back of his car." Josie shrugged. "One thing led to another. When I realized what we'd done, I was horrified. Allan was not. He kept telling me you can't get pregnant the first time. I told him, 'oh yes you can,' and I was in the middle of my cycle. Remember, this was before abortion was legal and way before any kind of morning- after pill. I guess Allen did some research, because a week later, he met me at the zoo at Clinch Park and gave me this fake diamond ring."

Josie waved her left hand adorned with a heavy platinum band holding two pear-shaped diamonds. "It turned my finger green. He told me we were now engaged, *if* it turned out I was pregnant. Fortunately, I wasn't, because two months later, by which time I knew I was safe, he got drunk yet again and took a young lady out in a rowboat during a party on Boardman Lake. They got rocking the boat, rather like we had been rocking his car, which then flipped over. The young lady swam to shore and emerged wet and spitting angrily that Allen had not even tried to rescue her."

Josie looked down, twisting the ring on her finger. "They called out to Allan. No answer. Then someone pointed to him floating. The boat had hit him when it flipped, knocking him out. He'd drowned."

If such significant facts had been left out by Dad, what about the rest of what he told me? Allison wondered.

"Then you ended up in California?" Allison prompted, but did not add married to an Italian waiter who could have been your son. Maybe her father had been wrong about that, as well.

"I wandered a couple of years, then ended up at a mobile home park for seniors near the Saltan Sea in Southern California. I made some good friends who had RVs and loved heading out to different places to stay. It was less expensive than cruises." Josie chuckled. "So, I got a used trailer and an old but lightly-used Ford Ranger pickup."

"A Ford?" Allison asked. "I thought you didn't like Fords."

Daisy made a face and interrupted. "What kind of RV?"

Josie answered Allison first. "Ford makes a good truck." Then Daisy. "A Jay Feather, light weight, pretty small. We'd go for a couple weeks over to Quartzite in Arizona or to Gunsight, a BLM area where you can camp for free. Of course, there are no amenities, but I went with good friends, Jan and Andy, Chris and Jessica, and two ladies, Mary and Haze. They were retired nurses who lived together. Were they lesbian?" Josie raised both her shoulders and her eyebrows. "Who knows, who cares? Mary had been married. Most likely they had to combine their incomes to have the lifestyles they wanted.

"Anyway, we had a blast, getting together for camping trips all over the west, dinners, playing cards, or we'd just walk over to each other's places to chat. The other woman with whom I spent time was a Greek lady, not much older than me in years, but looked and acted much older. She was bent over, shuffled along with a cane and later with a walker. She had no teeth, bad feet, a hearty laugh, and wicked sense of humor."

Josie paused and her expression softened. "Then there was her son, Petros, who came every other week to spend two days with her. He had a restaurant in San Bernardino, about a hundred miles away. He just shot down Route 10 to get to us. He had the same sense of humor and infectious grin. He was fifteen years my junior, but we soon started dating. His restaurant was open Wednesday through Sunday, so he'd drive over Monday morning, going against the rush-hour traffic and return Tuesday evening. I'd been living there for four years when his mother told us we had to either stop seeing so much of each other, as she put it, or get hitched. We got hitched, with his mom as matron of honor." Josie chuckled.

Allison grinned. Not a waiter and not Italian. A Greek restaurant owner, and not quite young enough to be her son, and his mother had ordered it. She found that part most humorous of all. She glanced at Rosie by the window who now leaned on the bed, raptly listening to the life stories she'd also never heard in their entirety.

The rain continued to fall, but not as blustery. Allison turned back to Josie, who was staring pensively into her lap.

"Once more, I didn't change my name. It would have taken the next year just to fill out all the forms. It was one of those incredibly long Greek names. I also did not move to San Bernardino. Petros had a tiny, one-bedroom apartment, so he came to visit every week, leaving the restaurant Sunday evening and heading back Tuesday evening. We took his mom home to Greece three times over the next three years, two weeks each time. I paid our plane fare over, and once there, we were put up and fed by family. She had nine siblings, six of whom were still living, and all their extended families." Josie shook her head in memory. "Even though I didn't speak the language, I was made warmly welcome. Many of the children spoke some English, so they would include me or translate what others were saying. Petros and I took his mother's ashes back to her hometown the year that she died.

"Nineteen months after his mother died, I was waiting for him to arrive as usual. It was only a two-hour drive, the restaurant closed at eleven, so he would arrive about 1:30a.m."

Allison felt as if the room was holding its breath. Except for a faint sound of hissing tires on rain-soaked roads outside, there was total silence.

Josie took a deep, ragged breath. "I tried calling his cell phone several times. Finally, a woman answered—not Petros. She asked who I was. I said I was his wife. She hesitated. I heard her speak to someone, then she said Petros had been in an accident, and it was bad. I needed to come to the hospital in Indio."

"I got there forty-five minutes later. There was no need to rush." Josie took a few deep breaths. "A drunk driver had swerved into the rear of his car on I-10. Petros had tried to correct after the impact, but his car was forced sideways across the lanes, where it was hit again by the other car, causing his to flip and roll several times down the interstate. He wasn't just dead; he was mangled beyond recognition. They strongly advised me not to do a personal identification. Later, Clayton read the autopsy report and said they were right not to let me see him."

Josie put her hands to her face, struggling to compose herself. Allison saw her lower lip quiver. "By that time, Petros wasn't the only one who was gone. Haze, who smoked like a chimney, had emphysema and dementia. Jessica had died after a massive stroke, and Chris had left. Jan and Andy also had health issues. It was time for me to leave. I called Clayton and told him I wanted to come home." She gave a little snort. "He panicked, thinking I meant *his* home. No, I wanted to go home to Traverse City.

"I was in rough shape, so he did the research and found a complex that had condos, senior apartments, as well as an assisted living facility. I opted for the condos, but he talked me out of it and recommended the senior apartments. I'd told him I was not sure about my driving anymore, I was still shaken, and he pointed out that I was also no longer used to winter driving. The apartments had buses that would take me shopping and so forth. I could keep a car if I wanted, but he suggested it was time to let it go. He filled out the paperwork, got me on the waiting list, and came down to help me move. I'd sold the camper and told him I could load half my stuff in the Ranger. He gave an emphatic *no*, and made me sell my truck. He hired a U-Haul and drove me back to Traverse City."

Daisy moved over to sit on the bed closest to Josie, gently resting her hand on her sister's shoulder.

"I honestly felt that I was building my own coffin. This was the end. No more vehicle and a boring home for ancient, drooling elders waiting to die." Josie looked up at her sister with a sparkle in her eye. "I was wrong! Within a week of moving in, I found a lady standing at my apartment door staring at my name plate. When she saw me, she asked if I was Josephine Shadduck. I told her that was me about seventy years ago."

Josie grinned delightedly and Allison was relieved to see it. "She squealed and said we went to school together, asked if I remembered taking piano lessons from Mary Morgan on Washington Street. She remembered both of us," Josie told Daisy. "Do you remember taking piano lessons with Mrs. Morgan?"

Daisy laughed. "Of course! She was a task master, or mistress." Daisy frowned. "So, who was this lady?"

"Arlene Shumsky. Do you remember her?"

Daisy nodded, then shook her head in amazement. "I do remember Arlene, and her older brother. He was cute. So, you like it at Cherry Ridge?"

"I love it! I've now met five ladies there who we knew from school. There is so much to do, always something going on—"

"Singing?" Rosie finally joined the conversation.

Josie chuckled. "Yes, and singing. There is a Sweet Adelines group as well as a choir who sing during our Sunday church services. We can attend events at any of the buildings, visit friends. There is a library, dining hall if we get tired of making our own meals, activities, movies, and bus trips to interesting places."

Rosie sighed, then murmured, "Can I move there?"

Josie turned to her. "There's usually a waiting list, but we could put you on the list."

Daisy leaned in and gave a quick head shake, whispering, "She can't afford it."

Josie snapped back, "I can."

Daisy looked hard at her sister. "You mean that?"

Josie nodded.

Daisy swung around and grabbed the smart phone off the bedside table. "Cherry Ridge, right?" She tapped, scanned, tapped, and frowned. "I can't do much from here. There's a way to ask questions but not get on any waiting list."

"Give me that." Josie grabbed Daisy's phone, punched in a series of numbers and waited through several rings. "Blast, answering machine. Clayton, can you contact Cherry Ridge and see if there are any apartments available, either building, but preferably the same one I'm in. Rosie wants to move there. Talk to you later."

"You mean maybe I can?" Rosie asked hopefully.

Josie reached over and took her baby sister's hand. "Yes, maybe you can. Clayton will check on availability."

Rosie smiled hopefully. "But I don't think I can afford it. Do they have any tiny, inexpensive apartments?"

Daisy looked down, embarrassed. Josie squeezed Rosie's hand. "We'll work it out. We will make it happen."

Allison remembered Daisy telling her, "*Make your dream happen.*" She watched these three sisters bonding, looking out for each other, and found herself wishing she had a sister, and also wondering why her father had such a poor opinion of these women.

Chapter 18

POOL SHARK

Rosie rooted through the nearly empty snack bag. While Allison hauled the last suitcase out to the car, staggering as she held the case out of the flooded parking lot, Rosie squeezed the last tube of yogurt into her mouth. Gray clouds wrung out the last drops of moisture. Iridescent circles formed in the parking lot puddles.

"We need to make a grocery run," Daisy said, plucking out the detritus, including a desiccated banana peel, which was all that was left in their depleted snacks bag.

Allison pulled the motel door closed at three minutes after the official 11a.m. checkout time. Daisy and Rosie stood on the sidewalk, trying to judge how far they'd have to jump to avoid wet feet. Josie walked down the way to find a place where the puddles were less deep and wide. "Wait," Allison called. Sighing, she scanned both directions. Deep puddles everywhere. "Wait," she repeated, holding her hand up before hopping and tiptoeing through puddles to the car. Allison backed away from the sidewalk, angled sideways, and pulled the car up so the passenger side tires scraped against the curb. She hopped out into the yards-wide puddle, came around, and held the door for Daisy to climb in the front. Rosie opened the back door and scooted to the far side. Josie waited for her to get settled, smiled her approval at Allison, then slid in, pulling the door shut behind her.

Thunder rumbled as they left the motel parking lot. Daisy leaned forward, peering up at fast approaching black clouds. "Oh my," she breathed, "that looks bad."

Rosie leaned sideways, craning around to see the sky above them. "Quick, find a place to eat! We need to eat first, then shop for snacks."

Josie glared at her baby sister. "Why do we need to hurry to eat?"

Daisy snorted as Rosie looked pointedly at Josie and started singing, *"Raindrops keep falling on my head."* Daisy laughed and responded with, *"Dancing in the Rain."*

Frowning up at the gathering dark, Josie nodded. "Understood. If we don't find a place soon, we get drive-thru."

"Golden Corral!" Rosie shouted, pointing down a cross street. "Turn left . . . right here, turn left." She waved excitedly.

Pulling into the left-turn lane, Allison glanced down the road, finally spotting the red sign for Golden Corral well down the way, more than a block away. Waiting for the light to change, she glanced back at Rosie. "How did you see that?"

Rosie giggled. "You can eat as much as you want. There are all kinds of food."

Daisy took over. "They have a chocolate fountain." She said, which prompted Rosie to make *yummy* sounds. "And watching the people there is nearly as entertaining as a visit to Walmart."

Navigating the busy streets, Allison pulled up to the Golden Corral entrance, letting the ladies off just yards from the door. The first huge plops of rain splatted against the windshield. The ladies dashed for the safety of the doors. Daisy turned back when they were safely under an overhang. "There's an umbrella in the trunk."

Allison found a parking spot as the black clouds opened. *In the trunk?* Allison sighed. The plastic shopping bags were also in the trunk. Then she spotted the nearly empty bag of snacks. Taking out the last couple of items, she pulled it over her head, took a deep breath, and ran.

Daisy held the door open for her. "You didn't bring the umbrella," she accused.

Allison pulled the bag off her head in the small entryway and draped it over a newspaper machine. "It was raining pretty hard." Wind ripped the nearly closed door from Daisy's grip, driving rain through the open doorway. A bolt of lightning ripped the sky open, followed almost instantly by a blast of thunder that shook the building. Someone in the restaurant shrieked as someone else dropped a plate.

Daisy ducked through the second door into the restaurant with Allison close behind. "Okay," Daisy said over her shoulder, "so it's raining. You could have grabbed the umbrella."

Allison stopped dead, ready to defend herself. Daisy shot a grin over her shoulder and led Allison to the pay line. "Come on, I'll introduce you to the chocolate fountain."

The storm flooded the parking lot, the streets, causing people to make Noah's Ark comments. The aunts ate, people-watched, and perused the food tables. The storm kept the lunch rush at a minimum, reducing the entertainment of people-watching.

"I've noticed most people in here are overweight."

"I've been in Golden Corrals where the crowd around the dessert table is four deep. You have to fight your way in."

"Do you notice it's the people who pile two and three plates high with fried food, greasy food, and chips who are the ones who loudly insist on a diet soda?"

"Did you see that guy put chocolate from the fountain on his fried chicken leg?"

"Be sure to try the carrot cake. It's one of the most popular items."

Allison watched the rain, half expecting the Buick to float away.

Finally, after over an hour, pointless conversation, new plates, and lemonade and iced tea refills, the rain let up and the black sky turned gray. Daisy shoved herself up, patted her stomach, and announced it was time for a snack run.

Seeing Allison's look of horror, she laughed. "Honey, you never grocery shop on an empty stomach. Remember, that was the plan—eat, then get snack foods."

. . . .

Once more, Allison pulled right up on the curb to pick up her aunts. A man scurrying by holding an umbrella in the remaining light rain stopped to escort the three elderly women one by one from the doorway to the car door. Once they were safely in, he gently closed the doors and hurried on his way.

Rosie twisted around in the back seat and trilled a thank-you to his departing back. He shot back a quick smile before ducking into the next store entrance.

At the end of the strip mall, Daisy pointed out a Piggly Wiggly grocery store. Allison eased through the inches-deep puddles. In front of the store, all four looked out at the rivers of water flowing beneath the car.

Daisy sighed and shook her head. "Let's go. Head for Savannah. We'll find something on the way."

Carefully, Allison pulled out into the road, trying to avoid the walls of water being thrown up by traffic moving too fast.

Allison stayed below the speed limit to avoid hydroplaning. The ladies remained silent, allowing Allison to concentrate. Josie broke the silence. "You mentioned a couple of times that you wanted to divorce Barth. Why didn't you?"

Allison glanced over at Daisy in the front next to her. She crossed her leg, jiggling her foot. A frown line etched deeply between her eyebrows, her mouth forming a hard line. Then to Allison's surprise, Daisy turned to her and snapped, "Do you have a bank account?"

"Yes."

"In your name?" Daisy demanded.

Allison glanced over at her aunt and nodded. "It's my college account."

"Credit card?"

Allison nodded again. "My dad gave me one for emergencies."

"No." Daisy spaced the words, "In . . . *your* . . . name."

Allison shook her head.

"Any loans . . . in *your* name?"

Again, a tentative headshake.

"Get your own credit card. Now. In *your* name!"

Josie shifted forward. "What happened?" she asked gently.

Foot still jiggling, arms crossed, Daisy turned to address both Allison and her sisters in the rear seat. "When we were first married, I did sewing jobs, alterations, repairs, making clothes to order. I was getting in a little money. I spent most of what I earned on things we needed around the house. After a year, I had a little over a hundred dollars saved up. I went to open an account at our local bank. I was sent to a manager who had me sit, smiled condescendingly, and told me I needed my husband's permission to open my own account."

The jiggling foot was now kicking the underside of the dashboard. "The following week, I brought Barth with me. The two men glad-handed and man-talked about the *little wife* and if Barth actually trusted me with so much money."

Josie nodded, sighing.

"Eventually, I had some part-time jobs, then I started working three days a week in a department store. They were just starting with store-linked credit cards. I was encouraged to get one. I did. I got myself a dress I would need for a funeral and a shirt for Barth. What fun. I paid off half of it, then needed a new tire for my car. The credit limit would not even cover a new tire."

Allison glanced over, seeing the fury in her aunt's expression.

"I took the card back to the business secretary and asked what was going on. She smiled sweetly and explained that it was in my name, *a woman. A wife.* I had no credit history. If it was in my husband's name, she informed me brightly, I'd have a much higher credit limit."

The jiggling foot got louder. "It was a few years after that that Barth bought his first Airstream trailer and wanted to travel. That meant I had to give up my job. By then, I was not in a good place." She turned to Josie. "That's when I wrote to you that I was considering divorce. I went to the bank and asked what I needed to do to take a large sum out of my . . . *my* bank account." She slammed her hand on the door elbow rest. "The manager was called. He took my elbow like I was disabled or incompetent and led me to a side office."

Daisy shook her head, then imitated a condescending male voice. "Do you have your husband's permission? A note, perhaps, giving us permission to give you this large a sum of money? I told him it was my money. He shook his head with a small smile and explained that it was *not* my money! He said my husband's name was first on the account and therefore I could not take it out. I just turned and left, furious, frustrated. I went to another bank and asked about their policy and how I could get a credit card. The teller had me fill out a form and said they'd get back to me."

Josie finished. "No credit rating, so no credit card."

"Correct," Daisy nodded. "I even went to a lawyer that a friend recommended. He told me that if the divorce was my choice, I could plan to live in poverty. Everything was in Barth's name. I would have to have his permission to remove MY money. I would have no credit rating, no chance of getting a loan." Daisy shook her head. "I felt like he was saying I was a prisoner." After a pause, she finished, "The lawyer said that's the way it was supposed to make me feel— helpless, totally dependent."

Silence enveloped the car.

"Ruth Bader-Ginsburg," Allison blurted. "Isn't that what she spent her life fighting for? To make it possible for a woman to buy a house in her own name, have a credit card in her own name, a loan."

Daisy nodded. "She had trouble getting into law school. She had trouble getting a job, even though her credentials were excellent, being told that giving her a job in a law firm would be taking a job away from a male." She looked sternly at her grandniece. "I'm glad you know of her. We, women, have had to fight to get what we have. Don't forget that."

Daisy crossed her arms, tapping her foot once more.

"Would you have done it? Would you have divorced Barth if you could?" Josie beat Allison to the question.

Thinking, frown line still deep between her eyebrows, Daisy responded. "No. I don't think so. I may have, actually I did, ask for time off. After a couple years of travel and rallies, I told him I needed some time to myself." She shook her head, relaxing into a smile. "Barth is so easy going. He's so frustratingly forgetful, often so childlike, but there isn't a mean or cruel molecule in him. I went along with his traveling for half of each year, and he puttered in his workroom and forgot I existed, except at mealtimes, for the other half of the year. I realized that we were good friends who lived together. And what's wrong with that?"

Silence descended, except for the hiss of car tires on the wet road.

· · · · · · · · · · · ·

The rain let up as Allison entered the city of Savannah, but the streets looked like rivers. Allison drove slowly, trying not to send up walls of water and to avoid the wake of other cars. They drove through the historic district, past old mansions, parks, and a place to pick up Old Town Trolley Tours.

Daisy pointed, "There, let's do that in the morning. Too wet now. I'll find a place for the night and we'll see some of the sites in the morning."

They found a grocery store and a motel just outside town on a street of small businesses. Josie pointed to the bar next to the motel. "Looks promising; let's check it out."

After checking in, hauling in luggage to their side-by-side rooms, using the bathroom, and freshening up, the ladies headed over on foot for the bar. Inside the door, the three elderlies stopped and surveyed the room. "Yup, it's got something for each of us," Josie nodded, a smile broadening as she spotted a pool table, karaoke, and a small dance floor. Off in the back of the bar—poker players.

Rosie clapped happily. Daisy gravitated left toward the pool tables. Josie strode to the rear and, after a brief exchange, was waved to an open seat at the poker table. Allison followed Daisy. They stood watching two men at one of the tables. "Do you play?" Daisy asked in a whisper.

"For fun, once in a while. I'm not any good. Actually, I'm pretty terrible."

Daisy smiled, then nodded as the man waiting for his turn glanced their way. The men finished and racked the balls again, ignoring Daisy and Allison.

Daisy got a beer and headed for the second table. She racked the balls, took a pull on her beer, then checked the pool cues. She felt the balance, looked down the length, and reached for the chalker. The two men smirked.

Daisy racked the balls and placed the cue ball, bent over the table, adjusted her position, checked again, and tapped the white cue ball. Rolling across the green cloth, it clacked firmly against the triangle of balls. One striped ball bounded toward a side pocket; a second meandered straight to a far corner pocket. With an approving flick of her eyebrows, Daisy lined up again. Another striped ball potted. Lining up again, she gently bounced the cue ball off the side, around a solid to pot yet another ball. The two men at the next table paused to watch. Daisy went to the rack and got the bridge, checked several angles. How was she going to avoid the solid colors and the eight ball while still getting one of the remaining striped balls in a pocket? She knocked in two. Allison heard the men share their appreciation of Daisy's shot. Three other men from the bar wandered over to watch.

Two striped balls to go. To Allison, it looked impossible to get either one. She heard the men whispering, discussing how they might try it. Daisy walked around the table, checking all angles, all sides, down the length of the pool stick. She finally stood on the same side of the table as one of the last striped balls. She hit the cue ball along its side, causing it to spin at an angle, almost in reverse back toward one of the striped balls, clipping it neatly into a side pocket. Several men clapped and nodded.

Allison realized she wasn't the only one holding her breath as that last ball crept toward the pocket. She heard Rosie hit and hold a high note in whatever Country Western song she was singing. The ball tipped slowly into the pocket.

Plunk.

Men cheered. Allison saw Josie look up from her new hand of cards to check them out.

"One to go." Daisy stood for a minute, looking at the eight ball. Again, the slow walk around the table. She smiled with a small headshake. Lining up the last shot, she again used a bank shot, cleanly knocking the eight ball into a side pocket, and smiled . The men showed their approval by patting each other on the back and buying each other beers. Daisy was ignored.

She smiled proudly at Allison. "I probably would not be able to do that again for another fifty games." Looking at Allison's expression of awe, Daisy chuckled. "Barth is an engineer. Pool is all about angles, velocity, point of impact, and trajectory. Want me to show you some?"

As she showed her grandniece how to choose a cue, she explained, "Pool is one of the few things Barth and I enjoyed doing together. He didn't care about winning, he liked the mathematics of the game. We might spend an hour going over a shot that I missed, with him resetting the balls exactly where they had been and showing me how to line it up, where on the cue ball to hit to get the correct trajectory, speed, or spin. He'd play for hours doing the same thing, just placing balls and experimenting on how they interacted."

After showing Allison how to break effectively, she continued. "Many of the RV resorts where we stayed had game rooms with pool tables. We'd usually find someone to challenge, but Barth wasn't into betting. He just liked the challenge of the game."

Allison lined up a shot. It looked straight forward. Daisy shook her head. "No, you're looking down on the balls, get down, bend over the table and line them up." Allison did as instructed and saw that she would have been slightly off. "Now, tap the ball right in the center."

The ball hopped up and bounced awkwardly to the right.

"Too low and slightly to the left." Daisy captured the ball and returned it to the same spot. "Again. Aim right here." Daisy put her finger on a spot on the cue ball. "Bend low, now gently touch the stick to that spot, then draw back and tap it."

Allison did as directed, shoving the stick toward the ball where it angled up and across the top of the shiny white ball, then shoving it to the side. Allison snorted in disgust. "I told you I was terrible."

"You're holding the stick wrong. It angled up because you were pushing slightly down. Here, hold it very lightly. Barth explained it as your arm is the fulcrum, not the power source. Let's try again."

The instructions continued, Allison bending low over the table, gently maneuvering one direction or the other, checking angles and replacing balls over and over until she got the results Daisy wanted.

Every so often, Daisy took a break from instruction and let Allison experiment. "I remember a day when two of my friends and I were at lunch together. Both their husbands were long gone. One of the ladies, she was Catholic, always referred to her husband as 'my dear sainted' or 'beloved sainted husband.' Our other friend pointed out, 'Now that they're gone, we think of our husbands as dear, beloved, and saintly. When they were alive, we called them lazy, no good, and worthless.' We chuckled, but I realized that wasn't Barth at all. He spent all his time puttering, creating, improving things, so not lazy. He definitely wasn't worthless. His skills and hard work had brought in enough money that he could retire early, and we could enjoy ourselves. That first Airstream he bought had louvered windows.

"On one of our first trips, he left them open when we drove, because it was so hot. The wind on the opened window panels stripped the metal fittings and left one window unable to be closed. Barth redesigned the fittings, made them stronger, angled them differently. Storage area inside was at a premium. He redesigned and replaced some of the cupboards to make better use of space. He drew up his designs and sent them to Airstream. They adopted the window design and some of the space-saving ones and paid him."

Daisy smiled fondly. "That's how he's made money since he retired. Sometimes he contacts the design department of a company and sometimes companies contact him. They send him a new product or design and let him play with it."

Allison lined up a bank shot and made it. She gave a little whoop and Daisy grinned, "See? You're improving. Good shot." And high-fived her beaming niece.

They took turns knocking a few balls into pockets, but it was getting obvious to Allison that Daisy's back was getting stiff.

She looked up to see a gentleman approaching—older, gray hair, nicely dressed, and good-looking.

"Ladies," he gave a slight, gracious bow. "I noticed your proficiency at the game, madam." He directed the comment to Daisy, but his eyes wandered to Allison. "May I interest you in a competition?"

"What did you have in mind?" Daisy asked.

He stepped closer. "Coin toss to see who breaks, then one shot each until one of us misses."

Daisy nodded. "And the prize?"

Again, the man's eyes slid sideways to Allison before returning to Daisy. He smiled roguishly, raising a single eyebrow. "I might suggest that I . . . entertain the loser in my room."

It was Daisy's turn to step closer, into his personal space, a touch of steel in her eyes. "Winner on top and chooses how."

Allison's eyes widened. The man fell back a step and chuckled, gently shaking his head. "Touché, madam. I did say, 'I might suggest.' Then how about the loser buys the winner a drink."

Daisy gave a curt nod and turned to rack the balls. The man dug in his pocket and pulled out a quarter. "If you would do the honor, pretty thing." He bowed gallantly as he handed Allison the coin.

Daisy frowned.

He chose a cue, placed the cue ball, then nodded for Allison to flip the coin. She thumb-flipped the coin, caught it, and covered it on her hand. "Call."

The gentleman won.

The first three shots for each were clean, neither taking particularly difficult shots, playing it safe. On the gentleman's fourth shot, he lined up, shifted slightly, and tapped the ball. His ball headed for the pocket, but brushed just to the side, where it rolled slowly away. "Bad luck!" he exclaimed. "I guess I must pay the price and buy you ladies a drink." He smiled to show no hard feelings.

Asking Daisy first and specifying, "And no beer. This is to be a mixed drink—a real drink." Daisy requested a Tom Collins. He nodded approval. "And you?" he turned to Allison.

"No, thank you."

"Oh, but you must. I insist." He looked her up and down. "Mmm, pretty thing like you, something fruity, a pina colada, or perhaps a mojito?"

Allison had never even heard of a mojito. "Ginger ale." She shifted uncomfortably.

The man frowned, but turned and placed their orders. He kept his back to them as the bartender returned with the drinks.

Rosie appeared quietly at Allison's side, whispering urgently, "Don't drink it!" She caught Daisy's eye and mouthed, *leave now!* Before the man turned around, Rosie had retreated quietly toward Josie.

"Ladies," he handed Daisy and Allison the ordered drinks.

Allison wasn't sure she should accept, but saw Daisy do so and followed her lead.

Daisy brought the drink to her lips, then looked over toward the poker tables where Josie folded her hand, scooped up her money, and stood with an apology to the table. Daisy handed the drink back to the waiting man. "It seems my sisters are leaving. You'll have to excuse us." She gave a quick nod to Allison, motioning her to put her full glass on the bar.

"Wait, but at least finish your drinks with me."

Rosie grabbed Allison by the arm and the four swept out through the door. During the short walk to their hotel, Allison could feel her aunt's tension.

Once in the safety of the hotel lobby, Josie turned to Rosie and Daisy. "All right, what happened?"

Rosie headed for the elevator. Daisy pulled her to a stop. Pointing to the fenced-in outdoor pool, "Let's sit out there."

Rosie shook her head. "The pool's closed."

Josie waved her hand toward the now clear, star-filled sky. "The chairs are not closed, nor is the night sky." She added, her voice softer, "We'll be safe out there."

Pulling four lounge chairs close together, Josie lowered herself onto one. "I believe I will likely need help getting up." Daisy smiled, agreeing.

Rosie giggled and sat carefully on hers. Daisy and Josie put the head rests up and laid back in their loungers, looking up at the night sky. Allison followed suit.

"Okay, what happened?" Josie asked again.

Rosie shifted uncomfortably before addressing Daisy. "You weren't paying attention. That man was watching Allison all the time you were showing her how to shoot. He watched her bend over the table, wiggling around to get a shot. You didn't see the way he . . . he ogled her."

Allison felt her color drain, remembering the way he had looked at her when he was speaking to Daisy. The comment he'd made about *entertaining* in his room. "When he ordered the drinks, he motioned to the bartender to make yours a double. Then he hid them from you. I didn't see if he did anything to them."

Allison remembered that by that point she could only see the man's back as well.

"All the time he was there watching you two, you never looked over at me or Josie, so he thought you two were alone."

"He purposely missed that last shot," Daisy added. "He had it lined up, then moved slightly to the side. I wondered about that."

"Lordy." Daisy breathed. "I'm glad we had you watching our backs."

"Being in bands, we went to a lot of bars and parties. It's a survival tactic to know what everyone is doing, where they are, and who might be dangerous. Guys in bands always have girl groupies fawning on them. Girls in the band . . . male groupies seemed to think we were there for the taking. So, when that guy referred to Allison as a thing, an object," Rosie shook her head.

"Red flag," Josie contributed.

Staring up at the star-filled sky, Allison took a deep, shuttering breath, trying to calm her racing heart.

Daisy reached out for Rosie's hand. "Thanks for having our backs."

Allison found her tongue. "Thank you, Aunt Rosie."

Rosie smiled back, gratitude lighting her wrinkled eyes. "That's what sisters are for."

Daisy reached for Allison's hand, and Allison tentatively held her other hand out to Josie on her other side. Josie gave it a gentle squeeze.

Allison felt warmth flow through her from each side. Warmth and a feeling of belonging.

That's what sisters are for.

Chapter 19

WOMAN OVERBOARD

Daisy stepped out of the elevator looking left at the pool where the ladies had bonded the evening before. Allison came toward her from the front doors, having taken the first two suitcases to the Buick.

"The sun's out. It looks like it will be a much nicer day than yesterday," Daisy greeted. Her smile seemed strained.

Hesitating, not sure if she should ask, Allison inquired, "Have you heard from Barth?"

Daisy pursed her lips like she was sucking a lemon. Then shaking her head, replied, "I heard from his friend, Daryl. He swears Barth left me a note. They decided that if I was going to be gone for several weeks, they'd go to the military antiques show they go to every year in Kentucky. Daryl felt that Barth deserved a road trip, as well."

Daisy turned away, but not before Allison saw her eyes swimming in tears. She took her aunt's elbow and guided her out by the empty pool, into the sunshine and warmth of a soft Southern morning.

"Daryl said. . . " Daisy choked on a sob, her hand to her mouth. "He said he wanted to get Barth around to visit as many of his friends scattered around the country as he could . . . while Barth still remembers them."

Allison took her aunt's free hand, the one that was not trying to hold back her sobs. "Is he really that bad?"

"I'm afraid it won't be long. Please don't tell my sisters. I'm not ready."

Allison nodded and waited quietly for her aunt to compose herself. Attempting to change the subject, she asked, "Where are we headed today?"

Daisy chuckled with a choking snuffle. "You've never asked that before! All these days on the road and you have never showed an interest in where we were going."

Startled, Allison took a moment to process, then replied with a *tug of the forelock* and an attempted lower-class British accent. "But Madam, I am but the chauffeur. It is not my place to ask where m'ladies wish to go, only to drive m'ladies there safely."

Daisy laughed. "This is your trip as well. Each of us chose three places we wanted to see somewhere along the Eastern Seaboard or on the way back up north."

Smiling and wondering which places each aunt had chosen, Allison ventured, "Assateague must have been one of Rosie's choices. Which were yours?"

"Well," Daisy settled back against the lounger, getting comfortable. "Josie chose the cities. She wanted to go to Philadelphia, Atlantic City, and it's her choice to go to Savannah. I chose Williamsburg, partly because your mother said you liked history." Daisy waved her hand dismissively. "I've been to most of these places, so I chose places I thought we'd all like. I chose the Jimmy Carter childhood home in Plains, Georgia. We should get there after we leave my friends in The Villages, which is my final place to visit, in Florida."

She smiled. "We'll stay there a couple days, do some laundry, and Rosie has requested a visit to a doctor for the arthritis in her knees."

"I've noticed her knees seemed more swollen. Is she all right?"

Daisy nodded with a slight frown. "She gets cortisone shots in her knees when they start hurting. It lasts anywhere from a few weeks to a few months. But we've been more active than she's used to. My friend has already set up an appointment for her."

"When? When are we supposed to get there?"

Daisy patted her knee. "We can get there day after tomorrow, or the following day. We're not rushed. I've been keeping them updated by text on our progress."

Allison nodded in relief. "So, what are the last two places that Rosie wants to visit?"

Shifting on the lounger, Daisy replied, "She chose a visit to the National Park site on the Montgomery to Selma Freedom Trail and the Vicksburg battlefield. She seemed to be very determined that we should visit both. She wouldn't say why."

"What about this *Okee-whatever* swamp we're going to? And the Johnstown flood site? Whose choices were those?"

Daisy grinned. "We left room for spontaneous choices. I've found in my years of travel that it's often the things you do because someone you met on the trip recommended it, or that you just decided on a whim to do, that are the ones which turn out to be the favorite things you did on that trip." She leaned toward Allison, "That also leaves room for you to make some choices. You chose Kitty Hawk. Are there other places you'd like to go?"

Thinking about it, Allison knew she couldn't add too many days to the trip. "I'd love to go to the Everglades and Florida Keys, but that's too far out of the way." Daisy nodded sadly. "But Vicksburg is in Mississippi. Is it near the Natchez Trace?"

Daisy grinned delightedly. "Yes! We can go up the section of the trace in Mississippi because the one place that all three of us chose is Corinth in the northern part of the state. Our great grandfather re-enlisted there during the Civil War. There is now a National Park site there. We were told we might be able to find out more about our ancestor at the visitor center."

"Wait a minute! We had an ancestor who fought for the South?"

Daisy laughed. "No, he *re-enlisted* there. He was in a Michigan regiment and their length of enlistment ran out while they were stationed in Corinth. We decided we knew nothing of what went on there." She frowned. "Do you know anything about Corinth? I've never heard of a big battle there."

Allison thought. "No. I don't think I've ever heard of Corinth." She broke into a grin. "Make that unanimous that we all want to go to Corinth to learn about our ancestor."

Daisy started to laugh, then saw the elevator door opening. "Oops! We'd better get going."

Josie and Rosie exited the elevator, hauling their stuffed purses, but nothing else. Frowning at not seeing the car out front waiting for them, Josie looked over toward the pool where she spotted her sister and niece, relaxing.

Allison sighed, gave Daisy a pained look. "Guess I'd better get to work." Starting to leave, she turned back and offered Daisy her hand. Smiling in gratitude, Daisy allowed Allison to haul her to her feet.

"I'll cover for you," Daisy whispered conspiratorially.

Allison found herself wanting to repeat what Daisy had said the night before. *That's what sisters are for.*

· · · · · · · · · · · ·

Under a brilliant blue sky, Daisy guided Allison to the Savannah Visitor Center. She dropped them in front then followed the signs to the free parking. By the time she returned, she saw Daisy waving tickets and pointing toward a waiting tour bus.

Breaking into a run, she caught up with the aunts as they began boarding the white Old Town Savannah bus. Daisy waited for her, ticket in hand. "We got here just in time! The bus is just about to leave." Hauling herself on board, she continued. "This tour is an hour and a half. Then we can find something to eat and be on our way."

Lunch sounded good to Allison. They'd once more had snacks from the bag for breakfast.

As usual, she sat next to Rosie. Though Rosie looked stiff and sore while walking, she bounced with excitement as the guide welcomed them all on-board. She hung on every word as they drove by the Sorrel-Weed House. "This was the boyhood home of Confederate Brigadier General Moxley Sorrel." The guide went on about his friendship with General Robert E. Lee, adding that the house was used in the opening scene of *Forrest Gump* and had been featured on *Ghost Hunter* TV shows.

Allison heard Rosie breathe, "Ooooh, ghosts!" then turn a bright smile at Allison.

The tour continued past pretty green parks every couple blocks, past the Cathedral of St. John, and then the Pirates' House. "Just a block from the Savannah River, this inn became a rendezvous for pirates!" Their guide informed them then went on to expound on the bar and restaurant fare.

Rosie turned excitedly to her elder sisters. "I'd love to have a drink there!"

"It's still morning, Rosie," Josie snapped.

"Lunch?" she asked hopefully.

Daisy turned back to look at her. "We were thinking of having lunch on the riverfront."

Rosie sagged back in her seat.

This time, it was Allison who pulled out her cell phone.

They drove by Ellis Park and City Market. Allison had to look twice to realize the man in a long coat and hat leaning against a fire hydrant was a statue. By the time they'd reached the River Street Market, Rosie had slumped lower, her enthusiasm exhausted. She leaned against the window, looking out at the bright sunlight sparkling off the Savannah River.

Allison sucked in a breath when she found the prices on the menu for the Pirates' House, then realized there was a lunch menu as well. Leaning forward, she showed Daisy what she'd found. Josie frowned. "I'd really hoped to wander the Riverside Market and eat somewhere there."

Daisy glanced again at the menu on Allison's phone. "Let's take a vote."

Rosie seemed to sag in resignation. Allison felt her frustration rise. Rosie never seemed to ask for anything.

Daisy looked first at Josie. "You vote for?"

Looking out at the receding market and eateries as the bus headed on toward the end of their tour, Josie glanced at Daisy. "I vote for the Pirates' House."

Rosie straightened in her seat, eyes lighting up, mouth in a perfect O. Daisy looked back at her and chuckled. "Me, too. I've already decided I want the She-crab soup and sandwich, and we have to try the fried green tomatoes!"

Rosie lit up like sunrise. "Me, too! Allison?"

"It's unanimous. We're going to the Pirates' House."

Josie took the phone, scrolling through the lunch menu, then turned back to share it with Rosie.

Allison smiled.

. . . .

Allison dropped the ladies off in front of the gray house with its bright blue shutters. Rosie, reanimated with delight, limped her way up the stairs to the railed porch. She returned to find the ladies scanning drinks in the bar.

"Skull Crusher!" Rosie cooed, pointing to a white skull mug.

Daisy and Josie got Pirate's Pleasure and Just Peachy. "Light on the alcohol, please, or we three are likely to sleep away our afternoon drive and miss the scenery," Daisy requested. "And what would you recommend virgin?"

Startled, Allison saw Daisy reach a hand toward her. "Our driver here, what have you got that would be interesting sans alcohol?"

Feeling a bit foolish, Allison glanced over the drink list, wondering which might be good *virgin*.

Asking that the drinks be brought to their table, the ladies were escorted to a candle-lit table in a room not yet filled with the lunch rush. Daisy got the soup and sandwich she'd decided on during the tour, with an appetizer of fried green tomatoes to share. Josie ordered honey pecan fried chicken from the dinner menu. Rosie showed great excitement over Okra gumbo and corn fritters with blackened shrimp. Getting into the let's-try-something-exotic attitude, Allison decided to try shrimp and grits, wondering, *what on earth are grits?*

Like the meal they'd shared back in Maryland, the lunch became a free-for-all of taste-testing what everyone else had ordered. The rum, schnapps, and bourbon added to the over-all levity.

"That was fun!" Josie said. "Good choice, Rosie."

Rosie beamed as she clutched her souvenir skull mug and inched her way painfully down the porch steps.

. . . .

Onward, that was Allison's directive when she brought the car around. Daisy sat up front to navigate, directing her out of Savannah to Interstate 95 then Route 84 to Waycross. "We should make it to Okefenokee Swamp mid-afternoon. We may have time to take a tour when we get there, otherwise we'll book one for tomorrow morning."

Allison drove while Rosie and Josie relaxed quietly in the back. She found herself relaxing, feeling good about the day, about the aunts, about the trip. Then the good feeling fled like a cat from water. Things were going too well . . . too smoothly. *Something* was going to go wrong.

Glancing her way, Daisy frowned and looked closer. "Are you alright? You look like you've got indigestion."

Allison shook her head, partly to say no, partly to clear her head and focus on driving. She murmured, "I'm fine."

Daisy held her phone in the air. "Did it! There is a tour at the northern end of the swamp that has a small museum dedicated to Walt Kelly, the creator of the Pogo books. They have a boat tour, and for the price of admission, we get to take a short train ride out to where people used to live on Pioneer Island. And we have time to grab a motel first . . . Allison, go straight into Waycross and we'll find a place to stay first."

Daisy directed her to a small motel outside of town, surrounded by fields already in flower. Daisy again got side-by-side rooms. Allison hauled in suitcases and walked around the premises while the aunts freshened up. The country road went off into the distance past farm fields and stands of pine and fruit trees. Two magpies scolded while flitting from the rooftop to a tree by the road.

Rosie came back out first, eyes alight with anticipation. "I can't wait to go on a boat into the swamp! It would be so much fun to actually see an opossum while there. Do you think we will?"

Allison shook her head with a smile. "I really don't know. Who were the other characters? Maybe we'll see a few of the Okefenokee Pogo characters."

Staring up at the sky in concentration, Rosie counted them off on her fingers. "Pogo the opossum, Albert Alligator, Howland Owl, Porky Porcupine, Churchy La Femme the Turtle, Miz . . . ohh, I can't remember! She's a French skunk, or probably an Acadian skunk." Rosie giggled. "Houn'dog, Miz Rackety Coon and Rackety Coon Chile, and there's a bug mother and her youngster who answers every question with Jes' fine!"

Daisy came out of her room, immediately accosted by her sister. "What was the name of the pretty lady skunk in the Pogo books?"

Daisy's mouth moved, eyes squinting in concentration. "You expect me to remember that?" She headed for the car, then yelled out, "Mam'selle Hepsibah!"

Josie closed the motel room door behind her. "What about Mam'selle Hepsibah? Is that the cute little skunk that all the Pogo characters mooned after?"

"Which ones do you remember?" Daisy asked.

They piled into the car amidst a chorus of names that Allison had never heard of.

"My favorite was the huge lady chicken, Sis Boombah."

"I liked the three bats and the buzzard who was the undertaker."

"I always got a giggle out of the angle worms and Bun Rab the rabbit and his drum."

That memory chatter continued as Allison drove to the Okefenokee Swamp Park. Daisy paid their way including a boat ride, leaving them an hour to see the other exhibits then take the short train ride. The sisters hustled over to the Walt Kelly Museum. Allison followed quietly behind as the three shared memories, laughed about remembered stories, and often fondly mentioned their father.

Will I think about my father that fondly when I get old? Do we have the kind of relationship they seem to have had with their dad? He seems to have had a wonderful sense of humor. Is my dad more like his mother, Anna, who they seem to dislike so much? I never got to meet Anna's husband. She remembered the snide comment Daisy had made about her the first evening of their trip. *"What did you expect from Anna's granddaughter?" I hope I'm not like Anna.*

They went into another building where an attendant introduced them to a large rat snake. Allison grinned as her three aunts were asked if they wanted to hold the large, somnolent snake. As children, her brother had introduced her to snakes, how to handle them, their biology, and what various snakes ate. Allison had no fear of them. She stroked the cool, dark scaly skin as Daisy took her turn holding the reptile. Daisy stood enraptured. "It's almost . . . soft. I thought it would feel rough and scaly."

Rosie then wanted a turn to hold the snake. Allison helped with the transfer, easing the snake from one elder to the other. Josie looked on before putting out a tentative finger to feel the rippling skin. With a look of wonder, she smiled, "It does feel soft. Cool and soft." Addressing Allison, she commented, "You seem to be comfortable around snakes."

"I have a brother." She explained with a shrug. "He collected garter snakes in the summer, then let them go after he'd kept them a while," Allison said. "He taught me how to hold them right, that when they bit you, they were really only afraid. After all, they're being held by a giant and of a race that often kill snakes on sight." Allison stroked the rat snake tenderly. "Most snakes are good. They eat the rats and mice that hang around farms, but unlike rats and mice, snakes don't transmit ticks or diseases, and they don't get in the house and chew up wires."

"So, you'd rather have a snake in the house than a rat?" Rosie joked.

Eyes alight, Allison replied, "We did! Late one night, after we kids were in bed, Dad was watching a horror movie. Right at a really tense moment, a snake that had escaped from my brother's terrarium fell from an overhead light onto my dad's shoulder. He screamed and shot out of the room. He was pretty angry when he came stomping upstairs to demand my brother find and capture that snake, NOW!"

Josie chuckled. "We didn't have brothers to show us such things. I had some rough moments raising a son. He liked to bring home bugs and frogs. One of his friends gave Clayton a tarantella to keep for a weekend. He had it out to play with it and it got away. I found it on the counter while making dinner. I was not happy. I probably looked and reacted a lot like your father did with the snake."

Leaving the snake behind, they proceeded on to the train ride.

"The tracks were laid on what appeared to be solid ground," the guide explained as the steam train chuffed along the one and a half mile of track. "Several small logging towns grew here in the swamp starting in 1909 when the Hebard Cypress Logging Company began operations in this area. The Waycross and Southern Railroad ran a track through a section of the swamp to haul the harvested wood to the sawmill in Hebardville. Over the years, spur tracks were built to reach the stands being logged, laying the tracks on pilings, really a bridge above the peat surface.

"This land is known as the land of quaking ground. Methane bubbles rise up, causing the land to undulate. In some areas, it's like walking on a waterbed. The train engines used here were small and generally traveled at speeds not much faster than we are traveling right now. One section of track with the weight of a locomotive on it sank out of sight into the swamp."

The train pulled into a clearing with a typical Southern two room dwelling, a *dog trot* separating the two rooms. The overhanging roof formed deep porches on either side. "During the logging years, this town had a population of about six hundred souls. The various towns of the Okefenokee had a population upwards of two thousand. The towns had stores, saloons, a church, schools, and even a movie theater. Besides the lumbermen, there were the railroad men who built and maintained the tracks and locomotives, and turpentiners who tapped the pine trees for turpentine." The guide pointed to a pine with slashes in the trunk, and a tin pan hung beneath the slashes catching the ooze emanating from rough bark. A large, rusted metal still behind the tree was used to distill the turpentine. They were also shown a cane press, in which sugar cane could be fed while someone pushed a long handle around the press, extracting the juice from the cane which could then be rendered into sugar.

"The Hebard logging company pulled out in 1927, but smaller operations continued into the 1930s. In 1937, the villages were abandoned and the land, stripped of any value, was designated the Okefenokee National Wildlife Refuge."

The ladies disembarked for a look around the cabin and clearing. Rosie, in obvious discomfort, needed the support of both Allison and the guide to step down from the train car. Inside the crude quarters, they found a bed made of cypress knees. A homemade cypress-log table took up most of the space in a side room with uncovered windows, letting in not only a nice breeze but insects as well. Dummies dressed like Ma and Pa Kettle perched in rocking chairs near the stone fireplace.

Holding Daisy's arm for stability, Rosie remarked quietly, "Daddy brought me a small cypress knee from one of his trips."

"I don't remember seeing that."

"That was the year I was the only one still at home. It was polished smooth. I used it as a doorstop when I didn't want my bedroom door slamming shut in the summer when windows were open."

Daisy smiled and patted her sister's arm, then turned and escorted her back to the waiting train.

. . . .

The boat for the swamp tour was small—a flat-bottomed skiff with four rows of seats. An older couple had the front bench seat. Allison and her aunts filled in the second. Behind them was a man and his wife, and in the last row sat a father and his three young children, each of whom was tucked securely into a proper lifejacket.

The small electric outboard motor kicked to life and the skiff pulled away from the dock into the murky black canal. Tall cypress and pine loomed overhead, casting a spiderweb of reflections in the still water. Rosie reached her hand over the rail and let her fingers trail in the water. "It's not cold," she announced.

The captain, standing at the rear holding the outboard's tiller, started his safety talk. "Please, no standing during the boat ride. Don't lean over the sides or reach for any branches or vines that dangle close to the boat." He then added with a conspiratorial smile to the children who turned to face him, "It may be a snake, not a branch. The water isn't deep. If you fall in, you can walk to shore, but there are critters in there!" He warned. "On our voyage through the canals, we will likely see birds such as anhinga, herons, ibis, as well as various ducks and woodpeckers. We will see turtles, likely an alligator, and possibly water snakes. The deadliest in the area is the Eastern Cottonmouth."

As they puttered through the relative silence, surrounded by the dense cypress forest, their captain pointed out a grebe, a shy wood duck paddling into a side channel and several ibis perched on a swaying branch. He called their attention to the call of a peewee, the distant hooting of a barred owl, and the "uh-oh" croak of a fish crow.

Having never been to a place like this, Allison became mesmerized by the variety of new plants, birds, and sensations around her. Except for occasional muttered comments from the man behind her, the noises were all those of nature.

The captain identified a flash of red as a pileated woodpecker. A ringneck duck burst into the air as they passed a side canal. The woman up front pointed to a snake slithering with ease through the dark water. Turtles plopped from logs, and kinglets flashed from overhanging branches. The guide pointed out what he called an alligator nest—a loose cave among dried grasses. One large alligator sunned itself on a bank and several smaller ones were seen sculling through the turbid water.

Three black vultures perched precariously at the top of a cypress. Rosie giggled and whispered to Allison. "He was an undertaker."

It took a moment for her to realize that Rosie meant the vulture character was an undertaker in the Pogo comics.

The boat entered a wider area of water. Nailed to a tree was a white sign with words that were both upside down and backwards. The captain pointed to it, then directed their attention down to the reflection of the sign in the water which clearly read *Mirror Lake.*

The man behind them stood up, rocking the small boat, causing undulations which distorted the sign's reflection.

"Sit down, sir!" barked the captain.

The man turned, snapping that he was switching places with his wife, then staggered in the swaying craft. Catching his leg against that of his wife, he tried to steady himself by flailing out, smacking Rosie between her shoulders. Yelping in pain and surprise, she fell forward off her seat. Allison lunged to catch her, fearing she'd hurt herself, which caused the craft to tilt further. The man, caught between narrow seats and his wife's legs, tipped and headed for the side.

Seeing the danger, the father in the last row shoved his children to kneel on the floor in front of them so they wouldn't be tossed overboard by the man's thrashing.

The captain kept shouting for him to sit down.

But momentum took over. Flailing wildly, the man pitched sideways, grasping at whatever came into his hand, which happened to be Allison's shirt and hair.

Feeling herself being pulled over, Allison grasped only air as the man pitched, shrieking, into the black, murky water, dragging her with him.

Both went under. Allison heard the engine prop switch off. She came up, blowing foul-tasting water, only to be shoved under by the man now screaming hysterically that he was being attacked by a snake.

Her hands brushed the silty bottom. Unable to rise to the surface, having only been able to gulp half a breath before being shoved under, her summer camp water safety training kicked in. *Do not try to save a drowning victim by jumping in the water with him. Drowning victims will often try to climb on top of their rescuer, pushing them under water, often resulting in drowning the would-be rescuer. If this happens to you, do not try to surface. Swim downward and away from the victim.*

Except there wasn't much down. Her feet kept kicking the slime and sucking mud at the bottom of the lake. She swam along the bottom, into reeds, weeds, slimy things, and silt. Kicking hard, she headed for the bow of the craft, away from the prop, just in case the captain found reason to start it up again.

She surfaced, blowing water and gulping air. The man continued to scream, insisting he was being attacked and bitten by a water moccasin.

The gentleman in the front seat extended a hand to her. Shaking her head, she indicated she was going to the far side of the boat, as far away from the man as she could get. Talking calmly, the gentleman kept track of her, calling encouragement. The captain extended the boathook toward the thrashing man, calling for him to grab hold, swim toward the boat, not toward shore.

Allison reached the far side of the craft as the captain pulled the man close on the opposite side. Kicking up to get her arms over the gunwales she paused to catch her breath. The father reached forward to help her in. Shaking her head, she told him to wait and have both of them pulled in at the same time so as not to dangerously rock the boat. Josie nodded her approval and put a comforting hand on Allison's slime-smeared arm.

"Vee in the water. Gator coming," The woman up front calmly informed them.

This caused renewed screams from the man who not only insisted the snake had him but that an alligator was about to bite off his leg. Seeing Daisy and Rosie getting soaked by his frantic splashing, the woman up front patted the seat next to her. "Keep your knees bent and pivot over to this seat. You don't want to be there when that man comes aboard."

The father and elder gentleman repositioned themselves to best haul Allison aboard.

Glancing their way and hearing what Allison had said about both coming out of the water at once, the captain grabbed hold of the kicking, screaming man as best as he could. "On three. One . . . two . . . haul!"

Allison gave a kick, popped out of the water like a cork, and found herself dangled in the air. The father held her with ease by one arm. The gentleman holding her other dripping arm, looking slightly damp, smiled in amusement at the other man's strength.

On the far side, the man came over the gunwale still kicking and thrashing. His flailing leg caught Rosie a sharp blow to the shoulder. Yelping, she clutched her upper arm. The woman next to her put an arm around her and clutched her close to protect her from further injury. The captain, with a barely concealed snarl, hauled the man toward the rear of the boat, causing the three children to huddle toward their father.

The man's fed-up wife snapped, "Oh, stop!" as the captain removed a slimy water plant wrapped around the man's leg, held it up, then tossed it back into the canal. The man wrung mud from his shirt and got seated while his wife snipped, "It was a water lily . . . not a snake."

Now sitting in a growing puddle next to Josie, Allison gratefully accepted the smile and emergency blanket the captain handed her. He winked and whispered, "Well done," before handing the other blanket to the grumbling snake-weed man. Josie scraped brown ooze from Allison's shoulder as she hunched into the blanket.

Holding her obviously painful shoulder, Rosie pointed to the approaching alligator, "Albert." She announced with a forced smile. Allison watched *Albert* approach, two nostrils and two eyes above the black surface of the water. Some kind of water muck lay between the two eyes. *Alligator turd?* Allison choked on a gag, wondering exactly what was in the water she'd gulped. Josie put her arm around her and pulled her closer. The prehistoric reptile slid quietly beneath the surface and under the boat.

"No snacks for you here," the woman said to the fading wake of its passing.

Daisy leaned over and pulled green slime from Allison's hair.

. . . .

Back at the dock, the man, still grumbling and snarling, was the first off, his wife snapping at him. "Shut your mouth and grow up. There was no snake."

The captain waited for them to leave. Looking down, stroking his mustache pensively, he asked, "If any of you are willing, could you come to the office in the gift shop? I'd like to get a few statements in case this guy wants to cause trouble."

Allison saw him casting surreptitious glances her way and realized she could also cause trouble. It seemed everyone was willing, or perhaps they'd all planned to go to the gift shop anyway. Allison and her aunts followed the captain into the office first.

"You were very impressive, young woman," he started. "Where did you learn your aquatic safety skills?" He leaned against the desk, smiling warmly.

Allison shrugged. "I have been spending summers as a camp counselor. We had to take water safety courses. Fortunately, this was the first time I've needed to use the skills I learned."

Josie scraped something green and stringy from Allison's hair. Brushing at her wet, stringy hair, Allison's hand came away feeling slimy. *Ick! Alligator turds?*

The captain looked uncomfortable. "I'm sorry, I shouldn't keep you. You need to get a shower and into dry clothes." He passed them each a pad of paper. Pausing at Rosie, "Ma'am, did I see you get kicked? Is your arm all right?"

Daisy moved in next to her sister, gently pulling up her loose short sleeve. "It's red. No bruise yet, but there will be one. How does it feel? Can you move your arm all right?"

Rosie moved her arm gently up and down, nodding briefly. "It's okay," She replied shortly.

Looking concerned, the captain continued. "Could you each write your version of what caused both people to fall overboard?" He then excused himself and went out into the shop.

Josie snatched up a pad and pen in her no-nonsense style, and wrote briskly. Daisy took more time, often stopping to think back, to get her facts straight. Rosie rubbed her sore shoulder reminding Allison that she'd been kicked in the right arm and that was the arm she needed to write. "You tell me what you remember, and I'll write it," she offered.

Rosie grinned. "What I remember is that you handled yourself like superwoman and the man was a silly goose!" She giggled. "And then Albert the Alligator came along." After getting out her silliness, Rosie went on to give a very precise description of the events, remembering what was said, word for word.

The captain returned as Rosie finished her narrative. He held out a new T-shirt to Allison. "You need to get out of your wet shirt. I'm sorry we don't carry any shorts or pants to offer you."

Allison shook open the light blue shirt to reveal the Okefenokee logo with Pogo standing off to one side. Rosie reached out with her left hand. "Oh, that's lovely!"

Remembering that she had been injured, the captain waved Allison to a bathroom to change out of her wet shirt, then retreated back into the shop. Allison exited the bathroom to find him returning with a woman carrying a second shirt, bright yellow, with the same logo on the front. She handed it to Rosie, who hesitated, then lit up with delight.

"Is that the right size? Would you prefer a different color?" the woman asked, pleased to see Rosie's reaction.

Looking at the shirt, holding it almost lovingly, Rosie answered. "I love the color. I don't have anything with me that goes with it."

Daisy spoke up. "We can fit in the same clothes. I have a pair of slacks you can use." Then turning to the woman, she thanked her.

Allison looked down at the dark puddle forming at her feet. She shivered in the coolness of the air-conditioned office.

"We need to get you back to the motel. A hot bath, a good meal, and you will be fine," Daisy said.

Allison chuckled and picked another wad of something slimy

and green out of her hair. "I think I'd better shower first, otherwise the bathtub water is likely to look like those canals."

"Let's go." Josie headed for the door.

"Dinner. I didn't see any restaurants out where we are," Daisy announced.

The woman listed several fast-food places near the major chain hotels.

Daisy shook her head and told them where they were staying.

Thinking for a moment, the woman's face lit up. "Do you like fish and chips? It's fresh fish."

Looking at each other, they nodded in agreement. Getting their room numbers, the woman waved them out of the office while she used the phone.

She came out looking pleased as Josie paid for a dark green fleece jacket. Daisy came up to the counter next with a red windbreaker.

"You'll have four fish and chips dinners, complete with coleslaw and French fries, and I hope lemonade is all right for a drink? And I asked her to include a side order of gator bites. It will all be delivered to your hotel rooms in two hours. That should give you time for a nice hot bath." She finished, addressing Allison. "Now get this girl home and out of those wet clothes."

Waving them out of the store, Daisy held out her hand to Allison. "I'm driving." Seeing her niece's hesitation, she *tsk*ed. "It's only a few miles to the motel. It's my car and you are shivering too hard to drive safely."

Allison reached for the keys, then suddenly went pale. "They went in the water with me! The keys were in my pocket. Will the electronics still work?"

Shaking her head, Daisy held out her hand. "The key will work."

. . . .

After stuffing her wet clothes into a plastic bag and showering off the mud and slime, Allison ran a hot bath, added the "soothing" bath salts Daisy had given her and sank blissfully into the heat and gentle steam of her scented bath. Sighing deeply, she lay back, resting her neck on the hard rim of the tub.

Drifting blissfully, muscles relaxing in the warmth, she experienced a sweet stretch of oblivion. Then the memories poured in—the motorcycles, the Adopt a Highway debacle, lip-locking Antoine, and finally taking a plunge off a tour boat. With a soft moan, Allison slipped under the water, from which erupted an explosion of bubbles as she burst into hysterical laughter. Coming up fast, wiping water from her face, and spitting out bath water, she heard movement out in the bedroom and concerned voices.

"Are you alright? We heard splashing," said Josie at the door.

Allison started to answer, but ducked back under the water when she felt another bout of hysteria emerging. She rolled to the side, sloshing water dangerously close to the rim of the tub.

"Allison! If you don't answer, I'm coming in."

One ear above water, she heard the order and came up for air. "I'm fine!" she sputtered, knowing immediately that she didn't sound fine.

The door popped open. Allison shrieked and tried to hide. "Oh, nonsense. We're all women here. We've seen it all." Josie stood in the door, frowning. Daisy peered over her shoulder with Rosie hanging back near the sink.

"But you haven't seen all of *me*," Allison squeaked.

Daisy grabbed a bath towel, flipped it open, and flung it into the water. Gratefully, Allison used it to provide her with some modesty.

"Now," Josie demanded, "what was going on in here? It sounded like either whales breaching or you drowning."

"I'd just realized—" Allison started choking, fighting back emotion.

"Oh, honey!" Daisy pushed forward, emanating concern. "I'm so sorry. We'll be with my friend in The Villages tomorrow. You can rest. It will be a nice peaceful couple of days."

Allison burst out laughing, waved her dripping arms in the air and shouted, "I love this trip!"

Shocked silence.

"You do?"

Rosie giggled.

Allison giggled.

Josie *hurrumph*ed, then turned to glare at her baby sister. "Now look what you've started."

Chapter 20

VISITING FRIENDS

Watching Allison load the luggage, Daisy commented, "I'm certainly glad you enjoy toting around a pack of seniors, being a luggage-llama, putting up with our eccentricities and. . . " Her voice trailed off. "You really meant what you said last night?"

Allison nodded, "I realized that I have never had so much fun!"

Josie prodded Daisy in the side. "I think you'd better tell her."

"Tell her? Oh."

Allison perked up, wary. "Tell me what?"

"Well," Daisy hesitated. "The reason Rosie and Josie agreed to visit my friend in The Villages is due to . . . uh, the reputation it has."

Allison waited.

Josie chortled. "It has the highest rate of new STDs in the country!"

Allison frowned, "ST. . . " her eyes flew wide open. "STDs! Sexually transmitted. . . "

Daisy shrugged. "Over fifty-five community. No longer afraid of getting pregnant."

Josie continued, "And Viagra is handed out like candy."

"People run around acting like teenagers, but without the concern of pregnancy or getting grounded by their parents. And everyone is of legal drinking age."

Allison looked from one withered face to another, wondering if they were kidding. They must be kidding! Then she recited as though reading a textbook chapter heading, "It is widely believed, based on anecdotal observation, that as people age into their senior years, they revert to childhood."

"Yup. That about sums it up."

. . . .

Daisy guided Allison though the sprawl that was The Villages, one of Florida's fastest growing communities for seniors. They drove down a four-lane avenue, past new houses and around a flower engulfed roundabout onto a two-lane major thoroughfare. They drove through the visitor side of a gate manned by an elderly gent who waved them by with no questions asked.

Must be we look like we belong here, Allison thought.

Driving was trickier than she anticipated. Golf carts of all sizes and designs whipped by on either side in golf cart lanes. There were underpasses and crossovers that Allison had to watch carefully, since some of the golf cart drivers seemed to be oblivious of auto traffic. There were pedestrian sidewalks, but no one was walking.

I'd be out walking, she thought.

They passed more roundabouts, community centers, shopping areas, a dog park, community pools and, of course, golf courses.

Finally, Daisy had Allison turn onto a quieter street, then right onto Cranberry Way, which curved gently past well-kept smaller houses with manicured lawns, flowering shrubs, and palm trees.

"Right here." Daisy directed Allison toward a dove-gray and white house. The door to the car-and-a-half garage gaped open, car on one side, golf cart on the other. A man turned from arranging boxes on a shelf on the golf cart side, waved to them, and turned to call to someone inside.

Slowly, Allison maneuvered the Buick onto the neat, decoratively coated driveway. A woman hurried out yelling something and gesturing. Allison powered down her window to listen.

"Pull way over to the side so we can get our car out! No! Not too far, not on the grass. Oh, you're about to hit the sprinkler head. Don't damage the sprinkler head! They're very expensive."

The husband took over, carefully guiding Allison to the exact edge of the pristine driveway. By the time she had parked and punched the trunk release, Daisy was out of the car and hugging her friend. Rosie and Josie followed more slowly. Allison took a moment to gather herself.

She heard the woman demand, "Does this car leak oil? It looks old enough to leak. Norman, get that sheet of cardboard. It needs to be under that engine."

Allison rolled her eyes and slowly exited, knowing full well who was going to have to crawl under the car to place the cardboard. She dutifully followed the directions to get the cardboard placed just right. Norman placed flower pots to hold the cardboard where it stuck out from beneath the car.

After directing the activities, exclaiming over the sisters, and barking orders at Norman, their hostess led the aunts into her neat, little house. "You must be ravenous. I'll make you something for lunch."

"We've eaten. We're fine."

"I have lunch meats and cheeses. We'll have sandwiches. And I have potato salad from the deli." The ladies and Norman disappeared inside. The door closed.

"No introduction. No thank you," Allison muttered under her breath as she hoisted the first suitcase out of the trunk. She shoved hers to the side and moved Rosie's back. They were staying in someone else's house, so no need to get those two out yet. As she hauled the second suitcase over the edge of the trunk, she heard a whirring sound, and watched the garage door power closed.

Nice. How long will it take them to notice I'm missing? She sighed. *Stop it. Just go to the front door.*

She dragged the two large suitcases across the driveway to the flagstone walkway that curved beside the garage to the small cement porch. At Allison's knock, small-dog barking erupted from inside. Allison glanced at the picture taped to the nearest window. It read, *In case of fire, please rescue our dog* and had a photo of a German shepherd. That was no shepherd barking.

The door cracked open, safety chain in place. "Who's there?"

"Umm, I'm with them. I'm—"

The door banged shut, the chain rattled, and the door reopened. Josie stood in the doorway. "What are you doing out there?"

Allison bit her tongue, did a quick count to ten, and answered politely. "I was getting the suitcases out, and the garage door closed."

Josie frowned in consternation. "You could have come in with us and gotten the suitcases later."

Daisy shoved her aside. "Oh, stop. Come in, Allison, and meet my good friend Jean and her husband, Norman."

Greeting the host and hostess, and realizing she would be getting no help, Allison propped the screen door open with one suitcase as she hauled the second up over the doorframe with a fox-red Pomeranian hovering, sniffing, and growling.

"Oh, don't leave the door open! The bugs will get in," Jean said.

Daisy tried to deflect. "Do you have a lot of insects here? I haven't seen any."

"Oh, no. The Villages sprays every insecticide known to man. No bugs dare to live here . . . birds either." Jean turned her attention back to the open door, as Allison tried to hurry to bring in the second suitcase without dinging walls, scuffing the tiles, or some other crime.

"Close the door! The lizards will get in! Belle, get out of her way."

Allison gritted her teeth, and looked above the door where two brightly colored fake geckos adorned the lintel.

Jean motioned. "This way. Did you wipe your feet? I insist that guests take off their shoes when they enter. I have several sets of slippers if you care to use them."

Allison dutifully kicked off her sandals, putting them next to four other sets of footwear. The little dog immediately started enthusiastically sniffing her discarded sandals.

"I don't want anyone's dirty feet on my carpets. Are your feet dirty? You've been wearing sandals. Where have you been walking?"

Allison accepted a pair of slip-on white terry scuffs with a red five written in magic marker on the toe. Josie, standing to the side, waggled her scuff-clad foot. Hers were marked with a purple three.

Guiding her through the immaculate dining area to a little hall leading to a guest room, Jean pointed. "Set that suitcase right here on the chair. The other one can go there on the table."

The tiny guest room had little space. A desk extended along the interior wall, and large windows looked out to the back of the house. A door led to a wooden deck with table and chairs, boxed in with planters on one side and flowering shrubs on the other. A covered grill sat out of the way next to the house.

Allison hoisted one suitcase up onto the arms of the chair. Going back for the second, she dragged it to the guest room and hefted the suitcase onto a small table which wobbled dangerously. Belle trotted in and put her paws on the table to sniff the new item invading her house, setting the table wobbling again. Allison hurried out, hoping the table wouldn't collapse on the dog.

Jean rummaged busily in the refrigerator while the aunts perched on chairs around the table. Josie sat woodenly, mouth in a severe, straight line. Rosie looked uncomfortable, jiggling her foot, clad in number four scuffs, attracting the attention of Belle. Only Daisy looked relaxed and content.

"I have lunch meats—roast beef, Black Forest ham, and hickory smoked turkey breast. They're all high end . . . Boar's Head. I don't buy anything else. There is also cheese—gouda, American and cheddar." She pulled out a loaf of whole wheat bread, mayonnaise, deli pickles, and a tub of potato salad. "I have this loaf and round, flat bread. It has less calories. Which would you like?"

Apparently giving up on convincing her friend that they had already eaten, Daisy got up to help and nearly tripped over the little dog who yelped.

"Oh, did you get hurt?" Jean rushed to the aid of her dog, scooping her up and addressing her in babytalk. "Is my Dora baby hurt? Mommy will kiss it and make it all better." Jean slathered the struggling dog with kisses and felt all her legs and ribs. "My precious Dora seems to be fine. You need to keep away from that big, clumsy lady."

Dora? I thought her name was Belle. Allison watched the display with distaste while Daisy stood her ground, trying not to roll her eyes too hard.

Sandwiches and chitchat done, Jean hopped up from her chair. "I'll call Peggy and tell her you're here."

While she was on the phone, Allison whispered to Daisy, "Should I get the other suitcases out?"

Daisy shook her head. "Let's say hello first, then deal with the suitcases. I'm sorry you got shut out and that we neglected to help you."

Allison could see Daisy was serious about her apology. She nodded, feeling mollified.

Neighbor Peggy met Jean and her entourage of visitors in the middle of the street, expressing her contagious exuberance with hugs and an enthusiastic welcome. She led them all to her house, almost directly across the street from Jean and Norman. After introductions, during which Daisy made sure Allison was front and center, Peggy grabbed Rosie by one arm, causing her to wince slightly, and took Allison's arm with the other. "Come on! I'll show you your room. It has a pull-out couch, but very comfortable. My daughter and her husband come to visit. Marty has a bad back. She can't sleep on anything but the best. You'll sleep just fine."

Guiding them in through her garage and down a short hall very much like the one in Jean's house, she took them to her spare bedroom. It was slightly larger than Jean's guestroom. Or maybe it was because the bed was a double rather than a queen size. The colors were peaceful soft blues and greens with colorful tropical fish decorating the walls. A net hung from one wall with ocean shells scattered through its webbing. Like Jean's guest room, large windows looked into a back yard. Houses were nicely spaced, offering some privacy.

After getting the grand tour of Peggy's three-room house, Daisy suggested they retire to their separate rooms and take time to get settled in. The suggestion was approved unanimously.

Jean nodded, looking relieved. "We all meet at my house for dinner at six o'clock . . . *six* o'clock," she repeated. "Understood?"

Josie looked away and rolled her eyes. Rosie nodded submissively. Allison found herself wanting to snap a salute and bark, *Ma'am! Yes, Ma'am!*

Daisy took her friend gently by the arm. "Of course we'll be there on time. After I unpack," Daisy led her friend to the door, Josie following behind. "I'd be happy to help you prepare dinner."

"Okay, then." Allison sighed with relief.

Peggy chuckled. "Jean's obsessive, but her heart's in the right place." She gripped Rosie's arm. Allison hesitated, watching. Her right arm, where she'd been kicked yesterday—no wince. "I am so glad you are staying with me."

"I'll bring in our suitcases," Allison offered.

. . . .

To Allison, the evening's meatloaf tasted like a McDonald's Big Mac without the lettuce. All the side dishes came from a deli. Space to sit was at a minimum—barely even elbow room—with seven people around a table made, comfortably, for four.

The ladies chatted happily. Norman grunted occasionally and shoveled food. Allison, perched on the dangerous looking folding chair, tried to stay still and not knock anyone's arm.

"Well, Allison," Jean addressed her for the first time, causing her to gulp down her mouthful of meatloaf. "I hear you just graduated from college. What is your field of study?"

"Actually, she'll be heading to *graduate* school in the fall," Josie announced. She smiled proudly at Allison while Jean and Peggy gave the appropriate "Oh my!" and "How wonderful," responses.

"I'm in counseling," Allison said, which was met with confused frowns and looks of consternation. "I mean, that's my field of study. I'm in the counseling program, for my degree." Allison wished her flimsy chair would collapse and she could sink through the floor.

"Oh." Peggy threw her a lifeline. Leaning forward with an encouraging smile, she asked, "What kind of counselor would you like to be?"

Allison hesitated, realizing she didn't want to say *school*. "There are many possibilities. I've been primarily working with children and adolescents."

"Oh, so family counseling?" Jean asked.

Once more, Peggy saw her hesitation and tossed her a life ring. "How about marriage counseling?" Shaking her head with a chuckle, she said, "We need some good ones."

"Did you use a marriage counselor?" Daisy asked, also noticing that Allison needed some help.

"We did." Peggy waved her bare ring finger in the air. "You can see how well that worked." She chuckled again. "The first counselor, the one I found, blamed all our problems on Jake, my husband. On the third meeting, he stormed out. He found the next counselor who blamed all the problems on me. I made it to the fourth session before flouncing out, fighting back tears. The next week, I got myself a divorce lawyer."

Her look changed to that look someone gets when the lightbulb goes off. "Now that's what you should become if you want money! Counselors don't make much, but a good divorce lawyer. . . " She shook her head in dismay or amazement. "You could live in a mansion and buy a yacht."

"But she'd have to start all over in her schooling," Daisy said.

"Then team up with a good divorce lawyer. You know, you counsel them, and then pass them on to the lawyer for a kickback," Peggy grinned.

Allison smiled, but Josie took the idea seriously. "How exactly would that work? Counselors gain their reputations by solving problems, not making them worse. Would she pass out the cards of lawyers, and to which one of the couple? Or would there be brochures for the divorce lawyer scattered around the waiting room?"

Peggy laughed, delighted that Josie was playing her game, and winked at Allison.

The one male voice entered the conversation. "You could counsel ex-cons. You know, help them reintegrate, find jobs, that kind of thing."

There was a thoughtful silence until Jean blurted, "Didn't you have a friend who did that? And didn't he end up in the hospital all cut up? Wasn't it like four hundred stitches after that ex-con sliced him up with a knife?"

Looks of shock swept the table. "It wasn't a knife. It was a letter opener," Norman corrected.

"That much damage from a letter opener?" Josie said. "How sharp was it?"

Norman's grumbled, "Not very," and was drowned out by Jean's screech. "It wasn't sharp until the con stabbed his friend's hand, pinning him to the desk, then broke off the blade of the letter opener and started slashing him!"

The ladies looked appropriately horrified. Any eating had stopped.

"Then there was the time he got beat up!" Jean belted out a few decibels higher.

Norman shrugged. "It wasn't so bad. They only kept him in the hospital overnight to make sure there was no severe kidney damage."

"And then one of his ex-cons fire-bombed his house," Jean continued at a pitch high enough that Allison feared hearing damage. The dog retreated to hide in her basket under a side table.

"The guy missed. The fire-bomb hit the wall, not the window. It just burned up the rose bushes and melted some siding."

Allison struggled not to chuckle, but Daisy burst out laughing. "Okay, I think counseling ex-cons is out, although it certainly sounds exciting."

Norman grumbled, "I'm taking the dog for a walk."

Belle—or Dora—leapt out of her basket, spinning in circles, yipping excitedly.

Norman took his plates to the kitchen, rinsed them in the sink, and tucked them in the dishwasher.

Belle—or Dora—spun faster, running to the door and back.

Norman rummaged through a drawer for a doggie poo bag, scooped up the extend-leash, and started a search for his favorite ball cap.

Belle—or Dora—yipped excitedly at Jean, squatted, and piddled.

"Oh, no! Adorabelle, bad girl!" She scooped up her offending pooch, shrieking, "Norman! She has to go *now*."

Allison caught Daisy's eye, and mouthed, *"Adorabelle?"*

Daisy, eyes dancing with delight, nodded, trying not to laugh.

"Yeah, yeah." Norman put on his cap, clipped the leash on the excitedly struggling little dog, took her from Jean's arm, and headed out the door. Jean rushed into the small kitchen, returning with a bucket of cleaning supplies, a sponge, and soapy water.

"Well." Peggy clapped her hands. "Let's clean up the table."

That seemed a safe thing to do. Teams formed since the kitchen was far too small for all five. Daisy and Peggy worked in the kitchen, rinsing dishes and loading the dishwasher, while Allison, Josie, and Rosie cleared and cleaned up the table, recapped and lidded leftovers and passed them to Peggy who loaded them back in the refrigerator.

It didn't take long.

As the ladies sank back in their seats at the table, Allison remained standing. "I think I'd like to take a walk."

Jean jumped up, offering rapid-fire directions. "You may see Norm out there, then you can join him and he can take you around. Otherwise, if you turn right down the street, you'll come to Tamarisk. Turn left and go down a ways and you'll come to Palm Court. Or you can go left out of the driveway along Cranberry to that road where you came in, that's Hydrangea. . . " Allison nodded, totally baffled, through descriptions of Strawberry Crescent, Tupelo, Sego Lily, Orange Grove, the community pool, a pond, but don't go near it, and do pay attention to the location of the water tower, which was a few blocks behind the house.

Meanwhile, Daisy quietly retrieved her fanny pack and pulled out her phone. As Allison headed for the door, Daisy handed her the phone, showed her the contacts list and Jean's number. "If you get lost, just call and Jean will talk you in."

Allison smiled her gratitude.

As she headed out the door, Peggy exclaimed, "Let's play Mexican Train!"

· · · · · · · · · · · · ·

After roaming the smaller streets, checking out the different house styles, garden decorations, and decorative driveways, Allison returned to Jean's house to find the five ladies and Norm crowded around the table playing Mexican Train and eating snacks. An octagonal piece of wood sat in the middle of the table with dominos of various colors and numbers extending in lines from seven of its sides. In front of each player were various numbers of tiles and a bone pile of upside-down tiles at each end of the table.

Allison watched a moment before getting up the nerve to ask, "Why do many of the golf carts have a . . . ahh . . . urinal strapped to the side?"

All the ladies turned startled eyes her way. Norm's mouth dropped open. A peanut fell out.

Allison squirmed.

Peggy burst out laughing, slamming her hand on the table, sending Mexican Train tiles bouncing and jigging, and causing her upper plate of dentures to fly out of her mouth, bounce twice, and career off the table onto the floor.

"Those are for golf balls!" she crowed, through her half empty mouth. "The golf carts have places for golf balls."

"Oh."

Daisy delicately picked up the ejected dentures, made a move to brush them off, and handed them to Peggy. "There's dog hair on them."

Norm picked up his dropped peanut, popped it in his mouth. "I need a beer."

Allison wanted to sink into the floor.

Jean jumped up and ran to the refrigerator. "Anyone else want a beer? We have only lite." Grabbing a beer for her husband, she turned and opened a lower cupboard. "Or I have whisky, Scotch."

She didn't notice how eyes lit up around the table. "Double or single malt?" Rosie asked.

Jean held up the bottle. "Glenlivet. Here's some vodka, Gray Goose, and a little peach schnapps."

Josie's hand shot up. "I'll take the schnapps."

Requests for Scotch on the rocks, vodka with lime and then, after asking for whiskey, straight, Peggy got up, went to the kitchen, rinsed her dentures briefly at the sink, and got down from a cupboard a squat, broad-based water glass. She poured it half full of whiskey, and plopped her dentures into it. Returning to her seat smiling smugly, she swirled her denture cocktail so it sounded like ice rather than false teeth clattering against the sides of the glass.

Allison slunk over the couch and sank down, wishing she could hide under the cushions.

Tiles were reorganized and play resumed.

A very raucous hour later, the Mexican Train became a catastrophic train wreck. Norman tossed back shots of whiskey with beer chasers. Rosie wove back and forth in her seat. Tiles littered both the table and the floor. Daisy now had a beer in a tall glass which she had salted to bring up a foamy head. Leaning over, she sucked foam off the top, coming up with a bubbly mustache and lopsided grin. Adorabelle had wisely fled her basket to go into hiding in the bedroom. Allison wished she could join her.

Allison thought of Daisy's comment, *No one can be grounded, and everyone is of legal drinking age.*

Laughter and confusion brought an end to the game. Tiles were repacked, a drink spilled, and the pack of elderlies looked in dismay at the tiles scattered on the floor. Allison, realizing she was the only one who wasn't at risk of falling over, roused herself from the couch to retrieve them.

She walked Peggy and Rosie back across the street to Peggy's house. Reaching the door, Peggy wove gently as she attempted to insert her key. Giving up, she waved off Allison's offer to help. "You wait here. I'll open it from the inside."

Concentrating on her walking, Peggy tottered unsteadily into her open garage, through the unlocked door from the garage into the house, and, moments later, Allison heard the lock tumble. Peggy pulled the door open with a smile, standing aside to wave them in.

After helping Rosie find her nightgown, checking the bruise on her upper arm and on her back between her shoulders, she helped her to pull off her sandals and support hose. Allison then retreated to the bathroom for a shower.

With Rosie out like a light, Allison crawled into bed, lay on her back, and gazed meditatively at the ceiling. *I definitely don't want to grow old. Heck, I'm not sure I want to grow up!* She sighed, then started to smile. *They certainly were enjoying themselves. Like children.*

Chapter 21

RAMPAGING GOLF CARTS

Allison awoke to blissful quiet. Only the gentle hum of the air conditioner intruded on the silence. Sun streamed through the large windows. She rose quietly, dressed, and headed out for a good walk.

She covered some of the areas she'd seen the evening before, but also found the community pool with its wall of post boxes next to the parking lot. She roamed on among larger, more expensive homes that faced on to the golf course. She eventually found Tamarisk Street, which she knew led back to Jean's. She turned toward the water tower, which Jean had listed as a landmark, and walked.

Thinking she must be close to Jean's house, she saw a man standing by the side of the street watching a small, fluffy, reddish dog sniffing around on a corner lawn. The dog squatted. The man dutifully pulled a poo bag from his pocket and scooped up the droppings. He walked slowly toward Allison without looking up. It was Norman. She started to call out a greeting, but then he stopped and looked furtively left and right, but not toward her. Taking a quick look at the house closest to him, he tossed the poo bag down the storm drain before hurrying on in her direction.

"Good morning, Norman," Allison greeted when he came closer. Looking up, startled, Norman hesitated as Adorabelle rushed to the end of her long leash, wiggling and grinning.

"Oh. Morning," he replied. Clearing his throat as Allison bent to greet the happy little dog, he continued. "Jean expects you in about a half-hour for breakfast." He then meandered on down the street, pulling the little dog after him.

Back in Peggy's house, Allison found the two ladies sitting quietly at the dining room table, sipping black coffee.

"Enjoy your walk?" Peggy asked softly.

"Yes. I met Norm out walking the dog. He said we're expected for breakfast in a half hour."

Rosie groaned.

While Rosie got dressed and ready, Allison put their first load of laundry in Peggy's machine. She'd kindly offered her laundry facilities rather than let the guests overwhelm Jean.

Allison once more held one elder on each side of her as they crossed over to Jean's house. The scene there was similar to Peggy's. Daisy and Josie sat at the table, quietly sipping black coffee. Jean, bustling around her kitchen, looked up as they entered. "Oh, good. You're here. The casserole is nearly ready."

Casserole?

"Good morning." Josie didn't sound like she really meant it. "We must have had fun. I don't remember how the evening ended."

Peggy kicked off her shoes and pulled out a pair of slippers from the bag she'd brought.

"Have you been out for a walk?" Seeing Allison nod, Jean abandoned what she was doing. "I don't want you on my carpets with dirty shoes."

Obediently kicking off her sandals, she started to help Rosie remove hers. Jean handed Rosie the same pair of white terry scuffs with the number four in green magic marker on the toe. "You'll wear the same ones while you're here. I wash them before someone else wears them," Jean chattered.

Slipping on the required scuffs, Allison helped Rosie and Peggy into their seats. She couldn't resist taking a closer look at Peggy's dentures as she helped her into her chair. Turning to the counter, she took the plates that Jean had laid out, setting them out in front of the quiet ladies. Utensils, glasses, and a jug of fresh orange juice completed the table setting.

The timer on the stove buzzed. Jean pulled open the oven door, peered in, then grabbed a mitt and pulled out a square glass casserole dish. Allison's eyebrows went up. *What in blazes is that?*

Jean cut the casserole into nine pieces, glancing toward the door for Norman.

Jean proudly set the dish on a hot pad on the table.

"What is it?" Rosie asked hesitantly.

"Breakfast casserole! I got it ready yesterday afternoon." Jean smiled, looking around at the doubt-filled faces. "First you put a layer of bread. I used whole wheat. Then cover it with six beaten eggs. Next a layer of bacon or sausage. I used turkey sausage. You can also add a layer of cheese, but we had cheese at lunch yesterday, so I didn't want to use it again. Cheese is binding, you know. Then it is finished with another layer of bread and six more beaten eggs. Also, some salt and pepper."

Allison put her hand to her mouth. *Eeww.* Thinking fast, she remembered a friend in college who was allergic to eggs. She would get congested and cough heavily when she ate them. "I'm allergic to eggs!" Allison blurted. Everyone turned to her, startled. "Sorry. It's not bad, I mean, I don't need an EpiPen or anything, but I get very congested, coughing, a really bad headache," she babbled, hoping her aunts would not point out that she had eaten eggs on several occasions on their trip.

"Oh."

Josie turned to glare in Daisy's direction. You didn't have to be able to read minds to see what she was thinking. *Why didn't I think of that?*

"What do you usually have?" Jean asked, obviously disappointed.

Allison shrugged. "Cereal. Yogurt. Fruit. I could have toast and some of the meat and cheese that you have from yesterday," she finished hopefully.

Jean shook her head in confusion. "But that's lunch meat. You can't have lunch meat for breakfast."

Daisy pushed herself up. "You get people served. I'll take care of Allison."

Norman rattled his way in, preceded by a happy, wagging little dog. He kicked off his shoes, replacing them with his own dark-green plaid slippers.

Daisy popped bread in the toaster, and while Jean's back was turned, pulled out ham and cheddar cheese from the refrigerator. "It's toast and a ham and cheese omelet, without the eggs. See? Breakfast!" Daisy whispered, with a grin.

Allison smiled gratefully. She buttered her toast as Daisy filled a large glass of orange juice. Daisy covered her sandwich with a napkin, and announced loudly, "Why don't you take it out on the back patio. You know where the door is."

Allison had the glass of juice in one hand and the plate with a covered sandwich in the other. Jean hopped up, bustled into the kitchen, pulled out an anti-bacteria wet wipe, and tucked it under a spare finger.

"Wipe off the table before you set anything on it."

Allison nodded, wondering how she was expected to wipe the table without setting anything down.

. . . .

So quiet and peaceful. Allison leaned back in the cast-iron patio chair. Yes, there had been a film of something on the table, probably pollen, so she'd wiped her chair as well. *No birds, no songs. Curious.* Occasionally, she heard the quiet putter of a golf cart going by or muted sounds of traffic from the main street a couple blocks away. She found she would very much like to spend the day right here.

The door opened, and Josie huffed out. She plunked down in the second patio chair. "Neurotic bundle of nerves!"

Feeling relaxed, Allison responded, "You or Jean?"

Josie rolled her eyes. "Oh, shut the door! Don't let the bugs in!" She mimicked Jean's screechy voice. "Take off your shoes! Your feet are dirty! Don't slam the microwave door! You'll damage the electronics!" Josie made a gagging sound. "How the devil did Daisy meet and befriend that woman? You and Rosie are lucky you get to retreat across the street and not have to put up with her even longer. This morning, it was all about her delicate stomach and what she could and couldn't eat because of her irritable bowel syndrome. And *Adorabelle?* Gad, if I had a name like that, I'd pee on the floor, too!"

Allison laughed. "The dog is pretty cute."

Josie shook her head in amazement. "The poor thing must have a golden personality to put up with those two."

Josie leaned back, eyes closed, enjoying the sunshine on her face. "Oh, this quiet out here is soothing."

Daisy poked her head out the door. "We're ready to go. Jean is going to take us on a tour and then we'll do some shopping. I'll put in the second load of laundry before we leave."

Josie groaned, pushed herself out of the chair, and followed her sister, holding the door as Allison grabbed her plate and glass to follow her.

Jean saw them coming, checked their feet for slippers, and then asked, "Did you put the chair cushions back in the bathtub?"

Josie came to a frowning stop. Allison halted, one foot raised, asking, "Cushions?"

Jean stopped what she was doing. "You did use the chair cushions, didn't you?"

Allison shook her head.

"You washed off the seats?"

Feeling a wave of relief, Allison nodded. "Yes, I used the wipe you gave me and wiped down the table and the chair." *Oh, happy day! I did something right.*

"Both chairs?" Jean shook her head in disgust. "I told you to use the cushions that are kept in the bathroom. We don't leave them out where they'll get wet or dirty."

"Wait a minute!" Josie barked. "You told Daisy and me last night about not using the bathtub because you use it to store the outdoor cushions. You never told Allison about it. You never told her to use the chair cushions or where they are."

Jean stared, her hands on her hips. "Did you sit in one of those chairs? Did you sit without wiping it off?" Jean turned, waving Josie to follow her. "Come with me."

As Josie stomped after her, Allison saw the yellow dust on the seat of her capris. She twisted around to peer at her backside. Belle followed Jean and Josie into Jean's bedroom. Belle followed happily, Allison with trepidation.

Jean showed Josie the two angled full-length mirrors, and had her turn so she could see the seat of her pants. "That's why we either wipe off the seats or use the cushions, which are kept inside so they don't get dirty."

Staring at her yellow-powdered derriere, Josie ordered, "Allison, in my suitcase is a blue pair of shorts. Please bring them. Jean, may I use your bathroom to change?"

Allison ran across to Peggy's house to put in a second load of laundry. She got back in time to hear an exchange between Daisy and Jean. "I never use dryer sheets; they cause cancer," Jean explained as she tossed three spiky blue balls into the dryer.

"But aren't those plastic?" Daisy asked.

"Of course. They prevent static cling without all the chemicals."

Daisy acted like she was thinking seriously, frowned, and countered, "But plastic is full of chemicals. Aren't you afraid the heat will release the chemicals?"

Jean turned, eyes wide, looking startled.

"I use natural materials." Daisy went on, "I have balls of wool that I put in."

Jean abandoned the laundry and rushed back into the house, shouting, "Norm? Norm! We need to get wool balls for the dryer!"

Allison stood, hand to her mouth. *That sure looked like payback!*

Daisy looked over with a devious smile, then shrugged. "Well, it's true. Plastic is full of chemicals; my balls of wool aren't." She closed the dryer door, adjusted the settings, and punched the start button.

"You're not worried about heated plastic dryer balls spewing chemicals on your clothes?" Allison grinned.

Daisy sent a sly glance at Allison. "Actually, I'm not sure if these are plastic or rubber." She shrugged. "I use dryer sheets. The wool balls don't work as well."

. . . .

Jean and Daisy climbed into the front seat of her white Prius, as Rosie and Josie crawled into the backseat, with Allison squashed in the middle. "Don't slam the doors! It could damage the electronics," Jean called as they maneuvered themselves in. Josie turned to Allison with a smirk and rolled her eyes.

Their hostess drove them all over the massive, sprawling Villages, where golf carts of all types whizzed along on both sides of the road. Jean took them through the high-end neighborhoods. Houses had birdcages—massive mesh screens that covered the patios and, in some cases, an outdoor pool, as well. Some sat on lots of several acres with perfectly manicured lawns and tasteful art works. They drove through new sections where land was just being cleared.

Each area had a theme and a town square including a park with bandstand, shops, restaurants, and usually a movie theater. Each area had a swimming pool and community center. Jean pulled into the parking area to show them around the one in her section. The inside décor was opulent—richly decorated rooms with large vases of flowers and clusters of overstuffed chairs and couches.

From there, Jean drove them out of The Villages into the surrounding communities. Daisy shook her head in wonder. "Back in the real world. The difference is quite striking."

"I can see why The Villages hold such an attraction." Josie looked out the window at the messy small businesses, unkempt lawns, run down houses—the real world.

Jean wheeled into the parking lot of a Beall's clothing outlet. "It is pronounced *Bells*." She pointed to the sign that had a bell shape over the name. "I do most of my clothes shopping here. Come on!"

Jean bustled them around the store, choosing tops, pants, shorts, skirts, holding them up to herself. Daisy did the same. Josie frowned and looked bored. Rosie wandered dreamily, fingering clothing, but not taking any from the racks.

It wasn't long before Jean had singled out Allison. "You really need this top. Look, it's your color." She pulled out shirts, blouses, shorts... "Where did you get your shorts? They're horrific! Did they come from Walmart? I've only seen you wearing T-shirts. You need something dressier."

Allison refrained from saying her shorts were from Kmart and that she liked them. They were comfortable. She liked her T-shirts and she had dressy things at home. She didn't bring them on a road trip. Then Jean veered into the shoe department. "Those sandals do nothing for you," she accused.

"They're comfortable for walking." *Okay, so I'm not a fashion model. My clothes are comfortable.* Allison decided she'd like to go back to being invisible and ignored. Then she noticed Rosie pulling out a colorful blouse. She held it against herself, then slowly put it back.

Jean pushed a pair of bejeweled strappy sandals in her face. Glancing at them, Allison shook her head. *Leave me alone! I don't need help choosing my own clothes. I have clothes at home.* She sighed and turned to face Jean. They had another twenty-four hours in her house. She was putting them up and letting them use her laundry and supplies. *Be nice!* "Please, Jean. I appreciate your help, but I'm not going to buy any new clothes today." She then turned her back and walked over to Rosie.

She watched her youngest aunt look at another blouse, fingering it, then turning away with an expression of longing. Allison realized she'd not seen Rosie pay for anything. She hadn't paid for any meal or any hotel room. She hadn't paid for gas or groceries. Allison remembered Daisy whispering, "She can't afford it!" when they were talking about her moving into the senior apartments where Josie now lived.

When Mom and I went to see her sing, we picked her up and dropped her off outside her run-down, red brick apartment building. Rosie never invited us in. Singing with small bands, singing backup in recording studios, singing for television and radio commercials couldn't pay much. I'm not the only one Daisy and Josie are paying for on this trip. That could definitely be a reason for her submission, for her just following along, not making demands.

"That's a nice blouse. I'm ready for lunch. How about you?" The yearning on her aunt's face was quickly replaced with a relieved smile.

"Me, too!" She leaned in conspiratorially. "You didn't miss anything with that breakfast casserole."

Daisy, looking their way, heard the lunch suggestion and repeated it to Jean, who was still choosing shoes and sandals for Allison. Josie heartily agreed.

Dismayed, Jean exclaimed, "But I thought we were going to shop for clothes!"

Daisy took her arm and smiled winsomely. "We did go shopping for clothes. We just didn't buy any."

Mollified, Jean led them back to her car, warned them all again not to slam the doors, and off they drove back into the neatly kept Villages, avoiding rampaging golf carts as they entered one of the town centers.

"This is one of my favorite places. We can eat outside on a shaded patio. They have couches set up with a coffee table if you just want drinks and finger foods. But we'll get a table. . . " Jean chattered on as they searched for a parking spot. In the end, it had to be a block away in a large parking lot. Even the parking spots for golf carts were full. Carts whipped around, circling like vultures, waiting for a space to open.

As they walked toward Jean's chosen eatery, Allison felt Jean adjust the collar of her shirt. "You would look so cute with your hair up. Can you use your barrette to wear it higher?"

Daisy snapped, "Jean!" reached over and adjusted Allison's collar again.

Frowning, Allison reached back to see what they were doing.

Josie cackled. "She was trying to turn the tag on your collar to the outside. That means you are *looking*."

Allison's eyes flashed wide open as she remembered Daisy saying The Villages had the highest rate of new STDs. She felt desperately to make sure the tag was tucked securely down, where it should be.

Jean laughed delightedly. "You're right. We don't want to give any of these old men a heart attack!"

Allison watched attentively through their lunch, looking for clothing tags hanging out. Much to her disappointment, she saw none. Jean didn't seem to be on the hunt. But her aunts spent the meal rubbernecking and occasionally ogling good-looking males who walked by.

. . . .

After a quiet drive back to Jean's house, the ladies retired to their rooms. Allison finished the laundry for Rosie and her, getting it folded and ready to repack. Since the squeaking from the bedroom had not ceased, Allison headed outside. Josie, wearing a diaphanous bathing suit cover, waved from Jean's driveway. "Norman is taking me to the pool. Any interest in joining me?"

With a delighted grin, Allison called out her agreement before dashing back in to change into her bathing suit.

She found Norman and Josie waiting in Peggy's driveway.

"It's certainly a beautiful day, perfect for sitting around the pool." Josie greeted her. Norm ignored the comment, putting the cart in reverse and tooling quietly up the road. "Norm says we have to keep these visitor passes on us while we're at the pool."

Still no reaction from their taciturn driver.

. . . .

Pulling into the pool parking lot, Norm came to a halt by the bank of post office boxes and turned to them with a brilliant smile. "Enjoy the pool! This a typical Florida day—bright, sunny, and warm." He helped Josie out and waited politely for Allison. "I'll get our mail and come back to pick you up in about an hour. Is that enough time? You don't want to stay out too long in this sun." He waved a hand toward the pool area and the umbrella-shaded loungers. "There's plenty of shade if you need it." He smiled at them again, leaning in toward Josie in case she had any questions.

"Thank you. I think an hour will be perfect. I appreciate the ride."

Norm's smile lit up his face.

"Yes, thank you," Allison added from beside him, but was ignored.

Josie led the way, commenting, "No wonder Jean yells so much. He's deaf as a post."

Josie shed her diaphanous peacock-blue cover to reveal a teal blue, modest suit, and carefully entered the pool. Allison noticed the scars on both her knees. *That's why she doesn't wear shorts. Both knees replaced.* Allison put their towels on a lounger. Two other pairs of ladies relaxed around the pool in loungers, two reading quietly, and two chatting. Joining Josie in the small pool, Allison smiled in bliss as she entered the walk-in warm water.

Josie swam ten laps, using different strokes, then did a few minutes of water exercise, showing Allison some of the exercises for her knees, hips, and lower back. After Josie retreated to a lounger to read, Allison continued to swim in leisurely circles around the pool.

. . . .

True to his word, Norm returned in one hour.

After changing out of her bathing suit, Allison returned to Jean's to find the garage door open and the last load of laundry in the dryer. After folding the clothes, she carried the pile of sparkly shirts and crop-length pants into the house. Entering the dining area, she saw the aunts around the table with Jean doing the talking.

"Yes, he's been going deaf for years. The hearing aids work to an extent, but he hates wearing them. He's still very active—golf, cycling, jogging." She leaned forward, putting her hand on Daisy's arm. "And how is Barth? Is the Alzheimer's getting worse?"

Allison saw Josie and Rosie freeze. Both sets of eyes turned to their middle sister. From her position, she could see tears gather in Daisy's eyes. Looking down, one tear spilled over to slide slowly down her flushed cheek.

"We didn't ask for help soon enough." She struggled to hold back a sob. "I teased him. When he'd forget something, misplace something yet again, I just laughed and called him 'old man.'

"Then one day, he got lost going to his friend's house. He drove all over, thinking he'd see something familiar. He did. Remember the state park I showed you outside Toledo that I said he and I liked?" She asked glancing at Josie and Rosie.

They nodded.

"He pulled up at the entry gate and asked where we were camped." Hand to her mouth, Daisy fought back a sob. "The girls there looked up the name and said no one by that name was registered. He looked so confused and asked that they check again. The older lady asked for his phone number, saying they'd look it up by phone. Turning away, she told the other lady to call me while she pretended to look it up on the computer. They got our address and printed out a Google map for Barth to follow home.

"After I got the call, I stood out on the lawn waiting for him to show up." She stopped again, taking a deep breath. "He was able to follow the map back, but he was so confused. He asked me why we'd come home early. I didn't know what he was talking about. It was Barth who decided to talk to his doctor, who ordered tests. The results were not good."

She put a napkin to her eyes, blotting tears. "If we'd acted sooner, the progress of the disease could have been slowed." She stopped, choked by emotion.

Jean patted her arm.

Hand to her mouth, lip quivering, Rosie placed her hand on Daisy's other arm. Josie, sitting across the table, facing her, frowned in concern, but remained quiet. Allison stood with her armful of clothes. Clearly, this was the moment Daisy had dreaded.

"I'm so sorry to hear. Is it all right for him to be home alone, without you?" Jean's concern, though well meaning, brought fresh tears from Daisy.

"He's taken off with a friend of his. He's fine, really." Taking deep breaths, Daisy excused herself. "Please, I'd like to go to our room for a moment."

Josie looked up and saw Allison, arms full, staring at them. Reading her expression, she asked quietly, "Did you know?"

Allison nodded. "Back when we were in Assateague, I found her outside at the ice machine, crying. She had been trying to reach Barth, and couldn't. Remember, when we were at her house, she'd been concerned because he wasn't there, and she'd expected him for dinner? She had been trying to reach him each evening and couldn't get ahold of him either at home or on his new cell phone. She seemed to be at her wit's end. I told her to call his friends. Maybe they knew where he was. That's when she came stomping in that evening at the motel, pretending to be angry at Barth."

Josie nodded, remembering those events. Then shook her head. "Allison, you brought up at her house that she seemed concerned, and I brushed it off. He's always been so scattered. That's why Daisy didn't take it seriously when he started forgetting things." She leaned back in her chair. "When we'd discussed this trip, she said something about . . . this may be her last chance. I asked about her health, and she just laughed and said it was fine. I didn't ask about Barth." Josie sighed.

Rosie sniffed, her hands shaking. Tears spilled down her wrinkled cheeks. Allison came over, putting the clothes on Daisy's abandoned chair. She put her arm around Rosie who leaned her head against Allison's shoulder.

Jean looked from one sister to the other. "She hadn't told you?" For once, she wasn't yelling.

Josie shook her head, then with a look of determination, she shoved herself up from her chair. "I can't believe I was so blind," she snarled, striding to the closed guestroom door. After a quick knock, she shoved the door open.

Looking stricken, Jean apologized, "I'm sorry. I didn't know."

"She needed to tell them. I think she was trying to figure out how. You just gave her a push." Allison kept Rosie held against her. Patting Rosie's shoulder, careful of her bruises, she suggested, "Let's go back to Peggy's and take a little rest before dinner." She made eye contact with Jean.

Jean nodded. "Peggy and Norm will be driving us to the square where we'll be eating tonight. We'll give you a call when we're ready to go. Will you two be all right?"

Rosie raised her head off Allison's shoulder and nodded. Allison helped her stand, helped her shed the number four scuffs and put on her sandals, then walked her slowly across the street.

· · · · · · · · · · · ·

On the golf cart ride to the restaurant, Peggy chattered. She wasn't in on the spilled secret, and neither was Norman. "This is the most dangerous time to be on the road, between five and six o'clock. Happy hour is over and all the men are headed home for dinner." She glanced over at her two passengers, a grin lighting up her face. "They are no longer just blind and deaf—they're also drunk as skunks!" She laughed and hit the accelerator to keep up with Norman.

He led the way, speeding down the cart lanes of the main road, sliding sideways around corners, whizzing across traffic and through underpasses, yelling to his passengers, "Hold your breath! The fumes get bad down here."

Peggy repeated the order as her cart entered the underpass.

Arriving before six, parking spots were available near the restaurant of Norman and Jean's choice. The specialty: ribs, baked beans, and coleslaw. Taking their drink orders, Norm went first, asking for "Ying-yang." Without batting an eye, the young waitress translated, "Yuengling," and turned to the next elder. Josie sputtered. Daisy bent to retrieve something she hadn't dropped under the table to hide her laughter. Impressed with the waitress's aplomb, Allison asked for the only non-alcoholic drink at the table, a lemonade.

She watched Josie and Daisy throughout dinner. Seated next to each other, they chatted, smiled, joked as though the afternoon's devastating revelation hadn't been made. It was Rosie, left out of the private bedroom conversation, who still looked stricken. Whatever Josie had said to her sister had drawn the two closer. Looks passed between them—small gestures and smiles.

I'll need to find a time to ask Josie what she said, how she handled it. Allison thought. *Hmm, grief counselor?*

Chapter 22

MEETING LUCIFER

After her last, early morning walk in The Villages, Allison helped
Rosie dress and pack. Sucking in a sharp breath of pain while
trying to put on her shoes, Rosie expressed her relief that she would
be seeing a doctor for her knees that morning.

Helping her across the street to Jean's house, Peggy chattering all
the way, they all felt relief when Jean asked if they wanted blueberries
in their pancakes. *No breakfast casserole!* The *yes* to blueberries was
unanimous. With a delighted grin, Jean dumped the entire container
of fresh berries into the batter. Shoes and sandals exchanged for
terry scuffs, Norm and the ladies crowded around Jean's small table
for their last meal together.

"I still have lunch meats. We could use it up to make sandwiches
to take with you." Jean offered as she slid golden pancakes, liberally
dotted with blueberries, onto a serving platter. "What are your plans
for today?"

Daisy looked at her sisters. Rosie rubbed a knee. "I'm just

relieved to be seeing a doctor about my knee pain. I'm so glad you were able to set this up for me, Jean."

Leaning over to pat Rosie's arm, Jean smiled warmly. "You'll like Dr. Aman. He's marvelous. I'm glad you'll be seeing him." Turning to the others, she pressed. "What else do you have planned? How far do you intend to go today?"

Daisy looked at Allison. "Anything you want to do or see?"

Remembering a conversation she'd had with Rosie the night before, she answered, "I guess I'd hoped to see a manatee. Is that a possibility?"

Norm shook his head, then fingered his dislodged hearing aid. "They're out in the Gulf by now. In the winter, they come up into the rivers."

Jean paused flipping the pancakes. "How about Homosassa? It's a wildlife park and directly west of here. It's pretty much on your way."

Peggy continued, "They have a manatee viewing area. It's one of Florida's natural springs. There's a pool with an underwater viewing area to see the animals. All the animals there are Florida natives."

"Yeah," Norman interjected, sipping his coffee. "That includes Lucifer. Those sneaky Everglades hippos are hard to spot in the wild." He grinned, taking another sip of his coffee.

Eyebrows raised, Daisy asked. "Lucifer is a hippo?" Turning to Peggy, "I thought you said they were all Florida-native animals?"

Peggy grinned. "Years ago, the springs was a wild animal park that housed and trained animals for TV shows. When it was transferred over to the state as a park, Lucifer went with it. He's been made an honorary Florida resident and has been there ever since."

Josie chuckled with a shake of her head. "He must be pretty old."

"Over sixty now." Norman shoveled warm, syrup-drenched blueberry pancakes from his loaded plate to his mouth.

Gently slapping the table, Josie announced, "We are going to Homosassa to visit Lucifer the Hippo and see manatees!"

She received a chorus of "Yay!"

. . . .

Jean waved them off an hour later, looking relieved that the four guests were out of her hair. Daisy, up front, read off the directions to the doctor's office, guiding Allison past golf courses, around flower-crowded roundabouts, and recreation centers.

"I can see why people like it here," Daisy said, gazing at packs of golf carts circling around a small park. "Boogying around in those golf carts was a hoot yesterday."

Josie snorted, "Yeah, we don't have good weather for such things where we live. I remember joining a friend for dinner at her family's house last Christmas. The drive was a whiteout. Her daughter picked us up, and after dinner, drove us back to the apartments. We couldn't see the road. I don't know how she made it safely."

Daisy chuckled, pointing to a golf cart that had a Mercedes hood ornament and another bright red one designed like a fire engine. "Jean said some of these golf carts cost as much as a car."

"Where on earth did you meet that woman?" Josie asked.

Rosie giggled. "I wondered the same thing."

Allison glanced at Daisy, also curious about such a friendship.

Daisy waved a hand airily and directed Allison left at the next corner. "We met at one the RV rallies we attended."

"I definitely do not see her in a tin can," Josie said. "What kind of RV did they have?"

"Not all the rallies were for Airstreams. Norm and Jean had a beautiful fifth wheel. She bragged over and over how little they'd paid for it, saying it was a floor model. Then when she tried to sell it, she went on and on about how it was top of the line and asked for nearly as much in her selling price as she bragged she'd originally paid."

Josie nodded. "That sounds more like what I'd expect. But how did you strike up a friendship?"

"It was more a friendship of Norm and Barth. Both Norm

and Jean worked in hospitals. Jean was in the infection control department, you know, cleaning and monitoring any kinds of contamination."

Josie shook her head. "That explains some of her behavior. And Norm?"

"He was in maintenance. He maintained equipment, all the sensitive monitors and machines that hospitals rely on. That's why he and Barth got along—both mechanical. Jean and I were along for the ride. The four of us traveled some together and we have stayed in touch for a number of years. They moved to The Villages a few years ago and, ever since, she's been telling me about it and insisting I come for a visit."

Daisy waved Allison into a parking lot of a hospital complex, then to a clinic off to one side.

· · · · · · · · · · · · ·

Rosie returned to the waiting room escorted by a nurse with whom she was in deep conversation. Her smile when she saw her sisters was one of relief. "Feel better?" Daisy asked, rising stiffly from the straight, lightly padded waiting room seat.

Nodding, Rosie finished her paperwork at the intake window and turned toward the door.

"Did you show him the bruises where you were kicked?" Josie asked.

Rosie nodded again. "The doctor looked at them and agreed that they were bruises."

Josie glowered. "That's it?"

Daisy snorted. "How many years of college did he have to attend to make that diagnosis?"

"The nurse said that I should stop at a drugstore and pick up some arnica gel. She said it would help if I rubbed that into the bruises. She said if we head west and go six blocks on Eleventh Street, we'll see a drug store that carries it."

In the back seat of the Buick, gently massaging arnica gel into Rosie's bruised shoulder, Josie turned her attention to Allison. "Have you got a boyfriend?"

"Uh, not right now."

"Oh, did you break up?" Daisy pressed.

"Well, no. I realized he was a jerk." Allison waited at a light and followed the signs leading her toward Interstate 75, then decided to add, "I have two male friends."

"Gay?" Josie asked.

Daisy whipped around to glare at her sister. Rosie gasped. Josie shrugged and met Allison's eye in the rearview mirror.

Allison seemed to straighten up before she answered. "I never have understood why you can only have one friend at a time, when it comes to the other half of the population. I've always had about as many male friends as female." She glanced sternly at Josie in her mirror. "Most of my female friends don't want to go to shoot-em-up movies, and my male friends weren't interested in making historical doll costumes." Allison found a straight stretch to lead-foot it around a semi-truck. She continued with a shrug. "Mom always said forget boyfriends, marry your best friend with whom you share interests and who you respect, and then let the love grow."

This was followed by thoughtful silence.

Looking out at passing citrus orchards, Daisy shrugged. "Makes sense."

Josie added, "Falling in love is actually a chemical reaction in the brain. It wears off in about three years. I've also read that people mourn the breakup with a best friend more deeply than with a marriage partner." After a moment of pensive silence, Josie realized aloud. "My two best marriages were with my best friend." Josie leaned forward leaning right up next to Allison's ear and asked, "So do you plan to marry either one?"

Shaking her head and laughing, she replied, "That's not in our plans . . . yet. And definitely not with Cass." She glanced over at her hovering aunt. "He's gay." She grinned and it was Josie's turn to chuckle.

After several miles of silence, Allison realized that Daisy was not giving her directions. "Do I go south on the interstate?"

"What?" Daisy came back from wherever she was, looking slightly bewildered. "Yes, south on 75 then take Route 44 West."

Shooting another glance at her Aunt Daisy, Allison asked gently, "Where were you?"

"Thinking about what you said." Her voice quavered a bit, sounding old. "I was trying to remember when I last felt that I loved Barth, I mean in a husband-and-wife kind of love."

Silence enveloped the car, as they waited for Daisy to finish her thought. "But he's my friend, my very good friend." Her voice took on strength. She turned toward Allison. "And that's all right, isn't it? I'm married to my best friend."

Allison blinked back tears. She heard Josie lean forward to put her arms around her younger sister, and heard her murmur, "Yes. That's all right."

There was no sound from Rosie, who leaned her head against the window, staring out.

Did she have a best friend that she regrets not marrying?

. . . .

After enjoying a picnic lunch overlooking the Gulf of Mexico, they drove on to Homosassa State Park. The tree-shaded visitor center entrance had a fountain topped by a manatee and baby. Rosie gazed up at it, trailing her fingers under the water spilling over the rim of the statue. Inside, a well-stocked gift shop invited them.

"Afterward," Daisy snapped, grabbing Josie's arm as she seemed magnetically drawn to a large, stuffed pink flamingo.

The wooden walkways and frequent benches and shelters allowed them to amble leisurely among the various birds and mammals that can be found in the state of Florida. Daisy pointed out spoonbills, herons, black vultures, and various owls. Josie stopped to gaze, enraptured, as the flamingos seemed to dance in unison. A red fox rested under a shading log. A Florida panther sat watching them from a stone wall. They passed the black bear and tiny Key deer and stopped to watch otters play.

Daisy read one of the signs explaining that all the animals here were unable to survive in the wild due to injuries or being orphaned and raised in captivity.

Rosie pointed excitedly. "There's Lucifer the Hippo!" Scurrying over, they gazed while Lucifer slept.

Finally, Josie had seen enough. "Well, that was exciting. Let's go find this underwater viewing area."

Wandering around the pond, they saw fish breaking the surface. Daisy and Rosie stopped to gaze into the blue-green water. No manatees.

Allison pointed to the stairs leading down to the underwater viewing area. Offering an arm to whichever lady needed it, she saw with relief that Rosie managed the steps on her own without wincing. Through the thick viewing windows, they saw fish—long ones, fast ones, silver scaled fish. No manatees.

All four peered from various angles, moving around to check all sides. No manatees.

Rosie sighed. "We'll keep walking and come back this way. We are in no hurry to leave." Daisy took Rosie's arm as they headed up the stairs to the walkway. They continued along, past the children's discovery center, stepping inside to enjoy the cool of air conditioning. Inside were various snakes, insects, turtles, and frogs.

Leaving the Discovery Center, they continued to the walkway over the Homosassa River.

Stopping to look down the river, Josie sucked in a breath and pointed toward a tangle of mangrove roots near the embankment.

A manatee!

The four quietly clustered at the railing, watching. The manatee drifted to the water's surface, nostrils emerging from the water. Expelled air caused a rainbow to form from its watery breath. Rosie's hands came up to her chest, eyes alight. Allison glanced at Josie and saw the same look of child-like amazement.

Josie glanced her way, breaking into a delighted smile. "This really counts!"

Allison raised a questioning eyebrow, still not willing to break the magical moment.

Josie whispered, "This one is in the wild, not inside the confines of the park. I've never seen a manatee in the wild. This is a first." She turned back to quietly watch, waiting for the massive gray animal to surface again for a breath.

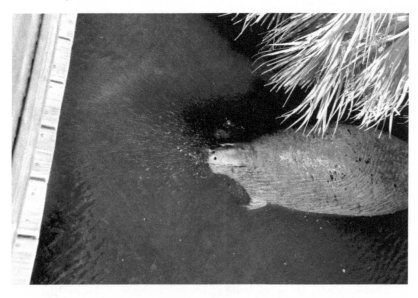

They stood, enraptured, watching for nearly twenty minutes until old knees and worn feet could no longer take the strain. Heading back around, they came once more to the enclosure of Lu the Hippo.

"He's up!" Rosie called in delight, tired knees and feet forgotten. She hurried over, followed by her sisters. Allison paused to look at a yellow sign announcing "Splatter Zone" that showing a hippo wagging its tail and water drops flying off it. Shrugging, she walked on.

The huge beast stood on his stumpy legs, munching on a pile of hay. The ladies piled up close to the barrier fence, watching enrapt as Lu lipped up hay and what appeared to be cubes of compressed grasses. With more than half the hay gone, the hippo shuffled around, turning his head away to look at the people gathered along the fence by his pool. Rosie pointed to his little tail with a row of bumps down its length ending in bristly black hairs.

Shuffling a few steps further, the stiff tail started to whisk back and forth, and faster and faster. Josie yelped. Daisy jumped back, brushing in surprise at a brown splotch that appeared on her chest. Rosie squealed as something slapped against her neck. Turning toward them in surprise, Allison was hit by a splat on her head. The stink was awful.

People on the other side of the pool laughed and pointed as the ladies scampered to get clear of the Splatter Zone—realizing too late what had been splattered at them.

Safely beyond the sign, they stopped and looked back as Lu continued to whip his tail back and forth, slinging hippo dung in all directions.

Allison groaned as she felt the stinky slime in her hair. "Not again!"

Daisy wrinkled her nose in distaste as she surveyed the brown splotches over her pink flowered blouse. Josie chuckled, flicking off the glob that had landed on her shoulder. Daisy glowered, scraped off a finger full of dung, and flicked it at her grinning sister.

"Oh, no, no, no." Allison grabbed Rosie by the arm and pulled her back. Rosie shook loose, scraped the brown stink from her neck, and flicked it at Daisy, hitting her in the butt. Wheeling, Daisy scraped and shot, hitting Rosie in the side as she shrieked and tried to spin away. Two pre-adolescent boys cheered them on.

Rosie threw up her hands laughing. "I'm out! That was my only hit."

Josie took the opportunity to catch Daisy in the back of the neck.

Feeling her neck, grinning like a little kid, Daisy shuddered. "*Eeewww,* that stink is awful!" Then spun and hit Rosie in the chest with a small blob. Chuckling, she motioned her sisters on and waved to the still laughing boys. "I think we'd better find some clean clothes to change into."

Relaxing, Josie walked by her, brushing at the brown stains on her blouse. Daisy lunged forward with one last smelly finger-full of dung, smearing it over her sister's shoulder. Leaping to the side, Josie glowered while Daisy laughed delightedly, and the two boys cheered and tried to find dung that they could fling at each other.

Parents raced toward the boys shouting, "Don't you dare!" and shooting dagger glares at the three octogenarian hooligans.

Staring in disbelief, Allison reached up and touched her hair, coming away with wet, odiferous fingers. She gagged.

Josie looked slightly green. Daisy held her hands out to her sides, looking down at the splatters on her pink print blouse. Pulling a face of total disgust, she looked up at Allison. "We cannot get in the car like this. Could you please bring us changes of clothes? We'll head for the bathroom and start cleaning up."

Relieved the poo fight was over, Allison pulled out the keys. "What should I get?"

While the ladies gave her change-of-clothes orders, they made their way back toward the visitor center. As Allison hurried back to the car to retrieve clean clothes, she heard Daisy challenge her sisters, "Race you to the bathroom!"

Half an hour later, the ladies left Homosassa State Park, hair wet, wearing clean clothes and carrying the poo-splattered ones, now rinsed and safely contained in plastic bags. Josie held a stuffed pink flamingo, waggling its long pink legs. Rosie gazed in delight at her purchase—a jelly fish in shiny blue, green, and purple fabric, long dangly tentacles hanging from it.

Allison shook her head. *It is widely believed, based on anecdotal observation, that as people age into their senior years, they revert to childhood.*

At least Rosie's knees no longer seemed to bother her.

· · · · · · · · · · · ·

Josie took the front seat, holding her flamingo. Daisy gave directions from the rear. Once headed north on Alternate Highway 27, Daisy asked her elder sister, "So you said this was the first manatee you've seen in the wild. Have you seen a hippo in the wild?"

Allison glanced over at her aunt, seeing her nod. "I've seen numerous hippos, black and white rhino, elephants, lion, hyena, wart hog, baboon—"

"Wait!" Daisy held up her hand. "Where were you when you saw all these?"

"Kenya. Arnie and I went there for three weeks just after he partially retired. He'd just sold one of his two smaller stores. One of the big chains moved into the area and offered him a good amount to buy him out. Anyway, vervet monkeys, three kinds of giraffe, eland, impala, waterbuck, leopard, cheetah. . . "

Glancing her way, Allison saw Josie staring out the window in concentration and counting on her fingers. "Topi, mongoose, two kinds of zebra, wildebeest. . . "

Daisy's hand came up, indicating for her to stop. "How many?"

"We saw twenty-seven mammals, birds like ostrich, bateleur eagle, marabou stork, superb starling, secretary bird, lilac-breasted rollers. . . "

"Yes, yes . . . and?" Daisy prodded.

"Nile crocodiles . . . big ones. And monitor lizards . . . big ones," Josie finished proudly.

"You count them and try to remember them all?" Allison asked.

"It's a competition we did when we traveled as children." Daisy leaned forward to explain. "We'd identify animals we'd see on a trip, or birds, or historic sites, then when we were headed home, Daddy would say something like, 'animals' and ask how many we had seen. We'd have to list all the animals we'd seen on the trip. It was fun. It meant that we really had to pay attention. It made us more attentive to what we saw and did."

"It was fun for most of us," Josie groused. "Anna thought it was stupid."

Allison flinched, and flicked her eyes to Daisy in the backseat. She saw her start to say something, look forward at Allison, and realize they were talking about Allison's grandmother. She snapped her mouth shut.

Rosie, glancing between her sisters, appeared uncomfortable. She raised her hand to her mouth, then gagged. She held her offending hand out with a look of disgust. "I still stink," she announced.

Daisy waved her hand as though to brush away the bad smell. "Me, too."

Josie rolled down her window a fraction. "It is getting a bit odiferous in here."

Pulling out her phone, Daisy announced, "We're stopping early today."

Rosie gagged again.

"Should I pull over?" Allison asked in alarm.

Rosie shook her head, and gagged once more, then frantically rolled down her window.

"Just keep driving. I'll find us a place to stay," Daisy ordered.

Thirty miles farther, they arrived at their hotel—two rooms, exercise room, pool, and laundry facilities.

Preparing for a shower, Daisy unwound her complex braids. "I guess these will have to go. Josie manages to rearrange hers so it looks almost as good as when she came out of the salon. There's no way I could achieve the same look again, and these now stink."

Rosie pulled her Obi Wan braid from its small, silk jewelry purse. "I'm glad mine is safe."

Allison gathered their soiled clothes to launder... and gagged.

Chapter 23

REGRETS AND RELEASE

With two rooms and an early bedtime, the crew got off to the earliest start Allison remembered them having. Loading themselves into the car, Rosie asked Daisy, "What did Jean say on the phone last night about us getting spattered with hippo poo?" and giggled.

Daisy grinned. "She said be glad we were not returning to her house. She would not have let us in, and she would not have let us wash our clothes in her machines." With a smirk, she slammed her car door hard. "My car isn't as wimpy and sensitive as Jean's." Then, imitating Jean's squawk, she mocked, "Don't slam the door! You'll damage the electronics!" Allison grinned. "I'm sure she's as glad to get rid of us as we are to be away from her."

After a huge breakfast insisted on by Josie, they arrived in Plains, Georgia, before eleven. Daisy guided them to the Jimmy Carter Museum housed in the old Plains High School. They learned of his early life, his courtship of Rosalyn, and his ten years in the Navy after graduating from the Naval Academy. After his father's death, Carter returned home to take over the farm.

Allison kept glancing at Rosie. *Something is wrong. She's distracted and apprehensive.*

Daisy pointed out the work the Carter Center was doing around the world. "Here, it tells about eradicating Guinea worm. Who would have chosen that as a project?"

Daisy pointed to the panels that described the pain and suffering caused by this parasite that invaded its host through the water they drank. It described the intense, burning pain that the adult parasite caused. The pain was so burning that people would go to water, often where villagers got their drinking water, to bathe and soothe their burning legs. Exposure to water caused the parasite to release thousands of eggs into that very water, infecting the next people who drank there.

After reading about it, Josie asked, "Are you saying they shouldn't have gone after this parasite?"

"No, I'm saying who else would have chosen something that no one outside of Africa had heard of? The Center was able to eradicate this parasite. No one else did a thing about it. The Carter Foundation made it happen."

They continued to the panels on Carter's work with Habitat for Humanity. "Have either of you ever worked on one of these projects?" Glancing at Allison, Daisy urged, "You should. Barth and I have helped on several Habitat for Humanity projects in our area. They take anyone. I did grunt work while Barth helped with design. We worked on one for a person in a wheelchair. Everything had to be specially designed, made at the right height for her. I was about her size, so Barth borrowed a wheelchair and had me try moving around the house as it was built, so they could put the sinks, mirrors, and counters at the right height for her. Hallways needed to be wider and room entries needed turning room so the wheelchair didn't keep bumping into walls."

Listening to Daisy's approbation, Allison commented, "You really respect Jimmy Carter. If he was such a nice guy, so successful, why was he only elected for one term as president?"

"Because he was too nice," Josie snarled. "But because he was president, he had clout. It's because of his term in office that he has been able to accomplish everything that he has."

Rosie remained silent.

As they headed back to the car, Allison dropped back to walk by Rosie. "What did you think of Jimmy Carter?"

Rosie's look of anxiety turned to momentary confusion. "Oh, I . . . I liked him. I voted for Carter, in both elections."

Do I ask her what she's thinking? Is this the right time? Daisy said one of Rosie's choices was the Selma Civil Rights site, and that's where we are headed next. Should I just wait and watch?

They drove the short distance to Jimmy Carter's boyhood home. The neat white house stood in a field of white gravel. Leaving the small parking area, Josie frowned at the gravel. "Someone didn't like mowing a lawn?"

Daisy smiled and shook her head. "No, it was to prevent bugs from getting into the house."

"Smart," Josie nodded.

They walked through the house, set up to the time before electricity was installed in 1938. "Jimmy was four when they moved here. He lived here until he went to the Naval Academy. Remember when I said the stands of trees were thanks to Jimmy Carter? It was here on this farm that his father told him that if land wasn't being used, plant trees on it. As Georgia's governor, Carter ordered the same thing. It's a crop that can be harvested by the next generation."

"Smart," Josie repeated.

Rosie said nothing.

They walked the grounds, Daisy and Josie chatting amiably, sharing memories of the President Carter years, commenting on signs they read, and listening with smiles of wonder at the stops where Jimmy Carter himself had recorded memories of his days on the family farm.

Allison walked by Rosie. "Are you all right? Do you want to drop back and talk about anything?"

Rosie shook her head and hurried forward to join her sisters.

Allison shook her head. *I blew it. What did I say wrong?*

. . . .

After breaking out the food bag and having a picnic in the parking area, the ladies chose their seats and the drive continued. Rosie had specifically asked that they stop at the White Hall Alabama Visitor Center of the Selma to Montgomery National Historic Trail in Lowndes County. Once more, she would not say why.

Trying to make conversation, Allison asked Josie, "What happened to your first husband? Did he remarry?" She couldn't remember his name.

"Preston? He died three years after I left."

Allison waited quietly. *Let the person gather her thoughts. Don't interrupt. She'll fill the silence.*

"Maybe if I'd still been there . . . Clayton blamed me for several years." Josie fell silent, leaning against the window.

Allison respected the silence.

"It was not your fault, Josie. He had a bad heart. You didn't know." It sounded like Daisy knew the story. Apparently, they'd had this talk before.

Josie looked at Allison. "It was winter, snowing pretty hard. Preston went out as usual to leave for work. After opening the garage, he did some shoveling." She paused again.

Allison nodded. Living in Upstate New York, she knew full well how many older men had heart attacks after a heavy snow. Shoveling could be hard work.

"Pres apparently collapsed near the garage. He wasn't visible from the road, so no one noticed. It wasn't until evening when someone saw the garage was open and there were no tire tracks in or out. A neighbor came up the driveway to check and saw Preston's legs. His body was hidden behind a drift of snow. The neighbor called 9-1-1 and went to check on him."

"He died of a heart attack?" Allison asked.

Josie shook her head. "Exposure. He died of exposure. If I'd been there, maybe—"

Daisy interrupted. "You've been through this. The kitchen was at the back of the house. You said you usually didn't hear his car leave. You've admitted you may not have noticed anything amiss until it was too late. He may have died even if he got to the hospital, or been left brain damaged. It wasn't your fault."

"I'm sorry, Aunt Josie. I understand that you must have felt guilt at not being there." Allison carefully avoided the placating, *I know how you felt*, because she had no idea how Josie would have felt.

"It got worse."

Allison glanced at her aunt. *How could it get worse than dying?*

"Preston hadn't changed his will. I inherited everything, including a substantial life insurance policy. I gave the house to Clayton, because it should have been his, and the life insurance as well to pay for the rest of his college. I kept the rest to live on. Those were the years I had almost nothing. I should have given it all to Clayton. It should have been left to him anyway. I was the runaway ex-wife." Josie fell into a stony silence.

Daisy reached forward to pat Josie's shoulder. "You needed the money. You don't know that Preston didn't purposely leave his will as it was. Assume that he wanted you to have something to see you through. You gave him twenty years."

Allison glanced over again, catching Josie's eye. "It sounds like you did what you felt was best. You thought of your son first, then kept what you needed. There's nothing wrong with that. After all, you didn't take a salary while you were his housekeeper, his cook, his social planner, and all the other duties you took on." *That is, there's nothing wrong with keeping the money unless there's something more you aren't saying.* "You said you felt you broke his heart when you left. He never hit you or was violent."

"I never said he'd never hit me," Josie corrected.

Stunned, Allison glanced at her again. "He was abusive?"

Josie snorted a laugh. "Not abusive. The first time he struck me was when Clayton was five. Preston came home a little after five o'clock and told me that he'd invited his boss and wife for dinner. They were arriving at six-thirty. I had just gotten back from the park with Clayton. We both needed to get cleaned up, the dining room was in its usual state of playroom, office, and storage. It needed cleaning. Then of course, there was what to have for dinner. I blew up. I demanded to know what he was thinking, to invite them without letting me know. He told me calmly that he had just then let me know. I asked what he thought we'd be having for dinner. He shrugged and said something elegant and simple. I demanded 'Like what? And who is going to clean the house? Who's going to clear out the dining room and get the table set?' He slapped me."

Allison sucked breath. "He hit you for that?"

"Yes, indeedy. He calmly told me I was being hysterical." Josie looked over at Allison. "Watch some of those old movies. When women get emotional, men slap them and tell them to snap out of it. Stop being hysterical." Josie shook her head, disgusted. "Then he told me I had plenty of time. I asked, calmly, what he was going to do while I got ready and made dinner. He said, go and relax. I nearly blew up again. I told him he needed to clear the dining room table and set it, then vacuum the floor. I grabbed Clayton and headed upstairs to shower and change." Josie paused, looking smug.

"What happened?" Allison asked, glancing at her aunt's expression.

"Boss and wife showed up. Preston had simply moved the junk from the dining room table to a couple extra chairs pushed against the wall. The plates he put out were lunch plates. He placed all the silverware on the same side of the plate. First thing I did when they arrived was apologize that I'd only been told at five that they were coming. I'd used a little cover makeup, but I could tell the wife could see the red mark on my face. She kept looking at it.

"The meal wasn't exactly elegant either. All I had that would serve four and a kid was hamburger. If I'd had time to think, I'd have cut up the potatoes and gotten them boiling for mashed potatoes. But I got dressed first. By that time, I only had time for boxed mashed potatoes. I rounded it out with a can of corn. The wife—I don't even remember her name—she fully understood what was going on, and I could see she was upset and concerned. Anyway, she kept telling me how nice everything was, how difficult it must have been to throw things together on such short notice. I caught Preston several times glancing at my reddened face and knew he was just dying to be able to man-speak to his boss that I'd been hysterical. He did, in their thinking, what a man needs to do when a wife gets like that.

"When dinner finished, I excused myself, saying I had to put Clayton to bed. The wife immediately said they had to go, collared her husband who had been hoping for a little guy time and some comradely drinking. She hustled him out of there. Preston was not happy."

"Did he do anything?" Allison knew she was the only one in the dark.

"Silent treatment. Which was fine with me. A week later, we had a dinner date with some friends. I handed Preston a stopwatch and clicked it on. I told him to keep an eye on it. I then took my shower, did makeup and hair. I already had my evening dress laid out. When I was done, I told him to hit stop on the watch. Then asked him how long. He was confused but said an hour and ten minutes. I then pointed out that the night he'd asked his boss over, he had given me and hour and fifteen minutes to get myself ready, clean the house, get Clayton cleaned up, AND make a dinner. The best way I can describe his reaction is, he pouted."

Allison pressed. "You said that was the first time he hit you. When was the next time?"

"It was two years later. I got *emotional* again. He slapped me and said I was hysterical. That time, I slapped him right back."

Allison shot a look at her aunt, eyebrows raised, amazed. "You hit him?"

Josie shrugged. "He hit me. I hit him."

"Well?"

"Tell her the rest of the story, Josie," Daisy instructed.

"What happened?" Allison wanted to pull over so she could look her aunt in the eye.

Josie smiled slightly. "The next day, he brought me flowers and apologized. As I said, he was a good man, most of the time."

Allison thought of the guys whom she'd dated, the ones who were friends. *What would I have done if one slapped me? Hit back? I don't think so. I'd be stunned. So startled, I'm not sure how I would react.* She looked over at Josie, her aunt who had fought back in her own way and in so doing, preserved her marriage. "Why did you marry him in the first place?"

Josie looked out the window, thinking a minute. "I'd finished college, had a bachelor's degree. At that time, we women were expected to find a good husband in college. I had two men interested in me; staid, calm Preston and wild, fun-loving Danny. Everyone," she looked pointedly over her shoulder at Daisy, "said I should marry Preston."

"Why? It doesn't sound like you loved him. Did you?" Allison realized in all her aunt had said, she'd never said she loved her first husband. She'd said he was a good man, but when referring to Arnie and Petros, they were her soul mates, she spoke highly and emotionally of them . . . but not Preston.

"I loved him in a way. It wasn't fall head over heels in love like in the movies. He was steady and stable and was already established in a good job. I knew he'd be a good provider."

Allison interrupted. "How about a good father? How about a good friend?"

Josie sighed. "He was a good provider and a decent person. I could have done worse."

"What about the other guy, Danny? Would you have been happier with him?"

Daisy let out a hoot of laughter.

Josie grinned. "Ahhh, no. He got married, and three years later that poor woman divorced him after he lost their house while gambling, was having yet another affair, and had worsened his drinking problem. Last I heard, he was in and out of rehab as well as jail."

Daisy laughed delightedly. "Aren't you glad you took our advice?" She leaned forward and patted Josie's shoulder. "After all, you got Clayton out if it."

"That I did."

. . . .

Late in the afternoon, Allison pulled into the White Hall Civil Rights Trail Visitors Center. Easing stiffly from the car, they made their way into the building. Rosie, still silent, followed in the rear.

After an hour inside, seeing the exhibits, the violence that occurred during the Civil Rights movement, the difficulty Black people faced trying to simply register to vote, the sisters and Allison headed out for a short walking path around the grounds.

They stopped before a photo of white canvas tents and trampled ground. The sign explained that in December of 1965, a city of tents appeared in the field in this spot. Following the passage of the Voting Rights Act of 1965, Black tenant farmers who dared register to vote were often evicted by the White landowners in Lowndes County. They were run off the farms that had been their homes and had provided their livelihoods. Some were able to move in with relatives. Some left the state. Others, who had nowhere to go, set up a tent city. Young White males were said to drive by, whooping and firing guns into the tent encampments, and of course, no legal actions were taken against them.

In December 1965, a city of tents appeared on this site. The temporary shelters were homes for evicted black sharecropper families. These farmers worked and lived their lives on white-owned farms in Lowndes County. But when they dared to register to vote, following the passage of the Voting Rights Act of 1965, white landowners ran them from their homes and livelihood.

The Davis family was evicted after 25 years, the Glover family after 35 years, and the Lusane family after 60 years. Some 40 families were turned out. Some moved in with friends or relatives. Others left the county. And still others left the state. Those who had no place else to go came here to Tent City. Walk the path and learn more about these people and their struggle.

After reading the sign, Allison glanced over and saw Rosie staring at the ground, shaking. Moving closer, she saw wet splashes hitting the dry walkway.

"Aunt Rosie, what is it? I think you need to tell us what's been bothering you. Why did you need to come here?"

By now, Rosie's sisters also faced her, watching tears weave a path through her wrinkles.

Daisy took her arm, leading her to a bench under a young tree. "Sit. You are going to tell us why you insisted on coming here. What happened?"

That's the skill I need to master. Give people wait time. Let them gather their thoughts. Let them fill the silence.

It took nearly five minutes before Rosie could speak.

"We were here in 1966. I mean, I was here with a band. One day, one of my friends in the band showed me a notice about recruiting people who would be willing to register Black citizens to vote. There would be a talk on it the next night. We went. We thought that since we'd be here for a couple months and our gigs were at night, it would be a good way to spend afternoons, going around registering people to vote."

They waited. Allison watched Josie and Daisy, again impressed by their patience.

"We went the next night. Most of the people there were White. Some groups had both races. Three young Black women came in, probably not more than late teens. I noticed them because they were dressed so nicely, shirtwaist dresses, gloves, hats. They looked like they were headed for church. They sat behind us, all the way in the back. I heard them talking quietly and caught their first names. A sign-in sheet came around and, out of curiosity, I checked their last names. We listened through the talk, a few people asked questions, then at the end, we were given the warnings. 'You may be beaten up. You may be arrested. And finally, ladies, you may face worse than beatings and arrest.'"

She fell silent again. Allison filled with questions. Her aunts had lived through the Civil Rights struggles. She'd only learned about it in books. *Rosie had been there.*

"When we left, Mark and I decided, joked, that maybe this wasn't for us. We brushed it off and left. Forgot about it." Rosie swallowed, struggling with her memories. "Back up in Chicago a few months later, going through some newspapers, I saw a tiny, three paragraph article. It was the photo that stopped me. It was one of the three Black girls we'd seen at the voter registration talk. It said she and a friend had been arrested. The friend had been beaten, and, the article didn't specify but hinted, that she was raped. She was released three days later, after others in the group kept up pressure to get her out of there and had paid her fine. But her friend was missing. The sheriff insisted she had not been arrested. She'd never been brought before a judge. No one had seen her since the two of them were taken."

Rosie stopped again. Shaking, hand to her mouth, the tears leaked slowly from reddened eyes. Daisy handed her a hanky.

"Did you ever find out what happened?" Allison asked.

Rosie wailed. "We didn't take it seriously! We had thought it would be fun. Those girls knew, they knew what could happen to them . . . all for the right to vote. We take it for granted! They were willing to be beaten and even die for it."

Allison remembered back to their time in Colonial Williamsburg, when Josie gave a similar lecture to the group of students. She remembered how she'd noticed Rosie upset, shaking, and had wondered why.

Josie slapped her thigh. "There must be records. Do you remember her name? There may be records right here where we can find out what happened." She stood, straight, determined.

Allison smiled. With her determination and no-nonsense, Aunt Josie would get to the bottom of this.

· · · · · · · · · · · ·

Rosie allowed herself to be pulled to her feet. They made their slow way back to the visitors center. Josie headed straight for the information desk, toward a Black ranger with a computer next to him. Allison thought she saw the ranger quail slightly at the approach of this wrinkled warrior woman advancing on him. Cocking his head in question and smiling slightly, he asked, "Is there a problem, ma'am?" He then saw Daisy carefully guiding her distraught, puffy eyed sister. His look turned to concern.

Josie placed both hands on the counter.

Aggressive and forceful, Allison thought.

"My sister here met a young woman back in 1966 at a voter registration talk. She later saw an article indicating that this young woman had been arrested and never seen again. Would you have access to any information about her?"

The ranger nodded in grim understanding. "It did happen to some. But I'm afraid without a name, I couldn't tell you more than that."

"Rosie," Josie snapped. "Her name."

Rosie mumbled a name, too quietly to understand.

"Louder."

Rosie straightened, taking strength from her determined sister. She stepped forward and repeated the name again.

Turning to his computer, the ranger typed in the name and year. After some frowns, scrolling, and a little more typing, he turned the screen toward Rosie. "Is this the article?"

Allison stepped closer to read it along with her aunts. The photo was of a very youthful, attractive girl, probably a high school senior photo. It told of her arrest and that her friends had not seen her since. The local sheriff denied having taken her into custody, and there were no records of her arrest. That was all.

Rosie nodded, answering almost in a whisper, "That's her."

The ranger turned the screen back and went on typing. Allison watched his expression go from grim to hopeful, to a slow smile. He turned the screen around again, showing an attractive older woman in a business suit. You could just make out a small scar on her right cheek and a slant to her left eye caused by a scar along her eyebrow and down the side of her eye.

Those are places where the skin splits easily when backhanded or punched, Allison thought.

"She did indeed go missing," The ranger told them. "After she was taken in by the sheriff, she was not booked, so there was no record. She was roughed up, but when people came looking for her, she was pushed out through a back door, at night, having been beaten up, so she'd have had trouble walking. A couple young men found her and did worse to her. She was badly hurt and scared, enough so that when she found a friend to drive her, she fled to relatives in another town. That's why the article said her friend had not seen her. It was written four weeks after her arrest. Her family was told where she was, but no one else, for over a month. She never went back home. She did, however, find work, saved money, and went to law school. This photo is her after she became a well-respected civil rights lawyer."

Rosie exclaimed, hand to her mouth, and a smile slowly lit up her face. Allison could feel her relief flowing into each of them. Even the ranger seemed affected by the intensity of her emotion.

"We went to that talk. But my friend and I just walked away. We didn't know how bad . . . we didn't know anything." Tears welled again.

"Ma'am," he spoke softly, "I think you did do something. Do you vote?"

Nodding vehemently, Rosie responded, "In every single election. And almost every primary. I've only missed three primaries."

The ranger continued. "You have done something. You care. You have remembered that young woman's name for how many years? Since 1966. You have remembered her name and worried about her. I'd say that's something."

Rosie smiled wanly, using a tissue to dab her eyes. "Thank you. Thank you for taking the time to—"

"To put your mind at ease," he finished. "I'm glad I could help."

．．．．．．．．．．．．

Leaving the building, Rosie walked on air. "She wasn't killed. She grew up and became a lawyer. She wasn't crushed or broken in spirit. She was strong!" Rosie's eyes lit up with their own fire.

Josie and Daisy could not have looked more pleased. "How long has this been weighing on you?" Daisy asked.

"Since October of 1966."

Josie, shoulders square, snorted. "What? Not the day and time?"

Rosie giggled.

Allison felt a wash of relief.

Tomorrow we visit the second of Rosie's choices. I wonder what mystery that will hold.

Chapter 24

ROSIE'S SECRET

"The National Park directions say the entrance is on Clay Street off of Route 20," Daisy announced, studying the directions on her smart phone.

"The map says it's right off 61 and we're on 61," Josie countered.

Allison gripped the wheel and kept her eyes on the road.

"Well, I'd rather follow the official directions," Daisy sniffed.

Josie rattled her map meaningfully. "We will be just fine on 61. Route 20 goes east-west."

"So? What has that got to do with the price of fish?"

Allison quickly flicked her eyes to the rearview mirror. That was the statement that would usually get a rise out of Rosie. But Rosie remained quiet, pensively staring out the window at the Mississippi countryside. Vicksburg National Military Park was the third place Rosie had insisted they visit on their trek. But she would not give a reason why.

Entering the southern reaches of Vicksburg, Daisy and Josie

lapsed into irate silence. Allison realized, taking another quick glance at the silent youngest aunt, that Rosie was the one who usually broke these moods. She was the one who giggled, or made a silly comment. She remained silent. After yesterday's emotional release, Allison had hoped to hear her youngest aunt's infectious giggles once more.

There! With a sigh of relief, Allison spotted a route sign for 20 along with the easily recognized light brown of a National Park sign for Vicksburg National Military Park. Route 61 joined with 20, heading east. "Aunt Daisy, Aunt Josie, 61 and 20 have joined. You were both right," Allison announced, trying to break the sounds of silence.

"Well, that's nice," huffed Daisy.

Allison exited on Clay Street and found the visitor center. Rosie was the last one to slowly pull herself out of her favored back seat behind the driver. Allison waited for her, offering a hand if she needed it.

Daisy waved her senior park pass at the desk, got the park map, and checked the show time for the video about the battle, or siege, of Vicksburg.

Over an hour was spent watching the movie and perusing the museum. The siege was long and brutal to the residents of the city. Starvation, constant bombardments, rifle trenches dug to get closer to the walls of the city, and hand digging a diversion canal to redirect the Yazoo River away from the city to prevent supplies from reaching it by water—all added to the suffering. There were naval battles along the Mississippi River, where, Allison learned, torpedoes were not shot by submarines, but instead were underwater mines suspended in the water to take out military vessels.

Returning to the car to begin the tour route, the early summer sunshine accentuated the vibrant green of the fields and fully leafed trees. A few remaining dogwood petals drifted to the ground. It was hard to imagine the horrors of battles fought in the area, the hardships, suffering, and ruination of the land from thousands of soldiers and horses and wagons and heavy equipment tearing up the earth. Now, there was only the muted sound of city traffic.

Allison held the back door of the car open for Rosie.

. . . .

At the Memorial Arch, the start of the auto route, all three ladies levered themselves from the vehicle. Josie snapped a photo. They spent a few minutes reading the signage, then got back in the vehicle. The seatbelt alarm bonged on the drive up to Battery De Golyer, and started again after their foray at Shirley House. Allison followed the loop around the Third Louisiana Redan, having also given up putting on her seatbelt after every stop.

By Grant's Headquarters, Rosie just sat and looked out the window as Allison and the sisters got out to take short walks and read the signs at each stop. Daisy kept looking with concern at her younger sister. Back in the car, Allison saw her put a hand on Rosie's arm and ask quietly if she was all right. Rosie silently nodded.

Rosie did get out when they got to the museum for the ironclad boat, the *USS Cairo*. But she kept looking distractedly down the road in the direction they would head. Allison could see cemetery headstones covering the undulating hills on the banks of the Yazoo River.

Daisy told them what she knew of the *Cairo*. "That was an ironclad gunboat that was sunk by an underwater mine on the Yazoo River in December of 1862. It's covered with steel plates to protect it from cannon fire. The wreck was found in the early 1960s, if I remember right. There used to be a video about raising it from the bottom. All the first attempts failed because it was both heavy and fragile. It kept breaking up whenever the attempt was made to lift it from the river silt. Then the guy who led the operation would have to raise more money to try again. When the Cairo was finally raised successfully in 1964, the guy in charge of the salvage had died. He never got to see all his efforts pay off."

Impressed, Allison asked, "How do you remember so much?"

Josie waved a hand dismissively. "She's always been like this, remembers everything. It can be quite annoying."

Daisy flashed a wicked grin and mouthed, "Everything!" She then rolled her eyes and held up her cell phone, motioning as if she were scrolling through internet webpages.

Rosie remained silent.

Allison smiled in understanding, remembering how often Aunt Daisy lay in bed at night looking at her cell phone. That's what she was doing. Not reading emails, but reading up on where they would visit the next day.

Next stop was the Vicksburg National Cemetery. All the stones were small, unobtrusive, but some were smaller than others. Driving slowly by, Allison saw that all that the smaller ones had on them were numbers. Daisy saw her look. "Those are the stone markers for the Unknowns, soldiers who fell in battle were often buried quickly, in mass graves. Often there was no identification left with them. Some had folded pieces of paper with their names and the addresses of loved ones. But by the end of the war, when the bodies were dug up to be reburied with military honors, those papers were gone or illegible. This cemetery has about thirteen thousand Unknowns."

Allison felt Rosie's hand on her shoulder.

"Stop here," her aunt directed, pointing to the small cemetery office building. She went in alone.

Returning fifteen minutes later, Rosie directed Allison along winding, tree shaded roads, past thousands of silent markers, lined up in military rows covering the rises and dips of the green lawns. Following the directions on the map she had clutched in her hand, Rosie finally had Allison pull over.

Easing herself from the car, she stood for a moment. This was a newer section, not Civil War. Daisy and Josie came and stood quietly on either side, silently awaiting what she had to show them.

With a gentle sigh, Rosie slowly made her way down the row of gray stone markers, checking numbers and names. Some had flags placed near them, and a few had pebbles placed on the stone. These markers had more recent dates on them, not the 1860s they had been seeing.

Rosie stopped, staring down at one. Her sisters moved in, flanking her.

Daisy put her arm around her sister's waist and asked quietly, "Is this someone you knew?"

Allison stepped closer, awaiting her aunt's response.

Her youngest aunt took a juttering breath. "He was my husband."

Shocked silence.

Both sisters stared at her in disbelief. Allison's mouth dropped open. She'd been told Aunt Rosie had never married. It was obvious her sisters had believed the same thing.

"Are you sure?"

Josie snorted derisively at Daisy. "That's the dumbest question I've ever heard."

Rosie choked out a half sob, half laugh. "You probably don't remember. I was still in high school, and I'd been chosen as a back-up singer for a struggling but good band performing in our area. One of their back-ups had gotten appendicitis. As soon as I graduated from high school, I left with them.

"I quickly developed a friendship with Andy. He was sweet, kind, he didn't drink as heavily as the others, and he protected me from them. He played bass as well as keyboard and had a velvety tenor. He could also sing falsetto like the Beach Boys. I really struggled not to laugh the first few times I heard him do it during our gigs." There was a ghost of a smile, and Rosie's eyes were lit with the warm memories of her friend.

"When the rest of the guys would party, Andy and I would have a beer, then slip out. Of course, the other guys would hoot and cat call about our slipping out to be alone. We'd walk city streets or drive out to forests or beaches or lakes and just walk and talk, endlessly.

We both liked the same things. We'd sing together, old songs, new, and often songs we'd both sung in our church choirs.

"Eight months after we met, he got drafted." Rosie glanced at Allison. "The Korean War had ended, but there was still unrest in that area. Vietnam . . . we knew war was coming there. Andy put on a brave face when he was with the rest of the band, but when we were alone, he cried. We'd watched the reports on TV. I knew all the guys were concerned about being drafted, but Andy was the first to have his fears realized. Finally, he calmed himself by suggesting that he could get into the Army band or, at worst, he could be trained as a medic or work at a MASH unit. After all, we weren't at war just then.

"A week before he had to report for boot camp, he stuttered around, hinted, then finally blurted out, 'Would you please marry me?' When he saw my hesitation, he begged me, *please*, he wanted to know that I'd be waiting for him. He said we could get the marriage annulled or get a divorce after it was all over if that's what I wanted. So, I agreed." She hesitated, then shook her head. "I mean, I agreed to marry him."

Rosie sniffed and held her hand over her mouth for several breaths. Her usually outspoken sisters remained supportively quiet, waiting.

"We started the paperwork and such, and the day before he had to leave for boot camp, we had a justice of the peace marriage. After basic training, Andy got one week off. He spent half with his parents, over the river in Louisiana, and then three days with me. I asked him when I could meet his parents. He shook his head and told me not yet, that they wouldn't approve. That hurt. For three days, we didn't leave each other for a moment, then he was gone."

Rosie stood, breathing deeply, tears sparkling in her eyes. At first, Allison didn't even realize she was singing, she started so softly and her voice quavered so. *"Tis the gift to be simple, tis the gift to be free. . . "*

Daisy joined in, singing mezzo-soprano in harmony, adding strength. *"Tis the gift to come down where we ought to be."*

Josie joined her deeper tenor voice in counterpoint. *"And when we find ourselves in the place just right. . . "*

All three gained confidence as they carried the simple melody. Josie went veering off in directions that made Allison smile. They were the variations from Aaron Copeland's version in *Appalachian Spring.* Allison saw a couple men ranging among the headstones stop to listen. A groundskeeper paused in his raking and looked up.

"We shall be in the valley of love and light!"

At the finish of the song, Rosie sank to her knees, Daisy slowly lowering herself beside her. It was clear old knees did not bend very easily. Both ladies ended up lurching forward to take the weight on their hands, then settling back, seated in the sun-warmed grass. Josie, with her hands on Rosie's shoulders, slowly lowered herself to kneel at her back.

Daisy rubbed her sister's shoulders and neck. Allison saw splashes of tears fall onto the bright blue, red, and yellow of Rosie's muumuu, colors totally at odds with her present mood.

"I don't know if either of you noticed. You were both out of college and married by then. For nearly a year, I had very little contact with Mama or Daddy, except for a phone call now and then from the road. Two months after Andy left, we'd written at least once a week. His letters sometimes came in a cluster, three or four at a time, but all sent at different times. His hopes of being in a band or being assigned to a medical unit had been dashed. When he'd asked his drill sergeant about those possibilities, the man laughed and told Andy that if he'd enlisted, he may have had a choice, but since he was drafted, he'd be put where he was needed. And where he was needed was in a base in Taiwan. But we weren't at war. There was no reason to worry."

Rosie choked on a sob. Once more, she needed to gather herself before going on.

"I had just sent a letter telling Andy that I was. . . I was . . . pregnant."

Josie gasped. Daisy tightened her hold around Rosie's shoulder. She urged softly, "What happened?"

"Two days after I mailed my letter, two soldiers in uniform showed up at my door, handing me a folded flag and their condolences." Rosie choked back a more intense sob.

Josie gently stroked her sister's curled red hair.

"He'd been killed in a training exercise! We weren't even at war. He died in an accident." She put a shaking hand to her mouth.

"I took to my bed. I tried to carry on, but I couldn't put my heart into singing. The band left me behind when they moved on. I had no money coming in. I rented a by-the-week motel room. I didn't want to go home. What would I tell Mama and Daddy? I had just talked myself into getting myself back together, to start eating right, get out, and find some work. I had a baby to care for! I still had something of Andy that I could love and cherish."

On the last sentence, Rosie lost all control of her voice, tears welling, throat closing off as sobs wracked her.

"Oh, God," Daisy murmured, dropping her head onto Rosie's shoulder and wrapping both arms around her.

"It started with cramps," Rosie's voice rose, sounding desperate, despairing. "Then horrible pain in my abdomen." Her sobs escalated, hysteria tinging her voice, "What had I done? I waited too long to take care of myself. It was all wrong. I should have loved that little being with all my heart, but I laid around feeling sorry for myself instead."

Daisy clung to her, rocking her, soothing. "It wasn't your fault," she crooned. "Miscarriages just happen. There's probably nothing you could have done."

"I was left with nothing." Rosie's thin frame quaked with sobs.

Hand to her mouth, Allison didn't know what to do. Then she realized she didn't need to do anything. Nearly sixty-five years since this terrible event happened, Rosie had the full support of her two sisters. They held her as she sobbed out the pain that she had held in for so long.

This time, it was Daisy who began to sing. *"The storm is passing over."*

Josie joined, singing a rich tenor, repeating the refrain. Deep and soulful, they sang a third time, *"The storm is passing over, Hallelu!"*

With a voice full of tears, Rosie joined in. *"Encourage my soul and let us journey on. Though the night is dark."* Rosie's voice grew in strength.

Daisy gripped her shoulder, lending her support. *". . . and I am far from home."*

Rosie's voice broke again, with a sobbed gulp letting her sisters lead with *"Thanks be to God."* She straightened her shoulders and joined back clear and pure, *"and the morning light appears."* The three wove a tapestry of their voices in a repeat of the chorus.

Allison felt her throat tighten with emotion. She saw a mother and son several rows over who had stopped to listen, quietly, respectfully, move on. Even the birds had stilled their cacophony to listen.

The sisters sat or knelt in silent tribute for a few moments. Josie, kneeling behind, still had her hands on her sister's shoulders. Daisy held Rosie's arm.

Rosie shifted stiffly.

"Oh, dear," exclaimed Daisy.

With a grunt, Josie rose from her knees, pushing down on Rosie, squashing her so she squeaked like a dog's toy.

Daisy rolled this way and that, trying to get seized knees and ankles to bend enough for her to try to stand. "A little help here."

Allison tried to lift her from behind, hands under her aunt's turkey-wattle arms, but it didn't work. She came around in front, analyzing the situation. "Here, do it like Josie. Put your arms on my shoulders and push up."

But Daisy couldn't get her feet under herself.

Allison, feeling a little desperate, looked around for help. Seeing none, she moved in closer, squatted facing her aunt and ordered, "Put your arms around my neck." She then put her arms around Daisy's waist. "Now, slowly, lift." Slowly, giving Daisy time to maneuver her uncooperative limbs under her, and with Josie at her back for stability, the two were able to ease her into an upright stance.

"Well done," Josie cheered.

"Help?" pleaded a muffled voice.

The three turned to see a blue, red, and yellow-clad, grass-coated, rear end stuck in the air. Rosie had succeeded in getting her feet under her, then using her hands for balance, had pushed her rear end up, but her hands were still firmly planted on the ground in front of her.

"What do I do?" she whimpered.

Daisy and Josie helped by roaring with laughter.

Again, Allison moved in front facing her, glad that Rosie had seen the doctor about her sore knees.

"Squat back down. Now put one hand on my shoulder." Josie once more moved in behind to stabilize her sister if she tilted backwards. "Now your other hand." Allison coached as she helped Rosie steady herself. "Now we stand." Allison took Rosie around the waist as she had Daisy.

"That was easy!" Rosie chirped as she brushed off the clinging grass.

Allison smiled, then looked down to brush off her knees and take a last look at the small headstone. Looking up, she saw the three sisters waddling stiffly back to the car, holding each other's arms for support.

Allison shook her head, amused at how easily they now moved on, then looked back down at the husband none of them had known existed. "Goodbye, Andy. Nice to have finally met you."

• • • • • • • • • • • •

Allison found her way back to the Natchez Trace, following the winding road over early summer hills.

Daisy broke the hour of silence, "So, are you over your crying jag now?"

Allison's eyebrows shot up. She glanced in the rearview mirror to see Rosie's reaction to such a terse statement.

Rosie giggled and touched her wadded up tissue to her nose.

Josie, in the front passenger seat turned back to Rosie. "Why didn't you tell us sooner?" She shook her head. "You didn't need to suffer alone."

Rosie again held the tissue to her nose as she turned away, looking out the window at the passing tupelo trees on the marshy verge.

Allison again glanced back, wondering if Rosie was going to answer.

Quietly at first, then gaining in strength, "I don't know. At times, I felt embarrassed. I'd jumped into marrying Andy. You were both busy with your own families. I didn't think you'd have time for me."

Josie snorted. Daisy sighed deeply and gave a headshake.

"Then when I lost my baby," she paused, "I blamed myself." All listened in silence.

"This may sound heartless, but I don't regret anything. I would have loved that child with all my heart. But over the years, I realized how many things I would not have been able to do, so many places I would have never seen, so many people I'd have never met." Taking deep breaths, Rosie again went silent, staring out the window.

Allison realized Rosie was struggling to express what she needed to say without sounding crass or cold-hearted.

"Do you regret marrying Andy? Does that make you feel guilty?" Daisy prodded quietly.

On an explosive breath, Rosie blurted, "Yes!" She gulped down a sob, sighed, and laid her head against the window. "I guess that's why I never told anyone. A part of me just wanted it to never have happened. I just wanted to get on with my life, and that made me feel so, so guilty."

Again, silence descended. Allison kept glancing at each of her aunts. Josie now faced straight ahead, wearing a look of consternation. Daisy leaned slightly toward Rosie, emanating concern. Rosie, forehead plastered to the side window, had her hand to her face.

With a deep sigh, Josie broke the pain-filled silence. "I felt that way myself. That's why I finally got a divorce. I loved my child, but wished I could have had a different life." She turned around to her youngest sister. "Honestly! I was jealous of you. You had the life I wished I'd had."

Daisy chuckled. "Sure. You thought she was living the life of sex, drugs, and rock-n-roll."

Rosie sputtered into laughter, spattering saliva onto the window. Josie barked out her boisterous laugh. "Rock-n-roll, yes, but I thought more beer and red wine rather than drugs, and I wasn't too sure about the sex part." She then leaned back conspiratorially as far as her stiff bones would allow. "How was the sex?"

Rosie lurched forward in her seat, swatting the back of Josie's. "Oh, you!" Settling back, primly, hands crossed demurely in her lap, she answered, "That's for me to know and you to never know."

It was Daisy's turn to laugh delightedly.

Allison smiled in relief. She found herself wishing for the first time in her life that she had sisters. Glancing in the rearview mirror, she addressed her youngest aunt. "This has been a very stressful, rough couple of days for you."

Rosie looked pensive, then replied softly, "No." Then with more feeling, "No." And finally, with a faint smile, a lifting of the tension on her wrinkled face, she repeated, "No. I feel so much better. Relieved.

"Yesterday," she said robustly, "I found out that the young woman I've felt guilty about for years, the one I thought had been killed, had been badly injured, yes, but she survived and was strong. She wasn't crushed. She grew to become a civil rights lawyer. And today, I finally introduced my sisters to Andy. I finally told them about the family I almost had, and I finally got to say a proper goodbye to a young man who loved me and who died too young." She sighed. "I feel like a horrible weight has been lifted, like I'm free, free at last." She relaxed back into the seat with a small smile.

Allison glanced back again. Rosie looked younger; so much stress had been released.

This is also what a counselor does. It's not all about solving problems. It's about relieving guilt, releasing stress. It's about letting someone share their darkest moments with someone who will listen without passing judgement. It's about support. It's about giving advice about where to go from here. And it's sometimes just telling someone that it's okay to feel as you do. It's okay.

Chapter 25

NATCHEZ TRACE

A llison swam in the hotel's pool as her aunts prepared for the day. Once more, Josie and Daisy had chosen to have two rooms. It was obvious to Allison that they were tiring. The aunts retired earlier and took longer to get ready in the morning. Allison knew the emotional turmoil had to have taken a toll on Rosie. She could see it in her face. Her color wasn't good.

Yesterday in the car was the first time she'd heard her aunts Josie and Daisy so short tempered. They had six days before Josie and Rosie flew home from Detroit. Five more days of travel. Maybe they should cut it short. Today, they would visit Corinth, the last place they had on their list to visit. What then?

Allison swam leisurely, enjoying the feel of the cool water as her thoughts swam.

Should I insist that we then head back to Toledo? Last night, Daisy got a call from Daryl that he and her husband Barth would arrive back at their house today. We could be back there in three days. Then the aunts could have two days to rest before flying out. I'm really feeling concern about their health and how tired they are looking.

Pulling herself out of the pool, Allison knew that the decision had to be made by the aunts themselves. Maybe there was a way she could suggest it. Wiping down with the towel and drying her hair, Allison realized, she needed to ask about her grandmother. *I still know very little about Anna. It's the one thing I hoped to learn on this trip. What was she really like?*

. . . .

Leaving Tupelo and the Natchez Trace, Allison drove the aunts north to Corinth. Daisy scrolled through her cell phone trying to find anything she could relay about what happened there.

"So then, tell me about our ancestor who fought there." Allison flicked a glance at Daisy's frown of frustration.

Josie leaned forward from her seat behind Daisy. "We're not entirely sure. His son said Milo mustered in the year 1862 in Flint, Michigan, but another source says it was an Ohio unit and another source talks about the Army of the Cumberland. All we know for sure is that Milo named his son Riley after a mess mate. We don't know if that guy lived or died or where they may have fought other than in Corinth or even what was important about Corinth. That's why we want to stop here."

"And Riley is your grandfather?" Allison asked.

"Riley Sweers is our grandfather, your great, great grandfather," Daisy answered.

"So that makes Milo your great, great, great. . . " Rosie made a show of counting on her fingers. "Grandfather!" and giggled.

Unable to help herself, Allison giggled, causing Josie to guffaw.

Daisy guided them to a parking area with a sloping hill and winding pathway up to the visitor center. Allison could see no easy way to get the aunts closer, but Daisy commented, "I'm interested to see the pathway leading up. Come on."

Intrigued, they all piled out, rather slowly. Slinging on fanny packs and dragging oversize purses.

The pathway did indeed prove interesting. Embedded in the cement were pieces of rifles, round bullets, belt buckles, shoes, caps, cartridge boxes and powder horns, everything that could have been found in the field after a battle. The walk winding up the hill was made slowly as they paused often to examine the various artifacts.

Pushing through the visitor center doors, the three ladies tromped up to the desk, hefting purses up onto the chest-high counter. Allison fought back a giggle. *No wonder they look like they're in such good shape! Those purses they haul around weigh a ton.*

The ranger looked from the bulging purses to the wrinkled ladies. "How may I help you?"

"We had an ancestor here."

"What happened here?"

"What battles were fought?"

"Ladies!" He held up his hand in a gesture to stop. "One at a time, please."

"You have a nice smile, young man," Daisy started. "We had an ancestor, our great grandfather, who re-enlisted here. We know nothing about what went on here in Corinth."

The ranger nodded. "What was your ancestor's name? I may be able to find you some information."

Josie took over. "Milo Sweers, from Michigan, but we are not sure if he was in a Michigan or Ohio regiment." She spelled out the name as the ranger wrote it down.

He smiled and pointed to the auditorium door. "Head on in there, and I'll start the video. Then you can look around the museum while I see if I can find anything on Milo Sweers." He flashed them a winning smile.

Corinth straddled the two main railway routes across the South. General Grant decided it must be taken. After landing part of his army at Pittsburg Landing, Tennessee, he was attacked and nearly defeated before reinforcements arrived. The Confederates retreated from Shiloh to Corinth and began extensive earthworks to protect the railroads. Federal forces, led by Henry Halleck, built their own rifle trenches and earthworks as they advanced. On May 29, 1862, the Federal forces took Corinth without a major battle.

A force of twenty-three thousand men remained to hold the town and railroads under the command of Major General Rosecrans. In early October of that year, Major General van Dorn's Army of West Tennessee advanced, hoping to take back their vital rail station. After a savage, hard fought battle with over seven thousand casualties, the Northern forces under Rosecrans kept their hold on Corinth. Images of the aftermath showed death, horrible injury, and devastation. The three aunts watched in silence. Allison wanted to take notes. When the film ended and the lights in the auditorium came up, the four sat quietly, each lost in her own thoughts and emotions.

Daisy finally broke the silence. "It was the first war on this continent during which photographs were taken. In previous wars, the men refused to talk about the horrors they had seen. Only those who had been there had any idea. With photographs, everyone had an idea of the horror of war."

Allison thought of the images, of a man with his leg blown off, bloated bodies splayed on the ground, a soldier who had had both hands amputated. "Did Milo tell about his years in the Army? Did he tell his son what it was like?"

Josie shook her head. "That's why we know so little. Grandpa, that is, Riley, said his father never talked about the war or his part in it."

Solemnly, the four filed back out to the main room. The ranger looked up from his computer. "I think I've found something, but it's for Milo S W E A R S."

Rosie giggled. "Swears. Milo swears! He would have been teased about that."

Josie nodded as a memory came to her. "Yes, I do remember that at some time after the war, Milo started spelling his name SWEERS. I'm not sure if it was officially changed. He did get some kind of military pension under the name Swears, but Riley always spelled his name with a double *e,* and that's the spelling on his marriage certificate."

The ranger flashed his winning smile at them. "Then I have your great-grandaddy's information. He was in the 10th Michigan infantry, Company C. From there, he was attached to Army of the Ohio while he was here, then to the Army of the Cumberland, which saw many of the major battles in the South. He re-enlisted as a corporal and mustered out as a sergeant." He handed them a slip of paper with the details written out for them. "If you want more information," he waved his hand to the glass-walled library behind the desk, "we can go in there and find more extensive records."

Rosie's eyes lit up. Josie smiled and mouthed, "Books!" and Daisy nodded emphatically.

The ranger led them into the glass-walled library. He searched among the volumes and came across the one containing information on the 10th Michigan infantry.

"Does it give a list of people in his company? Milo told his son, Riley, that he was named after his mess-mate," Daisy repeated.

The ranger flipped through pages. "Ah, here it is." He placed the tome in front of the three women, pointing to a list of names. Scanning down the list, Daisy asked, "Does it tell if they survived? Were injured? What happened to them?"

"If you find someone named Riley, I can look up the name and see what I can find."

"Oh my gosh!" Rosie pointed to a name near the bottom of the page. "Riley!"

The ranger turned it toward himself to read the first and last name. Josie then swiveled it back. "Keep looking. We don't want to miss a different Riley."

"But if there are two, how will we know which is the right one?" Rosie asked.

"Then we will have two answers to choose from," Josie replied.

Allison smiled. *Straight forward, no nonsense Josie.*

Finding no other Rileys listed, the ladies hefted the massive tome, passed it to Allison, and headed out to see what the winning-smile ranger had found in his computer database. He jotted some information, scrolled down, and jotted another note.

He looked up to see three wrinkled, hopeful faces. "Well. It looks like they signed up at the same time, were both here when they both re-enlisted and went on to fight in a string of battles— Chattanooga, Chickamauga, the Siege of Atlanta, and Kennesaw Mountain. They participated in destroying numerous railroads. It looks like Riley was injured at Kennesaw Mountain. From what I can find, he was discharged due to amputation at the rank of corporal, and his death is listed two years later." He pushed back from his computer. "I can't give you an address or family names, but now that you have his name, maybe that's something you can pursue in Michigan records."

Josie nodded. "That will give me something to do when I get home. You've been extremely helpful. Thank you so much."

Each of her sisters and Allison also offered their thanks. He pointed them out a rear door into a small patio with a water feature. "The blocks in the stream each represent a Civil War battle."

Daisy snapped a couple photos as Rosie walked quietly around the pond, examining the names on each of the jumble of stone squares seemingly tossed haphazardly into the water.

Daisy appeared to be drooping, Rosie was too quiet, and Josie had lost interest and wandered back in to look at the many photos of young men who had fought at Corinth.

"I think we should push on. You found the answers you sought." Allison gently took Daisy's arm.

She nodded, and let Allison guide her toward the door.

Walking back down the winding path to the parking area, Rosie stopped often to examine the artifacts embedded in the path. She reached out to gently touch those embedded on the cement walls along sections of the path. Allison thought about Rosie's tragically brief marriage and wondered if she were thinking of her Andy.

The silent drive from Corinth back to the Natchez Trace gave Allison time to ponder. The energy level of the aunts was waning. Should she suggest they head home?

· · · · · · · · · · · ·

"Look! They're blanketing the field! I have to stop!" Allison found a parking area close to a field of brilliant red clover they had been passing for the past several miles. "I'll leave the car here in the shade. I really want to walk over and photograph that field. It looks like a gem case of rubies on green velvet!"

Josie levered herself out of the rear seat, Rosie in her usual seat next to her. She opened her window and gazed at the sun-dappled leaves overhead, humming *Crimson and Clover* to herself. Daisy checked their plentiful food supply for a potential snack, *humph*ed, and wormed her way out the door, one hand on her hip as she creaked herself erect.

Allison darted down the road, scanning the gently rolling fields on each side, camera at the ready. Butterflies flitted among the bobbing clover, sucking nectar from the blooms. Camera clicking, Allison walked, crawled, and crouched through the fields and verges, looking for the best shots, trying to look nonchalant when the occasional car went by.

Back on the road, Allison paused in her shooting as a dark green van approached and passed, and then slowed. The brake lights came on.

Allison stood on the shoulder of the road where it dropped sharply to a gully.

The van pulled far to the right side of the road and made a U-turn. Tinted passenger windows hid the occupants.

Allison looked around. She was in the open, the parking area a good half mile back down the road. She'd likely fall if she bolted down the embankment. The safest escape route would be to run away from the parking area, passing the van as it came toward her, then into the field where there was less of a slope. From there, she could circle around and dash for the parking area.

The van slowed as it approached and the side door slid open.

Four Black ladies in full Sunday best peered out at her. Two more in the front seat turned toward her, looking concerned.

"You all right, honey? You need some help?"

The woman speaking sported a confection of yellow on her neatly coifed hair; tiny sunflowers and green leaves decorated the brim. Another lady wore a red velvet hat almost exactly the color of the crimson clover Allison had been photographing. Allison couldn't clearly see the two in the back row, except one had very sparkly strappy sandals. Two more well-dressed ladies occupied the front seats.

Taking a tentative step forward, Allison smiled and waved her hand at the clover bedecked field. "I was so taken with the beauty of the clover. I have been out photographing."

The ladies looked up and down the road. "Are you here alone? Where's your people, honey?"

Allison felt like she was back in the school hallway being quizzed by a teacher about why she was wandering the halls. "I left the car back in the shade in that parking area with my aunts."

The ladies looked at one another. One nodded, and whispers were exchanged. Yellow-hat leaned out the door. "Mind if we follow you back, sweetie? Don't want to scare you, but there was a problem," she stressed the word, "along here about a week ago."

Allison thought about the cars that had passed her on this lonely stretch, and about her fear when this van had turned around with the side door sliding open. She smiled graciously, "I would greatly welcome that act of kindness, ma'am. Thank you." Allison smiled more broadly.

The van kept pace until they were within yards of the parking area. It pulled in ahead of Allison, stopping a couple yards from Daisy's Buick. All six ladies emerged from the van as Allison hurried around the corner to join them. Six immaculately dressed and hatted Black ladies eyed three wrinkled White ladies dressed in a motley assortment of muumuus, capris, and sparkly T-shirts.

Yellow-hat remained the spokeswoman, waving back at Allison, "You ladies this girl's aunties?"

Josie stepped forward, but Allison hurried to intercept. "Aunt Josie, they stopped to check on me, see if I was all right. They were worried that I was out here alone. An incident happened about a week ago."

A frown fluttered across Josie's face. "Is that right?"

Daisy now stood by her side. "I can't imagine us being much help if we'd heard Allison shrieking for help." She turned on Allison with a concerned frown, "And YOU had the car keys, young lady. We would not have even been able to run the scumbags off the road if they took off with you." She looked proudly back at her car. "It's one reason I like that Buick. It's built like a tank."

Amused glances traveled among the six ladies.

"Well, we were just returning from our church choir practice when we saw your niece walking alone."

Josie extended her hand. "And we are most grateful you did. I'm Josie, and these are my sisters, Daisy and Rosie."

The various ladies introduced themselves, Ruth, Delia, Arabelle . . . Allison lost track of who was who, but caught yellow hat's name—Cassandra.

"Are you anti-Baptists?" Daisy asked conversationally.

Confused silence.

"You mean *Anabaptist?*" Cassandra asked politely.

Daisy considered this. "We saw a sign in a town yesterday advertising a gun-and-knife show at an *anti-Baptist* church. I didn't think churches would sponsor a gun show."

Two ladies looked like they may be offended and three looked thoughtful. One turned, hand over her mouth, and snorted mightily before shaking with silent laughter.

"I think you mean Anabaptist. Yes, I'm a little surprised they'd have a gun show, but really, the churches in many of these towns are also the community centers," Cassandra explained politely.

"Well, I'd heard how Southern Baptists weren't very. . . " Allison held her breath while Daisy searched for her footing, ". . . welcoming of Black people. Jimmy Carter wrote that wonderful letter saying he could no longer be associated with the Baptist church due to its intolerance. So, I assumed there might be anti-Baptists."

The one lady, Allison thought it might be Delia, burst into guffaws, knocking her little mauve hat nearly off her head. It dangled by one lone hairpin. One lady looked ready to *hurrumph*, but two others giggled, chuckled, and repeated *"anti-Baptist!"*

Rosie swayed gently back and forth, eyes dancing as she quietly hummed then began singing, barely audibly. Allison felt her skin prickle as she recognized the haunting rendition of the song the three aunts had sung the day before at Andy's grave, about the storm passing over. When Daisy had started it yesterday, her alto sounded like dark storm clouds scudding across the sky, carrying the storm away. In Rosie's clear soprano, it sounded like the clouds breaking up, allowing shafts of brilliant light to stream down. One of the church ladies standing close to Rosie picked up the tune, singing the first verse slow and yearning. The other ladies joined in, swaying to the tune, weaving their voices. Rosie's voice rose in volume for the chorus, syncing with the church ladies.

Then she took it, *"The stars have disappeared, and distant lights are dim,"* her clear soprano started quietly, then soared, *"My soul is filled with fears, the seas are breaking in."* Her eyes closed and her power brought tingles up Allison's spine into her neck.

Cassandra and her group let Rosie take it, becoming the background to her solo, then came in again for the chorus, blending, melding, and by the end of the song, challenging and competing.

Awed silence descended with the last notes of the hymn. With her hands clasped at her breast, Rosie whispered simply, "More."

And they sang, mixing old and new, traditional with spirituals. *Oh Mary, Don't you Weep* left Allison near tears. *Holy, Holy, Holy* soared and swooped on angel wings. *I'll Fly Away* brought two cars into the parking lot. One stayed, the couple getting out to stand by the car and listen. The other was hoping for a bear mauling and when they saw it was just a bunch of ladies singing, pulled out and gunned it, causing another car to pull in thinking the other car must be fleeing a bear mauling. The two girls in the car decided to stay, maybe hoping for at least a bear sighting, you never know.

After a brief conspiratorial consultation, the choir ladies started *Wade in the Water*, each taking a solo section. Ruth sang a strong tenor. Delia let her voice slide, warbling like a song bird. Rosie listened, got the feel for where Delia was going, and came in high and straight, cutting across the up and down drafts of Delia's rendition. The church ladies nodded and smiled at each other.

The ladies added some fun to *It is Well with My Soul*, causing a ranger to pull into the getting-crowded parking area, thinking someone was being attacked in a bear mauling. She was amused (and relieved) to find two sopranos competing over high notes.

They took it down to soft and yearning with *Are you Washed in the Blood*. Their audience had grown to eleven, and one dog.

Delia looked at Rosie's flushed face and nodded with a smile, "Last one. You ready for this, Soprano Lady?" She led the way into *Count Your Blessings*, taking it high and twining her voice with Rosie's, leading her up to the heavens as the other ladies anchored them to earth. They brought the volume down, the energy down, and drifted to a gentle stop. Their audience applauded. Seeing the show was over, folks smiled, some waved as they got into their cars to leave.

The ladies clustered around Rosie. "You come sing with us anytime. Come to our church, be in our choir, ya hear?"

And Rosie cried. Taking the arms held out to her for comfort, she folded herself into them and sobbed.

Allison looked on, appalled. Josie's mouth pinched into a hard line. "They kicked her out," Josie said, glaring at Allison. "Her performance choir that she'd been in for twenty years kicked her out before the Christmas concert. That's why she's upset."

"Why?" Allison demanded. "Her voice is beautiful!"

Josie snorted. "She was getting short of breath. She couldn't even get to the end of a song without fading out."

"But she's fine now! She sang beautifully."

Josie let out a deep sigh. "She went to the doctor. The shortness of breath was enough to scare her. Her doctor ran tests and said her shortness of breath was because she has congestive heart failure. He told her that if she watches her diet and takes care of herself, she has no more than five years to live."

Allison blanched, realizing that was the reason for those heavy stockings Rosie fought to put on each morning; they were for circulation.

Daisy breathed, "No!"

Turning sharply, Josie demanded of her sister, "You didn't know?" Daisy shook her head. "Then don't tell her I told you. I assumed you knew. That's why she's avoiding salt."

Daisy shook her head sadly. "No more margaritas. No more salt in her beer to bring up a good foamy head."

Shocked by Daisy worrying only about what Rosie could drink, Allison blurted, "But her heart!"

Josie turned on her. "That's not what bothers her. Singing is her life. Getting kicked out of the choir crushed her. That alone could have killed her."

They stopped talking as the church ladies backed gently away from Rosie, arms still extended for emotional support. One handed her a tissue, patting her shoulder consolingly.

Rosie dabbed her eyes, her nose, then blew. Allison remembered her grandmother holding a tissue to her nose and telling her to *toot*, but what came out of Rosie was the blaring shriek of a high-speed commuter train approaching a busy intersection. The ladies closest to her fell back a step. She held out the sodden shred of tattered tissue, and giggled.

Josie strode forward. "I am now doubly in your debt. Not only did you take the time to look after our niece, but also to share your voices and talents with my sister. You can see how much it meant to her." Josie's usually hardened eyes misted over.

There were several teary eyes among the church ladies as well. They each expressed the pleasure they'd had, how beautifully Rosie sang, and what joy it had brought to them as well. Each one reached out to touch Rosie once more before climbing sedately into their van.

Allison realized it was a let-down to see them leave.

The ranger still stood quietly, unnoticed beside her patrol car. She smiled, "Well, that's not something I see every day." She nodded after the disappearing van, "You've made some life-long friends there. When they invited you to join them, they meant it. Beautiful singing." She smiled at Rosie, climbed in, and buckled up.

Slowly, Rosie, Josie, and Daisy returned to their car.

"Did you get the photos you wanted?" Daisy asked.

"Yes, yes . . . NO! Oh, my gosh! I didn't take any of Rosie and all the ladies when they were singing!"

"Quick," Josie barked, shoving them all toward the car. "Step on it. We can catch them and make them pose for us."

Allison bolted into the car, cranked the engine over, thinking *Really?* Then looked out the window at the aunts standing, eyes sparkling, laughing at her.

· · · · · · · · · · · · ·

Driving to the end of the Trace, Daisy found them two rooms at a motel near Nashville. Once more, Allison dragged in all the suitcases. She found Daisy slumped in a chair on the balcony overlooking a suspiciously aquamarine-blue pool. After putting the two suitcases in the room, Allison came and leaned against the wall next to Daisy.

"You said Barth would get back home tomorrow."

Without speaking, Daisy nodded.

"I know you're worried about him." Allison glanced at her silent aunt. "Rosie doesn't look good. She's not sleeping well. I didn't know about her heart." Allison trailed off. *How should I word this?*

Daisy shifted, straightening up. "We have four days before Rosie and Josie fly home."

"Yes." Allison wanted to add, *we can use the time at your house, let them see the old neighborhood, spend time with Barth, whom I've never met.*

Daisy looked over the railing at the lit pool. She gazed out toward the lights of Nashville.

"This has been a wonderful trip, Allison. I don't want it to end. I don't think you could ever realize how much it has meant to us to be able to do this." Then she looked over at her grand-niece. "And one of the best parts was getting to know you." She sighed deeply. "But I think it's time to head home. If we pushed hard, we could make it tomorrow. Sorry, I should have said, if we made you drive too long, we could get home tomorrow. I really want to see Barth."

Allison started to say, she would, she'd drive all day and into the night.

"It's only about eight hours from here. But I'd really like to have one more day, one more night out. Let's stop at Abraham Lincoln's birthplace and childhood home, then through Lexington horse country. It's a beautiful area. The next day, we can make it home. We'll rest up there before Josie and Rosie have to fly home. It's been wonderful, Allison. I can't thank you enough for doing this for us. But it's time to go home."

Daisy slumped back in the chair. Allison could see her aunt's exhaustion.

She sighed, feeling relieved. Feeling disappointed. Feeling exultant, and proud, and so happy to have gotten to know her three amazing aunts.

Chapter 26

THE GOOD ONE

Allison told Rosie. Daisy told Josie. They both accepted the decision to bring the trip to an early end. Both seemed relieved.

For the first time, Allison felt sad as she hefted the four suitcases down the hotel stairs, across the parking lot, and heaved them into the car. *This is the second to the last time that I'll be hauling all four suitcases. Tonight will be our last night in a hotel, and I still haven't really learned what I wanted to about my grandmother, Anna.* Allison heaved the fourth suitcase in and rubbed sore hands against her thighs. She slammed the trunk of the Buick and smiled. *A Buick. An old lady's car. Someday, I'll own a Buick.*

Smiling, she headed back to the room. She found all three in Josie and Daisy's room, primping each other's hair.

Now. We don't have to push today. I'm going to ask now.

Allison plopped down on the bed, watching Daisy tease out Rosie's curls. Josie adjusted the blonde extension braid, winding it neatly around her head like a tiara.

"What's up, kiddo?" Daisy asked. "You look like you have something to say."

Rosie met her eyes in the mirror. Allison gave her red-haired aunt a tentative smile.

"Not something to say. I really hoped I'd learn more about my grandmother, your sister, Anna. I've heard a little, but what was she really like?"

Rosie, Josie, and Daisy paused what they were doing. They glanced at each other.

Allison squirmed. *Maybe I shouldn't have asked.*

Josie finished pinning her braid. "Imagine that you're a counselor in high school. A young lady comes in, furious, frustrated, angry. She stomps around your office ranting." Josie changed her voice in imitation of a high school girl. "I hate my sisters! They're self-centered, foul-mouthed hussies. I try, I try so hard to get them to behave, but no, oh no. The two older ones are sluts. It wouldn't surprise me if they drank. I try to tell them they shouldn't behave the way they do. They oughtn't use such language. They mustn't dress so outlandishly. They never listen. They just laugh at me, make fun of me. My younger sister is so selfish she doesn't even notice anyone else, much less care."

Daisy joined in, taking over the role of Anna. "My father doesn't care. He encourages their sick, stupid behavior. He joins in with their silly nonsense. And then they go off together, doing who knows what. My mother only cares about my younger sister. She spends all her time with *her*." Daisy spit the word *her*.

Allison felt her color drain. These were the same words her father had used to describe them. This was the way he had led her to believe her aunts actually behaved. She glanced over at Rosie.

Tears pooled in her silent aunt's eyes.

Josie, radiating anger, turned to Allison, demanding, "What would you say to that girl? What would you, as a counselor, say?"

Pondering, trying to process what they had just said about the way Anna viewed them, meshed with what her father had told her about her aunts, Allison hesitated. "I would first hear her out. I'd reflect back to her what she said she's feeling. 'You feel very frustrated by your sisters' behavior. It sounds like you don't get much support from your parents.' Once she's calmed down a bit, I might ask her why she feels it's her responsibility to make you behave better."

Josie snorted. "Because she's a controlling busybody. Honestly, I could not wait to get out of that house and away from her constant badgering and sniping." Allison glanced at Rosie and saw a tear sliding down her cheek, along the wrinkles by her mouth, to hang as a quivering drop on the point of her chin.

Allison continued, "I'd listen to what Anna had to say, let her express her anger. Then I'd hope to be able to talk to a sister, get the other side of the story." Allison spoke softly, calmly, as she would to a client who came to her upset.

Daisy shook her head in pained memory. Accepting that as a cue, Allison asked her, "What would you have told me if I'd asked you about your sister, Anna?"

But it was Josie who whirled, nearly shouting, pointing at Rosie. "Anna tortured Rosie! She never let up. She hit her, made fun of her, teased her . . . incessantly."

Rosie put both hands to her face, fighting to hold her emotions in check.

"Did it get any easier when we left, Rosie? When you were able to move into our room, did she stop?" Daisy reached over, gently touching her younger sister's arm.

Rosie shook her head, hands still covering her face.

"Why didn't you tell us?" Josie demanded. "Why didn't you tell Mama?"

Rosie's answer was barely a mouse squeak. "Because you didn't hear her cry at night."

Shocked silence.

With a frown of confusion, Josie lifted her hands in question. "What?"

Rosie lowered her hands and looked teary-eyed at her sisters. "You didn't hear her *cry* at night."

Allison felt heat rise to her face. Her stomach clenched. Rosie's pain, reflecting that of her sister, Anna, radiated.

"Cry?" The word exploded from Josie. "About what?"

Rosie looked from one sister to the other. "Didn't you see? Josie, you were so smart. We'd come along after you in school and teachers would comment that they hoped we were as smart and hard-working and intelligent as you were." She looked to Daisy. "We'd go to gym class and be asked if we were going to join sports teams and if we were anywhere near as good an athlete as you." Rosie didn't have to mention her own skill. "Daddy took you two camping. He took you fishing. He took you to ball games. He never took me or Anna."

"Neither of you wanted to," Josie countered. "Anna said over and over she had no intention of ever going camping just to get eaten by mosquitos, or to games just to watch a bunch of jocks throw balls at each other."

"Because she knew Daddy wouldn't take her!" Rosie wailed. "He never took her anywhere. Mama spent all her time with me. We were always going somewhere to sing or get lessons or practice or perform. And everywhere we went as a family, people commented on hearing me sing, or on Daisy's prowess at sports, or how brilliant you were. No one ever complimented Anna."

Daisy took a turn, answering her sister gently. "Did it ever occur to you why Daddy took Josie and me places so often?"

Rosie shook her head.

Allison leaned forward, waiting for the rest of the story. One of her professors had said this was when you often got the kick-in-the-gut piece that made you understand the family dynamics.

"Daddy saw how miserable we were with Anna constantly

pestering us. He took us so many places to give us an escape from her, to let us have some fun, to laugh. You know full well how she shut down any fun we had as a family, calling it stupid or immature or some other putdown. You saw how it made Mama wilt, how hard Daddy tried to keep the positive feeling going as Anna stomped out of the room or snarled her criticism. That's why he would take us places. He knew Mama protected you, got you out of there so you could find joy in your singing."

Rosie sniffed in misery. "But where was Anna's joy?'

There it is. The kick in the gut.

Allison gave the three sisters a moment to process, then broke the silence. "You've now answered your own questions."

Josie gave a bark of laughter. "Then why go to a counselor? If we can solve these things ourselves? Why would we need *you?*"

Allison smiled. "In seventy years, you never worked out the answer. It was when you asked me, put yourself in Anna's place, and then heard all three sides that you realized what was going on. That's why I said it's important to talk to other people in the family, siblings, parents." Allison thought about the things her father had told her, the one side she'd heard about her three aunts, and how very wrong they were. "Siblings usually take on roles—the smart one, the athlete, the silly one, the pretty one, the trouble-maker, and, one of the hardest roles . . . the good one. The roles of smart, athletic, and talented were taken. Was Anna pretty?"

Daisy shook her head, then looked up, her mouth an *O* of realization. "She tried! Remember? She wanted to go to a beauty parlor and learn how to use makeup. Mama wouldn't let her." She faced Allison. "Her hair was like yours, straight, brown . . . sorry, honey, but nothing special. Her features were plain."

Allison nodded. "So, she chose one of the most difficult roles. The Good One. You see it in so many fairy tales. Cinderella is always good and ends up with the prince. As girls especially, we're raised with such nonsense. Be good and submissive like Cinderella and you get your prince, or be beautiful and braindead like Sleeping Beauty or Snow White and you get your prince. Anna wanted to be noticed. She wanted desperately to be the *Good One*, trying to force your parents to see that she was better, *gooder* than you. But she didn't get the attention she craved, so she found herself in the opposite role . . . the Bad One."

For a time, the room was silent.

"That's sad. Explained the way you have, that's really sad," Daisy mused, finally.

"But she had a good life," Rosie finished. "She found a good husband, left the area, and had three nice children. She had a good life."

"Until she died," Josie snorted.

"No, wait." Allison held up one hand, turning to Rosie. "You said she left the area. Was that her choice or her husband's?"

"Well, she had two beaus. One was going into the family business in Traverse City, and the other had been hired by a manufacturing company that wanted him to move away to Syracuse."

Allison smiled and leaned back. "And she chose the one who was moving out of state."

"Is that important?" Daisy leaned in, curious.

Nodding, Allison answered. "It might be. Maybe by moving, leaving behind those who knew her, she could recreate herself. Now she could drop the role that hadn't worked and become someone new. My father always spoke of her as a *perfect mother*—sang them to sleep as children, read to them, made cookies and home-made bread. She organized wonderful birthday parties and decorated lavishly for Christmas. I guess that's why hearing such negative things about her behavior as a girl is such a shock. I've heard almost all wonderful things from my father."

"Saint Anna." Josie put her hands prayerfully together.

Daisy chuckled. "I'm just glad she found her way. I wish you'd been around for us to talk to sooner so maybe we'd have realized this when she was still alive." She continued pensively. "It could have made a difference. We could have rebuilt our relationships, maybe, and known her better."

Rosie wove her way between them to the vanity sink where she grabbed a tissue and honked impressively. She giggled. "I'm glad I wasn't the Good One."

. . . .

The travel that day progressed slowly, with several stops. First, Daisy insisted they detour to Mammoth Caves. They ate lunch there after insisting that Rosie and Allison get on the shortest of the cave tours. Allison wasn't sure that Rosie could do even that tour since it included a number of stairs up and down and some uneven paths. But using Allison for support and staying toward the back of the group so she wouldn't feel pressured to go faster, Rosie did fine and loved seeing the vast caverns she had heard so much about.

Back over to Interstate 65, they detoured over to Route 31 East to make a stop at Lincoln's birthplace. As with Mammoth Caves, Daisy had been several times and Josie had visited as well. As they showed Rosie the spring for which it was named and then a look through the museum, Allison walked the grounds, up to the marble building that contained the rough log cabin where Abraham Lincoln was born. Her aunts stayed in the visitor center, looking at exhibits and checking out the books. A light rain sent Allison scurrying back to join them. They drove on to Knob Creek, the cabin up the way where Lincoln spent his childhood before the family moved to Indiana. The rain let up for them to eat a snack outside, watching butterflies flit among blue and yellow wildflowers in the open meadow and listening to a serenade of early summer bird song.

Daisy guided her to the Blue Grass Parkway through Lexington horse country where they drove leisurely by white-fenced fields and perfectly manicured properties of the wealthy.

Leaving horse-country, Daisy guided Allison north to pull in at the fanciest hotel of the trip. As Allison brought the car to a halt under the overhang of the entryway, a young man ran out to help Allison haul the suitcases from the trunk, load them on a cart, and escort the ladies to the front desk. Another took the keys and parked the Buick for them. Rosie gazed around the opulent reception area. Marble tables stood firm under immense heavy vases of fresh cut flowers. Brocade sofas and chairs invited patrons to rest, to partake of coffee from a neat side table, or to lounge before the flickering gas fireplace.

Daisy got them checked in and the bellhop escorted them to their connecting rooms, asking several times if they had everything they needed. Did they need ice? Would they like a bottle of wine sent up? Allison asked how to get to the large swimming pool she had seen on the brochure on the counter.

"It's our last night out," Daisy explained. "We are going all out. There's a fine restaurant here and a nightclub. We intend to make full use of both. Who gets to shower first?" This last comment she directed at her roommate, Josie.

Allison turned to go back into the room she shared with Rosie.

"Do you have something nice to wear this evening?" Daisy asked.

Remembering back to first meeting Josie at the airport, when she realized in consternation that she had not brought anything dressy, Allison shook her head. "But I really liked that stretchy red blouse you loaned me when we went to the beer festival back in Virginia."

Daisy smiled at the memory. "That looked good on you." She went to dig it out of her suitcase.

After a luxurious shower with two massaging heads and thick, white, terry towels, Allison found Rosie still working on her make-up and hair. She'd removed her thick support hose to take her shower and chose not to go through the struggle of putting them back on for the evening.

Rosie looked over at Allison in her red blouse and black slacks, the dressiest thing she'd brought along. "You look fine. Why don't you go wander, find the pool, and meet us in the dining room in an hour?"

. . . .

The pool wasn't hard to find, and it certainly looked inviting. This would be the last chance for Allison to be able to swim in something warm, not recent-ice-melting cold, or muddy, or slimy with pond weeds. She sighed. Maybe while the aunts were in the nightclub, she could duck back here for a swim.

Forty-five minutes later, Allison waited in the posh sitting area, watching the bank of elevators for her aunts to arrive for dinner. She rose when they stepped out. Josie wore a swirling, pleated calf-length, silver-gray skirt and sapphire-blue silk blouse. Her blonde hair once more neatly piled and topped off with her crowning extension braid. Daisy, beside her, would have fit in at an upscale Hollywood soiree—lined silk slacks in deep gold, topped with a diaphanous ivory blouse; a chunky, gold druzy quartz ring graced one hand; an understated necklace of filigree gold beads finished off her look. She, too, had added some of the extensions to her updo. One braid had a gold cord braided into it, adding a bit of sparkle.

Rosie followed behind. Two strings of Flapper-length beads dressed up her blue, yellow, and pink muumuu. Allison grinned and waved to them.

"Wow, you look wonderful!" she greeted.

Josie preened, and Daisy replied with a lady-like dip of her head. Rosie giggled.

With dinner, the ladies ordered wine, Allison a ginger ale.

"Why don't you drink?" Josie asked brusquely.

Allison shrugged. "I could give you a number of reasons. My friends wanted to drink to prove they were grown up." She smiled with a small head shake. "I was enjoying being a kid. But I guess really—" She straightened up, hands folded on the table in front of her, and replied, "I guess I felt it just isn't ladylike. It isn't proper."

Josie and Daisy looked at each other, eyes large and round. Rosie put a hand to her mouth. Allison looked from one to the other, confused.

"It's like you were channeling Anna. That was her!" Daisy shook her head in wonder. "For a moment there, it was like we were sitting at the table with our sister."

Josie reached over to pat Allison's arm. "But we *like* you. Honestly, you're the way we wish Anna could have been."

With a look of amazement directed at her sister, Daisy breathed, "Yes!" Then to Allison, "You are the way we wish Anna had been. That's why I have so enjoyed this trip. I just realized it. It's like, finally, all four of us sisters being together and getting along."

Hand still to her mouth, Rosie nodded in delighted agreement.

Allison remembered back to that evening around the pool,

when they had all held hands after Daisy had commented, "That's what sisters are for."

"I'm glad I can be an Anna you like. My regret is that I didn't know you sooner. I have really enjoyed getting to know you, and. . ." she waved her hands expansively, ". . . everything we've done." She finished with a huge grin, echoed on the faces of her aunts.

Dinner consisted of wonderful food and even better conversation. Then it was on to the night club. Drinks and good music, but further conversation became difficult. Two drinks in, the music got fast and loud. On the horseshoe shaped bench seat, Rosie wiggled in time to the beat. Daisy leaned over to Allison. "This is when one of us should start dancing on the table." She shook her head. "Don't think it's going to be me this time. How about you?"

Making a show of peering carefully under their small oval table at the one supporting leg, Allison shook her head as well. "Table wouldn't support me. I'd end up in someone's lap."

Leaning in to hear what they were saying, Josie barked a laugh. "That's the whole point, honey." She smirked wolfishly.

Allison grinned and shook her head. Now that was the aunt her father warned her about!

She raised her hands over her head, swaying, tossed her hair and imitated Rosie, wiggling her butt on the bench seat. Daisy laughed and joined her, hands in the air. "If there can be chair-yoga, there can certainly be chair dancing!" she called out.

Josie joined them. Dance strobe lights glinted off her large diamond ring and the two clasp bracelets she wore—diamond and sapphires the same blue as her blouse.

Allison found herself smiling at her, thinking. *She is so put together.*

The music ended.

A waitress came by their table, placing fresh drinks in front of each. "Those gentlemen over there were impressed with your dancing and wondered if they could join you."

Seated on bar stools were two good-looking elderly men giving them a hopeful smile and finger wave.

Josie replied with a come-hither motion. Allison grinned. *What would Dad say? What would Anna say?* Allison knew what she'd say.

She leaned over so Daisy and Josie could both hear her. "Have fun. I'm going for a swim." And to Rosie, "I'll see you back in the room. Enjoy." She gave up her seat so the two gentlemen could sit down and join her aunts at the table.

Her swim lasted an hour. Another hour, she spent quietly at poolside reading a book Josie had picked up about the Lincolns. The underwater pool lights threw dancing patterns on the walls. Packing up, she wrapped herself in the thick terry towel and headed for their room.

Now what? None of them have returned. Do I check on them? Do I march down there demanding why they haven't come back, as Anna would? Is that what it would look like if I went to check on them? They're adults. Would they feel like I was treating them like children? Will I find out my father was right? Will I find them drunk and in some guy's bed?

Remember, Daisy said sisters look out for one another.

Allison plunked down on the bed, torn between getting dressed and going to see what her aunts were up to or going to bed and letting them have their last fling before heading back to a solitary apartment, senior living, and a husband with dementia.

That's what sisters are for. They watch each other's backs.

Allison got dressed and headed back down to the night club. She stood in the doorway. Josie swirled on the dance floor to a lively waltz. Her pleated skirt swung wide as she moved gracefully. Daisy sat at their table, smiling and laughing as she chatted with one of the two gentlemen who had bought them drinks.

Frowning, she didn't see Rosie. *Did I miss her on the way down from their room?*

Making her way over to their table, she smiled as Daisy looked up and acknowledged her. "How was your swim?"

Thanks, Aunt Daisy. I was wondering how I was going to start this conversation without it looking like I'm being critical of you.

"It was wonderful. I wanted to let you know that I was done and I'm ready to head for bed. Do you need me for anything?"

Daisy introduced her briefly to the gentleman at the table. A new dance started. Josie and her beau moved close and swayed gently to the music. And there was Rosie. She, too, had found a partner. She looked blissful as she moved to the music.

Daisy smiled her thanks. "We're fine. You've had a long day. Go ahead to the room. I promise, we'll be fine." Allison thought she was done, but Daisy turned back. "Thank you for checking on us."

"That's what sisters are for." Allison glanced again at Josie and Rosie. *I want to learn ballroom dancing. I want to have that look of bliss and delight on my face.*

She headed up to their room.

Chapter 27

HEADING HOME

The door eased open. Rosie tiptoed in, humming. Leaving the lights off, she stubbed a toe with a stifled yelp and whimper. Allison surreptitiously checked the bedside clock. *2:20.* Rosie had closed down the nightclub.

"You can turn on the light. I don't mind," Allison told her.

"Oh, did I wake you?" Rosie groped her way to the wall, feeling for the light switch.

Allison turned on the bedside lamp.

Rosie giggled. "We had such fun!"

"Did Josie and Daisy just get back as well?"

Rosie shook her head, curls tumbling, hand to her mouth, and her eyes lit with delight. "Josie is still out. She went for a walk with her gentleman!"

Allison sat up, now fully awake. "She went out? Out where?"

Stop. Don't be like Anna. Josie is an adult. She'll be fine.

Rosie's smile faded. "Do you think she'll be all right? Is something wrong?"

Allison forced a smile. "Just curious. I think she'll be fine. Time for you to get ready for bed. We have a long day tomorrow."

Rosie's smile returned. She dance-stepped over to her bedside lamp. "You can turn off yours. Oh, we did have fun! I wish you'd found someone as well." Gathering her nightgown and kit, Rosie headed to the bathroom, humming happily.

· · · · · · · · · · · ·

Allison awoke early, just as the sky began to turn pink. Gazing out the window, listening to Aunt Rosie's gentle squeaking, she thought about what her aunts had said. Her father had always told her how wonderful his mother, Anna, had been. But she knew that his siblings didn't feel the same way. Her father's sister had called Anna 'hard to please' and 'demanding.' His brother had mentioned once that she could be smothering.

Things now made sense. Anna, the Good One, had become Anna the Perfect Parent. Anna, the Good One, had alienated her sisters, had hurt her parents, had stressed her family.

Allison got up as the sun cast its rays across the roof tops. Leaving Rosie sleeping soundly, she dressed and headed out for an early morning walk. Stopping by the room next door, she listened at the door, wondering if she could hear both aunts. She heard Daisy's muted bombing runs, but nothing else.

A nearby park, populated with dog walkers and morning joggers, provided a relaxing place to take a stroll as the sun crept above a distant bank of clouds. Heat increased as the sun climbed higher. Joggers headed home to shower before heading to work. Dog walkers collected their balls, sticks, and poo bags. Allison headed back, hoping it wouldn't be up to her to rouse her sleeping aunts.

Listening at the doors, all remained quiet. It was only 9:30.

Plenty of time. Well, with a lot of help from Allison, it would be plenty of time to pack up and get out. She shrugged and wiggled into her still-damp bathing suit. One last quick swim in the hotel's wonderful pool.

Back in the room a half hour later, Allison became worried. None of the aunts had roused, still sleeping soundly. She took a quick shower, packed her own suitcase, put the wet suit in a plastic bag, and hauled it down to the lobby. No one waited at the front desk. Allison approached.

"May I help you?"

Allison gave their room number. "My great aunts had a late evening. They stayed until the night club closed and are still asleep. Is it possible for us to have a later checkout?" Allison stressed *great aunts* and wondered if she should have said octogenarian aunts.

The pert young lady turned to tap efficiently on her computer. After scrolling, tapping, with a gentle frown that would not disturb her perfect make-up, she turned back with a professional smile. "That does not seem to be a problem. We can move the checkout to noon or slightly later." She gave Allison an eyebrow-lifted 'anything else?' smile.

"Thank you . . . um." Allison never felt efficient or professional. "They'll be hungry. Should I make a reservation for lunch?"

"I can certainly help you with that." More perky efficiency. "Which dining area would you like?"

Feeling flummoxed, Allison looked around as though she could see both dining areas from where she stood.

Noting her confusion, the young woman pulled out a brochure, flipped it open, and showed Allison photos of the two dining rooms. One was fancy, candle-lit, and dark, where they had dined the evening before. The other looked more like a place to have a lunch that one could afford. She pointed to that one. "They were doing some drinking, maybe not next to a lot of noise or too sunny." The one photo showed morning sun bathing the nearby tables in light.

Tapping the keyboard with her long, perfect fingernails, Allison was told that of course an appropriate table could be found, one overlooking the back garden. She made the reservation for 12:15, lunch for four. "Thank you," Allison murmured as the young woman's attention switched to the man striding over from the elevator.

She dragged her suitcase out to the carefully camouflaged parking area, hidden behind a row of trees and flowering shrubs, loaded it into the Buick's trunk, and headed back up to the rooms.

I have to wake them.

Starting with Rosie, Allison called softly, then shook her shoulder gently. Rosie squeaked and thrashed against the covers. *"What?"*

Allison flashed back to the morning at Assateague when she was awakened by Rosie bouncing on their bed, chirping, *"Wakie Wakie!"*

"We need to get going. It's almost eleven."

"Ooohh! Oh no!" Rosie struggled to get herself untangled from the covers and get her legs to the side of the bed. "Are Daisy and Josie up? Am I late?"

"No, relax, Aunt Rosie. I've already gotten us a later checkout time. I haven't heard any sound from next door. I need to get them up as well. You start getting ready, and I'll see if I can get them up."

Rosie giggled. "We were up late. Josie went out walking after Daisy and I headed up to bed."

Allison had heard Daisy's unique snoring, but that was all. *Is Josie even here?*

Only one way to find out. Allison went to the room Daisy and Josie shared and rapped sharply on the door. She heard an explosive snort. Yup, Aunt Josie was in there.

She somehow had all three of her slow-moving, drowsy, aged aunts out of the room and down to the dining room by 12:30. She already had their suitcases loaded in the Buick. Last time. Last morning out on the road. Allison smiled at the memories.

Daisy and Rosie chatted happily after polishing off their first mugs of coffee and with a good start on the second. But Josie quietly stared out the window, gazing at the small garden behind the hotel. Inattentive, distracted.

This is not like her. Did something happen last night?

While waiting for their lunches to arrive, Allison got up the nerve to ask. "Is something wrong?"

Josie turned her gaze to Allison and her sisters. Dreamily, with a gentle smile, she announced, "I think I'm in love."

Allison's jaw dropped.

Daisy laughed aloud.

Rosie giggled.

"But you just met him!" Allison blurted.

No-nonsense Josie immediately returned. "That's why, at my age, you have to move fast."

"But he lives here! You'll never see him again."

Daisy laughed at Allison's consternation. "Oh, get over it. Josie, tell us all," she demanded.

"He doesn't live here. This is a hotel." Josie corrected her niece. "He lives in Chicago and has a daughter he visits several times a year who lives in Charlevoix." Josie added for Allison's benefit, "That's about an hour north of where I live. He said he'd come and visit." Josie went dreamy-eyed. "There are several hotels nearby, or he could use my pull-out couch and stay in my apartment." She sighed.

Rosie clapped her hands in delight. Daisy hooted and made a rude gesture, nearly knocking over her coffee.

"What is this Romeo's name?" Daisy demanded as the waitress set their sandwich plates in front of them.

Josie, eyes sparkling, hands clasped under her chin, gazed at the restaurant's crystal chandelier. "You met Charles last night. He's a retired lawyer—a family lawyer—not some shyster or ambulance chaser. His wife passed away several years ago and he has two daughters, the one in Charlevoix and one in Atlanta. He's sweet and dances beautifully. He still has hair and most of his own teeth."

Daisy burst into laughter. Even Rosie laughed, girlishly, aloud.

Allison choked.

It was almost 2 p.m. when the Buick was finally brought around, and all the aunts and luggage were loaded for the last day of driving. After circumventing Cincinnati, Allison had clear sailing.

"Oh, my gosh!" Eyes still on the road, Allison raised a hand to her face.

"What?" Josie scanned the road ahead. Daisy checked for idiot lights or car problems while Rosie stopped humming and leaned forward in concern.

"I just realized, Dad is the Good One."

That's why he never wanted me to meet you. That's why he could never say anything nice about you three. He followed his mother's lead.

Thoughtful silence filled the car.

Josie leaned forward and asked gently, "What about you? Don't drink, no boyfriend, no partying."

Allison thought, and felt heat rise to her face. She remembered her father's critical assessment of her wanting to be a counselor. "So, you want to tell people what they're doing wrong and how they should live their lives?" She thought about how much that had hurt. She thought about how much her father's opinion mattered to her.

Is that why I'm so unsure, so self-critical about going into counseling? So doubtful about my ability to be any good at it?

Slowly shaking her head, her concentration on the traffic on the highway, she responded, "No. No, I'm a Daddy Pleaser."

Daisy gazed at her, seeing the heightened color, the deeper breathing. "You're just realizing that, aren't you?"

Allison nodded. "It makes sense. It's why I believed everything he told me. I've always worked hard for his approval."

Which included not doing anything wild or inappropriate.

Josie, still leaning forward, asked, "And your brother?"

Allison nodded in realization. "He and Mom are close. They laugh a lot, joke around. They drink socially and my brother likes parties and getting wild. At least, what my dad considers wild."

"And that's why you don't," Josie finished for her. She then smirked wickedly. "So, are you going to drink now?"

Allison barely hesitated, made eye contact in the rearview mirror with her senior aunt, and shook her head. "No. I'm going to do what's right for ME." Flicking another glance at Josie, she continued, "And I do go to parties. I've been very popular, especially these last two years. I get invited to quite a few off-campus parties."

Daisy grinned and jumped in, "Designated driver."

Allison nodded. "Which makes me very popular." She then added, for Josie's benefit, with a mischievous grin, "I can get *drunk* on ginger ale and dill pickles, or good dark chocolate. I have been accused of being falling-down drunk, laughing and having a great time, on ginger ale and dill pickles."

Josie flopped back in her seat. "That, I'd like to see."

"Then as others start getting more wasted, I find my psychologist kicking in. As self-control weakens and alcohol takes over, I get to see more of what is hidden, what people work to control. And it isn't always pretty. That's another reason I don't want to drink. I've seen too many people do and say stupid things. I've heard too many guys say they don't remember the drive home, that their car knew the way. Or that they ran off the road and the car got them back on the road and home." She shook her head. "I don't want to be on the road with them. I don't want my friends who have only had a drink or two to drive home with someone like that on the road. In high school, I had a friend killed by a drunk driver."

The aunts remained silent, feeling that Allison had more to say.

"Girls in my dorm, they'd go to a party, get drunk, then come in upset, crying that they'd awoken in some guy's bed. Or, worse, that they passed out and realized . . . well, that they'd been raped. One girl in my dorm committed suicide after getting drunk at a party. I didn't know her well, but something happened, something bad enough that she couldn't live with it. That happened in my freshman year. I wish there'd been a counselor on hand. It may have saved her life."

Allison caught a glimpse of Josie reaching forward and putting a restraining hand on Daisy's shoulder as Daisy was about to say something. Josie made eye contact in the rearview mirror, stern, concerned, and silent.

She knows. She knows to keep her mouth shut. She knows that silence will encourage a person to fill that silence. Silence gives time for the person to gather thoughts, even for realization to occur. Well done, Aunt Josie.

"I usually went to parties with the same two to four friends." She flicked a glance back at Rosie. "I'm not as good at reading danger as you are. Or I wasn't paying attention. There were a couple times when one of our female friends had too much to drink and was being hit on. Remember, I mentioned Cass, my gay friend? He was good at reading danger signs. Just a few months ago, we were at a party. Cass came over and, like you, Aunt Rosie, said we should go. Our friend, Lacey, was very happy, and had found a very attentive admirer. He'd just bought her yet another drink. Cass stomped over and declared that Lacey was his girlfriend and they were heading out. Our other friend whispered to Lacey that the guy was trying to get her drunk, most likely to have his way with her. She threw the drink at him and we walked out." Allison pursed her mouth in consternation. "Cass had me drive to an all-night pancake house. He had us order food and coffee and got us all laughing and joking. We had more fun there than at the party. Cass is—" Allison shook her head again, self-doubt evident in her expression. "Cass is going to be a fantastic counselor."

"So are you!" Josie snapped. "You are going to be a very good counselor. Don't doubt yourself."

Allison noted the *very good* rather than *excellent*. Again, Josie seemed to know that using *excellent* would have rung false.

"Aunt Josie, you waited for me to continue. Where did you learn about wait time? That's a skill most people lack."

"You forget, Arnie and I owned bookstores. I have always read prodigiously. I did my share of reading psychology, sociology, journalism interviews, and true crime which included interrogation techniques. All of those talked about the importance of keeping your mouth shut. People tend to be uncomfortable with silence and want to fill it. It also gives the other person important time to process, to gather one's thoughts, and to find the correct way to express those thoughts clearly."

Allison nodded. "You did well."

Allison drove on in silence. Daisy gazed at her, taking in Allison's demeanor and expression, the pursed mouth and tense muscles around her eyes. "You are either thinking about something very deeply or we need to stop because you're going to erupt. Give."

Allison shot a glance at Daisy beside her, then flicked a look in the rearview mirror. "Well, I . . . uh. What if—" She frowned, hands gripping the wheel hard, eyes straight ahead. "What if I concentrated on counseling seniors?" she blurted.

Daisy stared at her, or at least in the direction of her right ear. Josie and Rosie stared at the back of her head.

Allison gritted her teeth.

"Aunt Daisy, you're facing . . . well . . . Barth's illness." She glanced sideways to see the reaction. "You must have questions. Wouldn't you like some support, someone with whom you could share your concerns, talk things through?"

Josie snorted. "People like that are called *friends.*"

"Friends can be critical of you. Friends can get caught up playing games like, *well, if you think that's bad . . .* or just mindless placating. What about you, Aunt Josie? If you hadn't gone to a financial counselor, you may have been taken for half your money, or more, when you married that guy in Colorado. Aunt Rosie, you finally revealed pain and heartache that has been with you for decades. Is it a relief to finally have it out and shared?" She flicked a look at Rosie, huddled against the window.

Rosie straightened slowly, pondering the question. "I feel much better. And you helped us all understand Anna. Is that what you would do? Talk, and listen, and help seniors find relief and release? It would be nice to face . . . well, face our demise with fewer regrets. It would be nice to heal old wounds, maybe even mend rifts in families before it's too late."

Rosie's statements once more brought thoughtful contemplation to the vehicle's occupants.

Daisy nodded thoughtfully. "That sounds like a very interesting idea."

"You could set up a practice going to senior living facilities, maybe rotating and visiting one every week or every two weeks." Josie shook her head contemplating the range of possibilities. "You'd be grief counselor, marriage, end-of-life. I've read there are counselors for people who are going blind or deaf, who help people and family members adjust to catastrophic injuries like after a bad accident, or in our case, aging."

Silence enveloped the car as they all thought about the possibilities.

"You do realize," Daisy began, "instead of seeing those you counsel grow up . . . you will see them age and die."

Casting a serious glance at her Aunt Daisy, Allison replied, "Yes, I have thought of that. But aren't all of us dying?"

Josie snorted. "That's the way some people look at it. I'm living. I intend to die living."

Allison remembered Josie saying that same thing the day the three sisters took off with the motorcycle guys. She nodded. "Yes, I remember you saying that before. So, I will be helping people who are living to hopefully enjoy living more. That's really what it's all about, no matter what age. Aunt Josie, you said people can talk to their friends rather than a counselor, but loneliness is a major problem among the elderly."

Josie nodded. "You also pointed out that friends make lousy counselors." Pursing her lips with a thoughtful frown, Josie added, "Friends can also be the reason we need counselors."

With a look of surprise, Allison nodded in agreement.

"I think you're on to something." Daisy patted Allison's tense shoulder. "It sounds like you've put some thought into this."

Allison relaxed into a smile of gratitude and relief. "I hope my parents agree."

No-nonsense Josie snapped. "It's your decision. You said earlier that you were going to do what's right for you, not what pleases either of your parents."

Easier said than done, she thought.

Chapter 28

ARRIVING IN TOLEDO

As they approached Toledo, Allison felt tension rising in the car. Daisy leaned against the passenger window, fist to her mouth, deep lines of worry at her eyes and mouth.

Rosie clasped her oversized purse in her lap, folding and unfolding the shoulder strap. On the other side of the back seat, Josie sat glaring out the window, legs and arms crossed, foot tapping arrhythmically.

"Aunt Josie?" Allison caught her senior aunt's eye in her rearview mirror. "You played a game with your dad on trips, naming animals or places you'd been. On our way home from a trip, Mom played *what did you like best?* So, each of you, what did you like best or remember most vividly on this trip?" She glanced at each aunt. Daisy straightened up, looking relieved and interested. Rosie's eyes lit up as she murmured a soft "Oooo." Josie shot her an analyzing glance and smiled.

Daisy answered first. "We did so much, it's hard to choose."

Allison nodded. She had them. With a slight, smug smile, she thought, *Maybe I will be a good counselor.* "Good point. In my family, we often found that it was something someone else chose or something we just did spontaneously that was a favorite because it was something we would have never chosen. Maybe it took us out of our comfort zone. So, each of you chose three places to visit. Name the one of those three that. . . " She realized that especially in Rosie's case, *liked* was not the appropriate word. ". . . impressed you the most. Then name one that impressed you that you did not choose."

Rosie's eyes sparkled with fond memories. "There were so many! I so enjoyed the afternoon we took off riding motorcycles."

Josie hooted. "That was a riot!"

Daisy smiled at Allison. "I know it scared the be-jeepers out of you, but it was a favorite for me, as well."

Allison rolled her eyes and shook her head. "Okay, you all agree that taking off with a motorcycle gang was your agreed upon highlight. It's certainly something I will never forget."

Josie guffawed. Daisy chuckled and patted her arm.

Rosie giggled.

So did Allison. "That's a tale I'm going to be telling for many years. And it will likely *improve* with the telling." She warned with a suggestive eyebrow waggle.

Casting a warm smile at Allison, Daisy started again. "Let's see, I chose Colonial Williamsburg, The Villages, and Carter's home in Plains. I'd been to two of them, so I have to say our trip to The Villages to visit Norman and Jean."

Allison nodded. That's what she'd expected. "That was quite an eye-opener."

"That was quite an eye-roller." Josie amended with an amused snort.

Rosie giggled. "And you thought the thing for golf balls on the golf cart was a urinal."

Allison shook her head in amusement. "A mistake I'd rather forget."

"Okay, Josie, your turn while I try to winnow down my choice for my other favorite," Daisy directed.

Allison recalled that Josie had chosen the cities. She remembered Rosie singing karaoke in Atlantic City and being called a cougar, but Josie hadn't been there for that.

When she glanced back and saw the wolfish smile emerging on her four-times-married aunt Josie, she knew what was coming.

"That kid, Antoine, in Philadelphia. I still remember the way you lip-locked him, Daisy."

Allison laughed. "I remember the way his arms stuck straight out, spasming!"

Hand to mouth, eyes sparkling, Rosie giggled.

Allison felt her heart swell. *I am so glad we were able to do this for Rosie. For all three of them. I'm so glad Mom got me to do this . . . and that I agreed.*

Rosie straightened up, staring ahead out the front window. "I got to see Banker Ponies frisking on the beach and racing at sunrise. I found out that a young lady about whom I've worried for years grew up to be a strong, dedicated lady." Gentle lines appeared between Rosie's eyes. "And I finally got to say goodbye to Andy with my sisters by my side."

Allison felt tears gather. A quick glance told her she wasn't the only one. Daisy reached over in the back seat and took Rosie's hand.

Clearing her throat, Daisy began on the second half of the challenge. "There are so many to choose from. But I see a pattern in my strongest memories." She gazed at Allison. "I was very impressed with how you handled being pulled off the boat in Okefenokee. I've been impressed with how thoughtful and patient you have been, taking us right up to entryways, pulling the car up close when it was raining, hauling our luggage without complaint. And, finally, how you have gotten us to talk, *seriously* talk, not just kibitz. In short, the high point for me has been getting to know you, Allison."

Okay, thought Allison, *that not only brought tears, but a quivering chin as well!*

Agreement emanated from the rear seat.

Allison was only able to murmur, "Thank you."

"Well, it's hard to top that." Josie finally broke the awkward silence. "So, what did I like best, other than getting to know Allison better. Oh, and learning about Rosie's past." She patted her baby sister on the leg. "And finding out that dear Daisy is still a darn good tour guide. Let's see. Playing poker in Atlantic City, even if I didn't win big; at least I didn't lose big. Meeting and smooching Antoine, then let's see. I guess getting sandblasted while watching horses run and poop on the beach was entertaining. Getting a wet T-shirt contest started at the beer festival. Well, I wish we'd stayed to see the outcome of that. Taking off on motorcycles was a lark, and when we pulled over and hopped out of the car when we saw that jail work crew," she chortled.

"Allison, I thought you were either going to melt into the seat or gun the engine and leave us behind. Then when Daisy got photos of the guy waggling his . . . his privates at us." Josie laughed so hard she snorted and started coughing.

Allison shook her head at the mental image. Not one of her fondest remembrances.

"Watching that guy fall overboard and scream about snakes in Okefenokee was definitely a high point. Then your friends in The Villages." Josie leaned forward to Daisy. "Where did you find those nuts? Finding out about your Andy was quite a shock, little sister. But that singing you did with the van full of church ladies blew me away. I wish we had gotten some photos of them. They were awesome, and so were you." She patted Rosie's leg again. More thoughtfully, she added, "I am also glad we visited Corinth. It gave me some small idea of what our great-grandfather went through in the Civil War. I'm glad he made it home in one piece." She sighed at the memory of the hardships the troops had faced during their stay at Corinth.

"Was there any one thing that stood out?" Daisy asked, turning around so she could see Josie behind her.

Slowly shaking her head, Josie replied, "The whole trip. The whole trip has just been beyond words, better than I could have ever dreamed. And a great part of it is thanks to you, Allison. We would have gone anyway, but you being our *designated driver* made it so much easier. I don't think we would have had the energy or ability at our ages to do half of what we did. Thank you. I don't think you can ever imagine how much this means to us."

Allison felt her chest tighten and tears gather again. She heard Rosie sniffle and start pawing through her handbag for tissues in the seat behind her.

Rosie honked.

Allison giggled.

"Enough drippy stuff," No-nonsense Josie ordered. "Your turn, Rosie."

Daisy interrupted while Rosie finished with her tissue, directing Allison off the interstate and onto a major four-lane into Toledo. Rosie dug in her purse, stalling.

Daisy guided Allison past the university and into a residential area. From there, she had to pay attention to directions, traffic, and pedestrians. Casting a glance back at Rosie, she could hear her humming softly, gazing out the window as she did. Listening carefully, Allison made out the song she'd sung at the Karaoke place in Atlantic City.

Motoring slowly down Daisy's street, Allison noted that her aunt was leaning forward, nervously watching as they got closer to her house. Soon, they both saw what Daisy had needed to see—Barth's dark blue Silverado pickup truck parked safely in the driveway. Daisy let out a swooshing sigh and leaned back. Allison pulled the Buick in next to the truck and popped the trunk.

"We're home!" Josie announced softly.

· · · · · · · · · · · · ·

Daisy gathered the items around her seat, seeming in no hurry to rush in to see Barth. Rosie sniffed and fiddled with her purse. Josie huffed and heaved herself out of the car. "It's over. We're back in the real world. Face it, head on." And she headed resolutely for the front door.

Levering herself out, Daisy followed, patting Barth's truck on the hood as she passed.

Rosie used the door to pull herself upright. Allison hopped out and offered her a hand. Rosie caught her eye. "Do you think he'll be all right?" she asked softly.

"Barth?" Allison asked. "Yes, I think he will."

They followed Daisy, Josie holding the door for them. Through the short foyer, Daisy entered the living room. They could hear the local evening news predicting a light rain that evening and another sunny, warm day tomorrow. Allison saw Daisy pause.

"I'm home," she sang out.

A few steps more and Allison could see Barth, a handsome man, still straight and tall. Light gray hair, slightly curling, drifted lightly just over his ears. Intense gray eyes centered on Daisy then tracked to Josie, then Rosie and Allison, his face fading into confusion.

"You've brought company," he stated.

"You remember my sisters, Josie and Rosie?" Daisy introduced them, putting a hand on each as she said their names. "And this is our grand-niece, Allison," she finished.

Barth smiled, taking Josie's hand and bringing it up as though to kiss it. "The oft-married, card-sharp Josie and our sweet voiced younger sister. Welcome. Now you." He turned to Allison, then looked to Daisy for guidance. "I don't believe I know you." His voice was hesitant.

Allison responded before Daisy could. "We've never met, Uncle Barth, much to my sorrow. I sincerely hope we can now see more of each other."

His gray eyes sparkled and a smile tugged as he took Allison's hand gently in his. He flashed a glance at Josie. "I see you have Josie's silver tongue. It will be my pleasure getting to know you, grand-niece. . . "

"Allison," She filled in for him.

He bowed gallantly over her hand, then turned to Daisy and waved a hand toward the kitchen. "Now I understand why Daryl had me order three pizzas. Ladies, dinner awaits. We have pizza, antipasto salad, and a bottle of wine."

Allison held back a few steps with Josie. "He seems fine."

Josie nodded. "But Daisy had to remind him who we were. He covers well, which is why it took too long to figure out what was going wrong." Josie slowed, putting a hand on Allison's arm. "It's not too bad yet, but it will get worse."

Clustered around the small kitchen table, three pizza boxes lined up on the counter containing something for everyone. Plates were loaded with antipasto, wine glasses were topped off (except no wine for Allison), and dinner stretched to over two hours as the ladies regaled Barth with stories from their trip. He joined in with memories of some of the places they'd visited. Like many with dementia, he remembered things in the past just fine.

Finally, the conversation got around to Barth's trip. Leaning forward in concern, Barth addressed Daisy. "Daryl said you didn't get my note. I expected you back from Detroit the day you picked up your sisters, but you didn't come home. Daryl and I had decided to leave the same morning we thought you were going to leave. But you weren't home, so I left a note."

Daisy shook her head sadly. "I'm sorry. I did try to call you from Detroit. I left a message on both phones that we would come in the following evening. When I got here, you and your truck were gone. I didn't find any note."

Barth shoved his chair back from the table, pushing himself to his feet. "I left it right under the phone where we always leave notes." He pointed to the wall phone, under which were a stack of phone books and takeout menus. "It was right here. I wrote it on the note pad in the drawer." He yanked open the drawer, pulling out and waving a note pad of flowered paper. Then his glance fell on it and his face crumpled. The note he'd left was still on the pad, which he'd put back in the drawer.

Slowly, Barth handed the note to his wife. "I did write it. . . " then his voice faded to that of a hurt, frightened child, ". . . and then I put it back in the drawer."

Daisy reached out her arms. Barth moved into her embrace, head sunk on her shoulder.

Looking on in dismay, Allison whispered, "Anyone could make that mistake."

Heaving on the sobs he tried to control, Barth clutched Daisy. "I'm sorry. I don't even remember you giving me a cell phone to keep on me. Daryl says I lost it. I don't even remember having it. I'm sorry!"

They couldn't hear what Daisy murmured back to him.

Josie motioned for them to quietly leave and give Barth and Daisy privacy. Slipping quietly out of the kitchen, Josie led them to the front door. "Time for a walk," she whispered, easing open the front door.

Allison looked back to the kitchen doorway, swallowing her own emotions.

They are best friends, and more. That will make this loss all the harder. . . for both of them.

Chapter 29

OVER, FOR NOW

Allison kept busy the two days at Daisy's house. She took after-dinner walks during which the sisters told her their memories of growing up in Toledo. It was nice when Josie joined Rosie and Allison for a walk, since most of Rosie's memories revolved around her years in Traverse City. Daisy drove them around the neighborhood, convincing Allison that her mother had been right to insist that Allison needed to be their driver on the road trip.

She got to know Barth. She found him to be sweet, and she understood why it had taken Daisy time to realize something was wrong and why Josie had thought his being forgetful was not a matter for concern. They'd be talking, playing a game, and Barth would drift off, staring into space, then hop up and run out to his shop, or grab a pencil and paper and start drawing a plan, oblivious to everyone around him. But on two occasions, he then looked up confused, disoriented. On those occasions, Daisy reached over and took the notebook from him and redirected him to something else, distracting him and redirecting his attention. His friend Daryl came over and regaled them with tales from their trip together. Most of the time, Barth joined in. Other times, it became obvious he had no memory of what Daryl was telling them. Daryl then asked him if he remembered, and named the place. Barth could remember things in the past. He'd then brighten up and tell of something that happened in that place years ago.

Allison felt touched and impressed at how well both Daryl and Daisy guided Barth to save him the pain and embarrassment of not being able to remember.

Allison also spent considerable time on Daisy's computer. She checked graduate counseling programs at colleges in western New York, northern Ohio, and Michigan. She found that Michigan State had a top-rated adult counseling program. Taking the plunge, she called, got information on transferring to Michigan State for the fall semester, and got the paperwork started. She found herself nearly hyperventilating. She'd done it.

What was I thinking? How am I going to tell Mom and Dad? I can't believe I actually had the courage to do what I know is right. Allison let out a *"Woohoo,"* and tried to high-five herself.

Her only worry during those two days was Rosie. She slept too much. She ate too little. Her level of energy had dropped and her breathing sometimes became labored. Allison helped her each morning to put on her support hose, fearing the swelling in Rosie's legs was increasing.

The night before Josie and Rosie were to fly out, Allison found the two elder sisters in conference. "Allison, can we ask one more favor from you?" Daisy began. Seeing Allison's confident nod, she continued. "We don't think Rosie should fly home. We're both worried about her breathing and getting to the airport alone. She said there is no one to pick her up. She plans to take a taxi. How is she supposed to wrangle that suitcase of hers? We are worried about her going back to her apartment alone."

Assuming they wanted Allison to change her ticket and fly home with Rosie, she nodded agreement.

"Airplane cabins are not pressurized to sea level. We both worry about Rosie's shortness of breath. We've rented a car. It will be brought around here tomorrow morning. We'd like you to drive Rosie home." Both aunts studied her expectantly.

The car's already rented. They knew I'd say yes. Of course, I'll say yes.

Allison nodded. "Of course, I'll drive her. I agree with your decision. I've been worried as well."

Daisy sighed with relief.

Josie relaxed. "We hoped you'd see it that way. Call or e-mail your parents about the change in plans. Can someone pick you up in Rochester?"

Nodding, smiling her own relief, Allison knew that her mother would understand and would gladly make the three-hour drive to pick her up in Rochester.

· · · · · · · · · · · · ·

Snacking in the car was all well and good, but both Allison and Rosie needed a break. They'd made good time after leaving Toledo, only being slowed down a little going around Erie. When Rosie suggested a late lunch/early dinner at Niagara Falls, Allison readily agreed.

The sun shone brightly on the tumbling falls. Rosie suggested they get a burger and sit out on a bench where they could watch the falls and tour boats that braved the spray and swirling waters. Helping Rosie from the car, steadying her as she used Allison's arm and the door to lever herself from her seat, Rosie then took her grandniece's arm, gripping hard as she took a hesitant step up the curb.

Allison tried to hide her concern. Daisy and Josie were so right when they cancelled Rosie's airline flight and insisted Allison drive their sister home.

After finishing half her hamburger, Rosie leaned her head against the back of the bench, enjoying the warm sun on her face. Allison could see that she once more needed a touchup on her hair color and a new perm.

"Allison," Rosie's voice was barely audible. Allison leaned toward her. Rosie opened her eyes to see her niece right there, looming. "Oh," she jerked back startled, then giggled. "I'm so glad you came with us. I had such fun." Rosie smiled, warm memories of the past weeks washing over her.

"I'm glad I got to come as well. I'm really glad."

Rosie smiled, her hands limp in her lap, gazing at the people strolling along the walkway at the river. "I guess we should get going."

Allison gently put her hand over her aunt's wrinkled hands. "If you're too tired, I can get us a room here. We can stop, I don't mind."

Rosie pulled herself together. "No, let's go on. It's only a couple more hours." She rocked forward and back a couple times, getting up momentum to rise. With a little help, Rosie got to her feet. Holding Allison's arm, they strolled slowly along the path, looking over the river at the Needle rising high, overlooking the falls on the Canadian side.

Rosie giggled and pointed. "Minions." Her face lit, the way Allison remembered it had at the beginning of their trip together.

Frowning, Allison looked where Rosie pointed, then laughed in surprise. A line of tourists wound down a steep trail, all draped in yellow ponchos to protect them from the falls' spray. Allison pointed out the boat in the river, just heading under Niagara's wind-driven spray. All the passengers lining the deck were draped in red ponchos. Rosie and Allison stood by the rail watching.

"I did that once," Rosie volunteered.

"It looks fun." They walked on.

Allison helped Rosie back into the front seat, helping lift her right leg up over the frame. "This car is smaller than Daisy's Le Sabre. That was a comfortable car," Rosie said as she pulled the seatbelt over and clicked it.

. . . .

Rosie remained silent during the two-hour drive to Rochester, humming quietly, too quietly for Allison to make out the tune. Driving up Route 490 into Rochester, buildings of the city center came into view, and Rosie pointed to her exit. They wound slowly through low rent residential areas, finally pulling into the parking area of a weathered, red brick apartment building. Allison realized this was the last time she'd be hauling a suitcase out of the trunk. Dragging the suitcase on her right, she offered her left arm to steady Rosie up the three steps to the cement stoop. The stained linoleum on the foyer floor crinkled at the edges. Rosie pushed the button for the ancient elevator. The door slid slowly open, revealing a once elegant interior. Once inside, it inched upward, rattling ominously. Rosie waited, hands clutching her large handbag in front of her with no excitement, no anticipation in her expression.

It took several minutes for Rosie to scrabble through her purse before she remembered she'd put her key for safety in a zippered side pocket. It then took three tries in the poorly lit hall to get the key in the lock. There was no one in the hall to call out a greeting. No doors opening to see who was here. No welcome home. Rosie pushed the old wooden door open, holding it for Allison to drag in the heavy suitcase.

Closing the door, Rosie turned, and stopped. Her shoulders sagged as she gazed at her home. Allison took in the living room and its galley kitchen. A faded floral couch slouched against one wall, a throw pillow at each end. The colors on the newer one may have matched the couch at one time, but now were too bright. An old analog television sat on a stand across from the couch. The side wall was the one area that looked like Rosie, covered with shelves of records, CDs, and even cassette tapes, all surrounding a high-quality stereo system and headphones.

In the galley kitchen, scarred Formica counters ran along one side. A small Formica topped table sat pushed against the far wall. Two chrome and red vinyl chairs, one with a taped-up rip, waited on two sides.

"Should I take this to the bedroom?" Allison asked. Rosie hadn't moved. She merely nodded.

Pulled shades blocked out what little light was left of the westering sun. Allison raised one shade, revealing the wall of the building next door. A single bed huddled in a corner, covered with a white chenille spread. A floral sheet covered the doorway of the small closet. Another stereo combo sat proudly on a battered dresser, surrounded by records and CDs. A bookcase bowed under heavy photo-filled biographies: Elvis, Elton John, Cher, The Beatles, Dolly Parton, Fleetwood Mac, The Supremes, and more. A comfy chair and footrest snuggled next to the bookcase.

Allison wasn't sure where to leave the suitcase. She hauled it up onto the bed and zipped it open.

Back in the living room, Rosie pushed the button on the phone's answering machine. Allison listened with her to the hang ups, robo calls, a wrong number, and the reminder of an upcoming medical appointment. No personal messages.

Rosie pressed erase, then stood upright, eyes scanning the small kitchen. "There's no food. We need to go to the grocery store." Her voice sounded plaintive, almost childlike.

"Let's make a list. I'll go to the store while you call Daisy and let her know you're home safely."

. . . .

Allison ignored the rickety elevator and took the stairs, shopping list in hand, leaving Rosie greeting Daisy and telling of their journey home. Her stomach felt sour, her chest tight. She remembered the rainy morning in the hotel room when Josie mentioned moving to Cherry Ridge, and how Rosie had asked if she could move there too. No wonder Rosie had never invited them in when she and her mother came to visit. She couldn't let go of the image of her aunt walking into her apartment and just shrinking, standing there drooping. She sighed.

Let Josie know, she thought, *let her know that Rosie really did need to move.*

. . . .

Sleeping on the couch wasn't too bad. There were lumps, and it was too short, but that's not what kept Allison awake. She needed to call her mother. She hadn't been ready to call her the night before. Ready, but not ready.

She heard music playing softly from Rosie's bedroom. She made their breakfast of eggs, low sodium turkey bacon, orange juice, and the cinnamon raisin bread that Rosie had so wanted. During breakfast, Rosie remained quiet, so Allison tried to finish the game they had started in the car, which had been interrupted when it was Rosie's turn.

What was your favorite place to visit? What surprised you the most? What left the strongest memory?

Rosie answered in monosyllables until Allison asked for *strongest memory.* That got a smile and a sparkle in her eye. "The Assateague ponies playing on the beach and silhouetted against the sunrise." She paused, then added, "And singing with the ladies on the Natchez Trace."

Allison started the clean up as Rosie sipped her second cup of coffee and popped her morning pills in her mouth one at a time, each followed by a sip of coffee.

Seconds after the clock ticked to ten, the phone rang. Allison grabbed it and handed the receiver to Rosie. "Is Allison still there?" She could clearly hear Josie's demand. "Tell her she's going to be needed next month to help you move. I've gotten you an apartment! When I got back, I checked at the office to make sure your name was on the list for an apartment. The manager told me one was coming open this month. They had tried to contact the first person on the waiting list and hadn't heard back, so yesterday, they called the second name on the list. You are third. I went to my apartment and came back with a check for the down payment. Slapping it on the desk, I told her 'a bird in hand.' She told me that if she hadn't heard anything by this morning, it was yours. Rosie, it's yours."

Rosie had her hand to her mouth. She gave a squeak of delight and surprise. "Mine? Is it in the same building as yours? It's on a ridge. Can I see Grand Traverse Bay?"

"Same building but a different floor. You will have a nice view, but it's not of the bay. We have a hill in the way. But there is a YMCA next door and a walking trail around an open field. There is a Great Wolf Lodge on one side and the junior high school on the other side."

"And the Meijers store is just down the hill. I remember from when I visited." Tears tracked down the creases in Rosie's cheeks. "When can I come?" she asked plaintively.

"The apartment will be cleaned and repainted and ready for you to move in on the first of August. Is Allison there for me to talk to?"

Rosie handed over the phone. Allison took it into the bedroom as Josie filled her in. "I will make sure I'm available to help Rosie move." Allison looked around the sparse bedroom. "There isn't much to move and most of it is pretty old and worn."

"Not a problem. Some things get left behind here. There are furniture sales and estate sales I can check out. I've got a friend here who *lives* to visit every garage and lawn sale listed in the newspaper. I can let her know and she'll keep an eye out for things we can use." After a slight pause, in a more concerned tone, Josie asked, "How is she?"

"Tired. It worried me when we came in. We came in the door of her apartment and she just stood. She seemed to shrink and deflate. I'm really glad she'll be near you and somewhere that she has company and activities—"

"—and singing," Josie finished.

Nodding in agreement, Allison thought, *and singing.*

Back in the kitchen, Allison found Rosie humming and dancing in place as she washed the rest of the breakfast dishes. Smiling, Allison retreated into the bedroom to call her mother.

Sitting on Rosie's bed, Allison went over what she needed to say. Would her mother understand? Taking a deep breath, Allison dialed.

Five rings, nothing. Then "Hello? Aunt Rosie?"

Allison relaxed into a smile. "Me, Mom. I'm at Rosie's apartment in Rochester. We made it here last night. She was really wiped out and I needed to do some grocery shopping for us, so that's why I didn't call." *Lame.* She knew full well her mother had waited up for her call. She found herself blurting, "Why, Mom? Why did I lose twenty-two years during which I could have known my aunts?"

"What? Allison, what's wrong? Are you alright?"

Allison mashed her bangs up, trying to regain control, taking a deep breath. "Rosie has congestive heart disease. Daisy's husband has Alzheimer's. She's devastated. Josie, well, she's eighty-eight. Who knows how long any of them will live . . . and I had a great time with them. I really had a great time."

Her mother laughed. "Even when they took off with the biker gang?"

Allison laughed as well. "Okay, it wasn't all smooth, but—" She got serious. "I'm not going to be a school counselor, and I'm transferring to Michigan State." There. It was out. Her mother was silent for a beat, then demanded.

"What? Are you sure? What are you going to do?"

"I'm going into counseling, but not children. I'm going to work with adults, specifically seniors. There is so much that these women have gone through, and they were strong. They had good people in their lives who helped them through the rough times. What about those who don't? I know it can be rough; the patients I work with will die, not grow up. But MSU has a top ranked program and I'd be three or four hours from Josie and Rosie in Traverse City or Daisy and Barth in Toledo."

"Now wait, Rosie is there in Rochester."

"Only until the end of July, then we're going to help her move to Traverse City."

"Now, wait!" her mother insisted, overwhelmed with all her daughter was dropping on her. "Aren't you getting a job? You still have two months to earn some money."

"The aunts paid me more than they promised, double, actually. Aunt Josie suggested I contact The Office for the Aging or maybe AARP, to see if there's someone I can talk to, maybe shadow. Seniors often suffer from depression, loneliness, isolation. They face the decisions of moving out of their homes, into assisted living, of losing their freedom when they can no longer get a driver's license. They are targeted by scammers. Women who are widowed often have no credit history, no work history, leaving them vulnerable financially. Office of the Aging or AARP may be able to recommend volunteer work I could do for the rest of the summer. But at the end of July, you and I are going to help Rosie move up to the senior living apartments in Michigan where Josie lives. She will have companionship, activities, buses to take her shopping and rides to medical appointments. Rosie was kicked out of her choir group because of her bad heart. There are people who live at the Cherry Ridge apartments who sing." Allison smiled at the memories of Rosie's singing. "She has a beautiful voice."

Allison stopped talking and waited. She could hear her mother breathing, but otherwise, silence.

"Mom?" More silence. Allison waited a full minute. Tentatively, she tried again.

"Mom?"

She heard a sigh. "I'm experiencing a paradigm shift. It's taking me a minute to readjust."

Allison moved uncomfortably, not understanding what her mother meant.

"I have always spoken to you—mother to child. Suddenly, I realize I'm not talking to my child." Her mother hesitated. Allison felt the blood drain from her face, a wave of anxiety. Then, taking another deep breath, her mother finished. "I'm speaking to a young adult. Are you sure this is what you want?"

Allison remained quiet for a moment before answering. "Yes. I'm sure. You know that song you like, *The Impossible is Possible.* Just before that song begins, a guy says '*You take all of this, you use it, but it doesn't give you the fire. Either you have the fire, or you don't have the fire.*' Working with children, I have no fire. But, Mom, spending time with my aunts, I've found the fire. I have the fire."

This was it. Allison knew that her mother could either hand her a gift of confidence, or rip it away from her and leave her staggering.

Once more, she heard breathing, an indrawn breath. "You've found the fire. I'll be there to help move Rosie, and I will be there to get you moved to MSU."

"Oh, and one last thing. I'm delighted . . . and proud of you!"

ACKNOWLEDGMENTS

I thank my mother, JoAnn, who shared ideas of what her wild grandmother and her independent sisters may have done as we roamed and explored together. She had a delightful and often off-beat sense of humor.

And to Karen Stupak who kept asking for the next chapters, encouraging, calling me from Sedona to reminisce, share stories of her travels, fact check my history, and let me know what octogenarian ladies really could and could not do!

CPSIA information can be obtained
at www.ICGtesting.com
Printed in the USA
LVHW091624091121
702889LV00014B/277/J

9 781646 634866